ZHANG WEI was born in 1956 in China's northern province of Shandong. He graduated from the Chinese Department at Yantai Normal College in 1980. Three years later, he became a member of the Chinese Writers Association, an organization for which he has served as the Chairman of the Shandong branch. His first novel, *The Ancient Ship*, was a bestseller and award-winner in China. One of the most widely respected fiction writers of the post-Mao era, Zhang Wei lives in Jinan.

ZHANG WEI

The Ancient Ship

TRANSLATED BY
HOWARD GOLDBLATT

HARPER PERENNIAL
MODERN CHINESE CLASSICS
London, New York, Toronto, Sydney and New Delhi

Harper Perennial
An imprint of HarperCollins*Publishers*
77–85 Fulham Palace Road, Hammersmith, London W6 8JB

www.harperperennial.co.uk
Visit our authors' blog at www.fifthestate.co.uk

This Harper Perennial Modern Chinese Classics edition published 2008
1

First published in China by People's Literature Publishing House in 1987

Translation copyright © 2008 by HarperCollins*Publishers*

Zhang Wei asserts the moral right
to be identified as the author of this work

A catalogue record for this book is available from the British Library

ISBN 978-0-00-728615-7

Set in Adobe Garamond

Printed and bound in Great Britain by Clays Ltd, St Ives plc

Mixed Sources
Product group from well-managed
forests and other controlled sources
www.fsc.org Cert no. SW-COC-1806
© 1996 Forest Stewardship Council

FSC is a non profit international organisation established to promote the
responsible management of the world's forests. Products carrying the FSC
label are independently certified to assure consumers that they come
from forests that are managed to meet the social, economic and
ecological needs of present and future generations.

Find out more about HarperCollins and the environment at
www.harpercollins.co.uk/green

There are things that people cannot imagine but nothing that people will not do.

Sui Jiansu

INTRODUCTION

The Ancient Ship (Gu chuan), Zhang Wei's first full-length novel, spans the forty years following the creation of the People's Republic in 1949. Published in August 1987, a little more than a decade after the calamitous Cultural Revolution, the novel was, by any reckoning, a groundbreaking work of fiction in terms of content, style, and historical viewpoint. The author, who began the novel when he was just twenty-eight years old, narrates the troubled early years of China's post-Liberation history in the fictional northern town of Wali. Three generations of the Sui, Zhao, and Li families, whose lives are closely and often contentiously intertwined, experience the Land Reform Movement, the Great Leap Forward, the famine of 1959–1961, the Anti-Rightist Campaign, and the Cultural Revolution (1966–1976), during which it is estimated that twenty to fifty million citizens died. The novel also reflects the late 1980s—a tense period during which Chinese society was beginning to look back on the ten-year frenzy that ended with the death of Mao and the fall of the Gang of Four (1976) and was bracing for the many modernizations heralded as the vehicles for making China an international power.

Like his fellow Shandong novelist Mo Yan, whose trailblazing *Red Sorghum* was published in the same year, Zhang Wei undertook to reexamine China's modern history, breaking free from the Party line to expose aspects of the national character that had been concealed or overlooked, often in the name of social stability, by fellow writers of the post-Mao era. *The Ancient Ship* is a character-driven novel; the nonlinear narrative highlights relationships among a cast of characters, most of whom are liberated from the stereotypes of their fictional predecessors. As critics have noted, typical characters give way in Zhang's novel to parodies of the idealized peasants and Party representatives. They put a face on the abstractions of political campaigns that created a climate of misery throughout China for more than three decades.

Life in Wali, to a large extent, revolves around the enterprise of producing the popular staple glass noodles (a form of vermicelli) on the banks of the Luqing River, once, but no longer, home to large sailing ships. The novel takes its title from the unearthed hull of an ancient wooden ship, a metaphor for China that is mirrored in the changing lives of the townspeople. With frequent references to three books—*The Communist Manifesto*, Qu Yuan's ancient classic *Heavenly Questions*, and a seafaring manual—members of the Sui clan ponder the role history has played in the evolution of the town of Wali, remnants of whose city wall date back to antiquity, and fundamental changes in society.

The Ancient Ship is, in many respects, a revolutionary work. Bold in its examination of a society in turmoil, yet lacking the parochial, nationalistic view of the world that characterized so much of the fiction of the period, it is a study in human relations, the inability of oppressed people to control their own fate, the struggle between tradition and modernization, and more. Stylistically, *The Ancient Ship* was enormously innovative for its time. The tone is often wickedly ironic as the novel moves back and forth in time and reveals the inner lives, the emotions, and the suffering—always the suffering—of its characters. Zhang Wei has created a landmark in Chinese fiction and a work that speaks to people everywhere. *The Ancient Ship* has long been a best-seller in China and Taiwan (more than twenty editions have been published, many of which are still in print) and is the recipient of several domestic prizes.

Zhang Wei, originally from China's northern province of Shandong, was born in 1956. He is a graduate (1980) of Yantai Normal College, where he majored in Chinese literature. His first published story appeared the year he graduated from college; in 1983 he became a member of the Chinese Writers Association, an organization in which he has served as the vice chairman of the Shandong branch.

✕

The translator has benefited from the gracious and helpful responses to queries regarding obscure references by the author and by the meticulous reading of the entire translation by Sylvia Li-chun Lin.

—Howard Goldblatt

THE
Ancient
Ship

Many great walls have risen on our land. They are almost as old as our history. We have built high walls and stored up vast quantities of grain in order to survive. That is why so many lofty structures have snaked across our dark soil and over our barren mountain ranges.

We have shed pools of blood at the bases of our walls to nourish the grass that grows there. In the Warring States Period the stately Great Wall of Qi reached the Ji River to the west and nearly all the way east to the ocean; at one time it split the Shandong Peninsula in two, north and south. But like so many walls before it, the Great Wall of Qi crumbled out of existence. Here is how the *Kuadi Gazetteer* describes it: "The Great Wall of Qi originates in Pingyin County in the northwest prefecture of Jizhou and follows the river across the northern ridge of Mount Tai. It winds through Jizhou and Zizhou, north of Bocheng County in southwestern Yanzhou, and continues on to the ocean at Langya Terrace in Mizhou." If you keep heading in that direction in search of other old walls, you will not find many relics. The capital of Qi was at Linzi. From the middle of the ninth century BCE emissaries bringing tribute to the throne entered the capital via Bogu. Then in the year 221 BCE the First Emperor of Qin vanquished the Qi, who had held sway for more than 630 years. Both the Qin and the Han continued to utilize the Great Wall of Qi, which did not fall into disuse until the Wei and the Jin dynasties. It stood for more than a

thousand years. The source of the Luqing River is in Guyang Mountain, where another wall once existed; whether or not it was part of
the Great Wall of Qi has never been determined, despite attempts by
archaeologists to find evidence.

From there the searchers followed the river north for four hundred
li to the strategically important town of Wali on the river's lower
reaches. The most conspicuous site there was a squat rammed-earth
wall that encircled the town. Mortar showed at the base. Squared corners, which rose above the wall, were made of bricks that had darkened to the color of iron and were still in fine condition. The surveyors,
reluctant to leave, stood at the base to touch the bricks and gaze at the
battlements. And it was during this northern expedition that they
made a startling archaeological discovery: the ancient city of Donglaizi,
which had stood in the vicinity of Wali. There they found a tall earthen
mound, the last remaining section of a city wall. What both amused
and distressed them was the realization that generations of residents
had used the mound as a kiln to fire bricks. A stone monument, with
an inscription in gold, had been erected atop the now abandoned
kiln, stating that it had once been the site of a wall surrounding the
city-state of Donglaizi; it was considered an important protected cultural artifact. The loss to Wali was patently clear, but the discovery
served as proof that their town had once existed within the walled
city-state of Donglaizi. Undeniably, that is where their ancestors had
lived, and by using a bit of imagination they could conjure up glimpses
of armor glinting in bright sunlight and could almost hear the whin-
nying of warhorses. Their excitement was dulled somewhat by disappointment, for what they should have found was a towering city wall
and not just an earthen mound.

The current wall, whose bricks had darkened to the color of iron,
trumpeted the former glories of the town of Wali. The Luqing River,
while narrow and shallow now, had once been the scene of rapids
cascading between distant banks. The old, stepped riverbed told the
history of the decline of a once great river. An abandoned pier still

stood at the edge of town, hinting at the sight of multimasted ships lining up to put in at this major river port. It was where ships' crews rested up before continuing their journey. Grand fairs were held each year on the town's temple grounds, and what sailors likely recalled most fondly as they sailed up and down the river was the bustle and jostling attendant on those annual temple fairs.

One of the riverbanks was dotted with old structures that looked like dilapidated fortresses. When the weather was bad and the river flowed past them, these old fortresses seemed shrouded in gloom. The farther you looked down the bank the smaller the structures became, until they virtually disappeared. But winds across the river brought rumbling sounds, louder and louder, crisper and clearer, emanating from within the walls of those fortresses, which created sound and harbored life. Then you walked up close and discovered that most of their roofs had caved in and that their portals were blocked. But not all of them. Two or three were still alive, and if you were to go inside, you would be surprised by what you saw: enormous millstones that turned, slowly, patiently, kept in motion by pairs of aging oxen, revolutions with no beginnings and no ends. Moss covered the ground in spots that the animals' hooves missed. An old man sitting on a stool kept his eye on a millstone, getting up at regular intervals to feed a ladleful of mung beans into the eye of the stone. These structures had once belonged to a network of mills, all lined up on the riverbank; from inside the rumblings sounded like distant thunder.

For every mill by the river there was a processing room where glass noodles were made. Wali had once produced the most famous glass noodles in the area; in the early years of the twentieth century, a massive factory had stood on the bank of the river, producing the White Dragon brand of noodles, which was known far and wide. Sailing ships navigated the river, the sound of their signals and churning oars filling the air even late into the night. Many of them brought mung beans and charcoal to town and left carrying glass noodles. Now hardly any of the mills remained in operation on the riverbank, and only a few rooms continued to produce glass noodles. It was a wonder that those ramshackle mills had survived the passage of time, standing opposite the distant crumbling wall in the twilight, as if waiting for something, or as if recounting something else.

Many generations of people had lived and multiplied on this walled stretch of land, which was neither particularly large nor especially small. The town's squat buildings and narrow lanes were evidence of the crowded conditions in which the townspeople lived. But no matter how many people there might be, or how chaotic their lives, a clear picture of the town's makeup appeared when you focused on clans, on lineage, as it were. Bloodlines provided powerful links. The people's fathers, grandfathers, great-grandfathers, and beyond—or, in the opposite direction, sons, grandsons, and great-grandsons—formed patterns like grapes on a vine.

Three clans made up most of the town's population: the Sui, the Zhao, and the Li, with the Sui clan enjoying more prosperity than either of the other two, for which residents credited the family's robust vitality. In the people's memory, the Sui clan's fortunes were tied to their noodle business, which had begun as a tiny enterprise. The height of prosperity was reached in Sui Hengde's day—he had built a factory that occupied land on both sides of the river; by then he was also operating noodle shops and money-lending ventures in several large cities in the south and northeast. He had two sons, Sui Yingzhi and Sui Buzhao. As children the brothers studied at home with a tutor, but when they grew older, Yingzhi was sent to Qingdao for a Western education, while Buzhao spent much of his time strolling aimlessly down by the pier until his brother returned. Buzhao was often heard to say that one day he'd board a ship and head out to sea. At first Yingzhi did not believe him, but his fears mounted, until one day he reported his concern to his father, who punished his younger son by smacking his hand with a ruler. As he rubbed his hand, Buzhao glared at his father, who saw in that look that nothing he did was going to change the boy's mind. "That's that," he said, and abandoned the ruler. Then, late one night, strong winds and the rumble of thunder startled Yingzhi out of a deep sleep. He climbed out of bed to look outside and discovered that his brother was gone.

Sui Yingzhi suffered from remorse over the disappearance of his young brother for most of his life. When his father died, he took the reins of the vast family holdings. His own family included two sons and a daughter. Like his father, he made sure that his children received an education and, from time to time, employed the ruler to ensure discipline. This period, spanning the 1930s and 1940s, witnessed the beginning of the Sui family's decline. Sui Yingzhi's life would end in a sad fashion, and in the days before his death he would find himself envying his brother, but too late . . .

Buzhao sailed the seas for most of his adult life, not returning home until a few years before his brother's death. He hardly recognized the town, and it certainly did not recognize him. He swayed as he walked down the streets of Wali as if they were an extension of his ship's decks. When he drank, the liquor dribbled through his beard down to his pants. How could someone like that be an heir to the Sui fortune? Morbidly thin, when he walked his calves rubbed against each other; his face had an unhealthy pallor and his eyes were dull gray. What came out of his mouth was unadulterated nonsense and unbridled boasts. He'd traveled the world over the decades he'd been gone, from the South Seas to the Pacific Ocean, under the guidance, he said, of the great Ming dynasty sea captain Zheng He. "Uncle Zheng was a good man!" he proclaimed with a sigh. But, of course, no one believed a word of it. He spun yarns about life and death on the open sea, often drawing a crowd of curious youngsters. Men sail by following an ancient navigational handbook, *Classic of the Waterway*, he told his audience, who listened raptly, hardly blinking, and he roared with laughter as he regaled them with descriptions of the fine women on the southern seacoasts . . . The man is destined for a bad end, the townspeople concluded. And the Sui clan will die out.

The year Sui Buzhao returned home ought to have been entered into the town's chronicles. For that spring a bolt of lightning struck the old temple late one night, and as people ran to save it, flames lit up all of Wali. Something inside exploded like a bomb, and the old folks informed the crowd that it must have been the platform holding the monk's sutras. The old cypress edifice seemed to be alive, its juices flowing like blood; it shrieked as it burned. Crows flew into the sky with the smoke as the frame supporting the great bell crashed to the floor. The fire roared, almost but not quite drowning out soft moans, high one moment and low the next, like the lingering echoes of the great bell or the distant strains of an ox horn. What petrified the people was how the flames rose and fell in concert with the sound.

The fire reached out at people nearest the burning building like red fingers, knocking down those who tried to put out the inferno. With moans, they stood up but made no more attempts to move ahead. Old and young, the townspeople stood around like drooling simpletons. None had ever witnessed such a blaze, and by first light they saw that the temple had burned to the ground. Then the rains came, attacking the ash and sending streams of thick, inky water slowly down the street. Townspeople stood around in silence; even chickens, dogs, and waterfowl lost their voices. When the sun went down that night, the people climbed onto their heated brick beds, their *kangs,* to sleep, and even then they did not speak, merely exchanging knowing glances. Ten days later, a sailing ship from some distant place ran aground in the Luqing River, drawing the curious down to the riverbank, where they saw a three-master stuck in midriver. Obviously the waters had receded and the river had narrowed; ripples ran up onto the banks, as if the river were waving good-bye. The people helped pull the ship free of the sandbar.

Then a second ship came, and a third, and they too ran aground. What the people had feared was now happening: The river had narrowed to the point where ships could no longer sail it, and they could only watch as the water slowly retreated and stranded their pier on dry ground.

A torpor held the town in its grip, and as Sui Buzhao walked the streets, deep sorrow emanated from his gray eyes. His brother, Ying-zhi, whose hair had turned gray, was often heard to sigh. The glass noodle business relied on a source of water, and as the river slowly dried up, he had no choice but to shut down several of the mills. But what bothered him most was how the world was changing; something gnawed at his heart night and day. As for his brother, who had returned home after so many years at sea, Yingzhi's sadness and disappointment deepened. On one occasion, women carrying noodles out to the drying ground threw their baskets down and ran back, agitated, refusing to put the threads out to dry. Puzzled by this strange occurrence, Yingzhi went out to see for himself. There he saw Buzhao on his back, lying comfortably on the sandy ground, naked as the day he was born, soaking up sun.

Sui Yingzhi's eldest son, Sui Baopu, had grown into a delightful, innocent boy who loved to run about. People said, "The Sui clan has produced another worthy descendant." Sui Buzhao doted on his nephew, whom he often carried around on his shoulders. Their favorite destination was the pier, now long out of use, where they would look out at the narrowed river as he entertained the boy with stories about life on the open sea. As Baopu grew tall and increasingly good-looking, Buzhao had to stop carrying him on his shoulders. So now it was the turn of Jiansu, Baopu's younger brother. Baopu, meanwhile, a good child to begin with, was getting increasingly sensible, so his father wrote out some words for him to live by: Do not be arbitrary, doctrinaire, vulgar, or egocentric. Baopu accepted them exactly as they were intended.

The first three seasons of the year—spring, summer, and fall—passed without incident, and when winter came snow buried the ice-covered river and the old mills on its banks. As the snow continued to fall, people ran to the Li compound to observe the meditating monk; the sight of the shaved-pated old monk reminded them of the splendid temple that had once stood in town and of the ships that had come there. Their ears rang with the sound of sailors hailing each other. When he completed his meditation, the monk told tales of antiquity, which were as incomprehensible to the people as archaic prophesies:

The Qi and the Wei dynasties contended for superiority over the central plains. When the residents of Wali came to the aid of Sun Bin, King Wei of Qi rose above everyone, to the amazement of all. In the twenty-eighth year of the Qing dynasty, the First Emperor traveled to the Zou Mountains south of Lu, from there to Mt. Tai, and then stopped at Wali to make repairs on his ships before visiting the three mystical mountains at Penglai, Fangzhang, and Yingzhou. Confucius spread his system of rites everywhere but eastern Qi, where the barbarians had their own rituals. The sage, knowing there were rituals of which he was ignorant, sent Yan Hui and Ran You to learn and bring some back from the eastern tribes. The two disciples fished in the Luqing River, using hooks and not nets, as taught by the sage. A resident of Wali who had studied at the feet of Mozi for ten years could shoot an arrow ten *li,* making a whistling sound the whole way. He polished a mirror in which, by sitting in front of it, he could see everything in nine prefectures. Wali also produced many renowned monks and Taoists: Li An, whose style name was Yongmiao and whose literary name was Changsheng, and Liu Chuxuan, whose style name was Changzheng and whose literary name was Guangning, were both from Wali. A plague of locusts struck during the reign of the Ming Wanli Emperor, darkening the sky and blotting out the sun like black clouds, creating a famine. People ate grass, they ate the bark of trees, and they ate each other. After sitting in deep meditation for thirty-eight days, a monk was awakened from his trance by acolytes striking a brass bell and immediately rushed to the entrance of the town, where he tented his hands and uttered a single word: sin! All the locusts in the sky flew up his sleeve and were dumped into the river. When the Taiping rebellion broke out, villagers near and far fled to Wali, where the town gate was flung open to welcome any and all refugees . . .

The monk's stories excited his audience, though the people understood hardly a word of what he said. And as time passed, they grew to accept the anguish of unbearable loneliness and suffering. Now that the waters had receded and the pier was left on dry land, the ship whistles they'd grown used to were no longer heard. That gave birth in their hearts to an inexplicable sense of grievance, which gradually evolved into rage. The monk's droned narration of olden days awakened them to the reality that the temple had burned to the ground, but that its bell remained. Meanwhile, time and the elements had peeled away layers of the imposing city wall, although one section remained in good repair, maintaining its grandeur. The absence of boisterous, agitating outsiders, people realized, actually improved the quality of life in town; the boys were better behaved, the girls more chaste.

The river flowed quietly between its narrow banks, its surface pale in color. The foundations of the old fortresslike mills were succumbing to the encroachment of vines. All but a few of them were quiet, but those that remained active emitted a rumble from morning till night. Thick moss overran the ground beyond the reach of ox hooves, and the elderly workers thumped the dark millstone eyes with wooden ladles, producing a hollow sound; the stones turned slowly, patiently rubbing time itself away. The city wall and the old riverbank mills stood peering at each other in silence.

Wali seemed to disappear from the memories of people in other places, and it was not until many years later that her existence was recalled; naturally, the first recollection was of the city wall. By then an earthshaking change had occurred in our land, characterized mainly by pervasive turmoil. The people were confident that it would take only a few years to overtake England and catch up to America. And that was when outsiders recalled the city wall and the bricks that topped it.

Early one morning crowds came to town, climbed the wall, and began removing the bricks. All Wali was in shock; agitated residents shouted their displeasure. But the people climbing the wall carried a red flag, which gave them implicit authority, so the residents quickly sent someone to get Fourth Master, a local man who, though only in his thirties, had earned distinction by being the eldest member of his generation in the Zhao clan. Unfortunately, he was then suffering from a bout of malaria and lacked the strength to climb off his *kang*. When the emissary reported the unwanted intrusion through the paper window of his room, Fourth Master's weak response had the effect of a command: "Say no more. Find their leader and break his leg."

So the townspeople snatched up their hoes and carrying poles and swarmed through the city gate. The demolition of the wall was at its peak, and the outsiders were surrounded before they knew what had happened. The beatings began. People who had been knocked to the ground got to their feet and shouted, "Be reasonable!" But all that got them was a defiant response from their angry attackers. "We're not about to be reasonable when a gang of thieving bastards comes to town to tear down our ancestors' wall!" More beatings ensued, for which the victims' only protection was to cover their heads with tools they had brought with them. "A good fight!" was the call. Decades of grievances had found an outlet. "Take that!" The Wali residents hunched over and looked around with watchful eyes before jumping up and bringing their carrying poles down on the panic-stricken outsiders' heads. Suddenly a painful shriek caused everyone to stop and turn to look. It was the group's leader—his leg had been broken. A local man was standing beside him, his lips bloodless, his cheeks twitching, his hair standing on end. It was clear to the outsiders that the people of Wali were not bluffing, that their attack was for real. On that morning the residents of Wali were finally able to release a ferocity that had been bottled up for generations. The outsiders picked up their crippled leader and fled. The wall was saved, and though the decades that followed would be unrelentingly chaotic, they had lost only three and a half old bricks.

The wall stood proudly. No power on earth, it seemed, was strong enough to shake it, so long as the ground on which it stood did not move. The millstones kept turning, kept rumbling, patiently rubbing time itself away. The fortresslike mills were covered with ivy that also created a net atop the wall.

Many more years passed. Then one shocking day the ground did in fact move. It happened early in the morning. Tremors woke the residents from their sleep, followed by a dull, thunderous noise that, in seconds, reduced the town's wall to rubble.

The townspeople were crushed, their hearts tied up in knots; as if on command, their thoughts roamed back to the time the old temple had burned down and the three-master had run aground in the river. Now their wall was gone, but this time the ground itself was the culprit.

As they sucked in breaths of cold air, they went looking for the cause. To their amazement, they realized that there had been omens of an impending earthquake, although, to their enduring sense of regret, no one had spotted them at the time: Someone had seen colorful snakes, more than he could count, crawl toward the riverbank; overnight a large pig had dug an astonishingly wide hole in its pen; hens had lined up atop the wall, cackling in unison before scurrying off together; and a hedgehog had sat in the middle of a courtyard coughing like an old man. But the people's unease was caused by more than just these omens. Far greater worries and alarms had tormented them over the preceding six months. Yes, there were greater worries and alarms.

Rumors flew over the village like bats. Panicky townspeople were talking about the news that had just come: Land was to be redistributed and factories, including glass noodle factories, were to revert to private management. Time was turning once again, just like the millstones. No one dared believe the rumors. But before long the changes were reported in newspapers, and a town meeting was called, where it was announced that land, factories, and the noodle processing rooms would be turned over to private management. The town was in a daze. Silence reigned as an atmosphere like that which had existed when lightning struck the old temple had the town in its grip. No one, not adults and not children, spoke; looks were exchanged over evening meals, after which the people went to bed. Not even chickens, dogs, or waterfowl broke the silence. "Wali," the people said, "you unlucky town, where can you go from here?"

The mayor and street monitors personally parceled out the land. "These are called responsibility plots," they told the people. That left the factory and glass noodle rooms. Who would take responsibility for them? Not until many days had passed did anyone come forward to assume responsibility for the factory. Now only the processing rooms remained. The mills stood on the riverbank, wrapped in quiet, inauspicious mystery. Everyone knew that Wali's essence—its misfortunes, its honor and its disgrace, its rise and fall—was concentrated in those dark, dilapidated old mills. Who had the courage to set foot in dank, moss-covered fortresses and take charge?

The people had long considered the milling of glass noodles to be a strange calling. The mills themselves and the places where the strands were extruded were suffused with complex, indescribable mystery. During the milling procedures, the temperature of the water, the yeast, the starch, the paste . . . if the smallest problem arose in any of the stages, the process would fail: Suddenly the starch would form a sediment; then the noodles would begin to break up . . . it was what the workers called "spoiled vats." "The vat is spoiled!" they would shout. "The vat is spoiled!" When that happened, everyone would stand around feeling helpless.

Many expert noodle makers wound up jumping into the Luqing River. One was pulled out of the river and saved from drowning, only to hang himself in one of the mills the next day. That's the sort of calling it was. Now who was going to step up and take charge? Since the Sui clan had operated the mills for generations, it made sense for one of them to assume responsibility. Eventually, Sui Baopu was urged to take over, but the forty-year-old red-faced scion shook his head; looking across the river at the line of mills, he muttered something under his breath, looking worried.

At that juncture, a member of the Zhao clan, Zhao Duoduo, shocked people by volunteering to take on the job.

All of Wali churned with excitement. The first thing Duoduo did after assuming responsibility was change the name of the enterprise to the Wali Glass Noodle Factory. People exchanged looks of incredulity as they realized that the industry no longer belonged to Wali, nor to the Sui clan. Now it belonged to the Zhao clan! Still, the old millstones rumbled from dawn to dusk. Where were they headed? People came to the riverbank to stand and gape at the mills, sensing that a bizarre change had occurred in front of their eyes, as extraordinary as hens lining up atop the wall or a hedgehog actually coughing. "The world has turned upside down!" they said. So when the earth moved that early morning, they were terrified but not surprised.

If there was a more immediate cause for the earth to move, the blame should rest with the drilling rigs out in the fields. For the better part of a year a surveying team had been far from town. But soon the rigs came so close that the residents grew uneasy. Among them, only the lean figure of Sui Buzhao was seen around the rigs, sometimes helping to carry the drills and winding up mud-soaked from head to toe. "These are for coal mining," he said to the gathered crowd. Day and night the drills turned, until the tenth day, when one of the town's residents stood up and said, "That's enough!"

"How do you know that's enough?" the operator asked.

"When you reach the eighteenth layer of heaven and earth, we're done for!"

The operator laughed as he tried to explain away their concerns. And the drills kept turning, until the morning of the fifteenth day, when the earth began to move.

People flew out of their windows. The rolling of the ground sickened them and made them dizzy. All but Sui Buzhao, who had spent half his life on ships and easily adapted to the pitching and rolling of the earth beneath him. He ran fast, but then a thunderous roar rose up from somewhere and froze people where they stood. When they regained their bearings, they ran madly to a vacant lot, where they huddled with the crowds already there. The lot was what was left of the old temple that had burned down. Most residents of the town were there, and they were shivering, even though it was not a cold morning. The sound of their voices changed—they spoke listlessly, feebly, and even the fastest-talking among them stammered. "What has fallen?" they wondered. No one knew; they shook their heads.

Many hadn't had time to dress, so now they frantically covered their bodies. Sui Buzhao was naked but for a white shirt tied around his waist. He ran around looking for his nephews Baopu and Jiansu and his niece Hanzhang, whom he found under a haystack. Baopu was dressed—more or less—while Hanzhang had on only bra and panties. Crouching inside, her arms crossed over her chest, she was shielded by Baopu and Jiansu, who was wearing only a pair of shorts. Sui Buzhao crouched down and looked for Hanzhang in the darkness. "Are you okay?" he asked.

"Yes," she replied.

Jiansu edged closer to her. "Go away!" he said impatiently.

So Sui Buzhao walked around the square and discovered that the clans were all huddling together; wherever you saw a group of people, you found a clan. Three large clusters: Sui, Zhao, and Li, old and young. No one had called them together—the ground had done that; three shakes here and two there, and the clans were drawn to the same spots. Sui Buzhao walked up to where the Zhao clan had gathered. He looked but did not see Naonao anywhere. What a shame that was. Naonao, barely twenty, was the Zhao clan's favorite daughter, a young woman whose beauty was spoken of on both sides of the river. She burned through the town like a fireball. The old man coughed and threaded his way in among the crowd, unsure which clan he should go to.

The sky was turning light. "Our wall is gone!" someone shouted. And that is when the people understood the origin of the thunderous roar. With a chorus of shouts, they ran, until a young man jumped up onto the abandoned foundation and shouted, "Stop right there!" They looked up at him, wondering what was wrong. He thrust out his right arm and said, "Fellow townspeople, do not move. This is an earthquake, and there will be an aftershock. Wait till it passes."

The people held their breath as they listened to what he was saying. Then they exhaled as one.

"The aftershock is usually worse than the first shaking," he added.

A murmur rose from the crowd. Sui Buzhao, who was listening intently, yelled, "Do as he says, he knows what he's talking about!"

Finally the square was quiet. No one moved as they waited for the aftershock. Many minutes passed before someone in the Zhao clan yelled tearfully, "Oh, no, Fourth Master didn't make it out!"

Chaos ensued, until another older resident cursed hoarsely, and everyone realized it was Zhao Duoduo. "What the hell good does all that shouting do? Go get Fourth Master and carry him over here!" Immediately a man broke from the crowd and ran like the wind down a lane.

No one in the square said a word; the silence was unnerving and stayed that way until the man returned.

"Fourth Master was asleep!" he announced loudly. "He says everyone should go back to their homes, that there won't be an aftershock."

The news was met with whoops of joy. Then the elders of each clan told their young to head back home. The crowds dispersed as the young man jumped down from the foundation and walked off slowly.

Three people remained in the haystack: Baopu and his brother and sister. Jiansu stared off into the distance and complained, "Fourth Master has become a sort of god, reigning over heaven and earth!" Baopu picked up the pipe his brother had laid on the ground, turned it over in his hand, and put it back. Straightening up to free his muscular body from its confinement, he looked up at the fading stars and sighed. After taking off his shirt and wrapping it around his sister's shoulders, he paused and then walked off without a word.

Baopu entered the shadow of a section of collapsed wall, where he spotted something white. He stepped forward and stopped. It was a half-naked young woman. She giggled when she saw who it was. Baopu's throat burned. A single tremulous word emerged: "Naonao." She giggled again, set her fair-skinned legs in motion, and ran off.

TWO

The Sui clan and the old mills, it appeared, were fated to be linked. For generations the extended clan had produced glass noodles. As soon as the three siblings—Baopu, Jiansu, and Hanzhang—were able to work, they could always be found on the sun-drenched drying floor or in the steamy processing rooms. During the famine years, of course, no noodles were produced, but once the millstones were turning again, the Sui clan was back at work. Baopu was happiest when things were quiet. Over the years he had preferred to sit on a stool and watch the millstone turn. Since it was Jiansu's job to deliver the noodles, he spent most of his time riding the horse cart down the gravel road all the way to the ocean piers; Hanzhang had the most enviable job: She spent her days on the drying floor, a white kerchief tied around her head as she moved amid the silvery glass noodles.

But now the factory had been taken over by Zhao Duoduo, who called his workers together on his first day. "I am responsible for the factory," he announced, "and I invite you all to stay on. Those who wish to leave may do so. If you stay, be prepared to join me in days of hard work!" Several of the workers were off as soon as he was finished. But not Baopu and his siblings, who left the meeting and went directly to their posts. The thought of leaving the business never crossed their minds, as if it was what they were destined to do, a job only death could force them to leave. Baopu sat alone in the mill, adding

mung beans to the eye of the millstone, his broad back facing the
door, the room's sole window high on the wall to his right. The view
out that little window was of the riverbank, the scattered "fortresses"
and the lines of willow trees. Farther off was an expanse of silver under
a blue sky. That was the drying floor, a place where the sunlight seemed
brighter than anywhere else and where the wind was gentler. Faint
sounds of laughter and singing drifted over from the sandy ground,
where young women weaved in and out among a forest of drying
racks. Hanzhang was one of them, and so was Naonao. Children lay
on the ground around the drying racks waiting for lengths of glass
noodles to fall to the ground, so they could run over and scoop them
up. Baopu could not see their faces through his window, but he could
sense their happiness.

The drying floor was the scene of intense activity even before sun-
rise. Older women gauged the direction of the day's wind by looking
up at the cloud formations and then positioning the racks accord-
ingly; they needed to be set perpendicular to the wind to keep the wet
strands from sticking together when gusts blew. Horse carts rumbled
up to deliver basketfuls of wet glass noodles; the snowy white, un-
blemished strands were hung over racks, where the young women
spread them out and shifted them with their dainty fingers all day
long, until they were dry and so light they fluttered gracefully like willow catkins with each breeze.

People said that White Dragon glass noodles had earned their reputation not only because of the extraordinary quality of Luqing River
water, but also because of the young maidens' fingers. They touched
the strands with great care, from top to bottom and from left to right,
like strumming a harp. The colors of the sunset played on their faces
as light retreated from the noodles until, finally, they could tolerate no
colors at all; they had to be the purest white.

As the women's bodies warmed under the sun, one of them began
to sing softly. The notes went higher, and everyone within earshot
stopped to listen. When finally she realized she had a rapt audience,
she stopped and was rewarded with applause and laughter. The loud-

est voice on the drying floor belonged to Naonao, who was used to doing whatever she wanted, even cursing at someone for no apparent reason. No one on the receiving end ever minded, knowing that was just how she was. She'd learned disco from TV, and sometimes she danced on the drying floor. And when she did, the others stopped working to shout, "More, more, more . . ." But Naonao never did what others wanted, so instead of dancing, she'd lie down on the hot sand and expose her fair skin to the sun. Once, as she lay on the sand, she began to writhe and said, "Day in and day out there's something missing." The others laughed. "What's missing is a goofy young man to wrap his arms around you!" an elderly woman said. Naonao jumped up from the sand. "Hah!" she exclaimed. "I'm afraid that particular goofy young man hasn't been born." The others applauded gleefully. What a happy scene it was, with laughter all around as they turned and headed back to the noodles.

Hanzhang generally kept her distance from the center of activity and on some days would hardly talk to anyone. She was tall and thin, and had large, dark eyes and long lashes that fluttered constantly. It was common for Naonao to slip under drying racks to run over to Hanzhang, filled with chatter. Hanzhang would just listen.

Then one day Naonao asked, "Who's prettier, you or me?" Hanzhang smiled. Naonao clapped her hands. "You have a wonderful smile. You always look so down in the dumps, but when you smile you're really pretty." Hanzhang didn't say a word as her hands kept flying over the racks. Naonao babbled on, even took Hanzhang's hand and held it up to get a closer look. "What a lovely hand, with such pretty little nails. You really should paint them red. Oh, have you heard? From now on, when you paint your nails, you won't have to use oleander. Now they have oil you paint on, and your nails are red." She lifted Hanzhang's hand, and when she lowered her head she could see Hanzhang's pale upper arm up the sleeve, which so unnerved her she dropped the hand. The skin was so nearly transparently thin Naonao could actually see the veins beneath the surface. She then looked at Hanzhang's face, which was slightly sunburned. But the skin on her neck and spots covered by her bandanna were the same color as her arm. Naonao held her tongue as she studied Hanzhang, who was carefully separating two strands of glass noodles that were stuck together. "You Suis are strange people," she said as she quietly went to work beside Hanzhang, who sensed that there were more knots in the noodles than usual, too many for her to handle. After separating several that were stuck together she looked up and sighed and noticed that Naonao was gazing off in the distance. She turned to see what Naonao was looking at. It was the mills across the river.

"Isn't he afraid at night, sitting there all alone?" Naonao asked.

"What do you mean?"

Naonao looked at her. "Your brother! They say the old mill is haunted . . ."

Hanzhang looked away and straightened some strands. "He's not afraid. Nothing scares him."

The sun was high in the sky, its rays reflected off the noodles, the riverbank, and the water. Children with baskets waited in the shade of willows, their eyes fixed on the shiny strands of noodles. Every day they waited for the dry strands to be taken off the racks so they could run over and throw themselves down on the hot sand, but lately the drying women had been getting miserly. After taking away the noodles, they even raked the sand under the racks, which meant hardly any pieces were left. But that did not stop the children from waiting, nor did it quell their excitement.

The moment the women raised their rakes, the children let out a whoop and charged, falling to their knees and scrounging for broken pieces. Some put their baskets aside and frantically scooped up sand with their hands and then sat there picking through the pile. The workers inevitably dropped strands onto the sand and stepped on them, and anyone who found a half-foot length would jump up in delight. As the sun crept across the sky, the children under the willows put their baskets over their heads, took them off, and put them back again, displaying their impatience. The oldest among them was only eight or nine, and since they had nothing to do, their parents sent them out to gather some noodles, which could be sold on market days. While they waited they asked each other how much they'd earned in the past.

But today the widow Xiaokui brought little Leilei over to sit beneath a willow tree. Leilei was a boy who refused to grow, and it didn't seem to people that he was any taller now than he used to be. The other children laughed, and one of them mocked him in a loud voice, "Of course *we're* not going to be able to pick as much as him . . ."

Xiaokui just stared at the drying floor without saying a word, her hand resting heavily on Leilei's head. He looked on blankly, his lips turning dark as he snuggled up close to his mother. She was watching Hanzhang work the racks and saw her remove a long strand, then pick up her rake, which she raised above her head. "Go on, run!" Xiaokui said to her son, who ran out onto the drying floor, but not as fast as the other kids, who had sharper eyes and stronger legs. They elbowed their way up to Hanzhang and sprawled on the sand. Xiaokui tried to spot her son, but there were too many kids, too many grimy hands blocking her view. She stood up, straightened her hair, and walked out among the children.

Hanzhang gave the ground a quick rake and drew a line in the sand in front of each area she raked; no one was permitted to cross that line to scavenge for broken noodles. She kept her eyes on all those black hands sifting frantically through the sand and moving immediately to each new open spot. But when she looked up she saw Xiaokui, digging through the sand beside Leilei, and for some unknown reason, the hand holding the rake began to quiver at the sight of mother and son. Seeing that Hanzhang was looking at her, Xiaokui stood up, brushed the sand from her hands, and took a step forward to grab her son's hand. With a look of embarrassment, she smiled at Hanzhang, who nodded in return before looking down and continuing to work. But now she was having trouble holding on to her rake; her hand was shaking so badly she kept knocking strands of glass noodles to the sandy ground. Children scrambled forward, their faces red from excitement. Finally, Leilei managed to crawl up to the front, where he grabbed a handful of noodles and squeezed them so tight he looked as if he'd never let go.

Once dried, the noodles were laid out atop burlap sacks, piling up until there were little mountains of the white strands. A line of horse carts rode up, the drivers shouting for the women to load up. Jiansu drove his cart to the farthest pile of noodles, but instead of stopping he snapped his whip in the air and circled the drying racks. His bell rang out, and he whistled as he sped behind the women, frightening them. All but Naonao, who ran up to his cart and gestured. "Stop!" she cried out. Jiansu slowed down enough for Naonao to jump onto his cart. "Now make him run fast!" she shouted. His whip cracked in the air and away they went. Eventually, Jiansu drove up to a pile on the edge of the drying floor, where he and Naonao loaded up his cart. He was so much taller than Naonao, his legs so much longer, that he had to squat down when the two of them lifted up one of the piles.

"Be careful," he said, "or I'll toss you onto the cart along with the noodles."

"Don't be so cocky!"

Jiansu gleefully pushed his hair back, reached out, and wrapped his arms around the girl and the load she was carrying. *Thump!* He tossed them both into the cart.

"Wow, you're strong!" Naonao said joyfully as she lay in the bed of his cart. "Stronger than the mighty Wu Song, and twice as bad!" The other women, drawn to the scene, clapped approvingly. One of them, a middle-aged woman, pointed and said, "Those two are having so much fun you'd think they were a couple!" That was met by shouts of delight. Naonao looked down from the cart and stood up high. "What the hell do you know!" she barked, pointing at the woman.

Zhao Duoduo came to the drying floor, as he did every day. The women were clapping and giggling when he walked by, and when they saw that that angered him, they quieted down. With a dark expression, he walked over to Jiansu's wagon and glared at the two of them. "What are you looking at, old Duoduo?" Naonao said. "You don't scare me." Duoduo smiled, showing his front teeth. "I know I don't. You scare me. I just came to tell you that starting tomorrow you'll work inside. You'll make more money there."

She pouted. "You won't scare me there either."

Duoduo watched her jump down off the wagon and narrow her eyes as she tried to catch her breath. A drop of sweat fell from her neck to the ground. Then a commotion behind him caught Duoduo's attention. He turned and saw a bunch of kids with baskets, shouting and chasing after Hanzhang, who was waving her rake in the air. "Damn!" he cursed as he went over to see what was happening. The kids were digging frantically in the sand with their grimy hands, which entered and emerged from the sand at about the same time, clasped together; if no noodles came out with them, the fingers separated for the next try. The kids' eyes were fixed on the little spot of ground in front of them, and they saw nothing else. When Hanzhang shouted something, the kids looked up to see, just as a large foot stepped down on their hands. It was big enough to bury most of them. Young eyes traveled up the leg. Discovering it was Duoduo, they burst into tears.

"You little thieves!" he cursed as he looked into each of their baskets.

"Uncle Duoduo . . . ," Xiaokui called out. He bent down and pinched Leilei's ear without looking at the woman behind him. The boy's yelp of pain was followed by an explosion of tears; he dropped his basket. The foot lifted up off the hands, which returned quickly to their owners. Then it kicked out backward, knocking over Leilei's basket and spilling the noodle pieces back onto the sand, like embroidery needles. The kids stared wide-eyed as Xiaokui stumbled backward and sat down on the sand with a thud.

For a long moment the drying floor was silent before Hanzhang decided to go over and scoop up Leilei's noodles for him. Duoduo glowered at her as she set down her rake. "Stop right there!" he shouted. Hanzhang froze. By then the children were all crying. The other women were off a ways, loading the wagon, where the horse announced its presence between the shafts with loud whinnies. The sound of a bell added to the confusion, that and the curses of the man directed at his animal. From where he stood, Sui Jiansu took a look at Zhao Duoduo, then walked over, stood beside Hanzhang, and lit his pipe. He glared at Duoduo as he smoked.

"What the hell do you want?" Duoduo asked, his anger building. Jiansu just puffed away and said nothing. "Well?" Duoduo asked, his voice thick.

"Second Brother!" Hanzhang said softly. But still Jiansu said nothing. After casually smoking all the tobacco in his pipe, he tapped the bowl to empty the ashes.

Duoduo's glance shifted from Jiansu to the children. "Who the hell do you think you are at your age? Make me angry and you won't live to talk about it!" He turned and walked off.

Hanzhang grabbed Jiansu's sleeve and said softly, "What's wrong, Second Brother? What is it?"

"It's nothing," he said, grunting derisively. "I just wanted him to know he'd better start treating members of the Sui clan with respect from now on." That elicited no response from Hanzhang, who looked across the river at the old mill. Evening mist rose from the river, through which the silent mill gave anyone who saw it an uneasy feeling.

The old mill stood silently, but if you listened carefully, you heard a low rumble, like distant thunder, settling over the wildwoods beyond the riverbanks and into the autumn sunset. The millstone turned slowly, patiently rubbing time itself away. It seemed to put people increasingly on edge; maybe one day, sooner or later, it would infuriate the town's young residents.

～

The young heir of the Li clan, Li Zhichang, fantasized that he could find a way to turn the mill by machine. Not much given to talking, he entertained a host of fantasies in his head. And when he related one of them to Sui Buzhao, his only confidant, the two of them would get excited. "That's an interesting principle!" the older man would say with an approving sigh. Li Zhichang's favorite pastime was reading up on math and physics, memorizing formulas and principles. Sui Buzhao never could remember the things Li Zhichang told him, but he was drawn to the word "principle" and would submit these principles to his own unique interpretations. He urged Li Zhichang to share his plans for revamping the mill with a geological survey technician, also surnamed Li.

"Can do," Li replied. So, by putting their heads together, the three men came up with a workable plan. Now all that remained was to build and install the machinery. Belatedly, it occurred to them that they needed Zhao Duoduo's approval before anything could be done. So Sui Buzhao went to see him.

At first Zhao said nothing. But after thinking it over, he said, "Go ahead, mechanize one of the mills. We'll give it a try."

Li Zhichang and Sui Buzhao were thrilled, as was Technician Li. They went right to work. Any parts they needed they had made in the town's metalwork shop, billing the factory for the costs. The last item was the motor. Zhao Duoduo gave them the least workable diesel pump in the factory. Now the question was, which mill should they target for the new equipment? Sui Buzhao recommended the one run by his nephew. Baopu, who seemed pleased by the news, called his ox to a stop, unhooked the tether, and took it out of the mill.

Work began. For days the mill was the scene of bustling activity, observed by crowds of local residents. Sui Buzhao was in perpetual motion. One minute he'd be bringing oil or a wrench, the next he'd be moving the gawkers back. Finally, the motor sputtered to life, and when it was running at full speed, the millstone began to turn. The rumble was louder than usual, as if thunder had drawn near. They added a conveyor belt to feed the soaked mung beans into the eye of the millstone at a constant rate. The liquid poured out and flowed down the revamped passage into the sediment pool. It was immediately obvious to everyone that the age of feeding the beans with a wooden ladle had come to an end. But someone was still needed to spread the beans evenly on the belt, so Baopu continued sitting in the old mill, as before.

Now, however, it was no longer possible for him to enjoy the quiet solitude, since a steady stream of town residents dropped by to see how the motor did its job and were reluctant to leave. The praise was practically unanimous. The sole exception was an odd old man named Shi Dixin, who was generally opposed to anything new and unfamiliar and, for added measure, was feuding with Sui Buzhao; he was particularly unhappy about anything accomplished with Sui's participation. He watched for a while and then spat angrily on the rumbling motor before storming off.

Women from the processing room were frequent visitors; that included Naonao, who stood there sucking on a piece of hard candy and smiling. When she was around, the motor noise didn't seem as loud as at other times, since it was nearly drowned out by her shouts. If she was in a good mood curses flew from her mouth. She cursed the millstone; the millstone did not curse back. She cursed people; they just smiled. She ran around, touching this and rubbing that, and sometimes stomping her foot for no apparent reason.

One day she reached out to touch the conveyor belt; Baopu ran up, wrapped his arms around her, and dragged her over to a corner, where he pushed her away as if singed by her touch. Naonao looked at him as if seeing him for the first time. Then, in a shrill voice, she said, "Shame on you, how dare you." Turning to look at him one last time, she ran out of the mill. Everyone present laughed, but Baopu, acting as if nothing had happened, went back to his stool and sat down.

As time passed, fewer people came around. Then one day, as Baopu sat alone looking out the window, he saw Xiaokui, basket in hand, and her undersized son, Leilei, standing on the riverbank and gazing at his place. He faintly heard the boy ask his mother, "What's a machine?" That sent a charge through Baopu, who jumped up and shouted through the window, "Come over here, boy, the machine's right here!" There was no response.

Whenever Sui Jiansu returned from making a delivery he went into the mill to keep his brother company. Maybe because he was so used to driving his cart all over the landscape, he simply could not understand how a healthy young man could sit quietly all day long, like an old codger. His brother wouldn't say a word, almost as if he had no interest in anything that occurred outside that room. So Jiansu sat and smoked his pipe awhile before walking back outside, feeling he'd carried out his sibling responsibilities. When he gazed at Baopu's broad back, it looked as heavy as a boulder. What was stored inside that back? That, he figured, would always remain a mystery. He and Baopu had the same father but different mothers, and he did not think he'd ever understand the eldest son of the Sui clan.

When he returned from the drying floor that day Jiansu told Baopu how Zhao Duoduo had yelled at Hanzhang and Xiaokui. Baopu didn't stir. "Just you wait and see!" Jiansu said callously. "The Sui family will not carry their whip forever."

Baopu glanced at his brother and said, more to himself than anything, "Making glass noodles is what we do, it's all we do."

Jiansu cast a cold glance at the millstone and said, "Maybe, maybe not." What he wanted more than anything was to get Baopu out of that hard-luck mill and see that his brother never stepped foot inside it again. Baopu may have been born to make glass noodles but not to sit on a stool and watch a millstone turn.

Everyone agreed that Baopu was the best glass noodle maker in town. What no one knew was who he had learned the art from, and they all figured that it was the Sui clan's natural calling. A few years earlier, when they had suffered a spoiled vat, Baopu had left a lasting impression on the people. On that unfortunate morning, a strange smell emanated from the processing room, after which the starch produced no noodles. Eventually, some finally emerged, but in uneven thicknesses that broke up when they touched cold water. Finally, even the starch stopped coming out. The shop losses were substantial, and up and down Gaoding Street, the village area within the confines of Wali, shouts of "Spoiled vat! Spoiled vat!" were heard. On the fifth

day, a master noodle maker from the other side of the river was sent
for at great expense. As soon as he entered the room he frowned.
Then, after tasting the paste he threw down his fee and ran off. The
Gaoding Street Party secretary, Li Yuming, an honest, decent man,
was so upset by this development that his cheeks swelled up overnight. At the time, Baopu was sitting in the mill woodenly feeding
mung beans into the eye of the millstone. But when he heard there
was a spoiled vat he threw down his ladle and went into the processing
room, where he hunkered down in a corner and smoked his pipe,
observing the looks of panic on the people there. He saw Secretary Li,
whose face was distorted—thin above and thick below—attach a piece
of red cloth to the door frame to ward away evil spirits. Unable to
keep crouching there, Baopu knocked the ashes out of his pipe, got
up, and went over to the sediment vat, where he scooped out some of
the liquid with a spoon. Everyone stopped and gaped at him. Without
a word, he scooped the liquid out of one vat after another. Then he
went back to his corner and crouched down again. Later, in the middle of the night, he started scooping again. Someone even saw him
drink a few mouthfuls of the starch. The diarrhea hit him at daybreak,
when he held his hands against his belly, his face a waxen yellow.
Nonetheless, he went back and crouched in the corner. That is how it
went for nearly a week, when suddenly a familiar fragrance emerged.
When people went looking for Baopu in his corner, he was no longer
there, and when they tried to strain the noodles they saw that everything was back to normal, with Baopu sitting in his usual spot in front
of the millstone.

Jiansu found it impossible to understand how anyone could be so
stubborn. Given the man's talents, why didn't he become a technician?
It would mean a doubling of his wages and prestige, not to mention a
more relaxed job. But Baopu shook his head every time the issue came
up. Quiet was too important to him, he said, although Jiansu found
that hard to believe.

The day after Jiansu told his brother about what had happened at
the drying floor, he drove his cart back onto the gravel road to the port

city. As it bumped and rattled along, he held his whip close to his body and was reminded of what he'd said: "The Sui family will not carry their whip forever." Angered by the thought, he lashed out at the horse. The round trip took four or five days, and on the road home, as he neared town, he spotted the riverbank line of "fortresses" and the old city wall. The sight energized him.

The first thing Jiansu did after bringing his cart to a halt was go see his brother. He heard a rumble when he was still quite a distance from the mill, and when he walked in the door he saw the gears of the machinery and the conveyor belt. He was dumbstruck. With a tightening in his chest, he muttered in a shaky voice, "Who did this?" Baopu told him it was Li Zhichang and their uncle. Jiansu cursed, then, without another word, sat down.

Over the next several days, Jiansu stayed away from the mill so as to avoid the confusing sight of those spinning gears. He predicted that before long, all the mills and processing rooms would be mechanized, which would be a boon for the Zhao clan. He paced back and forth on the sunset-drenched riverbank, staying as far from the mills as possible. The distant strains of a flute came through the mist, played by the bachelor everyone called Gimpy, a shrill, jumpy sound. Jiansu stood looking down at the shallow water and thinking about his uncle, who had helped Li Zhichang in the project; nearly cursing out loud, he cracked his knuckles.

Coming down off the riverbank, he rushed over to see his uncle.

Sui Buzhao lived a fair distance from his niece and nephews in a room outside the compound, where he'd lived ever since leaving the sea behind him. No lamps had been lit and the front door was open. Pausing in the doorway, where the smell of liquor was strong, Jiansu heard the sound of a bowl banging on the table and knew that his uncle was home. "Is that you, Jiansu?" Sui Buzhao asked.

"Yes," Jiansu replied as he stepped inside.

Sui Buzhao was sitting on the *kang* in the dark with his legs crossed, dipping his bowl into a liquor vat. "Drinking in the dark is the way to go," he said, offering a cup to Jiansu, who took it and drank. Buzhao wiped his mouth with his sleeve. He slurped his liquor; Jiansu never made noise when he drank. Sui Buzhao had often eaten raw fish aboard ship, washing it down with strong liquor to smother the fishy smell. Jiansu, who seldom drank, accompanied his uncle for nearly an hour, with grievances and anger burning inside him.

Suddenly Buzhao's bowl fell to the floor and shattered, the sound causing Jiansu to break out in a cold sweat. "Jiansu," his uncle asked, "did you hear Gimpy play that flute of his? You must have. Well, the damned thing keeps me awake at night. I've spent the last few nights wandering through town, and I feel like I'm ready to die. But how could I expect you to know?" He grabbed his nephew's shoulder; Jiansu wondered what was troubling his uncle as Buzhao drew back his hand and massaged his knees. Then, without warning, he put his mouth up to Jiansu's ear and said loudly, "Someone in the Sui clan has died!"

Jiansu stared blankly at his uncle. Even in the dark he could see two lines of shiny tears running down the old man's face. "Who?"

"Sui Dahu. They say he died up at the front, and it might be true . . . I'm the only person in Wali who knows." The old man's voice had a nasal quality. Though a distant younger cousin, Sui Dahu was still a member of the Sui clan, and Jiansu took the news hard. The old man went on: "What a shame, he was quite a man. Last year, before he left, I went over to drink with him. He was only eighteen, didn't even have the hint of a moustache." Shrill notes from Gimpy's flute came on the air, sounding as if the player's tongue was a frozen stick. With the flute music swirling around Jiansu, the hazy image of Dahu floated up in front of him. Too bad! Dahu would never again set foot in Wali. As he listened to the icy strains of flute music, Jiansu had a revelation: We're all bachelors, and Gimpy's flute plays our song.

Sui Buzhao was soon so drunk he fell off his *kang*, and when Jiansu picked him up he discovered that the old man was wearing only a pair of shorts; his skin was cold to the touch. Jiansu laid him out on the *kang* as he would a misbehaving child.

Not until three days after his ferocious drinking bout did the old man finally wake up. Even then he spoke gibberish and kept tripping over his own feet. So he propped himself up against the window and informed anyone who would listen that a large ship had pulled up to the pier, with Zheng He himself at the tiller, and he wondered why he was still in the town of Wali. Jiansu and Baopu watched over him; Hanzhang cooked for him three times a day. When Baopu began sweeping the floor and removing cobwebs from the window, his uncle stopped him. "No need for that. I won't be here long. I'm getting on that ship. Come with me, and we'll sail the seas together. Or would you rather die in a dead-end town like this?"

Nothing Baopu said could change his uncle's mind, so he told him he was sick. "I'm sick?" the old man shouted, his tiny gray eyes opening wide. "It's this town that's sick. It stinks. Can't you smell it?" He crinkled up his nose. "At sea we deal in nautical miles, which equal sixty *li,* although some stupid bastards insist it's only thirty. To test the depth, measured in fathoms, you drop a greased, weighted rope into the water, it's called a plumb . . ." Baopu stayed with his uncle and sent Jiansu to get Guo Yun, a doctor of Chinese medicine.

Jiansu left and returned with Guo Yun.

After feeling the old man's pulse, Guo Yun left a prescription that would bring him around in three days. Hanzhang sat at the table watching, and when Guo Yun stood up to leave, he turned, spotted her, and froze. Her brows looked penciled on, two thin black lines. Her dark eyes shone, though her gaze was cold. The skin on her face and neck was so fair, so snowy white, it was nearly transparent. The elderly doctor stroked his beard, an uncomprehending look on his face. He sat back down on the stool and said he'd like to feel Hanzhang's pulse. She refused.

"You're not well, I'll bet on it," he said as he turned to Baopu. "In nature growth is inevitable, yet moderation is essential. Without growth there can be no maturation, and without moderation growth is endangered." Baopu could make no sense of that, but he urged Hanzhang to do as the doctor said. Again she refused. Guo Yun sighed and walked out the door. They watched his back until it disappeared.

THREE

In the end Sui Jiansu quit his job at the factory, surprising many people, since a Sui had never before given up the calling. For him, however, it was an easy decision. After visiting the commerce office and checking with the Gaoding Street Party secretary, Li Yuming, and Luan Chunji, the street director, he received permission to open a tobacco and liquor stall. A month later he found an empty building just off the street, ideally located to expand his business into a shop. He went to the mill again to talk his brother into joining him in the venture, but Baopu shook his head. "Well, then," Jiansu said, dejected, "since your calligraphy is so good, will you paint a shop sign for me?"

The old millstone rumbled. Baopu took the writing brush. "What's it called?"

"The Wali Emporium."

So Baopu laid a sheet of paper on the stool, but his hand shook uncontrollably when he dipped the brush into the ink, and he could not write the sign.

Ultimately, Jiansu was forced to ask the elementary school principal, Wattles Wu, to write it for him. The principal, a man in his fifties who had layers of loose skin on his neck, refused to use bottled ink; instead he had Jiansu make traditional ink on his long ink stone. It took Jiansu an hour to liquefy the ink block, after which the principal picked up a large, nearly hairless brush, soaked it in the ink, and began writing on a sheet of red paper. Jiansu watched as three thick veins rose on the back of the man's slender hand, and when they retreated, the words "Wali Emporium" appeared on the paper. The characters for the word "emporium" were truly unique and, for some strange reason, conjured up the image of rusted metal. After Jiansu pasted it over the doorway he leaned against the door frame to look up at the sign. This was going to be an unusual shop, he was thinking.

The first week he was open, Jiansu sold only three bottles of sesame oil and a pack of cigarettes. Sui Buzhao was the first customer to step through the door of his nephew's shop, but he merely looked around. On his way out, he recommended that Jiansu sell snacks to go with cups of liquor straight from the vat. He also urged him to paint a large liquor vat on the wall. Jiansu not only accepted his uncle's suggestions, he went further by pasting posters of female movie stars on the outside wall. All Wali elders had been in the habit of going over to the local temple to drink, and the painted liquor vat invited nostalgia. As a result, most of his early customers were older, but the younger folks weren't far behind. The place quickly became a hub of social activity.

One day, after business had started taking off, an elderly woman, Zhang-Wang, who coupled her maiden name with that of her deceased husband, entered with a request for him to begin stocking her handicrafts.

By "handicrafts," she meant things like homemade sweetened yam-and-rice balls on sticks, clay tigers, and tin whistles, things she had been making and selling for decades, even during difficult times. She also told fortunes, some openly, others on the sly, to make a little extra money. Already in her sixties, she was a chain-smoker; the corners of her mouth were sunken, making her look older than her years. She had a thin neck and a pointed, turned-down chin, and her face was forever dirty. Her back was bent, her legs shook, and she made constant noises even when she wasn't speaking. But the things she made were of the highest quality. Take, for instance, her clay tigers. She fashioned them so they had the same down-turned mouth as she, giving them an elderly yet proud, kind and gentle appearance, like their maker. And she kept making them bigger and bigger, until some were the size of pillows, toys that needed to be shared by two children at a time. She suggested that they be displayed on top of the Wali Emporium counter on consignment.

With a broad smile, Jiansu stared at the dust that had gathered on her thin neck and chatted with her casually, while she removed cigarettes from a rack and smoked them one after the other, never taking her eyes off Jiansu. He was by then in his mid-thirties, with slick black hair and a pimple here and there. He possessed a long, handsome face, an alert, vigilant face that showed a bit of cunning. Needless to say, he was a favorite of the women. But he was still unmarried, primarily a result of his clan's situation; no one wanted to marry their daughter to either of the Sui brothers, him or Baopu. Baopu had once been married to the daughter of the family's handyman, but she had died of consumption early on. He had not remarried.

Zhang-Wang, who knew that Jiansu was neither as open nor as guileless as his older brother, smirked as she looked at him, revealing blackened teeth. He blushed and urged her to say what was on her mind, even jokingly calling her an ugly old woman. When she took a few clay tigers out of her pockets and placed them on the counter, the similarity of their faces made him laugh. Reaching out to touch his bicep and chest, she said, "Aren't you the strong boy!" When he wouldn't stop laughing, she reached around and spanked him lightly. With a frown, she said, "You should be more serious when you're talking to your old grandma!"

"Um," Jiansu grunted, and stopped laughing. So they began negotiating the price and split for the handicrafts, and while they hadn't reached an agreement by the time he lit the lamp, the deal was struck before she left.

From then on, Zhang-Wang came to the shop every day to move her clay tigers around on the counter. Sales were up: Many women bought the toys for their children, and if the children themselves came, she taught them new ways to play with them, with a little tiger attacking a big one by banging its head. But, they said, that would quickly lead to cracked heads. "Then what?" "Come buy new ones," she'd say. As time passed, there was more business than the two entrepreneurs could handle during the day, so they started lighting a lamp and staying open longer. One night a group of old men sat beside the liquor vat drinking and snacking till the middle of the night.

Jiansu often slept with his head down on the counter, and Zhang-Wang delighted in blowing cigarette smoke at his red lips. In his eyes, she was a good assistant, and part of the shop's success was her doing. "The tigers are our protectors," she said. He gave the clay figurines, with their downturned mouths, a doubtful look. "Tigers are mountain spirits," she added. When business was slow they talked about all manner of things, but his uncle, Buzhao, was one of her favorite topics. She'd laugh and show her dark teeth. "That old man is skin and bones, but he still won't behave himself. When he was younger plenty of pretty girls got their taste of those old bones, including me. He's never had an unskinny day, but he's always been good at what he does.

"Do you know why he and Shi Dixin are mortal enemies?" she asked one day. Jiansu stared at her curiously and shook his head. So she took a cigarette from the rack, lit it, and told her story.

"Well, it was all on account of something really small. Back then, before your time, there was a lot more going on in Wali than now. And whenever you find a lot going on you'll also find men who behave badly. Keep that in mind. When they're ill mannered, they expend what energy they have on women's bodies, leaving none for the things they ought to be doing. Men like your uncle, for instance, couldn't even carry a lump of bean flour weighing three catties; they'd trip all over themselves and drop it, turning it into a pile of snow. Everyone always had a big laugh over that. And those sailors, well, the minute they stepped ashore they were like wolfhounds, their eyes bright red, throwing a fright into anyone who saw them, but once you got to know them they were all right. Your uncle learned how to treat people from those sailors, and that means that the Sui clan has at least one man who doesn't follow the straight and narrow. That said, he did wind up doing one thing that benefited the people in town. What was that? He brought a dirty, black object to town from a ship. It had a smell somewhere between fragrant and stinky. Some people said it was from a musk ox, with something added. If a local girl's belly started to grow, your uncle held whatever that was up to her nose a couple of times, and she immediately lost fluids from both ends, which restored her to the way she was before. You can see how much trouble that saved. But damned if Shi Dixin, that big phony, didn't find out about it and take out after your uncle, who ran straight to the pier, with Shi on his heels. One fleeing, one chasing."

Zhang-Wang lit another cigarette and blew the smoke out through her nose. "Shi ran like crazy and still he couldn't catch him. So heaven intervened. Just as your uncle was about to reach the pier, his legs got all tangled up and he crashed to the ground. Weird old Shi ran up and twisted his leg. Your uncle threw sand in Shi's face and received a second twist in return. Back then there was more sand on the riverbank than there is now, and your uncle's face was all bloody from scraping on the ground. Curses flew from his mouth, but Shi didn't say a word. He just picked up a rock and smashed your uncle's hand with it, which gave him the chance he was looking for to grab that thing. Now, that's when the real fighting started. They were both covered in blood. Shi Dixin predicted that sooner or later that thing would bring down the town of Wali, but the town's young men all thought it was great. A knock-down, drag-out fight was inevitable. But then, when Shi felt his strength about to go, he flung the damned thing into the river, and that brought the fight to an abrupt end. The two men, battered and bloody, just stood there glaring at one another . . ."

Jiansu didn't make a sound for the longest time after Zhang-Wang had finished telling her story. He'd been mesmerized by a fight that had occurred decades before. If he'd been around at the time, he was sure that the only thing that would have wound up in the river would have been Shi Dixin himself.

Workers from the noodle factory often killed time in the shop, the older ones drinking straight from the liquor vat, the younger ones eating Zhang-Wang's homemade sweets. After holding them in their mouths awhile, they'd pull them out into long, thin threads. The sweets alone attracted young men and women to the shop. They'd chew and pull and giggle, and if Jiansu saw one of the girls chewing a piece, he might just grab hold of it, pull it into a long thread, and wrap it around her neck.

One day Naonao came in wearing her white work apron, her arms exposed. Having just learned how to disco, she couldn't wait to put on a show. Sticking out her hands, she ah-ed and ooh-ed a couple of times, under the hypnotic stare of Jiansu, who was clutching the twenty fen he'd just been given. He went up to her when she began to chew one of the treats. Her dark, shining eyes rolled as she surveyed the items on the rack and slowly moved the wad around in her mouth. Jiansu was just about to reach out and pull it when Naonao poked him in the chest. He stumbled backward, feeling a numbing sensation—she'd probably hit an acupuncture point. He sat down and looked up with cold eyes at the fireball that was Naonao, rolling around in front of the counter and from there out the door. He took a deep breath.

It was Duoduo's first spoiled vat since opening the factory.

It lasted five days, and even though the losses were lighter than those from the spoiled vat of years before, Duoduo was frantic. Feeling helpless, he went several times to the mill, begging Baopu to come to the factory as a technician, but Baopu refused each time, preferring to feed the saturated beans into the eye of the millstone with his wooden ladle and then sit on his stool to watch the stone turn. Duoduo would curse him as he left the mill, vowing to shoot the wooden-headed man one day. "His head's made of wood, why not shoot him?" As commander of the Gaoding Street militia during land reform, Duoduo had already shot several people, and he couldn't think of a better

candidate for a bullet than this member of the Sui clan. But Duoduo
was getting on in years, and he no longer had a rifle. So he returned to
the factory, where he was asked why he hadn't brought Baopu with
him. "He's too busy sitting like a block of wood in the mill!" he replied, turning livid with rage.

Back and forth he paced, finding it impossible to control his nerves,
until another member of the Sui clan came to mind. Without a second thought, he went to the Wali Emporium and asked Jiansu to take
over as technician. Jiansu said no. Duoduo smiled and said, "There's
never been a member of the Sui clan who wasn't born to this calling.
Give it a try. I'll pay you top wages. There's always been someone who
could right a spoiled vat."

Jiansu laughed to himself, knowing that Duoduo had actually set
his sights on Baopu. While Jiansu was thinking the offer over, Zhang-
Wang joined the conversation, urging him to take what looked to be
a fine opportunity; just how good he wouldn't know until he gave it a
try. "What about the shop?" Jiansu asked.

The dark folds on Zhang-Wang's neck jiggled as she gave him a
hard stare and said, "The shop will still be yours, I'll just run it for you.
I've been taking care of business all along, haven't I?" Jiansu looked
out the door into the sky and smiled.

So Jiansu returned to the factory, leaving the Wali Emporium in
the hands of Zhang-Wang, who sat behind the counter for two hours
every day. Business did not suffer a decline. Without telling anyone,
she added orange peels to the liquor vat and diluted it with cool water.
She carefully organized the rest of her day, her early-morning hours
with household duties and, when the sun was up, massaging Fourth
Master's back. All these she handled easily, though the man's back
caused her a bit of apprehension. Only two years away from his sixti-
eth birthday, he was still healthy and energetic. But there was a noticeable thickening of his back. She had massaged that back for decades
with hands and fingers that had grown dexterous from fashioning her
clay tigers. Her massages brought Fourth Master unparalleled pleasure, but in recent days she had begun to feel her strength ebb. One

day, while she was kneading his back, she told him that Hanzhang, his foster daughter, ought to take over. He responded by shifting his rotund body, which was covered only by a towel for modesty's sake, and snorting. It was the last time she brought up the subject. The red, round sun would be making its way into the sky when she left Fourth Master's house and went to the shop to sit behind the counter, slightly out of breath.

As for Jiansu, who found the factory more to his liking, he stayed away from the shop, going back no more than once a month to attend to the accounts. The factory, big as it was, was still run more or less as a workshop; only the name had changed. But many of the former workers, unwilling to work for Zhao Duoduo, had left, and the majority of their replacements were women. Two shifts kept the factory running around the clock. As the nights grew longer, the heated air had a soporific effect on the workers, and the sight of all those women nodding off beside the starch vat and under the water basin was a delight. As technician in charge, Jiansu was not required to keep to a rigid schedule; he could check on the work any time he wanted.

After the sun went down, he changed into a light purple fall jacket and a pair of straight-legged indigo pants that he tucked into shiny high-topped rubber boots. Thick black hair made his face appear unusually fair. One after the other, he studied how each of the women looked as they slept, a trace of derision at the corners of his mouth. This turned his face even paler and lit up his eyes. After he'd stood there awhile, they would wake up, one after the other, and yawn.

A chubby woman by the name of Daxi started coughing any time she saw Jiansu and did not stop until her face was red. She was not one of the better workers, and when she washed the noodles, they often fell to the floor in front of the cold-water basin. Once, while she was coughing, Jiansu walked up and kicked the gooey mess, which stopped the coughing fit. She belched and stared at him, but he strode past her, his rubber boots making squishing sounds. At that sound the yawning women got to their feet and went back to work sifting the noodle mixture. Their white aprons fluttered in the room's heavy mist; the unique fragrance of the shop began to spread like perfumed rouge.

An iron strainer full of holes hung above them, and when the sticky bean starch was poured into it, silvery threads of glass noodles streamed through the holes and into a steamy pot, where they turned clear. Sitting up high working the ladle was a swarthy man who, on this particular day, had just awakened when Jiansu entered. With a shout, he pounded on the strainer ostentatiously, his head swaying, filling the room with a rhythmic banging sound. Jiansu sat down to smoke, eyes sparkling behind a patch of hair that had fallen over his forehead. For half an hour he didn't say a word; then he jumped to his feet and ran out, not looking back, passing by the women like a flash.

Jiansu ran out onto a tall concrete platform, where he stopped to catch his breath as he looked up at the moist stars in the sky and listened to the sounds of water flowing in the Luqing River. The millstone was still turning, still rumbling; he turned toward the row of small windows on the riverbank, through which light shone weakly. Baopu would be behind one of them, sitting on his stool and tending the millstone. Jiansu wished the window would open to let the light out, if only briefly. With a sense of disappointment he stepped down off the platform and walked to the building around the corner from the processing room, stopping just outside. Light emerged from inside, as did the sound of snoring, and he knew that the factory manager, Duoduo, was sleeping in there. Taking hold of the handle, he held his breath and opened the door slowly. Once inside, he quietly closed it behind him and turned around. Duoduo was on his back, warmed by the heated *kang*, wearing only a pair of black underpants. Made of thick, hard material, and shiny, they were disgusting. The older residents of Wali, with the exception of Sui Buzhao, were all getting fat. Duoduo's fleshy belly was distended. His beard was graying, the skin on his face was sagging, and there were strange purple splotches on his cheeks. His slightly green lips were parted, revealing one of his front teeth. As he studied the face, Jiansu discovered that the left eye wasn't completely closed, and that made his heart lurch.

He stayed perfectly still, except for his hand, which he passed over the slightly open eye. It didn't flicker, and he breathed easier. Duoduo's prominent Adam's apple moved in concert with his loud breathing. He had, for some reason, placed a cleaver on the windowsill near him. Although there were rust spots on the back edge of the blade, it appeared to be quite sharp. The blood drained from Jiansu's face when he spotted the cleaver. He stood there a while longer and then left quietly.

The Midautumn Festival was only a few days away, and the accounts had been settled. The factory had brought in an astonishing amount of income, especially since becoming mechanized. In a week's time the mill went through at least a thousand more pounds of mung beans than before. Each time Duoduo came by to inspect the millstone he left in high spirits. He had his bookkeeper tally up the mechanized production and was told that at this rate profits would soar. So, since midautumn was nearly upon them, he decided to host a dinner for Li Zhichang, who had contributed so much to the mechanization process; Technician Li; Sui Buzhao; and especially Sui Jiansu. He hired the government chef, Fatty Han, the finest cook in all of Wali.

When he was in a good mood Duoduo was a generous man; this was one of those times, so he told the night workers they could come in shifts to enjoy some good food and spirits. Rumor had it that Fatty Han had 160 different tofu recipes. Maybe that rumor had influenced Zhao Duoduo, for this time the ingredients he supplied the chef included a dozen or more baskets of broken glass noodles from the previous spoiled vat. That didn't bother Fatty Han, who merely shed the vest he normally wore, now that he had a more difficult meal than usual to prepare, and was naked from the waist up. He devised twelve dishes for each table: There were reds and there were greens; there were dishes so sour it made the guests shiver and others so sweet the room was filled with the sound of smacking lips. Not long into the meal, the diners' shirts were soaked with sweat as they contentedly caught their breath. After the meal, Duoduo told his bookkeeper to determine how much it had cost. The dozen or so baskets of noodle pieces were not worth much, and most of the money had gone to the purchase of sugar and vinegar, plus the pepper the chef had stolen from the municipal cafeteria.

The eating and drinking continued until two in the morning, with three shifts taking part. Jiansu drank cautiously that night, keeping his eye on all the others. Sui Buzhao, who was mightily drunk, was bending the ear of Technician Li, passing on stories about Uncle Zheng He. Zhao Duoduo's face was dark, almost purple; still sober, he toasted Jiansu. "The people of this town are too shortsighted," he said. "They laughed at me, saying I was wasting my money by putting a Sui on my payroll. But I knew what I was doing. I figured that if I had a member of the Sui clan working with me, there's no way this factory could have a spoiled vat."

Jiansu drained his glass and glowered at Zhao Duoduo. "You're good at account keeping," he said in a soft voice before sitting down and glancing over at Li Zhichang.

"The girls are getting drunk!" someone shouted as Jiansu quietly left the table. He walked into the processing room feeling the effects of alcohol, his face turning pink. He saw that some of the giggling girls' faces were also slightly red. But they kept working, just a bit wobbly, pulling the strands this way and that; harmony reigned. Enveloped by mist, Jiansu lit a cigarette. Daxi was the first to spot him, but she pretended he wasn't there and pulled the noodles like a madwoman, the best she'd ever looked at work. The swarthy man with his metal strainer, sitting high above them, was singing as he worked. It was a song no one knew, but they were all pretty sure it was not for mixed company. Naonao was drunker than any of the others. At first, like them, she swayed as she worked, but then she began to spin and fell in a heap, happily chatting away. Parts of a woman's body that ought not to be exposed were, but just for a moment, before she straightened her clothes and stood up. Now she was steady on her feet, but Jiansu began to sway and had to support himself with his hand on the wall. The swarthy man above was still banging his ladle and singing his off-color song. With difficulty, Jiansu walked out the door and somehow made his way back to where the others were still drinking. He leaned up against his uncle.

Just before he fell asleep Jiansu vaguely heard his uncle say something about "a leak on the port side" and immediately felt as if he were sailing on the high seas. That continued for a while, and when he heard his uncle say, "We're in port," he woke up. The first thing he saw after opening his eyes was Zhao Duoduo, neck stretched taut as he listened intently to Li Zhichang, whose voice gradually reached Jiansu. What he heard sobered him up in a flash. He was talking about buying a used piece of machinery from the prospecting team and turning it into a generator, which would light up all of Gaoding Street. He said he'd already spoken with the street director, Luan Chunji, Party Secretary Li Yuming, and Fourth Master, who had given his approval. At this point Li Zhichang grew animated, talking about how he wanted to apply scientific principles to the entire noodle factory. Pouring the starch into hot water, the sedimentation process, and sifting would all be accomplished by machines. The first step would be to install variable gears, large and small, and though others might not believe him, three or four of the gears had to be the size of peaches.

Given his experience in the old mill, Duoduo was eager to believe what he was hearing. He toasted Li Zhichang. When Jiansu coughed loudly, Li turned to look. Jiansu glared back. That had the desired effect: Li stopped talking. A few minutes later, Jiansu got up and walked off. A moment after that, Li made his excuses and left.

Together the two men stepped onto the concrete platform of the drying floor, where they were refreshed by a cool breeze. Neither spoke. They stood there for a long while before Jiansu reached out and took Li's hand, squeezing it tight. "What do you want from me?" Li asked.

"I want you to give up your plans."

Li freed his hand. "I can't do that," he said, "and I won't! We're buying the machinery, end of discussion. And the variable gears will be installed. It's something I have to do. Lights will shine in Wali, you have my word on that."

Jiansu's eyes flashed in the starlight as he pressed forward and said in a low voice, "I'm not talking about a generator. I'm talking about putting variable gears in the noodle factory. I want you to stop that."

"That can't be stopped," Li replied stubbornly, "none of it can be stopped—the mechanization plan must go forward."

Jiansu held his tongue and ground his teeth. Li gave him a puzzled look, and when Jiansu's hand sought out Li's, it was feverish. Li pulled his back in alarm. Jiansu gazed at the little window far off on the other side of the river. "The noodle factory is mine," he said, seemingly to himself, "mine and Sui Baopu's. Listen to me, Zhichang. When the Sui clan takes back the factory we'll go ahead with your damned plans." Li took a couple of steps backward and gasped. "You don't believe me?" Jiansu said. "It won't be long. But don't tell anyone."

Li kept retreating and wringing his dark hands. In a quaking voice, he said, "I won't tell, I won't tell a soul. But I won't give up my plans for the gears, not unless Sui Buzhao tells me to, only him."

With a sneer, Jiansu said, "Then go ask him. But you'll have to wait until he returns from his sailing trip with Uncle Zheng He."

The conversation ended there.

As promised, Li Zhichang did go to see Sui Buzhao, who was hesitant, and Li knew that Jiansu had already spoken with him. At that moment he understood the depth of the enmity between the two families. So long as the Zhao clan was running the factory, his gears would turn only in his mind, day and night, making sleep all but impossible. There were times when golden gears seemed to be turning just above his head, and he'd excitedly reach up to touch them. There was nothing to touch, of course. In his dreams he'd hook his finger around one of them and give it a kiss. Now all the plans he'd drawn up had been nullified on the night of the Midautumn Festival, in a scene he played out in his head over and over: He and Jiansu were standing shoulder to shoulder on the concrete platform, buffeted by cold winds. Jiansu's hand had been so hot he had to let go, and he knew he must no longer let those gears come to him at night. And yet, the fervent images burned their way into his breast, day and night. He must keep his passions in check. The only person he had to listen to was Sui Buzhao, who could give Li a new lease on life.

Li Zhichang had mixed feelings toward the older generation. He hated them, and he loved them. His grandfather, Li Xuantong, who had not considered himself an ordinary mortal since the age of fourteen, had shaved his head and traveled to a distant mountain to become a mystic. His father, Li Qisheng, had operated machinery for a capitalist in northeast China, making his return to Wali an inglorious one. People said that no respectable man would do what he did. Though he later tried to redeem himself through good service, the townspeople refused to forgive him. In their eyes, Li's family was synonymous with abnormality, to be neither understood nor trusted. Once the smartest boy in school, after finishing the fifth grade Zhichang was ready for middle school but was told he could not continue his education. The reasoning was convoluted, but it rested primarily on the fact that his father had operated machinery for a capitalist. An elementary school education was deemed sufficient for someone like him. He returned home burdened with unquenchable loathing for both his father and his grandfather.

In his nineteenth year something happened that left Li Zhichang with eternal regret. What he experienced that year made him realize that a man must always behave scrupulously; he must neither be slack in his work nor allow himself to get carried away with it.

Early one warm spring day, a feverish Li Zhichang walked alone on the bank of the river; never before had he felt such a need for something as he did now. He wanted it desperately. Sunset colors created a beautiful reflection on the water; budding new leaves on the floodplain willows swayed in the breeze like bashful maidens. He wanted it desperately. He strolled aimlessly for a while before crossing the floodplain to head back. But when he reached the willows, his throat turned hot and began to swell. He stopped, feeling weak, and sat down on the hot sandy ground. Time for pleasure.

Li Zhichang did not make it back home until nightfall, feeling more relaxed, his hands unusually soft. He slept well that night.

The next morning he drew curious looks when he was out for a walk. "Did you have a good time out in the willow grove?" a boy asked. With a malicious laugh, another boy went up to him and said, "In books they call that masturbating." Li felt an explosion go off in his head. He turned and ran, heedless of everything around him. Damn it! he cursed inwardly. Goddamn it! Laughter was following him. "I saw you!" someone shouted. "I saw everything!"

The young Li Zhichang refused to go out after that. His gate remained shut, and after several days had passed, people began to sense that something was wrong. So Li Yuming, the Gaoding Street Party secretary, and a clan member tried Zhichang's door. Not only was it locked, apparently something was blocking it; it may even have been nailed shut. With a sigh, Li Yuming left, saying that the boy would have to get through it on his own. Others tried their luck but with the same result. Sighs were heard all over town. "The Li clan, ah, the Li clan!"

Last to show up at Zhichang's door was Sui Buzhao, possibly the only person in town who understood the Li clan, and someone who had become a friend to the young man. He asked him to come out but was rebuffed. So he pounded on the door and cursed. "Uncle Sui," Li answered weakly from inside, "there's no need to curse. I'm not worthy of your friendship, I've done a terrible thing, and all that's left for me is to die." Sui Buzhao pondered this for a moment before leaving. He returned with an ax, with which he easily broke down the door. By then Zhichang was skin and bones, his face ashen, his uncombed hair in tangles. He stepped unsteadily up to Sui. "Uncle," he said, "be kind and use that thing on me."

The blush of anger rose on Buzhao's face. "Fine," he said as he swung the ax handle and knocked Li Zhichang to the floor. Li struggled to his feet and was promptly knocked down again. With his hands on his hips, the older man swore, "I must have been blind to befriend such a coward!" Li hung his head and said he was too ashamed to go outside.

"What's the big deal?" Sui growled.

After getting Li Zhichang to wash up and comb his hair, Sui Bu-zhao told him to step outside and walk with him, holding his head high. This time the people looked on with sober expressions; no one laughed.

In a word, what happened that day nearly destroyed Li Zhichang. But Sui Buzhao's ax had indeed given him a new lease on life. At night, as the golden gears turned above his head, he experienced both excitement and agony. He dared not try to touch them. He knew that sooner or later he would install them in the noodle factory, but impatience lay just below the surface, the same sort of impatience that had overcome him that day when he'd sought pleasure in the willow grove. Maybe, he thought, the passion he was experiencing now was an off-shoot of the same force that had nearly destroyed him. It was sheer agony, and there was nothing he could do about it. What he needed to do was join Technician Li in setting up a generator for Gaoding Street and turning Wali into a town where the lights shone brightly. Too many people had suffered as a result of insufficient lighting in town.

A resident had once gone to the Wali Emporium to buy one of Zhang-Wang's clay tigers, and she had taken advantage of the weak light to sell him a cracked model. Then there was the fellow named Erhuai, who was responsible for maintaining the floodplain; he was known to run like the wind through the shadows, a rifle slung over his back, reminding people of Zhao Duoduo as a young man. Li hated the way the man scurried through the darkness.

Li often stood outside the old mill on the riverbank. That is where the first gears were already turning. The millstone rumbled like distant thunder. By looking through the window he could see the most taci-turn member of the Sui clan inside. He too was beginning to take on the man's disinclination to utter a sound. The man seemed to contain as much power as the millstone itself as it tirelessly ground everything in its path, smoothly, steadily. But he did not utter a sound.

On one occasion the man stood up and, with his long wooden ladle, broke up a clot of mung beans on the conveyor belt. On his return to his stool he glanced out the window and raised his ladle. Li Zhichang looked in the direction of that glance and saw Jiansu, who was walking lazily up to the mill, pipe in hand. Once inside, Baopu offered his brother the stool, but Jiansu said no. "I was afraid you were getting drunk the other night," Baopu said, "so I waited for you in your room . . ."

Jiansu just smiled. Then, abruptly, the smile vanished. His face was slightly pale, much the same as that night on the platform. He hung his head and knocked the ashes out of the bowl of his pipe. In a soft voice he said, "There's something I've been meaning to talk to you about. I was going to mention it when the idea first came to me, but I got drunk that night and had no desire to sleep the next day. People said my eyes were bloodshot. I decided I wouldn't come see you after all. I didn't want to tell you what I had on my mind."

Baopu looked up at his brother, a pained look on his face. He stared at the tip of his ladle, dripping with water. "Go ahead, don't hold back. What was it you wanted to talk to me about?"

"Nothing. I've changed my mind."

"Go ahead, let's hear it."

"No, not now."

The brothers went silent. Baopu rolled a cigarette. Jiansu lit his pipe. The smoke clouded the air in the mill as, one puff after another, they created layers of smoke, all of which slowly settled onto the mill-stone, as it turned slowly, taking the smoke with it, until the swirls stretched into a long tube and drifted out through the window. Baopu smoked on and on, finally flipping away the butt. "Keeping it inside will only make you feel worse. As brothers we ought to be able to talk about anything. I can tell it's something serious, and that makes it even more important to tell me."

Jiansu paled. The hand holding the pipe began to tremble. With difficulty, he put away his pipe and uttered a single, softly spoken sentence: "I want to take the noodle factory back from Zhao Duo-duo."

From where he stood just beyond the window, Zhichang heard every word. As soon as that sentence was uttered, a crack from some-where inside the mill gave him a start; it sounded like someone had smacked against a steel rod. He thought something might have hap-pened to one of the gears, but the mill kept turning. Baopu stood up, his eyes lighting up beneath the heavy ridge of his brow. He nodded. "I see."

"The noodle factory has always carried the name Sui. It should be yours and mine." Jiansu's eyes bore into his brother.

Baopu shook his head. "It's nobody's. It belongs to the town of Wali."

"But I can take it back."

"No, you can't. These days no one has that power."

"I do."

"No, you don't. And you shouldn't have such thoughts. Don't for-get our father. At first he thought the mill belonged to the Sui clan. This misunderstanding ruined his health. Twice he rode his horse out to pay off debts. He returned home the first time, but the second time he threw up blood, staining the back of his horse. Our father died in a sorghum field—"

With a shout Jiansu slammed his fist down onto the stool. Then he crouched in pain, holding the stool with both hands.

"Baopu, you, you . . . I didn't want to but you made me tell you! You've taken the fight out of me, put out the fire, like smashing your fist into my head! But I'm not afraid. Don't worry, I won't stay my hand on this. You want me to spend the rest of my life sitting in the mill, like you, listening to the millstone rumble tearfully in circles, is that it? Never! That's something no member of the Sui clan ought to do. None of our ancestors was ever that gutless . . . I won't listen to you. I've held this inside me for decades. I'm thirty-six this year and still not married. You were, but your wife died. You should have a better life than most people, but you just sit in this mill, day in and day out. I hate you! I absolutely hate you! Today I want to make this perfectly clear: I hate the way you spend your days in this old mill . . ."

Zhichang stood beyond the window, stunned. He saw large beads of sweat roll off of Jiansu's forehead and cheeks.

FOUR

Sui Baopu recalled how little time his father had spent at the factory during Baopu's teen years, preferring the solitude of the pier, where he could ponder things and gaze at the reflections of ship masts in the water. He would not return home until dinnertime. His stepmother, Huizi, was in her thirties. With her lips painted red, she would sit at the dinner table eating and keeping a worried eye on her husband, while Baopu watched anxiously to see if she swallowed the color on her lips along with her food. His stepmother, the pretty daughter of a rich man from Qingdao, liked to drink coffee. Baopu was a little afraid of her. Once, when she was in a good mood, she took him in her arms and planted a kiss on his smooth forehead. Sensing her warm, heaving breast, his heart raced as he lowered his head, not daring to let his gaze linger on her snow-white neck. "Mama," he blurted out as his face reddened. She murmured a response. That was the first and last time he called her that. But he stopped being afraid of her.

One day Baopu found Huizi crying bitterly and writhing on the *kang,* nearly breathless. It wasn't until later that he learned why his stepmother had been so grief-stricken: Her father, it turned out, had been murdered in Qingdao, caught selling land and factories for gold bullion to take out of China. Baopu was at a loss for words.

After that he began spending time in the study, which held many scrolls and more books than he could count. He found a date-colored wooden ball, so red it shone, and when he held it in his hand it felt incredibly smooth and very cold. There was also a box that played a lovely tune when he touched it.

One evening, when his father was in the middle of dinner, Zhang-Wang from the eastern section of town dropped in to borrow some money. He politely invited her to sit and poured tea for her. Then he went into his study to get the money, which she tucked into her sleeve and promised to repay after she'd sold a hundred clay tigers. "Don't worry about it," he said. "Go spend it any way you like." Huizi glowered at him; Zhang-Wang noticed.

"How's this?" she said. "Since I feel awkward taking your money, why don't I tell your fortune?" With a wry smile, Father nodded his approval. Huizi just snorted. Zhang-Wang sat down in front of him, so close it made his lips quiver, and reached her hand up the opposite sleeve, where she counted on her fingers. She announced that he had a pair of red moles behind his left shoulder. The soup ladle fell from Huizi's hand. As Zhang-Wang studied his face, her eyes rolled up into her head, and all Baopu could see were the whites. "Tell me the day and time of your birth," she intoned. By this time Father had forgotten all about the food in front of him. He told her what she wanted to know in a weak voice. She began to shake; her eyeballs dropped back into place, and she fixed them on Father's face. "I'm leaving, I must leave," she said, raising her arms. With a parting glance at Huizi, she walked out the door. Baopu watched as his father sat like a statue, mumbling incoherently and rubbing his knees the rest of the day.

Over the days that followed, Father seemed laden down with anxieties. He busied himself with this and that, not quite sure what he ought to be doing. Finally he dug out an abacus and began working on accounts. Baopu asked what he was doing. "We owe people," his father replied. Baopu could not believe that the richest family in town owed money to anyone, so he asked who it was owed to and how much. Suddenly the son was interrogating the father. "All the poor, wherever they live!" his father replied. "We've been behind in our obligations for generations . . . Huizi's father was too, but then he refused to pay, and someone beat him to death!" Breathing hard, by then he was nearly shouting. He was becoming skeletal; his face had darkened. Always nicely groomed in the past, he now let his hair turn lusterless and ignored the specks of dandruff. Baopu could only gaze at his father fearfully. "You're still young," his father said, "you don't understand . . ."

In the wake of this conversation, Baopu vaguely felt that he too was one of the destitute poor. From time to time he strolled over to the riverbank to watch the millstone rumble along. The man tending the stone at the time kept feeding beans into the eye with his wooden ladle; white foamy liquid flowed from beneath the stone, filling two large buckets, which were carried away by women. It was the same scene he'd witnessed in his youth. After leaving the mill, he'd walk over to the factory where the noodles were made and where steam filled the air with a smell that was both sweet and sour. The workers, male and female, wore little clothing, their naked arms coated with bean starch. As they worked in the misty air, they moved rhythmically, punctuated by cadenced shouts of "Hai! Hai!" A thin layer of water invariably covered the cobblestone floor. Water was the irreplaceable element here. People were continually stirring huge vats to wash the white noodles. On one of his visits, a worker spotted him. "Don't splash any water on the young master!" she yelled anxiously. Baopu left in a hurry. He knew that one day this would no longer be his and that he was in fact born to be one of the destitute poor.

Father continued to spend time on the riverbank, appearing to be settling into deeper nostalgia for the ships that had visited from afar. One time he brought Baopu along. "This is where Uncle Buzhao sailed from," he said, and Baopu could tell that his father missed his brother. On their way home, his father looked over at the old mills, drenched in the colors of the sunset, and stopped.

"Time to pay off our debts," he said lightly.

So Baopu's father mounted the old chestnut he'd had for years and rode off. A week later he returned, his face glowing, the picture of health. He tethered the horse, brushed the dust from his clothes, and

called the family together to announce that he had been repaying
debts and that from that day on, the Sui clan would operate only a
single noodle factory, since the others had all been given away. They
could hardly believe what they were hearing. The silence was broken a
moment later: They shook their heads and laughed. So he took a
folded piece of paper out of his pocket. A red seal appeared at the bottom of several lines of writing. Apparently a receipt. Huizi snatched it
out of his hand and fainted dead away after reading it, throwing the
family into a panic. They thumped her on the back, they pinched her,
and they called her name. When she finally came to, she glared at
Father as if he'd become her mortal enemy. Then she burst into tears,
her wails interspersed with words no one could understand. In the
end, she clenched her teeth and pounded the table until her fingers
bled. By then she'd stopped crying and just sat there staring at the
wall, her face a waxen yellow.

The incident frightened Baopu half to death. Though he still didn't
understand what lay behind his father's actions, he knew why his father felt as if a burden had been lifted. The incident also revealed his
stepmother's stubborn streak. It was a terrifying stubbornness that
eventually led to her death, one that was far crueler than her husband's.
But Baopu would not know that until much later. At the time he was
too concerned with learning how his father had found the people to
take over the factories. He knew that the Sui clan holdings, including
factories and noodle processing rooms in several neighboring counties
and a few large cities, could not have been disposed of in a week.
Moreover, the money he owed was to the poor, and where would he
find someone willing to accept such vast holdings in the name of the
poor? Baopu pondered these questions until his head ached, but no
answers came. And the millstone rumbled on, as always. But Father
stopped going there. From time to time unfamiliar boats would come
to town to transport the noodles, and many of the people who had
helped with the work quit to go elsewhere, leaving the Sui compound
quiet and cold. His stepmother's injured hand had healed; only one
finger remained crooked. No one ever saw her laugh after that. Then

one day she went to see Zhang-Wang to have her fortune told. She didn't say a word after returning home with a pair of large clay tigers. They would await the birth of Jiansu and Hanzhang, for whom they would be the first toys.

◁

Large public meetings were held in town, one on the heels of the other. People with large land holdings or factory owners were dragged up onto a stage that had been erected on the site of the old temple. The masses flung bitter complaints at them; waves of loud accusations swept throughout Wali. Zhao Duoduo, commander of the self-protection brigade, who paced back and forth on the stage, a rifle slung over his back, was responsible for an intriguing invention: a piece of pigskin attached to a willow switch, which he waved in the air. In high spirits, he used his invention as a lash on the back of a fat old man who was the target of criticism. The old man screeched and fell on his face. The people below the stage roared their approval. Duoduo's actions also spurred the people into climbing onto the stage to beat and kick the offenders. Three days after the first session, a man was beaten to death. Baopu's father, Sui Yingzhi, stood between those on the stage and those below it for several days, and in the end he felt that his place was up on the stage. But members of the land reform team urged him to go back down. "We've been told by our superiors that you are to be considered an enlightened member of the gentry class."

◁

Sui Buzhao returned to Wali on the day Hanzhang was born. He had a fishing knife in his belt and he reeked of the ocean. He was much thinner than when he left and his beard was much longer. His eyes had turned gray but were keener and brighter than ever. When he heard about all the changes in the town and learned that his older brother had given the factories away, he laughed. "It ends well!" he said as he stood near the old mill. "The world is now a better place."

Then he undid his pants and relieved himself in front of Sui Yingzhi and Baopu. Yingzhi frowned in disgust.

In the days that followed, Sui Buzhao often took Baopu down to the river to bathe. The youngster was shocked to see the scars on his uncle's body: some black and some purple, some deep and some shallow, like a web etched across the skin. He said he'd been nearly killed three times, and each time he'd survived despite the odds. He gave Baopu a small telescope he said he'd taken from a pirate, and once he sang a sailing song for him. Baopu complained it was a terrible song. "Terrible?" his uncle grunted. "It comes from a book we sailors call the *Classic of the Waterway*. Anyone who doesn't memorize it is bound to die! Uncle Zheng He gave me this copy, and I couldn't live without it."

When they returned to town he retrieved the book, which he'd hidden behind a brick in a wall. The yellowing pages were creased and dog-eared. With great care he read several pages aloud; Baopu didn't understand a word, so the old man shut it and placed it in a metal box for safekeeping. He spoke of his disappointment in the receding waters of the river and said that if he'd known that that was going to happen, he'd have taken Baopu to sea with him. The two of them spent most of every day together, and as time passed, the youngster began to walk like his uncle, swaying from side to side. Eventually, inevitably, this made his father so angry he swatted the palms of the boy's hands with an ebony switch and locked him in his room. With no one to accompany him, the lonely old man hesitated for several days before wandering off to another place.

Zhao Duoduo often came by to pass the time. That was the only thing that could get Sui Yingzhi to put down his abacus. He'd come out to pour his guest some tea. "No, thanks," Zhao would say, "you can keep working." Yingzhi, put on edge by the visit, would return to his study.

One time Zhao came to speak to Huizi. "Do you have any chicken fat?" he asked with a smile. When she gave him some, he took his revolver out of the holster and rubbed chicken fat into the leather. "Makes it shine," he said as he stood up to go. But when he handed the dish back he placed it upside down over her breast . . . Huizi spun around and picked up a pair of scissors, but Zhao was already out the door. The dish crashed to the floor, bringing Yingzhi rushing out of his room, where he saw his wife holding scissors in one hand and wiping grease from her breast with the other.

On another occasion, when Huizi was in the vegetable garden, Duoduo sprang out from behind a broad bean trellis. She turned and ran away. "What are you running for?" he called out. "It's going to happen sooner or later. Who are you saving it for?" Huizi stopped, smiled, and waited for him to catch up. "That's the idea," Zhao said, gleefully slapping his hand against his hip. He walked over, and when he was right in front of her, she scowled, raised her hands as if they were claws, and scratched both sides of his face like an angry cat. Despite the pain, Zhao pulled out his revolver and fired into the ground. Huizi ran off.

A month passed before all the scratch marks had scabbed on his cheeks. Zhao Duoduo called people to a Gaoding Street meeting to discuss whether or not it was reasonable to still consider Sui Yingzhi an enlightened member of the gentry class. Yingzhi was summoned to the meeting, where a heated discussion ensued until Duoduo abruptly held his finger up to Yingzhi's head like a pistol and said, "Bang." Yingzhi crumpled to the ground as if he'd been shot and stopped breathing. They picked him up and rushed him home, while someone ran to get Guo Yun, the traditional healer. They did not manage to wake Sui Yingzhi until late that night. His recovery after that was slow; he walked with a slouch and was rail thin. Day in and day out Baopu heard his father's coughs echo through the house. The meeting had sapped his vitality. He was like a different man altogether.

"We still haven't paid off all our debts," he said to his son one day between coughs. "Time is running out. It's something we have to do." His coughing fit that night lasted into the early morning, but when the family awoke the next day, he was gone. Then Baopu found blood-stains on the floor, and he knew that his father had ridden off on his chestnut horse again.

The days that followed passed slowly. After a week of torment, Sui Buzhao returned from his wanderings and laughed when he learned that his brother had ridden off again. Just before nightfall, the family heard the snorts of their horse and ran outside, happy and relieved. The horse knelt down in front of the steps and whinnied as it pawed the ground. The animal's gaze was fixed on the doorway, not the people; its mane shifted, and a drop of liquid fell into Baopu's hand. It was blood, fresh blood. The horse raised its head and whinnied sky-ward, then turned and trotted off, the family running after it. On the outskirts of town, the horse ran into a field of red sorghum and fol-lowed a path where the leaves were spattered with blood. Huizi's jaw tightened as she ran, and when she saw the trail of blood she began to cry. The horse's hooves pounded the ground, managing to avoid all the sorghum plants. Baopu wasn't crying, didn't feel sad at all, and for that, he scolded himself. The sorghum field seemed to go on forever, and the horse picked up the pace until it stopped abruptly.

Sui Yingzhi was lying in a dry furrow, his face the color of the earth beneath him. Red leaves covered the ground around him, though it wasn't immediately clear if that was their natural color or if they were bloodstained. But one look at his face told them he'd lost a great deal of blood before falling off the horse. Sui Buzhao sprang into action, picking up Yingzhi and shouting, "Brother! My brother . . ." Sui Yingzhi's mouth twitched. He searched their faces, looking for his son. Baopu knelt beside him.

"I know," he said. "Your heart was too heavy."

His father nodded. He coughed, and a thin stream of fresh blood seeped from his mouth. Sui Buzhao turned to Huizi. "The coughing has destroyed his lungs." Huizi bent down and rolled up her husband's pant leg. The flesh was flabby and nearly transparent, and she knew that he was dying from the loss of blood. "Jiansu! Hanzhang! Come see your father!" she shouted as she pushed the two younger children up in front of Baopu. Hanzhang bent down and kissed her father, and when she straightened up there was blood on her young lips. She gazed up at her mother with a frown, as if put off by the taste. Only a few minutes of life remained in Sui Yingzhi. He mumbled something and closed his eyes.

Sui Buzhao, who had been holding his brother's wrist all this time to check his pulse, let the arm drop. Loud wails burst from his throat; his frail body was wracked with spasms of grief. Baopu, who had never seen his uncle cry, was stunned. "I'm a no-account vagabond," his uncle said through his tears, "and I know I'll not die well. But, you, brother, you lived an exemplary life, educated and proper, the best the Sui family had to offer, yet you bled to death out on the road. Oh, the old Sui family, our family . . ."

The old horse's head drooped, its nose spotted with mud; it wasn't moving. Holding their breath, they lifted Sui Yingzhi up and laid him across the horse's back.

"A member of the Sui family has left us," the old men of Wali were saying. The town's spirit seemed to have died, and two consecutive rainfalls did nothing to change that. The streets were so deserted it felt as if most of the residents had been swept away. The old man who worked the wooden ladle in the mill by the river said, "I've watched the mill for the Sui family all my life. Now the old master has left us to open a noodle factory on the other side, and I should go with him. He needs my help." He said this half a dozen times, and then, one day, as he sat on his stool, he simply stopped breathing. The old ox kept turning the millstone, uselessly, ignorant of what had happened. The town's elders narrowed their eyes when they heard the news. Staring straight ahead, they said to anyone who would listen, "Do you still say there are no gods?"

Huizi bolted her gate and refused to open it for anyone, so Baopu opened a side door to let his uncle, whose room was on the outside, into the compound. Buzhao knew that no one could keep Baopu away from him anymore, but then he noticed a somber look on the youngster's face. When he spoke to him of his adventures on the high seas, the boy lacked the interest he'd displayed in the past, not regaining it until the day Buzhao took the old seafaring book out of its metal box and waved it in front of him.

On days when Jiansu came to Buzhao's room, his uncle would hoist him onto his shoulders the way he'd done with his older brother and carry him out through the side door, down to the river or into one of the lanes to buy him some candy. He could see that Jiansu was smarter than Baopu, a boy who learned fast. He decided to let Jiansu play with the telescope, and he watched as the boy focused on the girls bathing in the river. "That's really neat," Jiansu said with a click of his tongue as he reluctantly handed back the telescope.

Buzhao hoisted him back on his shoulders and sort of stumbled along. "We're a team, you and me," he said.

Jiansu spent so much time on his uncle's shoulders that people called him the "jockey." Sooner or later, Sui Buzhao said, he'd leave to go back to sea. That is what made his life interesting and what would make him worthy of the town. He told Jiansu to wait for that day, saying he had to find a flat-bottom boat, since the river was so shallow. Not long after that, someone actually came forward with a beat-up sampan, and Sui Buzhao could not have been happier. He fashioned a tiller, plugged up the holes with tung oil, and made a sail out of a bedsheet. People came to gawk at the boat, maybe touch it, and, of course, talk about it. Excitement was in the air. "That's called a boat," adults would tell their children. "Boat," the tiny voices would repeat.

Sui Buzhao asked some of the young men to help him carry the boat over to the abandoned pier, where a crowd waited patiently, having heard that something was in the air. Sui Buzhao saw Baopu in the crowd, which further energized him, and he began to describe the boat's functions to the crowd, stressing the use of the tiller. The people pressed him to put the boat in the water. He just rolled his eyes. "You think it's that easy? Have you ever heard of anyone putting a boat in the water without chanting to the gods?" At that point he stopped surveying the crowd and assumed a somber expression as he offered up a chanted prayer, thanking the gods for keeping the nation and her people safe and offering up sacrifices of food and spirits to the ocean, island, earth, and kitchen gods to watch over ship and crew.

$$\prec\!\!\!\sim\!\!\!\succ$$

A profound silence settled over the crowd as the hazy image of a distant mist-covered ocean came into view, with bare-armed men pulling at their oars, their lives in imminent danger, or of a ship brimming with treasure that disappears in the mist. Truly, the vista is of men and ships, with fortune and misfortune giving rise to each other. The elders could still remember ships' masts lining the old pier and the fishy smell that hung in the air. Ships old and new fighting for space, one nearly on top of the other, as far as the eye can see. Ten thousand sailors breathing on myriad decks, as lewd, murky air assails the face. Commerce is king in Wali, where silver ingots roll in from everywhere. Suddenly a cloudburst, but the rivergoing ships stay put, like a swarm of locusts . . .

The townspeople gathered round Sui Buzhao and his boat, making hardly a sound, exchanging glances as if they were all strangers. After rubbing their eyes they saw that Sui Buzhao was already sitting aboard his boat, still on dry land, and as he sat there, he raised the telescope hanging from his belt, an invitation for Jiansu to come along with him.

With a shout, Jiansu took off toward the ship as if possessed, but Baopu grabbed him by the shirt and refused to let go, no matter how hard his brother struggled to break free.

Foul curses tore from Sui Buzhao from where he stood in the cabin. With a wave of his hand he signaled them to pick up the boat, with him in it, and carry it over to the water. Bursting with excitement, that is what they did, and the instant the hull touched the water it came to life; a welcoming sound arose from somewhere inside. The sail billowed and moved the boat swiftly away from the bank as Sui Buzhao stood up and let the wind muss his hair. The crowd saw him put his hands on his hips, then slap his thigh and make faces. The women lowered their heads and scolded softly, "Shame on him."

The spell was broken when the boat reached the middle of the river. "A fine boat!" the people shouted. "And a fine captain!" "Good for you, Sui Buzhao!" "Come back and take me with you!" . . . As they shouted their encouragement, the boat began to turn with the current, moving in a slow circle, just like the millstone. Then, as it picked up speed and everyone expected it to take off, it abruptly sank beneath the surface, leaving nothing behind but a swirling eddy. If Buzhao didn't bob up in a hurry he'd be lost, everyone knew. So they waited, but there was no sign of him as the surface smoothed out and the river returned to its original state. Wrapped in his brother's arms, Jiansu wept. Baopu held tight, his arms trembling.

Immersed in grief and disappointment, the people were suddenly amazed to see a head burst through the surface near the bank. Who was it? Why, none other than the stubble-faced Sui Buzhao.

Back on dry land, he ignored the whoops of joy as he walked off, swaying from side to side and dripping water. Heaven willed the ship to sink, people were saying. Maybe Wali is not supposed to have boats. If it hadn't sunk, Sui Buzhao might have left town and never returned. Yes, they all agreed, as they chided themselves for not even considering where the man might have wanted to sail off to. Their eyes were on Jiansu. How lucky you are, they said, how very lucky. But there were those who accused Buzhao of having a sinister side. How could he think of taking a mere child with him? Baopu, who would have none of that, took his brother by the hand and walked off, following the trail of water left by his uncle.

For days Sui Buzhao was too embarrassed to leave his room. Then he fell ill. When, many days later, he finally emerged from his room, he was terribly gaunt. He had tied a strip of blue cloth around his forehead, almost as if that were all that kept his head intact.

A boat had sunk out of sight, but a few years later, a large ship would see the light of day, and its appearance would rock the entire province. That event would occur at about the same time as the assault on the town wall, making it one of the most feverish years in memory.

Sui Buzhao had his head buried in his seafaring bible when he heard someone outside his window shout, "A team of irrigation repairmen has found a buried ship!" He knew that everyone in town was engaged in digging in the ground for one reason or another, so maybe someone had dug up his boat. His heart racing, he ran outside and headed for the riverbank. When he reached the old pier he saw that the whole town had turned out, forming a crowd a few hundred yards from the riverbank. He started running, stumbling and falling several times before he reached the crowd. Fortunately for him, he was thin enough to squeeze his way up front, where he saw piles of excavated mud. Dirty water was flowing down a man-made ditch; something had been moved to higher ground. "My god!" The declaration burst from his throat when he saw it.

It had once been a large wooden ship whose deck had long since rotted away, leaving a sixty- or seventy-foot keel with a pair of iron objects—the remnants of two cannons—lying athwart it. A rusty anchor lay to the side, along with other scattered, unidentifiable items, turned black by gooey mud. A pair of iron rods lay across what had been the bow of the ship, seemingly some sort of staffs that had been stuck in the deck. A strange odor rose from the pit, attracting a hawk that was circling above them. The smell turned the people's throats dry, inducing a sense of nausea. The keel, exposed to the dry air, had already begun to turn red. Water seeped from holes in the wood, white at first, then red. Before long, people smelled blood and backed away from the sickening odor. The hawk was still circling, carried by the air currents.

The man in charge of the dig was crouching off to the side, having a cigarette. "That's enough gawking," he said as he stood up. "We've got work to do. We'll chop it up and carry the wood back to the kitchen for kindling."

Sui Buzhao was in motion before the man's words had died out. Standing as close to the keel as possible, he shouted, "Don't you dare! . . ." Shocked silence. "That's my ship!" he said, pointing to the relic. "It belongs to Uncle Zheng He and me." His words were met by laughter. Again the man in charge told his men to go on down and start working. "Hey, you!" Sui Buzhao's gaunt white face turned purple; the blue headband went pop and fell away, like the broken string of a lute. He ran down, picked up the rusty anchor, and raised it over his head.

"Anyone who so much as touches my ship gets this!"

Baopu and Jiansu were among the onlookers. Jiansu cried out to his uncle, but Buzhao didn't hear him. He stood firm, gnashing his teeth, his wispy beard quivering. Someone commented that the ship must have been buried for centuries and might even be a national treasure. When he recommended holding off until they could get an expert opinion, the others agreed. So the man in charge sent someone to get Li Xuantong.

The man returned to report that Li was meditating and was not to be bothered. But he had recommended his good friend, the herbalist Guo Yun. Half an hour later, Guo arrived at the site, and the crowd parted to let him through. Hoisting the hem of his robe as he negotiated the muddy ground, he walked up to the keel, knelt down, and studied it carefully. Then he circled it, like a grazing sheep. Finally, he narrowed his eyes and stretched out his arms as if feeling for something, though there was nothing within two feet of his reach. He groped the air for a moment, a series of snorts emerging from his nose as his Adam's apple rose and fell. He pulled his arms back and gazed skyward, just as some bird droppings fell onto his upturned face. He was oblivious. Then he looked down and gazed at the ditch, staring at it for a full half hour, during which the crowd held its collective breath. The unbearable anxiety was palpable. Slowly the old healer turned to the people.

"Which direction was the bow pointing?" he asked.

No one knew. At first, all anyone had cared about was chopping the keel up to feed the kitchen stove, so they'd carried it up willy-nilly. No one could recall which way it was facing.

"Who cares which direction it was facing?" the foreman said.

The old healer's face darkened. "That is critically important. If it was facing north, it was headed for the ocean; south, it would have wound through the mountains. And if it was facing Wali, it would have stopped at our pier." The people exchanged glances but said nothing. "This was a warship that sailed on our Luqing River and was sunk during territorial battles in the old days. It is a true national treasure. No one is to touch it, young or old. Post a guard, day and night. We must send our fastest messenger to the capital to report this find."

"I'll go," Sui Buzhao volunteered as he laid down the anchor and elbowed his way through the crowd.

Baopu took Jiansu home and went looking for his uncle. He was nowhere to be found. Then when they were crossing the path they heard weeping inside. It was, they discovered, Hanzhang, so they rushed in to see what was wrong. Their sister was lying on the *kang* crying. Taken aback by the sight, they asked why she was crying. She pointed to the stable. They ran outside and went to the stable, where they saw that the old chestnut was dead. Their uncle was there, too, trembling uncontrollably and muttering something incomprehensible at the dead horse. Baopu knew instinctively that his uncle had planned to ride the horse to report the finding. But now he couldn't. Baopu and Jiansu fell to their knees at the horse's side.

Eventually, people at the provincial capital sent a team of experts to remove the old ship, and the residents of Wali never saw it again.

Many years before the old ship was excavated, that is, the spring after Sui Yingzhi died, his second wife, Huizi, followed him in death. The impressive main house of the family estate burned to the ground that day, incinerating Huizi amid the cinders on the *kang,* a sight too gruesome to behold. Baopu, the only witness, secretly buried her. Jiansu would later ask how she had died, and Baopu would reply that she had taken poison, which was true. But there were many things he did not reveal to his younger brother. Now that the main house was gone, the foundation had been converted into a vegetable garden tended by the two brothers and their sister. Late at night, moonbeams cast their light on the bean trellises, from which crystalline drops of dew fell to the ground.

Baopu recalled how, six months after his father died, Sui Buzhao came to see Huizi. "Sister-in-law," he said, "I think you should move out of the family home." She said no. "Now that my brother has passed on," he said, "you don't have the good fortune to hold off the evil tied up in this house." But she ignored him. Several days passed before Buzhao, his face beet red, his body trembling, returned. "Huizi!" he called out after barging into the house. "Huizi!" He fidgeted with his clothes. When she came out and saw him, her surprise was mixed with annoyance.

"What do you want?"

He pointed outside. "My room out there is neat and tidy. I even sprayed perfume on the floor." She just stared at him, not sure what he was getting at. His chin quivered, and he blinked nervously. Finally, with a stomp of his foot, he said, "Come live with this wretched man, what do you say?" Hardly able to believe her ears, she reached out and slapped him, giving him a bloody nose. "I mean it, you should come with me," he said, biting his lip. He was obviously not going to be easily put off, so she picked up a pair of scissors. He turned and fled.

"I'm afraid there's no future for your stepmother," Buzhao said to Baopu. "She tried to stab me with scissors. Instead of thanking me for my kindness, she treats me like a stranger. I've been a useless vagabond all my life, but I've never had an indecent thought where she is concerned. I may be dirt poor, but I don't owe anyone a cent, just what she needs to get through life. Well, to hell with her! She's never gone to sea, never seen the world. There are plenty of women down south who have moved in with their brothers-in-law after losing their husbands. But, like I say, to hell with her! She has no future!"

Sui Buzhao left and never again entered the main house as long as Huizi was alive. Before long his prediction came true. Some people came to drive her out of the house, which they said now belonged to the town. Baopu urged his stepmother to move, but she set her jaw and refused. She didn't say a word; she just refused to move. In the end she sent the three children over to side rooms, leaving her alone in that big house. Seeing how stubborn she could be, her brow creased in an expression of strength and hostility, Baopu was reminded of how she had injured her hand by pounding on the table after his father had returned from paying off debts.

After Huizi died along with the main house, militiamen kept watch over Baopu and his siblings for a long time before letting them be. All this time Zhao Duoduo led a team of people in searching the site for hidden treasure, poking the ground with metal poles. To their enormous disappointment they came up empty.

Now that the side buildings were occupied by the brothers and their sister, Sui Buzhao often came over to where the main house had stood. Baopu tried to talk him into moving back into the compound, but he said no. So the three children occupied one of the buildings and used the others for storage. Few books were left from their library, but as political ill winds began to blow, Baopu hid what few remained in a casket. As Hanzhang grew older she more and more closely resembled her mother, but she had the temperament of her father. She moved into one of the other side rooms to be alone.

Around the time of Sui Yingzhi's death the people who had worked for the family left, all but Guigui, who had nowhere to go. When she wasn't cooking for the brothers and their sister she sat in the doorway of one of the buildings shelling beans. She was three years younger than Baopu, with whom she'd bathed together when they were both children. Now when she shelled beans she often looked over at him and blushed. One night, after the brothers had fallen asleep, Guigui saw that the lantern was still lit, so she went into their room; she stopped when she noticed Baopu's muscular shoulders as he lay asleep in the red light of the room. One of his legs was sticking out from under the quilt. She had never seen so much of him uncovered. Worried that he might catch cold, she covered his legs and then his shoulders. The smell of his naked body brought tears to her eyes. She dried her eyes, but the tears kept coming. Then she bent down and kissed his shoulder. He was sleeping so soundly he did not wake up. But Jiansu did, in time to see Guigui bending over his brother's shoulder. He sat up to see what she was doing. Only half awake, he mumbled, "Hm?" Guigui stopped and ran out of the room. Suddenly wide awake, unable to go back to sleep, Jiansu blew out the lantern and lay there smiling.

From that night on, Jiansu was always on the lookout for contact between Guigui and Baopu, and he discovered that she was actually quite pretty, while his brother was a very strong man. He could have his way with her any time he wanted. A year passed and Baopu and Guigui were married, forcing Jiansu to move into a room by himself, one next to the eastern wall. From then on he could not escape the feeling that his brother's room was filled with mystery, and he sometimes went in to see what he could see. Guigui had stuck one of her paper-cuts over the window—a crab with a date in one of its claws. The place had a different smell, not sweet and fragrant, but warm. It was a wonderful room.

Jiansu's own room, cold and forbidding, was only a place to sleep. Most of the time he spent with his uncle, who captivated him with tales of strange things, especially those from his seafaring days, so exciting Jiansu that he listened with his mouth hanging slack. Sometimes he went into the woods to walk aimlessly, searching the trees for birds and daydreaming. As time went on, he could no longer do that; he was like an ox in a halter, tied to a plow with no fun to be had anywhere. He and his brother worked the fields all day long, where he suffered cuts from hoes and scythes and bled like a sapling. His blood was fresh, new, bright red. Scars appeared all over his body as he grew strong from the hard work.

On one occasion the team leader sent him down to the riverbank to cut brambles for a fence. When he got there he spotted a girl of sixteen or seventeen who was also cutting brambles, and when she called him Brother Jiansu, he had to laugh. I'm a brother, all right, he was thinking, one who's looking for a girl just like you. Hot blood that had flowed through his veins all those years suddenly pooled in his throat, and it burned. Although he barely spoke to her, he kept looking over. As a lively, cheerful girl, she'd have loved to talk to him, but he refused to give her the opportunity. What he wanted was to squelch her cheerfulness and turn her into a different kind of girl. The second day passed the same way, and then the third. On the fourth day, as he was once again cutting brambles, he had a perverse desire to chop off his own hand. At about midafternoon, Jiansu shouted to her, "Look, a thorn pricked my hand!"

The girl shrieked, threw down her scythe, and ran up to him. "Where? Let me see!"

"Here, right here!" he said. Then, when she was close enough, he grabbed her around the waist and pulled her to him.

She squirmed like a snake, struggling to break loose. "Brother

Jiansu!" she said. "I'll scream. Let me go!" she demanded. "Let
me go!"

For some strange reason, all Jiansu could do was mimic her:
"Brother Jiansu!" he said. "Brother Jiansu!" To calm her down he
began stroking her hair, basking in the feeling of its silkiness. As he
stroked, he could sense a change in her movements. Slowly she stopped
resisting, and after a moment, she laid her head on his shoulder.

There was only dim moonlight that night as the girl slipped quietly
into the compound, where Jiansu was waiting for her beneath the
broad-bean trellis. He carried her into his room, where the only light
came from the hazy moon. She sat down and reached out to touch his
face with both hands. "I won't let you see me," she said.

He touched her face with one hand. "And I won't let you see me,"
he said.

Brushing his hand away, she said, "But that's why I came here, to
see you. I'll look at you awhile, but then I have to go." Not tonight,
Jiansu was thinking, you can't go away tonight. He wrapped his arms
around her and kissed her. Thrilled by the kiss, she kissed him back—
on the neck and on his eyes. Touching the fuzz that grew on his upper
lip, she said, "Very nice."

Jiansu was trembling all over. "Are you ill?" she asked anxiously. He
shook his head and began to undress her. She asked him to let her go,
but he was breathing too hard to speak. By then she was no longer
speaking either, as she took off everything but a pair of knit underpants with purple and yellow stripes. Jiansu clenched his fists; his
muscles rippled as she bashfully laid her head against his arm, pressing
hard against him, as if she wanted to wrap herself around him. Her
skin was slightly dark and chilled, but amazingly soft. Her body reminded him of a sash—long, thin, and soft. Her skin shimmered in
the moonlight; her small hips were round and firm. "You can't leave,"
Jiansu said softly. "Why would you want to do that?" The girl began
to cry, and as she wept she wrapped her arms around his neck.
She kissed him and she cried. Tears wetted Jiansu's face, but they were

her tears, not his. After a while, she stopped crying and simply gazed at him.

A wind came up in the middle of the night. Jiansu and the girl slipped out of his room. They stopped beneath the trellis to say goodbye. "If your parents ask, just say you lost your way," he said.

"Um," she muttered. Then, before she walked off, she said, "You're the worst person I know. You've ruined me. I won't say bad things about you behind your back, but I won't do anything with you again. You're terrible, you've ruined me . . ."

Jiansu tried to console her: "You're not ruined. You're lovelier now than ever. I won't forget you, not till the day I die, and I'll never forget tonight . . . remember this, you're not ruined, not by a long shot."

The next morning Jiansu met his brother at the neighborhood well. Baopu sensed a change in his kid brother—he was more upbeat than usual; he studied Jiansu as his brother filled the buckets and then carried them inside for him. Baopu invited Jiansu to sit for a while; Jiansu turned down the offer, and when he stepped out the door he raised his arms and exclaimed, "What a beautiful day!"

"What did you say?" Baopu asked. Jiansu just turned and looked at his brother, grinning from ear to ear.

"What a beautiful day!"

The lamp in Jiansu's room often stayed dark, its occupant missing most of the night. He began losing weight, and his face and hands were permanently scraped and bruised from work; his bloodshot eyes, which were retreating into their sockets, showed the effects of a lack of sleep, though they were still bright and lively. For Baopu it was a particularly bad time. Guigui had been stricken with consumption years before, and though she struggled to keep going, she did not make it through the year. She died in his arms, feeling to him as light as a bundle of grain stalks. Why, he wondered, did she have to die now, after having lived with the disease for so many years? Back then they had been so desperate to find food that he was reduced to removing talc weights from an old fishing net and grinding them into powder.

Their uncle spent his days sprawled atop rocks on the bank of the Luqing River trying to catch little fish. Baopu recalled how, toward the end, Guigui had been too weak to even chew a tiny live shrimp, and how it had squirmed down into her empty stomach on its own. Thrilled to see that the bark of an elm tree was edible, Jiansu had shared his find with his sister-in-law. Baopu would have chopped the bark into tiny pieces if his cleaver hadn't been taken away the year before to the outdoor smelting furnaces. The family wok had met the same end. So he chewed it up first and then fed it to his wife to keep her alive. But only for three years or so, until she left the Sui family for good. Baopu slowly climbed out of his grief a year after burying Guigui. By then Jiansu had nearly grown into a young man, and one day, when Baopu went out to pick beans, he spotted Jiansu hiding beneath the trellis with a young woman.

〜

The noodle processing rooms on Gaoding Street reopened that year. Since there had been no mung beans for years, noodles had been out of the question. But now the old millstone was turning again, and that's where people could find Baopu, sitting on a stool, just like all the old men who tended millstones, a long wooden ladle resting in his lap. White liquid flowed into buckets, to be carried away by women. One of them, called Xiaokui, regularly showed up earlier than the others and waited in a corner with her carrying pole. One morning she brought over a cricket cage and hung it up in the mill. When he heard the chirps, Baopu went over to take a look. Xiaokui was standing beside the cage, leaning against the wall, her hands behind her. Her face was red, bright red, and her nose was dotted with perspiration. The ladle in Baopu's hands shook. With her eyes focused on the little window in front, she said, "You're very nice." Then she added, "Such a lovely sound."

Baopu stood up and hit the millstone with his ladle. The old ox looked at him, concern, if not fear, in its eyes. The bucket was nearly full of bean starch. Two young women came in, hoisted it up on their carrying pole, and took it away with them, leaving a little pool of water on the spot where the bucket had sat.

As he glanced down at the water on the dusty floor, for some reason he thought back to when he and Xiaokui were children out catching loaches in the bend of the river. Wearing similar red stomachers, they laughed as the slimy loaches slipped out of their hands. He also recalled going over to the noodle factory and seeing her sifting bean residue, turning the white mixture into a ball. She held one of them up when she spotted him. What would he do with one of those? he wondered. But now, thinking back, he recalled the somber but reserved look on her face as she held it up for him.

Xiaokui returned to the mill and caught Baopu's eye. She stood calmly, blushing slightly, her dark eyes glistening. Not particularly tall, she had a slender figure. His eyes fell on her breasts, which were heaving rhythmically, as if she were in a deep sleep. The air was redolent, not with perfume, but with the smell of a nineteen- or twenty-year-old virginal young female, the unique aroma of a gentle young woman who knew what it meant to love and was instinctively good natured. Baopu stood up and went to look at the trudging ox. The aging animal shook its head in a strange fashion. Baopu fed mung beans into the eye of the stone, the ladle in his hand in constant motion, and it was all he could do to keep from flinging it away. But then it fell out of his hand and landed on the stone, which carried it along until it was opposite Xiaokui, where it seemed to turn into a compass needle and point directly at her. She took a step forward. "Baopu," she said, "you, me." He picked up the ladle, putting the millstone in motion again. "When you finish here, instead of going home," she said softly, "can you meet me down on the floodplain? When you finish . . ." Sweat beaded his forehead; he stared at Xiaokui. The next bucket of liquid beans was full, and another young woman came in to remove it. Later that day, when it was time for the next shift, Baopu, finished for the day, left.

Breaking from his normal schedule, instead of crossing the river at the floodplain, for reasons he could not explain he decided to go around it. He walked slowly, his legs feeling unusually heavy. After a while he stopped. The sunset blazed across the sky and turned his broad back bright red. He shuddered in the sun's dying rays and then took off running back toward the floodplain as fast as he could, muttering things no one could understand. His hair was swept back, he lurched from side to side, and his arms flailed out from his body. Deep imprints in the ground were created with each flying step. Then he stopped abruptly, for there in the densest part of the willow grove stood Xiaokui, her hair tied with a red kerchief.

Baopu stood motionless for a moment before walking slowly toward her. When he reached her he saw she was crying. She said she'd thought he was walking away from her.

As they crouched down in the grove, her tears were still flowing. Baopu nervously lit a cigarette; Xiaokui took it out of his mouth and threw it away. Then she laid her head against his chest. He put his arms around her and kissed her hair. She looked up at him and he wiped away her tears with his callused hand; then she lowered her head again. He kissed her, and kissed her again. "Xiaokui," he said, shaking his head, "I don't understand you."

She nodded. "I don't understand myself," she said, "so of course you can't. You sit there on a stool with that ladle in your hand, never saying a word. You look like a stone statue, but with energy bursting to get out. I have to admit I'm scared of anyone who won't talk, but I also know that sooner or later I'll be yours."

Baopu lifted up her face and looked intently into her flashing eyes. He shook his head. "I'm part of the Sui clan," he said. "Why . . . would you want to be mine?"

She just nodded. Neither of them spoke as they leaned against one another until the sun had disappeared below the horizon. Then they stood up and began to walk. When it was time to go their separate ways, Baopu said, "You and I are people who have little to say." Xiaokui rubbed his rough, callused hand and raised it to her nose to smell it.

Baopu had trouble sleeping after Xiaokui had smelled his hand, he realized. He tossed and turned, and when he finally fell asleep someone came up and lifted up his hand. He held out both hands for her, his heart filled with happiness. She walked out of the room, and he followed. Moonbeams created a haze in the air. She was walking in front of him, but when he blinked she was gone. Then she leaped out from behind, her body as light as a bundle of grain stalks. Oh, it was Guigui. "Guigui!" he shouted "Guigui! . . ." He reached out, but pristine, pale moonbeams were all he touched.

He didn't sleep that night, but that did not keep him from going to the mill the next day, where only her cricket cage remained; Xiaokui did not show up to carry off buckets. He fed the crickets some melon flowers. When he went over to the processing room, he saw that she was washing the noodles, her arms red from being submerged in water. He did not call out to her, since Li Zhaolu was sitting above her banging the metal strainer, chanting as he did: "Hang-ya! Hang-ya!" The people below said, "He sure knows how to bang that!" Baopu looked up at the coarse old man, who had his eyes fixed on Xiaokui on the floor below. Without a word, Baopu walked back to his mill, where the stone creaked as it made one slow revolution after another and the ox's head swayed in concert with the sound.

Baopu forgot what it was like to enjoy a good night's sleep. How had he gotten through the past twenty years? he wondered. He regularly stumbled into Zhao Family Lane and lay sprawled beneath Xiaokui's rear window, where no one could see him. She had told him she was to be married to Li Zhaolu, and there was nothing she could do about that, since the decision was made when Fourth Master nodded his approval. Baopu lost hope. That nod of the head had sealed the matter. So he abandoned his fantasies and went back to sitting quietly on his stool in the mill. And yet, desire burned in his heart, tormenting him. When a splitting headache set in, he wrapped his head with a piece of cloth, which lessened the pain at least a little. This reminded him of when the old ship was excavated, since his uncle had

worn a headband that day, and he now realized that the old man too
had likely been suffering from a headache; he had taken the loss of his
boat badly and had been in low spirits ever since.

Not long after Baopu started wearing a headband, Xiaokui married
Li Zhaolu. Baopu collapsed when he heard the news and lay numb in
his room. Then news reached town that Li Zhaolu had fled to the
northeast and slipped into one of the cities there, where he planned to
make his fortune and then send for Xiaokui. Sure enough, there was
no trace of Zhaolu in town, and Xiaokui had moved back into the
family home on Zhao Family Lane.

One stormy night, as thunder rumbled, lightning struck a tree near
the old mill. Everyone in town heard the fearsome noise. Wakened by
the thunder, Baopu could not go back to sleep and suffered the rest
of the night from a headache so bad he had to put the headband back
on. As the rain fell outside he imagined that he heard Guigui calling
him from far away. So he threw his coat over his shoulders and ran
outside, racing across the muddy ground and through the misty rain
with no idea where he was going. But when he wiped the water from
his face and out of his eyes, he found he was standing beneath Xiaokui's
window. His blood surged. He banged on the window. She was leaning against the sill, weeping, but refused to open the window. Baopu
felt the blood rush to his head, turning his cheeks feverish; with a pop,
the headband snapped in two, like a broken lute string. He drove his
fist through the window.

Suddenly feeling cold, he held her in his arms and felt her heat
burning into his chest. Unable to stop shaking or breathing hard, she
held her arms crossed in front of her. When he pulled her arms away,
she rubbed his rough, callused hands. She was breathing hard in the
darkness, almost choking. "Ah, ah," she said, over and over. Baopu
loosened her long hair and removed the little clothing she was wearing. As if talking to himself, he said, "This is how it is. I can't help
myself. I've been like this every day. Lightning split something in two.
Are you scared that you can't see anything? Pitiful people, like this,
like this. The cricket cage in the mill was blown brittle by the wind. It

crumbled when I touched it. A poor, pitiful man. What can I do? You think I'm a terrible person. Like this, like this. Your hands, oh, oh, I've got stubble all over my face. I'm so stupid, like a stone. And you, and you. More thunder, why doesn't lightning strike me dead! All right, I'll stop talking like that. But you, your hands. What do we do? You, little Xiaokui, my little Xiaokui . . ." She kept kissing him, and he stopped talking. When lightning lit up the sky, Baopu saw she was sweating. "All I can think of is taking you back to my room, where we would seal up the door and never go out again. The millstone can turn on its own. And that's how we'd be, in our own home." Xiaokui did not say a word, it seemed; her eyes reminded him of the night beneath the willow tree that year, and he recalled what she'd said then: "Sooner or later I'll be yours." And he had whispered to her: "That's good."

For several days after the thunderstorm, Baopu slept through the night. He was also moved to go to his brother's and his sister's rooms in order to share his happiness with them. Hanzhang always looked healthy and happy, while Jiansu was in a permanently foul mood. As the circles around his eyes grew darker, he told his brother he'd been spurned, which didn't surprise Baopu, who just sighed. Apparently, fate had dictated that this generation of the Sui clan could fall in love but that marriage was beyond their reach.

Several days later Li Zhaolu returned from the northeast. After a year of trying to make a living far from home, his skin had taken on a gray pallor and his cheekbones were more prominent. He said he planned to go back, and he'd only returned home to start a family. So he spent a month in Wali, after which he said, "That'll do it," and headed back to the northeast. This time he did not return. News of his death arrived six months later. He had been buried in a coal mine cave-in. His widow, Xiaokui, was no longer willing to step foot beyond Zhao Family Lane. Then one day Baopu spotted a woman in mourning apparel. Xiaokui.

Xiaokui gave birth to little Leilei. Meanwhile, Baopu's health deteriorated, until one day he fell seriously ill. Guo Yun checked his pulse and his tongue, then examined his arms and his back. Lesions had

broken out on the skin, he was feverish and thirsty, uncontrollably
agitated, and his tongue had changed color. The old man sighed. "The
unhealthy external heat has not dissipated," he said, "and the unhealthy internal heat has risen. The outer and inner heats feed off each
other, disrupting the state of mind and internal organs." He then
wrote out a prescription, which Baopu took for several days, improving his condition somewhat, although the lesions did not go away. So
Guo Yun gave him a prescription for them: two taels of raw gypsum,
three tenths of a tael of glycyrrhiza, three tenths of a tael of figwort,
four tenths of a tael of bluebell, a tenth of a tael of rhinoceros horn,
and a tael of nonsticky white rice. Baopu followed the healer's instructions meticulously; once he was on the road to recovery he looked
through some medical books. He discovered that Guo Yun had used
a formula that produced only temporary benefits and was not a cure.
When he asked if that was true, Guo Yun nodded and said yes, stressing the importance of serenity and a moderate use of herbs and tonics.
What mattered was breathing exercises and a calm spirit. Baopu met
this with silence, firm in his belief that any member of the Sui clan
who contracted this illness had no hopes of ever being cured.

Every few days Baopu suffered from insomnia, tossing and turning
restlessly, as he had for nearly twenty years. He would get up and walk
in the compound, though now he avoided standing beneath Xiaokui's
window. In his imagination he heard Li Zhaolu banging the strainer,
he heard the collapse of the mine, and he heard Li Zhaolu's cries for
help. He also saw a look of denunciation in the man's eyes from beyond the grave. With Xiaokui's mourning garments floating before his
eyes, Baopu walked over to the bean trellis, sometimes recalling that it
had been built on the floor of the main house in the estate; his heart
would pound. As the only witness to the fire that had destroyed the
main house, he had seen Huizi die, had seen the terrifying writhing of
her body on the *kang*. He did not dare tell Jiansu any of this, though
he worried that the boy already knew and that it was what burdened

his mind. When Jiansu reached adulthood, he had the eyes of a panther searching for prey, and Baopu hoped he'd never see his younger brother pouncing to rip and tear with his teeth.

As the eldest son of the family, he could not rid himself of the feeling that he had failed Hanzhang in his responsibilities to her. She was now a thirty-four-year-old woman who, like her brother, had known love but not marriage. Her uncle had once arranged a marriage for her with Li Zhichang, to which she had agreed. But two days before the wedding she had changed her mind. Li had paced the drying floor for several days bemoaning his fate, assuming that what had happened beneath the willow tree that time had created resentment in her mind. But she begged him to leave her, saying she was unworthy of being part of the Li clan, which she revered. Over the days that followed she grew increasingly wan, until her skin was nearly transparent. She actually grew lovelier by the day, and frailer. From time to time she visited Fourth Master, returning home more obstinate and unruly than ever. She was a dedicated worker, never missing a day. When she returned home from a day on the drying floor, she wove floor mats from tassels of cornstalk to add to the family's income.

Baopu sat in the mill gazing at the drying floor, thinking about his hardworking sister and growing increasingly melancholy. He was on edge for days after the blowup with his brother in the mill, and he felt as if something were gnawing at his heart. Then one afternoon he threw down his ladle in a fit of pique and walked over to the drying floor, where a chorus of women's voices came on the wind before he reached it. One horse cart after another drove up to the racks, with their silvery threads waving in the air; the horse bells and the women's voices merged. Baopu skirted the area of greatest activity and headed for a corner, where he saw his sister standing next to one of the drying racks. She did not see him coming. As her hands flew over the strands of noodles, she was looking up, a smile on her face, gazing through the gaps in the racks at the other women. The sight flooded Baopu's breast with warm currents of joy, and he decided not to get any closer.

The noodles around her were as clean and clear as crystal, uncontaminated by a single blemish; the sand at her feet shimmered slightly. For the first time Baopu detected the harmonious relationship between his sister and the drying floor. He reached into his pocket looking for some tobacco but left it there as Hanzhang spotted him; by the look in her eyes, she was surprised to see him, and when she called out to him, he walked up. First he looked into her face, and then he turned to look elsewhere. "You never come out to the drying floor," she said. He looked into her face again but said nothing. He wanted to tell her that he and Jiansu had had a fight, but he swallowed the words.

"Guo Yun says you're sick," he said. "What do you have?"

With a look of alarm, she pressed herself up against the drying rack and grabbed threads of noodles with both hands. "I'm not sick," she said with a grimace.

"Yes, you are," he said, raising his voice. "I can see it in your face."

"I said I'm not!" she shouted.

Feeling hurt, Baopu lowered his head and crouched down to stare at his hands. "It can't be like this, it can't," he said softly. "No more . . . everything has to start from the beginning, and it can't be like this." He stood up and looked off in the distance, where the old mills stood at the riverbank, dark and forbidding, like fortresses, and quiet. "The Sui clan," he said, almost as a moan, "the Sui clan! . . ." He gazed off in the distance for a long while before spinning around and saying sternly, "You have to get whatever it is treated! I won't let you turn into someone useless like me. You're still young! I'm more than ten years older than you, so both you and Jiansu are supposed to do as I say, to listen to me."

Hanzhang held her tongue. Baopu kept staring at her. She looked up at him and began to tremble.

In the same stern tone of voice, Baopu said, "Answer me. Are you going to have that treated or aren't you?"

Eyes open wide, Hanzhang looked into her brother's face without so much as blinking. She held that look for a moment and then stepped up and wrapped her arms around his shoulders. She begged him not to mention her sickness again, never again.

SIX

"Another member of the Sui clan has died!" The news traveled stealthily through town for several days. At first no one knew who had died, but word slowly leaked out that it was Dahu, who had been sent up to the front. Half the town knew before anyone told Dahu's family. Word came first from a mine prospecting team. A young worker's elder brother who had been in Dahu's team wrote home. Then Technician Li told Sui Buzhao, and the news continued to spread until one day people saw Dahu's mother carrying a set of her son's clothing as she ran wailing up and down the street. "My son!" she was crying, "my unmarried, teenage son! . . ." People stood around gaping at her. Now that she had been notified of her son's death, she sat down on a rush mat and wept until she lost her voice. A pall settled over the town and did not lift all that afternoon. Even the workers in the noodle factory were silent. After Zhang-Wang closed the Wali Emporium, old men on their way to have a drink turned back and went home. When night fell no one lit lamps; people groped their way through the dark to sit with the old woman as she mourned her loss.

A tiny, three-room hut with incense curling into the air produced the smell of death familiar to all the town's residents. Several chests were piled up to form a sort of pulpit covered by a mat and a bedsheet. Various bowls and cups vied for space with gray-yellow candles on top. The bowls were mostly filled with glass noodles dyed in a variety of colors, topped with slices of egg-filled pancakes and decorated with lush green cilantro. Behind were photographs of the only person qualified to enjoy the offering. The photos, all of them small, were fitted into a large frame. The one in the middle, in red and yellow, had been taken six months after Dahu left home. Dressed in an army uniform, he struck a handsome, commanding pose, which had drawn the admiration of nearly every girl in town. Under the flickering candlelight, old folks leaned on their canes and bent forward to examine the photo.

At midnight Zhang-Wang came over with a stack of coarse yellow paper and a bundle of incense sticks, which she handed to the old woman, who then told her young son to record the items in pencil. With a solemn look, Zhang-Wang mumbled something before taking a twig from the old woman to draw an oval shape on the ground. She burned the yellow paper in the middle of the oval. Still mumbling, she sprinkled liquor around the flames; a few drops fell on the fire, which leaped up suddenly. The smoke got thicker, making people cough and tear up. Zhang-Wang sat down on the largest rush mat, her eyes downcast, her sleeves and her shoulders drooping. Her dusty neck was slender but strong, and with her chin pressed inward, she began to chant in a low voice like the whir of a spinning wheel. The people around her began to sway to the rhythm of her chants, the range of their movements widening as they went along, as if they had been dumped into a giant washbasin and were being stirred rhythmically. That went on till daybreak; Zhang-Wang never wavered in her chanting, but some of the people fell asleep and slumped to the ground. The old folks held on to their canes with both hands, their heads drooping down between their legs, their purplish mouths hanging slack. Some of them dreamed they were in the old temple listening to monks reciting sutras; they barely managed to escape when the temple caught fire. It was daylight when they finally woke up. The windows were red from the morning sun and the candles had burned down. Zhang-Wang rose from the rush mat to leave but was stopped by the old woman and her son, who held tightly to Zhang-Wang's sleeve.

Mother and son let her go only after she told them what they wanted to hear.

～

The Sui clan moved to the yard in front of the hut when the sun was high in the sky and set up a rush tent. They placed a vermillion table and chairs inside and set the table with tea servings. It was late in the afternoon when all was ready, and Zhang-Wang brought in five or six strangers with musical instruments; they sat wordlessly at the table. Then, at a silent signal, they picked up their instruments and began to play. And that was the cue for Zhang-Wang to enter the tent, where she sat on a rush mat that was spread out on the ground. The music was indescribably moving; there were people in town who had never heard ancient music like that before, and others who had a vague recollection of hearing it in the past. People streamed over, crowding the tent until latecomers were forced to stand outside. The noodle factory was virtually empty; when Duoduo came over to find his workers, even he was captivated by the music.

The musicians, whose sallow faces were unfamiliar to the townspeople, had exhausted their emotions over a lifetime of playing and now performed their mournful songs with expressions that revealed no emotion. One of them, who seemed not terribly bright, was barely holding on to his instrument and playing nearly inaudible sounds, calm and unhurried. People sat on the ground, their eyes closed as they listened intently, feeling as if they had been transported, trance-like, to a mystical land of wonder. When the musicians stopped to rest and drink a cup of tea, the listeners, near and far, exhaled loudly. At that moment it dawned on someone to ask who had invited this musical group, and they were told that Zhang-Wang had made the arrangements. That surprised no one. A moment later the music started up again and the people once more held their breath and narrowed their eyes. But then a shrill noise cut through the music. All eyes popped open to search out the source. The music stopped.

Someone spotted Gimpy, who had slipped in among the others

and was sitting tearfully on the doorsill. He had taken out his flute. Angered by his presence, they told him to leave, but he began to play his flute, undeterred even when someone in the crowd kicked him. Erhuai, the pier guard, walked up with his rifle and threatened to snap the flute in two. But Gimpy held on to it for dear life, rolling on the ground to protect his treasured instrument; finally, he managed to run off.

The musicians played till late into the night, when everyone's hair was wet with dew; moisture on the stringed instruments altered their sound until they seemed to be sobbing. Then the shrill sound of a flute came on the wind from the floodplain, each note like a knife to the heart. There is nothing quite like the sound of a flute at night, and the full extent of its mystical power was felt by the townspeople that night. The sound was mistaken by some for a woman singing or a man sobbing, boundless joy pierced through with limitless sadness. The tune was as cold as autumn ice, constantly rising and falling like a barrage of arrows in flight. When and why had Gimpy decided to play the flute like that? No one knew. But the music quickly immersed the people in thoughts of their own suffering and their own pleasures. They were reminded of how Dahu had gone down to the river as a boy, naked, to spear fish, and how he had walked around tooting on a green flute he'd fashioned from a green castor bean plant. Once he'd climbed an apricot tree and tasted some of the sap, mistakenly assuming it would be much like one of Zhang-Wang's sweets. As shrill notes from the flute continued to drift over, the people conjured up an image of Dahu lying on the ground in his tattered uniform, his forehead ashen white, blood seeping from the corner of his mouth. The musicians in the tent began to sigh; one by one, they laid down their instruments and, like everyone else, listened intently to the flute. And so it went until the music stopped as abruptly as it had begun. The sense of disappointment was palpable as people looked around helplessly. Stars hung low in the clear, bright night sky as the dew settled. Erhuai, still carrying his rifle, came running over, stepping on people as he went to clear a passage. Everyone turned to look.

"Fourth Master!" they shouted in unison.

A man in his fifties or sixties walked slowly up a path that had been opened for him, casting glances all around from his glimmering dark eyes. Then he lowered his eyelids and looked only at the ground. His shaved head and beardless face glinted in the starlight. His neck was fleshy, the skin moist and ruddy. Thick around the middle, he stood straight when he walked; his reddish-brown jacket was ringed at the waist by a stiff leather belt. He wore a somber look that day; his eyebrows twitched. And yet his face emanated kindness and gentleness, even with his mouth tightly shut, which both consoled people and filled them with resolve. The clothes he wore were handmade, with close stitching and neatly placed buttons, the sleeves cut to show off his powerful shoulders and upper arms. He had large hips that moved easily as he approached the tent. Not until that moment had anyone noticed that the street director, Luan Chunji, and Party Secretary Li Yuming were behind Fourth Master, who stood at the opening to the tent and coughed softly. The musicians, who sat impassively when they were working, now stood up and bowed, forcing smiles onto their faces. Without a word, Fourth Master signaled for them to sit down. Then he bent slightly at the waist and poured each of the musicians a cup of cold tea before turning and walking over to the hut.

All sounds came to a halt. The old woman grabbed her young son's hand and rushed up to Fourth Master, taking tiny, rapid steps. She was choked with tears. Fourth Master took her hands in his and held them for several minutes, and as her shoulders slumped and heaved and quaked, she seemed to be getting smaller. She was too grief-stricken to speak for a moment. "Fourth Master," she managed to say, "what happened to Dahu has upset you! What do I do? How do . . . I do it? I am fated to suffer, the whole Sui clan is fated to suffer. Fourth Master, this has upset you." He let go of her hands and walked up to look at Dahu's photograph, where he picked up a bundle of incense sticks and lit them, then bowed deeply as Zhang-Wang stepped out of the shadows and stood beside him. Her lips were pressed together more tightly than ever; her face looked very old as she glanced at the wrinkles on Fourth Master's neck. Noticing a leaf on his clothes, she removed it.

Next to enter the hut were Luan Chunji and Li Yuming, who tried to console Dahu's mother, telling her what a good son he was, the pride of Wali, and urged her not to be too sad; they wanted her to shun superstitions as much as possible. A little of that can't hurt, they said, but her heroic son deserved something better. Overhearing what they said, Zhang-Wang narrowed her eyes and glared at them, exposing her black teeth. They quickly turned away.

No one else spoke, inside or outside of the hut, for a long while, for the most solemn moment had arrived. People outside could not see what Fourth Master was doing, but they assumed that he was involved in some sort of mourning ritual. The Sino-Vietnam war had seemed alien and distant to them, but now it was linked directly to the town of Wali, right there where they could touch it, as if the fighting had broken out at the foot of the city wall. Cannon fire rocked the town; the iron-colored wall of ancient Donglaizi was spattered with blood. Wali had sent not just one of its sons to fight, but the whole town . . . Fourth Master emerged from the shack, walking slowly, as always. This time he did not stop at the tent but continued on.

His back rocked slightly as it disappeared into the darkness.

The flute started up again. Regaining their sense of responsibility, the musicians signaled each other with their eyes, and the music recommenced.

Baopu sat in the midst of the crowd, feeling like a man carrying a heavy boulder on his shoulders. He wanted to cry but had no tears to shed. The chilled air cut into him. Finally, wanting to hear no more of the flute or the musicians, he got up and left. When he walked past a haystack, some twenty or thirty feet from the hut, sparks flew out. "Who's in there?" No response. He bent down to get a better look and saw his uncle, Sui Buzhao, curled up amid the loose straw. And he was not alone: Li Zhichang, Technician Li of the mine prospecting team, and a laborer were in there with him. Baopu edged in and sat down. His uncle, who was leaning to one side, was muttering between drinks he took from a bottle. The younger men were talking, with an occasional interruption from Sui Buzhao. The air grew increasingly cold as Baopu listened to the conversation about the front lines and about Dahu, which was to be expected. But what he heard loudest of all were the sounds of the flute and a constant rumbling. Did it come from the mill or was it the sound of heavy guns? He wasn't sure. But the distant image of a smiling Dahu took shape in the hazy night air. With the sound of heavy guns to the rear, Dahu waved to him, put on an army cap camouflaged with leaves, and ran off.

≈

Following several months of training, Dahu and his men had driven off to the front. A place like this was particularly hard on soldiers from the north. They would be sent into the fighting in another month, and they seemed anxious to get started. Get it over with early was how they saw it. Dahu was promoted to squad leader during his first month at the front. Dahu, whose name meant "great tiger," was called "Squad Leader Tiger" by everyone, including Fang Ge, the company commander, who said, "Now we need a Squad Leader Dragon to realize the saying 'Spirited as a dragon, lively as a tiger.' " Dahu told him about a friend named Long—"dragon"—but he was in a different company. Fang Ge took the news with obvious disappointment as he walked along, resting his hand on the back of his squad leader's neck. He was especially fond of this handsome, clever, yet reserved son of the Luqing River, who had all the qualities of a man who could be relied upon to get the job done.

A few days earlier he had sent Dahu for ammunition for the company. Carts from the other companies had returned empty, while his had rolled in with a full load. "The person in charge of the armory must have been a pretty girl," Fang Ge teased him. Dahu just smiled. Next he was sent to scare up some prefabricated steel frames for camouflage to supplement the ones they had. Dahu happily took on the assignment, for during his training he'd met a pretty girl named Qiuqiu who lived in a nearby village. At the time she was off making bamboo cages in another village, and he hoped to give her a ride back home while he was on this assignment. Everything went according to plan: he brought back several steel frames and the pretty girl.

The company was planning a banquet for the upcoming May Day celebration, to which the local villagers would be invited. Soon after this special holiday they were to be sent to the front, so it was time for the finest liquor and everyone's favorite songs. For Dahu it was also a chance to see the girl he'd fallen for. All the time he was singing, drinking, and dancing, he had one thing on his mind, and when he finally managed to see her, he was bursting with desire. The temperament and traits that seemed to exist in all members of the Sui clan were displayed with extraordinary tenacity in Dahu. He was like a man on fire, pulsating with passion. This was further evidence, if anyone needed it, of how members of the clan generated more fervor than anyone, no matter where they went, fervor that nothing and no one could constrain. At the banquet he sang a special song, one the others had not heard before but which everyone in his hometown, young and old, knew by heart. It had come generations before from sailors who had tied up at the Wali pier.

"Clouds often hang on the Kunlun glass. Beating gongs and drums, we set off on a decorated ship. When it reaches Chikan, the ship turns and heads toward Mt. Kunlun. The mountain is truly tall, but with a following wind we pass it quickly. The ship will not put in at Pengheng port but will head straight to Mt. Zhupan, whose peak shines bright. Mountains of bamboo line both east and west. One of the two Luohan islands is shallow, and we reach Longya Gate after passing Baijiao. The man sails for barbarian lands in the South Seas and the Western Ocean; his wife and child burn incense at home. She kneels to pray for a good wind to send him safely to the Western Ocean. The man sets sail for the South Seas and Penghu to sell tortoise shells and turtle boxes. He keeps the good combs for his wife and sells the bad ones. The now finished ship looks newer than new, with a hawser like a dragon's tail and anchors like a dragon's claws. It will fetch a thousand pieces of gold in Hong Kong and Macao."

As Dahu sang along, someone rang a small copper bell as accompaniment.

It was a simple song with few highs and lows, but inexplicably a strange power emanated from it, eerily taking the listeners into a semiconscious state. Everyone was seemingly lost and dazed.

"That's strange, Dahu," Fang Ge said. "I've never heard such a wonderful song."

His nose beaded in sweat, Dahu replied shyly, "Have you heard of Wali? Well, everyone there knows it."

When his comrades told him they'd never heard of the town of Wali, he sat down dejected, as some of the soldiers followed his song with one of their own, "Well Water at the Border Is Clear and Sweet." But it sounded plain by comparison.

As soon as the singing was finished, the drinking began, with good liquor and plenty of it. Everyone was in a festive mood when one of their superiors came up to toast his men. When that was done, he walked off, and the serious drinking commenced. Fang Ge reminded them that this was International Labor Day and that fighting a war was a form of labor, which meant it was their day to celebrate. The political officer gently corrected him, saying it was their day to celebrate because they were fighting to protect their countrymen's labors. White foamy liquor filled the glasses, and when one of them broke during a toast, another quickly took its place. One of the men, his neck red from drinking, urged Dahu to sing another Wali song. Dahu ignored him. He could think of nothing but the girl Qiuqiu. A disco song was put on a tape deck, background to the men's drinking. "Victory is ours!" someone shouted, but for Dahu there was only a buzzing in his ears. Seeing that no one was paying attention to him, he slipped away and headed for the bamboo grove.

Darkness reigned in the dense grove, the bamboo stalks swaying in the night winds, movements that reminded him of Qiuqiu's lithe figure. He was breathing hard; a sweet warmth rose up in his heart. When he reached a stand of dead bamboo he took five paces to the left and ten paces forward. Then he crouched down and waited, barely able to keep from shouting. After about ten minutes, a breeze bent a nearby stand of bamboo, and when the stalks straightened up again, Qiuqiu stepped into the clearing and wrapped her arms around him. He was trembling. "How can you fight a war like this?" she asked. He just smiled. Their bodies were entwined. "Your hands are so cold," she said. Then: "Oh, how I'd like to give you a good spanking!" Dahu held his tongue as he placed one hand gently on the nape of her neck and reached under her blouse to touch glossy skin that emanated intense heat. When his hand stopped moving he rested his head on her breast. Ashamed and overjoyed at the same time, she pummeled his back with her fists, but they were little more than love pats. There was no sound from him. Had he fallen asleep? Wind whistled through the bamboo grove and carried with it the sound of distant artillery. The thuds were particularly ominous that night, since when morning came, the wounded would be brought back from the front. Qiuqiu and other village girls had organized a unit to clean the wounded soldiers. She stopped hitting him when the gunfire commenced, and Dahu looked up. "When do you leave?" she asked.

"The day after tomorrow."

"Scared?"

Dahu shook his head. "A fellow from my hometown, Li Yulong, went up to the front over a month ago." Someone coughed nearby. The sound so surprised him he was about to remove his hand when a beam of a flashlight hit him in the face. Before he could say a word, the man called out his name; it was a voice he knew—one of the regiment officers. He let go of Qiuqiu and stood at attention.

Dahu spent the rest of that night confined to quarters, since his actions on the eve of their departure for the front were considered a serious offense. Though Fang Ge, his company commander, was fond of him, he was powerless to come to his defense. A company meeting was hastily called the following afternoon, at which the regimental decision was to strip Dahu of his unit command but give him a chance to redeem himself by being assigned to the dagger squad.

Qiuqiu wept at the company campground and refused to leave.

Grabbing the company commander by the sleeve, she said tearfully, "He did nothing wrong. What did he do? He's about to go into battle. Give him back his command, you can do that at least." Her eyes were red and swollen from crying. Dahu stood off to the side looking at her with cold detachment. "Dahu, it's all my fault," she said. "I'm to blame!"

Dahu clenched his teeth and shook his head. "I'll see you when the fighting's done, Qiuqiu." With one last lingering look, he turned and walked away.

As he passed the row of tents Dahu took off his army cap and crumpled it in his hand. His freshly shaved scalp made him look like a teenager. He walked on aimlessly until he found himself in front of the large surgical tent. He heard moans from inside. This was no place to stop, but before he could leave, an army doctor came out and laid a large basin by the tent opening. Dahu went up to it but stepped back and cried out in horror when he saw what was inside—a bent and bloody human leg. He staggered off, his heavy steps reflecting his mood. But he hadn't gone far before he turned and headed back to camp. It was suddenly important to learn the name of the comrade-in-arms who had lost his leg. It was, the doctor informed him, Li Yulong! Dahu's legs came out from under him; he buried his face in his hands.

Dahu stepped on the dying sun's blood-red rays as he made his way back. On the way he encountered armed soldiers escorting prisoners. He glared hatefully at the gaunt, sallow, pitiful enemy soldiers, their lips tightly compressed. How he would have liked to pick up a rifle and put a bullet in each of them. One, he saw, was female. He stood in the fading sunset watching them pass.

Dahu's unit moved out the following day.

Every day, without fail, Qiuqiu climbed the highest hill in the area, gazing out at puffs of smoke from the big guns. "Dagger squad," she muttered. "Dahu." When she shut her eyes she conjured up the image of the bamboo grove and Dahu's head resting on her breast. But then the number of wounded increased, and her unit was so busy attending to the injured soldiers that she had little time to go out alone. It was hard to look at the soldiers carried back on stretchers, their uniforms soaked in blood, the looks on their faces too horrible to bear. Some were little more than skin and bones, with pale, brittle hair and uniforms shredded almost beyond recognition. Only by actually seeing them would anyone believe that human beings could be reduced to that condition and still be breathing.

The women soon learned that the enemy had sealed off these latest arrivals in the mountains for nearly three weeks, with no food or water. How had they survived? Impossible to say. What could be said was that they had not surrendered. Most were country boys who had been in the army a year or two, joining up directly from the farms for which their fathers had been assigned responsibility. Raised to be frugal and obedient, one day they were tilling a field, the next they were fighting for their country. Supplied with more canned food than they'd ever seen before, they ate with a sense of shame as they thought of their fathers, who were still out working the fields. The girls changed uniforms and cleaned wounds, barely able to keep their hearts from breaking.

Late one afternoon the first wounded members of the dagger squad were carried in. Qiuqiu could not hold a pair of scissors, not even a bandage. She shivered as she went up to look at each man carried in. Her heart sank as she checked one face after another. Finally, she bent over to clean the blood from a dead soldier with the top part of his head missing. She removed his torn, bloody uniform and emptied his pockets. There among his meager possessions was her own hankie . . . she screamed. People rushed up to her. Her face was buried in her hands, which were shaking uncontrollably, streaking her cheeks with blood that was still dripping through her fingers. She stood like that for a long moment before she was suddenly reminded of something. She let her hands down to search for the serial number on the man's uniform, her eyes clouded by tears. And then she fainted.

Just before the sun went down, an urgent signal sounded in the mountains. Heavy artillery continued to send sound waves through the air. Thrushes sang in the bamboo grove, as before. The autumn winds had blown to the east of the mountains the day before; today they were blowing back. Night had fallen, immersing everything in its inky darkness.

The sky darkened until Baopu could not see a thing. The thrushes' songs grew indistinct in the darkness of night. Now the mournful strains of a flute alone held sway.

The young man from the Sui clan who was now sleeping for eternity could hear the flute being played on the bank of the Luqing River, and his soul would follow the familiar tune all the way back to Wali.

After letting his hands fall away from his face, Baopu looked at the people around him. Technician Li of the survey team and Li Zhichang were silent; Baopu's uncle lay on the straw, dead drunk. Suddenly he began shouting shrilly, but no one could understand a word, though the cadence was of a seagoing melody.

Li Zhichang turned to Technician Li and said hoarsely, "Wouldn't it be wonderful if there were no more wars? That way people could devote themselves to the study of science."

Technician Li shook his head. "War is inevitable. The world has never known total peace. A good time is any time people aren't fighting a world war."

"Do you think one of those will break out any time in the next few years?" Li Zhichang asked.

Technician Li smiled. "That's something you'll have to ask those running the show, the higher up the ladder the better. But there isn't a person alive who's willing to give you a guarantee one way or the other. My uncle is a military expert, and I'm always looking for a chance to get him into a debate. It's great fun. One of our favorite topics is what they call 'Star Wars.' "

Baopu, who was listening in on the conversation, was reminded of the nickname people in town had given Technician Li: Crackpot.

"Last time you went too fast," Li Zhichang said. "I'd like to know more about those Star Wars. You were saying something about a NATO and a Warsaw Pact. What's that all about? I mean, like they're a couple of persimmons, one softer than the other . . ."

The laborer standing beside Crackpot laughed, but Crackpot cut him off. "I don't know which persimmon is softer, but those are military blocs. NATO is led by the United States; the Soviet Union leads the Warsaw Pact."

"I've got that," Li Zhichang said.

Crackpot continued, "If those two persimmons ever bang into one another, they'll both be crushed. They are the key to whether or not there'll be a world war. Both sides need to be careful not to cross the line. The year the Soviets shot down a South Korean airliner, America sent its army into Grenada. Then the Americans announced plans to place midrange missiles in Western Europe, so the Russians countered by upping the number of missiles siloed in Eastern Europe. They also broke off weapons talks on three occasions and boycotted the Olympics. It was tit for tat, with both sides digging in their heels, till they reached an impasse. Relations between the two countries were deteriorating rapidly, and the rest of the world looked on anxiously, detecting the smell of gunpowder in the air. The US and USSR faced off like that for more than a year before relaxing tensions a little. In the end the foreign ministers of the two countries sat down in Geneva and talked for more than seventeen goddamned hours . . ."

"Everything was ruined by people who knew nothing about water," Sui Buzhao bellowed, his body twisting in the hay. "After Uncle Zheng He died, the goddamn ships, all eight or ten of them, sank, killing all those people. There were cracks in our hull and we tried to stop the leaks with our bare bodies. They didn't trust the *Classic of the Waterway,* so they deserved to die, disregarding even the life of the helmsman. How the hell could it end well? I puked until there was nothing but bitter bile in my stomach, and the barnacles cut me bloody when I went down to stop up the leaks. I bled while reciting the *Classic of the Waterway* until I was hoarse. The ship sailed to Qiyang zhou, and as stated in the book, 'You must fix your direction with care and make no mistakes in your calculation. The ship cannot veer. If it heaves to the west it will run aground, so you must heave east. If you heave too far to the east the water will be dark and clear, with many gulls and petrels. If you heave too far to the west, the water will be crystal clear, afloat with driftwood and many flying fish. If the ship is on the right course, the tails of birds will point the way. When the ship nears Wailuo, seven *geng* to the east will be Wanli Shitang, where there are low red rock formations. The water is shallow if you can see the side of the boat and you must be careful if you see rocks. From the fourth to the eighth month, the water flows southwest, and the currents are quite strong . . . ' But no one paid any attention. These men finally had to cry when the waves rose up around midnight. It was useless to cut the mast, for the current ripped the ship apart. I'll curse them for the rest of my life because of what happened to that ship."

"All arms races are fierce competitions," Crackpot continued. "They start out on land or at sea, but that doesn't hold their interest for long, so then it moves to outer space. When the Americans say they're going to do something, they do it. They decided to put up their Strategic Defense Initiative in three stages: The tests would take them up to 1989, they'd finalize the design in the 1990s, and the program would be functional by the year 2000. Maybe earlier. Then they could shoot down any missile, no matter where it came from, using guided weapons with lasers or particle beams. At that point it would no longer be necessary to fight on land. Everything would be taken care of out in space. Space, the new frontier. The Star Wars initiative is part of what the Americans call advanced frontier strategy. The newspapers call it a multilayered deep-space defense system. If they're allowed to actually succeed in this, the long-standing balance of power between the US and the USSR will no longer hold, and that will be a challenge to the whole world."

Crackpot ignored Sui Buzhao's shouts as he carried on a lively one-sided conversation with Li Zhichang, who nodded and occasionally made a mark in the dirt with his finger, as if recording scientific data.

"What I don't understand," he said, looking in the direction from which the notes of the flute carried over in the darkness, "is how the foreigners can spend all that money making enough atomic bombs for any contingency and still not be content."

Crackpot slapped his knee. "The more A-bombs you have the less you have to be content about. That's the whole point. Consider this: A few powerful countries have labored for years to produce nuclear weapons, more than they could ever use, and they could double their present arsenal, and it wouldn't make any difference. There are so many of the things that no one dares to use a single one. Whether you launch the first attack or not, that's the end for everyone. It's a perfect example of the concept that when things reach an extreme they develop in the opposite direction. When the number of bombs reaches a certain point they can't be used and have to lie sleeping in their silos for all time. But if the Americans' Star Wars initiative becomes operational and can intercept the other guy's missiles in space and keep them from hitting friendly targets, that changes everything, don't you see?"

Li Zhichang murmured his understanding of what he was hearing but didn't say anything. Then, as if awakening from a dream, he blurted out, "My god! If they can do that, what'll happen to us?"

He received no answer. None of the men around the haystack had an answer to that question. Sui Buzhao, whose trancelike state allowed for some sorrow, picked this moment to leave the broken old ship and lie down exhausted on the hay. Silence lay over the men and the haystack. The stars were enormous, some shining like bright lanterns. The sharp, mournful sounds of the flute still sliced through the night. Chilled winds cut to the bone. Baopu rolled a cigarette and lit it, then curled up as far as his back would let him.

After fiddling with his liquor bottle, Sui Buzhao stood up unsteadily and, his steps wobbly, paced back and forth in front of the haystack, his tiny eyes poking through the darkness. There were no more conversations; everyone stared at him. He flung his bottle through the air; it hit a wall and broke. "Good shot!" he cried out. Then he laughed. "Two masts with one goddamn shot . . . don't act so surprised! An armada of warships came from the south to wage war on Wali. There were corvettes, frigates, corsairs, towered ships, and bridged ships. They didn't know we had a giant ship of our own in port, a seven-thousand-tonner with four or five hundred men and six cannons. I stood on the dock with my telescope trained on their sailors, black men who weren't wearing pants. That infuriated me! 'Set sail at once and engage the turtle scum!' I shouted. Our ship pulled noisily away from the pier and moved out with a following wind. Li Xuantong wanted to come aboard and fight with the rest of us, but I told him to stay ashore and keep reading his sutras. It was a battle for the ages, recorded in the history of our town. You can check it for yourself . . . it happened in 485 BCE . . . and people were still talking about it hundreds of years later. Wali's brilliant reputation was well deserved, and talented people came from miles around. Fan Li, the old man, was not valued in foreign countries, so he floated over from the Eastern Ocean in a basket. The banks of the Luqing River were so cold that year that the frost settled on the corn before it could be harvested, and it would have been lost if not for Zou Yan from the west bank, who blew his flute and melted the frost. Gimpy's playing cannot compare. He just spends his time on the floodplain, but I wouldn't be surprised if he was a reincarnation of Zou Yan. A few years after the melting of the frost, the First Emperor of Qin rose to power, and Xu Fu, from the Xu family in East Wali, was possessed. He insisted on taking me to meet the First Emperor. Not me. I preferred to practice meditation with Li Xuantong . . ." At this point in Sui Buzhao's narration, his legs got tangled up and he stumbled to the ground. That broke the trance that held the others, who rushed over to help him up.

Li Zhichang stayed where he was, however. He had been listening to Sui Buzhao with the others, but not a single word got through to him. He was still thinking about Star Wars. Since he did not grasp all the details and had many questions about related issues, such as the effects on politics and the economy, when Crackpot came back and sat down, he asked him to tell him more.

"I could talk all day and still not be finished," Crackpot said with a shake of his head. "We'll get back to it some other day. It's an important, serious issue, and I wish there was someone in town who'd debate it with me, the way my uncle used to—"

"Not me!" Li Zhichang said. "I can't."

The sky was beginning to lighten up in the east, creating an air of tranquillity. Baopu was thinking about the dim candle that burned in Dahu's house and how the wick was flickering. Zhang-Wang, a hard look on her face, was seated on a rush mat, and everyone was waiting for dawn to break. Gimpy's flute was not as crisp as it was at night; now it had a delicate, gentle quality. And the winds were no longer so cold, warmed, it seemed, by the strains of the flute. Baopu was reminded of his uncle's strange comment, that Gimpy might be a reincarnation of Zou Yan.

SEVEN

Leilei was no taller than a few years before, it seemed to Baopu, and hadn't changed a bit. By counting on his fingers he tried to fix the boy's age but couldn't do it. The boy's head was nice and round, shaved on all four sides, with just a tuft of hair on the top. He had a gray pallor on his skin, which never seemed quite dry. The outer corners of his eyes turned strangely upward, just like his father's, Li Zhaolu's, and he had thin, curved, almost feminine brows, much like those of his mother, Xiaokui. Baopu wished he could somehow hold the boy in his arms. He often dreamed that he had his arms around him and was kissing him. "You should call me Papa," he said to the boy in his dreams.

Once, when he was walking by the river, he spotted Leilei coming toward him carrying a live fish, its head hanging low and twisting from side to side. When he spotted Baopu he stopped and looked at him, the corners of his eyes inching upward. It made Baopu feel awkward, almost as if Zhaolu were looking at him. It was an agonizing moment, for he knew that sooner or later that look would compel him to reveal what had happened on that stormy night. So he crouched down and rubbed the tuft of hair as he studied the boy's face. Everything below those eyes resembled him, Baopu discovered. With a muttered oath, he stood up and hurried off. But then he stopped and turned to take another look. Leilei was still standing there, not moving. Abruptly he held up the fish and shouted: "Pa—"

It was a shout Baopu would never forget, and one night, when thoughts of Leilei came to him, he murmured: "Not bad. I've got a son!" But then feelings of self-reproach gnawed at him, creating a desire to say that to the boy's mother. Yet as soon as he was outside and washed in the moon's rays, he realized he was being ridiculous—Leilei had clearly gotten those eyes from Li Zhaolu. Counting backward, he tried to calculate when Zhaolu had come home for the last time and then recall the date when the old tree by the mill had been struck by lightning. His heart was pounding as he relived the night of passion and joy they had shared. No detail escaped him: Xiaokui's moans of pleasure, her frail figure, and the two sweaty bodies as lightning flashed outside the window. The night was hideously short, and he recalled Xiaokui's cry of alarm when the sky began to lighten up in the morning. She was holding him as he lay, utterly exhausted, as if he had only minutes to live. She shook him, maybe thinking he was in mortal danger, and began to cry. He sat up but lacked the strength to jump out her window.

The rain had stopped by the time he was on his way back to his room, and that is where his reminiscences always ended. He concluded that such heart-stopping joy had to have produced fruit, a realization that made him break out in a cold sweat. Time and again he asked himself if there was a chance that he could someday claim the boy who refused to grow up.

The next emotion to torment Baopu was profound remorse. He had watched Xiaokui limp along dragging the boy with her all these years, and he'd never once offered to help, to his everlasting feelings of guilt. There were times when he turned his thoughts upside down, telling himself that Leilei was definitely not his son, and that invariably lifted an emotional burden from his shoulders.

Xiaokui wore her mourning garb for a year. Such attire had likely been outlawed in other places, but not in Wali. Rather than diminish in number, complex funeral rites and strange customs had actually increased in recent years. Where death was concerned, only the eyes of the spirits were watching. For the better part of a year, Xiaokui was seen on the streets and in the lanes clad in funereal white, a reminder to the townspeople not to forget to grieve. When Baopu saw the white garb he immediately thought of Zhaolu, who had died in the far-off northeast provinces. He did not have to be told that if the people in town knew what had happened between him and Xiaokui, he would never be forgiven, for that was what people called "stealing a man's wife when he's down." Zhaolu could not experience the loathing of a man whose wife had been taken from him, for he was already in the ground. This thought made Baopu cringe. But no one in town knew, and no one could imagine that their taciturn neighbor was capable of what had happened on that stormy night. Baopu censured himself anyway.

In the end, Xiaokui shed her mourning garments, and a huge sigh of relief was let out all over town. The mill seemed to turn faster; the color returned to Xiaokui's face. She was often seen in Zhao Family Lane with Leilei in her arms.

They met once. Her burning gaze made Baopu lower his head and hurry away. From then on he avoided the ancient lane. On another occasion he saw her deep in conversation with Sui Buzhao, who was nodding, his tiny eyes shining. Later that night his uncle came to his room and smiled as he fixed him with a stare. Baopu could barely keep himself from sending the old man away. But then his uncle said, "This is your lucky day. It's time for you to have a family. Xiaokui—"

A shrill shout burst from Baopu's throat, to his uncle's astonishment. With a cold, hard look, Baopu said, exaggerating every word: "Don't mention that to me ever again!"

～

Ever since his teens, Baopu had been unhappy with his uncle, owing mainly to the day he had tried to tempt Jiansu into going out into the river with him on a boat that immediately sank, scaring Baopu half to death. A later incident only increased his disgust for the man. Early

one cold morning, during the lunar New Year holiday, Baopu and
Guigui rose early to celebrate, as custom dictated. First one, then the
other washed up with bath soap they kept in a small wooden box, filling the small room with a pervasive fragrance. Guigui urged him to
wear the leather, square-toed shoes left to him by his father. The sky
was lightening, but the streets were still deserted. In a campaign to do
away with superstition, officials had forbidden the use of firecrackers
and paying New Year's calls. So Baopu summoned Hanzhang and
Jiansu to his room and had Guigui go for their uncle while they placed
dumplings with yam fillings on a cutting board. Guigui had not been
gone long when cracking noises erupted on the street. At first they
thought someone was setting off firecrackers, but Jiansu ran out to see
what it was and reported that a couple of local carters were riding up
and down the streets, their heads beaded with sweat as they snapped
their whips in the air.

Water boiled in the wok as they waited for their uncle. But Guigui
returned alone, red eyed, and said she'd pounded on their uncle's door,
but he was inside snoring away. When he finally woke up, he refused
to get out of bed. Even when she told him they had prepared dumplings, he said he wasn't getting up, not for anything or anyone. She
stood there until water began dribbling out under the door onto the
ground, and it took only a moment to realize that he was on the other
side relieving himself. She came straight home and announced that
she never wanted to see that man again. Baopu and Hanzhang were
beside themselves, but Jiansu merely looked out the window and said,
"That uncle of ours is really something!"

As he dumped the dark dumplings into the boiling water, Baopu
summed up his view of the man: "He's the sinful member of the Sui
clan."

～

Baopu's uncle stood in his room that day wanting to continue with
what he'd come to say about Xiaokui, but the determined look on
Baopu's face kept him from doing so. Caught off guard by his nephew's

attitude, he turned and left, stumbling along as always, with Baopu's eyes boring into his back; he wondered if the old man had learned of his wretched secret.

Much later that night, Baopu was out pacing the yard. Finally, unable to restrain himself, he went to his brother's room and knocked on the door. Wiping his sleepy eyes, Jiansu let him in and lit a lamp. "I couldn't sleep," Baopu said. "I have to talk to someone. I'm really depressed."

Jiansu, dressed only in a pair of shorts, crouched down on the *kang*, his skin glistening in the lamplight, as if oiled. Baopu took off his shoes and joined him on the *kang*, sitting cross-legged. "I've been there," Jiansu said, "I know how it feels. But time took care of it. If I'd carried on like you, I'd have been skin and bones by now."

With a forced smile, Baopu said: "I guess I've gotten used to it. I'm in the habit of feeling sinful. I'm used to suffering."

The brothers smoked in silence until Jiansu, pipe in hand, lowered his head and said, "There's nothing worse than waking up in the middle of the night. There are so many things on your mind at this time of night that if your thoughts take an ugly turn, you can forget about getting any more sleep. Going outside and letting the dew wet your face helps a little. Or, if your heart seems on fire, you can pour cold water over your head. I hate waking up in the middle of the night."

Seemingly oblivious to what his younger brother was saying, Baopu asked, "Jiansu, who would you say is the most sinful member of the Sui clan?"

With a grim laugh, Jiansu replied, "Didn't you say that's what our uncle is?"

Baopu shook his head, tossed away his cigarette, and looked at his brother without so much as blinking.

"No, it's me!"

Jiansu shoved the pipe back in his mouth and bit down hard. He gave his brother a strange look. "What are you talking about?" he said with an angry frown.

Baopu rested his hands on his knees and arched his wrists. "I can't tell you now, but believe me, I know what I'm saying."

With a bewildered shake of his head, Jiansu smiled grimly. Then he took his pipe out of his mouth and laughed. Surprised by that laugh, Baopu frowned. "I don't know what you're referring to," Jiansu said, "and I want to keep it that way. You didn't kill somebody, did you? Become an outlaw? All I know is that members of our clan are in the habit of making things hard on themselves right up to the day we die. If you're a sinful man, then everybody else in Wali deserves to be killed. My days are not pleasant—sheer torture, if you want to know— and I don't know what to do about it. I often suffer from a toothache that makes that side of my face swell up, and I have to stop myself from picking up a hammer, knocking out every last tooth, and letting the blood flow. What am I supposed to do? Why does it happen? I don't know. So I suffer. I know I should do something about it, but I don't. Sometimes I feel like picking up a hatchet and cutting off my hand. But what good would that do? I'd be gushing blood and rolling around the ground in agony, minus a hand, and drawing a crowd of people whose only reaction would be to look down on me for being a cripple. I just have to put up with things the way they are. That's the punishment for being born a Sui! During the crazy times a few years back, Zhao Duoduo came into our yard with a bunch of men and a steel pole with the idea of digging up buried treasure left by our ancestors. That was like stabbing me in the chest. I watched them through the window and—I'm not joking when I say this—I cursed myself the whole time. Myself, not Duoduo and his men, and I cursed our ancestors for their blindness in setting up a noodle factory on the banks of the Luqing, ensuring that future generations could neither live nor die well. As I grew into adulthood I imagined myself with a wife, just like everybody else. But what woman would willingly marry into the Sui clan? You were married once, so you know what I mean. Nobody gives a damn about us. They see we're alive and breathing and never give a thought to what our lives are like. You're my brother, look for yourself, just look!" Jiansu's face was red. Tossing away his pipe and knocking his pillow to one side, he crawled under the covers to fetch a little book with a red cover. He opened it, and several photographs of women fell out, all local women who had married. "See those? They were all in love with me, all former lovers, and all were stopped from marrying me by their families. Why? Because I'm a Sui! One after the other they married someone else. One married a man in South Mountain who then hung her up from the rafters. I can't forget them. I look at their photos at night and meet them in my dreams."

Baopu picked up the photographs and held them until his hand was shaking so hard they fell onto the bed. Wrapping his arms around his brother, he held his face next to his, where their tears merged. Though his lips were quaking, Baopu tried to console his brother, but even he wasn't sure what he was saying.

"Jiansu, I hear what you're saying and I understand completely. I shouldn't have come over. I'm just adding to your suffering. But like you, I can't bear it any longer. What you said about our family was right. But you're young, after all, you're still young, and you were only half right. There are other things you don't know. What I mean is, there's something else that causes us to torment ourselves. And it might be worse, even harder to bear. That's what I'm facing, that's what it is . . ."

With Baopu gently patting his brother's back, they both calmed down after a while and sat down on the *kang*. Jiansu angrily dried his tears and then looked around for his pipe. After lighting it and taking several puffs, he gazed out the window at the darkness. "Uncle has feasted and drunk like a sponge all his life," he said softly, "which means he hasn't suffered the way we have. Papa lived a proper life and died trying to settle accounts. You and I were shut up in our study so you could practice your calligraphy and I could prepare the ink for you. Then after Papa died, you put me back in the study, where you taught me all about benevolence and righteousness and made me repeat the words to you. You taught me how to write the words 'love the people,' which I did, one stroke at a time."

Baopu, his head lowered, listened silently to his brother. The image

of a burning house flashed before him, red fireballs descending from
the eaves and burning in all directions. The whole house was engaged
as his stepmother writhed on the *kang* . . . He jerked his head up as
he felt compelled to tell his brother about Huizi, tell him how his
mother died. But by gritting his teeth he managed to keep from saying anything.

They stayed up all night.

The riverside mill rumbled along. Baopu, wooden ladle in hand, sat
motionless twelve hours a day, until he was relieved by an older worker.
It was a job for old men who had sat on the same sturdy stools for
decades. When one of them, who had worked for the Sui clan all his
life, saw that Sui Yingzhi had died, he'd said, "It's time for me to go
too," and he died there on the stool. With their stone walls, the old
mills were like ancient fortresses carved into the riverbank and drawing generations of people to them. Moss that grew on the ground
beyond the paths trampled by ox hooves, a mixture of old and new
growth, looked like the multihued fur of a gigantic beast. The old man
died and a master miller hanged himself because of a ruined batch,
but neither drew a sound from the mill itself. They were the soul of
the town. During hard times there were always people who ran to the
mills to do things in secret. Then during the reexamination period
following land reform, whole families fled from Wali after first stealthily performing kowtow rites in the mills. Villagers burned spirit money
to memorialize the forty-two men and women buried alive in a yam
cellar by the landlord restitution corps, and the mill did not make a
sound. It had only a single tiny window, its only eye. Tenders of the
millstone gazed at the open fields and the river through that eye.

The first thing Baopu saw when he looked through that window
each day was the partial trunk of the tree of heaven taken down by a
bolt of lightning. At the time people had discussed the destruction of
the tree, but it was soon forgotten by all except Baopu, who continued
to study it. His face darkened when he examined its ruined state. A

tree so thick at its base that two people were needed to circle it with their arms was now split down the middle, exposing a white core that had the look of a shattered bone. A lush canopy that had only recently created welcome shade, the branches emitting refreshing moisture, was now nothing but splintered debris. A dark liquid had congealed at the outer edges of the wood core, the bloody seepage from the lightning strike. A strange odor emanated from its depths, and Baopu knew it was the smell of death. Thunder and lightning are bullets from the universe's rifle. Why had that particular tree wound up in its crosshairs? And why that night? Heavenly justice has a long arm.

He had bent down to pick up pieces of the tree and carried them back to the mill.

The abandoned mills were left over from the heyday of the glass noodle industry. Many had rumbled loudly during their youth, but after Father died in a field of red sorghum, the mills began dying off, one after the other. They had been built on the bank of the river for its abundant supply of water. Then one day Baopu stumbled across stone troughs that showed that the millstones had once been turned not by oxen but by water, which was why the Luqing River was shrinking. That discovery had people believing that the excavated ship had sailed down a raging river and that the Wali pier had indeed been the site of a forest of ships' masts. Vast changes occur as the constellations change places, making predictions of the future impossible. The old mills slowly ground time itself away. Once the mill was mechanized, the conveyer belt and the gears that turned it dazzled the people's eyes, an example of how abruptly the world can change. People flocked to see the motor-driven millstone, which brought life to the mill. But now that the novelty had worn off and they had stopped coming, Baopu looked out the window and spotted Xiaokui, market basket in hand, and Leilei, the son who never seemed to grow. He called to the boy, but there was no response.

He was reminded of the night many years before when he and his brother had wept together. Two grown men airing their teary complaints until the sun came up. That night left a permanent mark on Baopu's heart. He could not sleep for thoughts of the woman and her son. Then one day he saw her at the riverbank, where she was gathering castor beans. As determination filled his heart, he walked up to her.

Xiaokui ignored him, concentrating on gathering the beans, so he fell in beside her to help, not saying a word. They worked in silence. When her red plastic basket was nearly full, Xiaokui sat down and cried. Baopu took out his tobacco pouch but spilled the tobacco on the ground.

"Xiaokui," he said, "I want to tell you something about me . . ."

She looked up and chewed on her lip. "Who are you? For ten years you haven't said a word to me. For ten years I haven't so much as seen you. I don't know you."

"Xiaokui!" he cried out. "Xiaokui!" She slumped to the side and cried bitterly.

"I know you hate me," he said in a frantic tone of voice, "that you've hated me all these years. But you could not hate me as much as I hate myself. For years you and I have hated the same person, someone who ruined your life and proved unworthy of the friendship of Li Zhaolu, who died in a coal mine far off in the northeast provinces. That person must pay for his sins. He has no right to ever give another thought to that stormy night or to step foot in Zhao Family Lane."

Xiaokui sat up and glared at him. Her lips were quivering. "Unworthy of Li Zhaolu? How? I vowed to give myself to you years ago. Zhaolu may have died in the cave-in, but his fate was no worse than mine. I've suffered so much, it would have been better if he'd taken me to die with him. But no, he abandoned me and Leilei. I mourned him for a whole year, longer than any other Wali widow has ever mourned her husband. Worthy or unworthy, I have to go on living just the same. And I need a man. I keep thinking about that wretched cricket cage that hung in the mill . . . when I can't sleep I curse the heartless man in that mill . . ." Teardrops hung from her lashes.

Baopu's heart was broken by this outpouring of grief, and he was speechless. Then, as he crumbled dirt clods and gasped for breath, he said, "Listen to what I have to say. You may have plenty of self-awareness, but you don't know men, especially the men of the Sui clan. For us life has always been a bitter challenge, and that has turned us into cowards. For men like us, maybe wasting our lives in a mill is the best we can hope for. I want you to know that not a day goes by that I'm not petrified by the image of Zhaolu's eyes burning holes in me. The pain in my heart keeps me awake at night, and when I recall what happened beneath the willow tree that night so many years ago, I'm reminded of how a few days later you stopped coming to the mill. I know that someone must have seen us, that the Zhao clan had their eye on me. Then you told me how Fourth Master nodded his approval of your marriage to Zhaolu, and I was disconsolate. I was like a madman that night the lightning struck. Somehow I had found my courage. I knew that if I went to you after Zhaolu died your family would recall what had happened in the past and, by following the vine to find the melon, label you a fallen woman and me an evil wife-stealer. We would not have been able to hold our heads up. When I think about the window I smashed, my heart begins to pound. I never did learn what you said to the Zhaos when they asked what had happened. It's these things that keep me awake at night. That and how my father spent his last days settling accounts, how in his single-minded obsession to pay off his debts he coughed up blood all over his chestnut horse. I know that future generations of Suis will never again owe money to anyone. But I owe a debt to Zhaolu, and that thought is more than I can bear!"

Xiaokui gazed at Baopu, who was so overwrought his face was beet red. He was shaking all over, and she was so stunned by his outburst she couldn't speak. Suddenly he seemed like a stranger, though she'd known him since childhood. She was amazed to learn about the thoughts that had filled his mind, including the question of what had happened after he broke the window. No one had even asked about it, since so many windows had been broken during the storm. And she wondered who the Sui clan had owed; she had no recollection of his father going out to repay debts. Baopu must have gotten confused over time, since so many of the things he talked about were beyond her understanding. How he must have suffered, day and night, over the years. She saw light glinting off hair that had turned gray. Inexplicably, his face was red, and he seemed to be holding up well. But the look of sorrow stamped on his face was indelible and it was clear that his eyelashes had been worn down by tired fingers. Xiaokui's heart stirred. She heaved a long sigh and saw that Baopu's gaze was frozen on her. There was a question in her eyes.

"Whose child is Leilei?" he asked in a barely audible voice.

That was the last thing she expected to hear. She was confused. "He's mine," she muttered, "mine and Zhaolu's . . ."

Baopu did not believe her.

Sensing herself about to lose control, she looked away and said breathlessly, "What sort of question is that? All you ever do is entertain crazy thoughts, thoughts that must surprise even you. At this rate you'll have me as confused as you are. How could you think such thoughts, Baopu? I really don't think you understand a thing. Have you been listening to me? Have you heard what I'm saying?"

Baopu kept staring, unwilling to believe her.

Meeting his gaze, she shouted: "Why are you looking like that? I tell you he's Li Zhaolu's son!"

Baopu's head drooped like a grain stalk beaten down by hailstones. "That can't be," he muttered, wringing his hands. "It simply can't be. Leilei and I have reached an understanding. He and I have said everything that needs to be said. I believe him, and I trust my own knowledge—"

"Leilei hardly ever says a word, there's no way he could have told you anything. I know what I know."

"You're right," Baopu said with a nod. "He didn't actually say the words, but our looks said everything that needed to be said. You may not know it, but some things can only be said with the eyes. I understand him and he understands me."

What could Xiaokui say to that? Her anger was tempered by pity. Years of resentment and bitterness were swallowed up by a warm current that enveloped her. Her chin began to quiver, then her shoulders lifted. She crouched down, fell to her knees, and wrapped her arms around Baopu. "Baopu," she begged, "get rid of those crazy thoughts so we can live together. Save me and save yourself . . ."

Baopu rested his callused hands on her shoulders until her body relaxed. Then he took her in his arms and kissed the top of her head. When he laid his hand on her breast he felt her heart pounding. Xiaokui buried her face in his chest, desperate to breathe in his manly scent. She forgot that she was in the bean field, where the sound of gently flowing water in the Luqing River came on the wind. She was immersed in the pleasure of feeling his hand, which was slowly, gently stroking her, a sensation she wished she could feel until the sun sank in the western sky, even until the end of time. "Tonight," she said without thinking, "Leilei will be asleep. I'll leave the window open." The hand stopped abruptly, and she looked up, surprised and fretful. Baopu's forehead was creased as he looked through the gaps in the bean plants at the riverbank, where Party Secretary Li was walking with a group of people down Gaoding Street, engaged in a spirited conversation. Struck by a powerful impulse, she pulled his hand away.

"Stand up," she said. "We don't have to hide behind bean plants. Stand up! Let them see us. We belong together. We've always belonged together!"

She leaned over, kissed him, and stood up straight.

The people on the other side of the river stopped to look at her. "Out gathering castor beans, are you?" Secretary Li shouted in greeting.

Xiaokui nodded. In a voice so low only he could hear, she urged Baopu to stand up. He wouldn't. "Yes," she replied weakly, "I'm gathering castor beans."

Tears slipped down her cheeks.

Baopu never did stand up that day, even though it could have been his last chance to do so. When darkness fell he slinked back to his room, shamefaced.

And so, when Li Zhichang led the old ox out of the mill for the final time, Baopu sat on his stool, as always, accompanied now by the whirr of a motor. His blood, which had nearly congealed in his veins for years, was flowing freely again among the castor plants. He knew that Xiaokui loved him still and, there in the castor bean field, had given him the opportunity to be with her. He had let that opportunity pass. Once again in his place in the mill, he assumed that there would not be another. But he could not get thoughts of Leilei out of his mind. Xiaokui had said what she said to make him feel better, but it had not put the matter to rest, and he had a hazy notion that only he and Leilei could do that. Passing up this opportunity could well turn out to be something that Sui Baopu would regret for the rest of his life.

In the days that followed, every time he walked past the bean field or was outside on a stormy night, a sense of unease overcame him. One night he walked into the field, alone, and found the spot where he and Xiaokui had met. He reached down and touched the nonexistent footprints and other traces of that day.

The night after he'd called to Leilei to come see the machine, a storm raged. He lay on the *kang* but could not sleep, feeling as if something were gnawing at him, and nearly crazed with desire. Thunder crackled, and his desire was greater than ever.

In the end he climbed down off the *kang* and went outside. The window in his brother's room was dark, the one in his sister's room bright. Nothing could stop him as he ran out of the yard, his clothes quickly drenched by the rain. It was cold, almost icy, just what his overheated body needed. The rain dripped from his hair, and he could not keep his eyes open, but in his imagination he felt her soft hand stroking his beard as he wrapped his arms around her frail, light-as-air body. He came to a teetering stop and looked up to see Zhao Family Lane, shrouded in blackness. The window was dark, and he imagined he could hear the gentle sleeping sounds of Xiaokui and Leilei. Never again would that window open for him. Thunder rumbled and lightning flashed, illuminating his waterlogged body. One bolt was so close it felt as if it had crashed on top of him. He spit out the water in his mouth and began cursing himself. Balling his hand into a fist, he thumped himself in the chest, so hard it knocked him off his feet and into the mud, where he rolled around painfully on the sharp-edged gravel. For hours he lay where he fell.

From time to time Baopu got up from his stool to spread beans on the conveyor belt with his wooden ladle. White liquid with a green tinge flowed from the bottom and was carried in a trough straight through to the sediment pool; there was no more need for anyone to come carry it out in buckets. The old man who was supposed to spell him spent more and more time at Zhang-Wang's shop drinking and often showed up late. When he did arrive he reeked of alcohol and was half asleep.

This time, when Baopu was relieved, the lane seemed all but deserted. The few people he saw were hurrying along. As he wondered what could have happened, he spotted Xiaokui, holding Leilei by the hand. She ignored him. Hesitating briefly, he then fell in behind her. A crowd had formed at the city wall, many of them pointing excitedly to a well in the middle of a field. Baopu ran over to see what it was.

Someone in the circle around the well frame shouted. Leilei jerked his hand free and threaded his way up front. Instinctively, Baopu was right behind him, all the way up to the front, where he saw stacks of iron pipes of various lengths. The coal prospecting team, all wearing hats woven of willow twigs, were hard at work, and Sui Buzhao was right in the middle. Baopu stopped short of the work site, but not Leilei, who ran up to the pipes in time to see Sui Buzhao and the other men dig a black object out of one of the pipes and smash it to pieces. Leilei rushed over, jumped up in front of Sui Buzhao, and snatched pieces out of the old man's hand.

"Mama," the boy shouted, "it's coal!"

The grown-ups in the crowd were astonished that the little boy was the first to figure out what the object was. Xiaokui, who had worked her way up front, snatched Leilei up in her arms and handed the coal back to Sui Buzhao. There were, people saw, tears in her eyes, and they whispered that the sight of the coal had reminded her of Zhaolu, buried under a mountain of the same. Leilei had proved himself worthy of his coal-mining father, knowing instinctively what the black object was, yet Baopu was surprised that the boy had known what it was without being told. After watching mother and son leave the area, his uncle and the coal they'd brought up held no interest for him. But as he headed home, he turned for one last look at the well site, where he saw the eccentric Shi Dixin off by himself, glumly smoking his pipe.

By the time he turned back, Xiaokui and Leilei were nowhere to be seen, and he suddenly felt a powerful hunger and crippling exhaustion. With difficulty he made it into his yard, where he saw Li Zhichang pacing back and forth anxiously. It dawned on him that he hadn't seen Li in the crowd. Rather, he was looking up at Hanzhang's window. After watching for a moment, Baopu walked up to Li, whose passions had, to his great surprise, burst into the open. Baopu saw that the man's face had lost its luster. Feeling compassion, he laid his hand on his shoulder and said, "You need to eat, you can't go on like this."

Zhichang nodded. "She won't open her door," he said. "She ignores me. But she loves me, I know she does, so I'll keep waiting until she comes out."

Baopu took Zhichang's icy hand in his and said, "You were like this a few years back, but I thought you'd come out of it."

Zhichang shook his head. "You don't come out of something like this. As long as the flame burns in my heart I'll keep at it. Dahu was the latest upstanding member of the Sui clan to leave us, and when I was in the haystack that night listening to Gimpy's flute while Technician Li talked about Star Wars, all kinds of thoughts ran through my mind, and I realized how slow I am in everything. There's so much I ought to do, but I don't, and other things I don't do as well as I should. I knew I had to move faster. Variable gears can't stop, and neither can love. The lights I put up still haven't been turned on, though Wali's streets should have been lit up long ago. The person I love won't speak to me, though we were fated to be together back when we were kids. I let other things get in the way, and by messing up one thing I wound up messing up everything. But it's too late for regrets. How about it, Baopu, will you help me?"

Sparks seemed to fly from his eyes, and Baopu knew exactly what Zhichang was feeling. "You Lis are good people," he said as he grasped the man's arm. "I'll do what I can. I'll try as hard as if I were doing it for myself." He crouched down and said, "But you're going about it all wrong. If you really love her, you have to stop acting like this. If she refuses to come out much longer she could get sick. Now that you've let her know how you feel, leave as quietly as possible. You really should." Zhichang stared at Baopu. "I mean it, you need to leave."

So Li Zhichang walked out of the yard reluctantly, leaving Baopu resting on his haunches to silently smoke a cigarette. Obviously, Dahu's death had spurred Zhichang into starting up something that had lain dormant for so long. That came as a major surprise. But the anxieties Baopu had felt in recent days were also tied up with the death of Dahu. He couldn't say why, exactly, but he felt as if a force were driving him to do something. Just what that something was he couldn't say, yet he had a sense of urgency. This was no way to live; it took too much out of a man. Baopu envied Li Zhichang's clarity of purpose and the way he kept his eye on his goal. "Variable gears can't stop, and neither can love." Baopu blew out a mouthful of smoke, stood up, and went over to knock on Hanzhang's door.

The door opened. His sister appeared to have just returned from the drying ground; she carried the smell of the glass noodles. Her face had lost its color, her eyes were sunken and dark, yet she remained calm as she watched her brother walk in. "You heard it all, I guess," Baopu said. She nodded and smiled. She didn't look unhappy. All the things he wanted to say to her remained unspoken. Zhichang had said he knew she loved him, and one look at his sister convinced Baopu that he'd been right. Hanzhang was as lovely as Huizi had been. But she was also becoming as cold as his stepmother. It was that trait that upset Baopu. He recalled what a gentle, lovable child she'd been, and he'd envied her innocence and cheerful nature. He wished she could have stayed that way forever, the embodiment of that Sui trait. But it was not to be, and he could only sigh.

With a smile on her lips, Hanzhang stood up, as if she hadn't a care in the world. She had the figure of her mother in her youth. She walked over to the window and then came back and sat down. "What did you want to say to me, Elder Brother? Go ahead."

What *did* he want to say to her? Where to start? Did he want her to go take care of what was making her sick? Have a long talk with Li Zhichang about their future? There was a sense of urgency about both of those but no reason to bring them up again.

"I came to tell you they found coal today," he said matter-of-factly.

EIGHT

Zhao Duoduo slept in the factory director's office; most nights he slept straight through till morning, snoring so loudly he could overwhelm the rumbling of the old mill. His wife had died when he was only forty. One night she'd picked a fight, so angering him that he had climbed on top of her and gotten rough. When he was finished, she was dead. Now he slept alone in his office, a cleaver on the windowsill by his side; it was an old habit.

During land reform, Fourth Master had been worried that someone might try to get to him at night, so Zhao had slept in Fourth Master's place. Someone did come at midnight one night. Zhao continued snoring until the intruder got close enough for him to use his cleaver. He'd been young back then, and it was the first time he'd killed a man. Normally, only hunger could wake him up at night, and during those chaotic times he had developed a habit of eating in the dark. As for food, he'd consume anything that was edible, especially when he patrolled the village with a rifle slung over his back. When his name was mentioned in town, people would say, "He'll eat anything." He had eaten field mice, lizards, snakes, porcupines, toads, earthworms, and geckoes. One autumn day after a rainstorm, he spotted some purple earthworms as big as his pinkie crawling on the ground. He squatted down, picked them up, and flattened and stretched them thin, one by one, before tying them into a bundle like a pile of leeks as thick as his arm. After covering the earthworm bundle in mud, he roasted it over flames from dry bean stalks. When that was done, he peeled off the mud to reveal a stick of steaming, fleshy red meat. Holding it like a pig's leg, he ate it under the terrified gaze of onlookers. Maybe as a result of his indiscriminate diet, he gave off a strange smell, so strong that people in Wali could sniff him out at night. He kept a small cooking pot he'd gotten during the war years in his office, and Erhuai, who passed by the factory on his night patrols, often brought him things to eat. After becoming a night watchman, Erhuai seemed almost like Zhao Duoduo's clone.

On occasions when he had trouble sleeping through the night, Zhao often took a leisurely walk around the processing room. Not particularly susceptible to cold, he usually wore only a pair of loose white underpants, exposing his bulging muscles and tough skin to the cold. By this time women on the night shifts were working two extra hours and were required to wear white aprons printed with "Wali Glass Noodle Factory." Another regulation required them to stack their hair on the tops of their heads and cover it. All this was Zhao Duoduo's doing, ideas he'd copied from an electric fan factory during a tour organized by the county chief, Zhou Zifu, who had brought some "entrepreneurs" together to learn from a more advanced enterprise. That was how Zhao Duoduo learned that he had become an "entrepreneur." During the visit, the factory leadership had briefed them on "TQC," a management model adopted from the Japanese in which importance was placed on the flow of "information." Duoduo was so impressed he decided to adopt the system. So upon his return, he extended the work period and had the workers wear aprons and cover their heads. He even held a factory-wide meeting to promote TQC (which sounded like "kick the ball") and underscore the importance of information.

He had his bookkeeper report to him daily and asked the workers in his clan to tell him what they heard from the others. On his night visits to the processing room, he would amble along leisurely in the watery mist. If he did not hear the banging of the metal strainer, he'd look up and shout, "How about a taste of my branding iron?" which immediately produced the sound he was waiting for. He'd kick a girl if she dared to fall asleep by the paste vat and comment to himself that "kicking the ball" was great fun. With their hair stacked on the tops of their heads, which pulled the corners of their eyes upward, the girls presented a sort of comical look, which always got a laugh out of Duoduo. He was happy with their appearance, especially their pudgy faces, which turned red in the steam. Red too were the words on their aprons: "Wali Glass Noodle Factory."

One night he kicked Naonao, who was dozing off, and she shocked him by kicking him back. "Ow," he yelled, but he wasn't angry. As for the heavyset Daxi, he enjoyed watching her jiggle as she worked, and he pinched her when the mood struck him. If she shrugged her shoulders to shake off his hand, he'd curl his fingers into a ball and twirl his hand over her head to make her dizzy. Then he'd take the opportunity to poke her in the chest.

Inevitably, Jiansu ran into Duoduo in the processing room. Separated by watery mist, they formed eye shades with their hands, and when they saw who it was, they walked across the slippery floor toward each other. Neither said a word at first; they merely laughed tentatively. A roll of dark fat was pushed up by the band of Duoduo's white underpants, and Jiansu couldn't take his eyes off it. Duoduo, on the other hand, stared at Jiansu's legs, which reminded him of the old chestnut once owned by Sui Yingzhi, a frustrating image, for he'd always wanted to patrol the town on that horse but had never gotten the chance to do it. The horse had died before he could carry out his other wish, which was to fire a bullet into its head.

Duoduo rubbed his hands and patted Jiansu on the shoulder. "Best worker in the Sui clan," he said. Jiansu just looked at him out of the corner of his eye, then surveyed the processing room, bloodshot eyes highlighting his pale face. His glossy, dark hair was uncombed, and when he pushed back a strand that had fallen over his brow, Duoduo was reminded of the black bristles on the old chestnut's forehead. He swallowed hard. What a fine horse that had been. There was a period of time when he'd often dreamed about it. Once he'd seen Sui Yingzhi ride over from the floodplain, the horse's mane waving in the air, its tail raised as it ran; it was an intimidating presence to him. He'd been armed at the time and felt his palms itch. What a magnificent horse that had been.

Duoduo hitched up his underpants to loosen the band and lowered his head. "Were you just over at the mill with your brother?" Jiansu shook his head. The mere mention of Baopu's name always brought a sense of discomfort to Duoduo; he hated the silent man who sat in the old mill all day long. Jiansu and Duoduo walked around the room. "I'm using the kick-the-ball management system these days," Duoduo said. "It works. You have to admire those Japanese for thinking up something like that. Now all we have to worry about are Li Zhichang's gears. We need to do something about that." Jiansu clenched his teeth at the mention of Li. As they drew close to the girls they stopped talking. Daxi gave Jiansu a look and coughed. Then her face and neck turned red. "Well, well," Duoduo said. But Jiansu ignored him; he was looking at Naonao, who was hard at work.

Over a period of months Jiansu had grown increasingly agitated. The kick-the-ball management style was forcing him to act. If he appeared weak or was hesitant, he'd never forgive himself. He knew it was simply a matter of time before the noodle factory would fall more or less permanently into Duoduo's hands. The date for bidding on the lease was nearly upon them, and everyone in Gaoding Street displayed the same terrified anxiety. Like a hawk, Zhao Duoduo had his eyes on his prey and would swoop down as soon as he could to clamp his iron claws around the factory. The Zhao clan was becoming the most powerful family in Wali, having gradually taken over from the Sui clan, beginning in the 1940s, and was in clear ascendance. Duoduo was only one of the clan's iron claws but the toughest to deal with. A powerful force would be needed to break off each knuckle, since the claw would never cramp up on its own. From the beginning Jiansu had worked hard to learn every aspect of the enterprise—raw materials, capital investment, equipment depreciation, wages, promotion and retention, marketing expenses, taxes, and investments in infrastructure—and he had proceeded cautiously. Clearly, the Zhao clan was reaping huge profits from the factory, which meant that a majority of the townspeople was sacrificing for the greed of a small minority. His difficulty lay in finding concrete and accurate numbers that could be consolidated as evidence when the time was right.

Jiansu cautiously approached local government officials. He wanted them to take note of his presence, which he considered to be an important aspect of his endeavor. He had, for instance, talked to Party Secretary Lu Jindian about restoring Wali's former glory through the revival of the glass noodle industry. Both men were excited by the prospect. Jiansu also believed that applying modern science to the old production methods was critical. His next step was to invite the bookkeeper to share a drink at the Wali Emporium, convinced of the importance of striking up a friendship with the black-clad man with a lean, gaunt face. The bookkeeper grinned, exposing his blackened teeth, and cursed Duoduo with each mouthful of liquor. He even said that Duoduo had "touched" every girl in the processing room, like playing with beads on an abacus. He didn't stop grinning until Zhang-Wang laid down the clay tigers in her hand, walked over, and slapped him. When they left the shop this time, they had their arms around each other, like best friends.

From then on, Jiansu busied himself at night with the accounts, a task that was actually better suited to his brother, Baopu; but Jiansu did not want to involve him, not yet. Though it might turn out to be a huge mess that could never be untangled, he was intent upon getting at least a basic outline. Duoduo might be able to deceive everyone, but not the young man with the pale face and burning eyes. Late at night he would lock his door before opening the little notebook crammed with minutely written numbers and start to check the accounts. The factory employed 112 workers who processed 15,000 *jin* of mung beans each day. Before the old mill was mechanized, they could process 11,500 *jin* during the busy season and 5,300 *jin* in the slow season. There were three busy months out of eight, which made 1,830,000 *jin;* when added to the 1,150,000 *jin* produced during the five months following mechanization, the grand total reached 2,980,000 *jin*. Dazed by that huge number, Jiansu paced the room anxiously, muttering, "Two million, nine hundred and eighty thousand!" The stones in the old riverside mills rumbled on.

Jiansu was amazed that a mountain of beans had been consumed in slightly over a year, since Duoduo took over. The weather varied from season to season; so did the rate of production, but the difference was negligible: On average, a *jin* of noodles required 2.58 *jin* of raw materials. That meant that the Wali Glass Noodle Factory had produced over 1,150,000 *jin* of noodles in thirteen months.

The sale of the million-plus noodles had been a complicated process. The price had risen and fallen three times since January. After the opening of coastal cities, White Dragon Glass Noodles enjoyed a substantial jump in exports, from 19 percent to 51 percent. Export noodles sold for 2.53 yuan per *jin*, while the domestic sales ran at about 1.16 yuan. Jiansu gasped when he was confronted by the enormous gap between export and domestic sales; his skin tingled. He vowed to put together a powerful export team when the day came for him to take over the factory. Many years earlier, ships transporting noodles from Wali to the South Pacific had crowded the river; the forest of masts was one of the most beautiful, captivating images anywhere in the world. Jiansu cracked his knuckles and banged on the table, producing a searing pain, and as he cradled the sore hand in his other hand, the image of a young girl cutting brambles flashed before him, and he closed his eyes. The burning body of that girl had rested on his muscular arm, seemingly about to start spinning. He had carried her into this little room from under the bean trellis . . . A tear rolled from the corner of a tightly shut eye. Jiansu bit his lip and picked up the account again. This time he discovered that the gross profit from the 586,500 *jin* of exported noodles reached 1,483,845 yuan, while the gross profit from 563,500 *jin* of domestic sales was 65,366 yuan. That meant the factory had earned 2,137,505 yuan in thirteen months, after deducting the average transportation costs and losses.

Jiansu's heart was in turmoil after seeing that figure, which he committed to memory. He was compelled by the glorious number to speculate on the Sui clan state of affairs in the 1920s and 1930s. It had been a wealth several times greater than the current number and had extended the clan's influence well beyond the Luqing River, according them a prominent position in local history for decades . . .

Each account took considerable time to go over, and since he did not know how to use an abacus, he performed his calculations with a red pencil and was reminded of what his brother had said about how their father had gone over the accounts day and night the last few years of his life. At the time Jiansu had found it ludicrous, but now he understood. If he kept at it, the number would get smaller, as deductions were made for wages, the cost of raw materials, marketing, taxes, and more. But he still would not have the net profit, because the by-products—bean dredge and bean milk—could be used to make alcohol, animal feed, and fertilizer. Variances in quality commanded a range of prices, but they all had to be included in the income from the noodles, which meant another large account for Jiansu, who was slowly entangled in the giant net. It got tighter and tighter, until he found himself completely enmeshed in it.

When he made his nightly visits to the processing room, those minutely written numbers swirled in his head. Amid the white steam, the row of paste vats, hot-water basins, and cold-water basins looked like a single column of giant zeros. The people worked in the mist to keep adding numbers to it, and he had no idea what would come from this calculation, in which over a hundred people participated. Numerous silvery noodles were pulled from the hot-water basins to the cold-water basins before pink arms tied them into a bundle and hung them to dry, constantly adding numbers to the total. He rounded off the numbers, noting the accumulation. The decimal system was unchanging. Tangled noodles bobbed in the water and formed their own bundles; the floating noodles now stood orderly to the right of the decimal point. The man with the strainer hovered over the vats and kept banging, turning the starch into tiny round milky white threads that contributed to that giant number. Every digit was the same as an iron wheel, like the variable gears designed by Li Zhichang. Each one, smaller than the one to its left, was strung together by those tiny round threads. When Li Zhichang's gears were finished and put into use, they would revolve in the misty room and add a new tail to the end of the number . . .

Whenever Jiansu stared at the vats, Daxi started coughing. He was about to move off one time when a fleshy palm fell on his shoulder. He could tell whose it was by the smell, but he didn't turn around. Duoduo said, "I can't sleep, damn it. Let's get a drink." He dragged Jiansu toward the door, but they stopped when they reached Daxi. "Your coughing is a sickness," Duoduo said. "Lucky for you it's one that every man knows how to cure."

They moved a squat white table over to the *kang* and sat down to drink. Since a fire was burning in the opening beneath them, they were soon sweating. Duoduo pulled a bottle of Maotai from his bedroll. "My present to Fourth Master, but I need to check it out first. The last time it took him only a sip to know it was fake, and he threw it out the window. Hmm, is this the real thing or not? Yes, it is." That night Jiansu left most of the liquor to Duoduo, who rocked back and forth and stared at Jiansu, whose head seemed to get bigger one moment and smaller the next—a bizarre sight. A typical Sui clan sight, perhaps. Duoduo laughed and rubbed his eyes. "Jiansu, do you think someone is plotting against me?" Jiansu held his tongue. "I'm doing so well," Duoduo went on, "they're jealous. But I'm just starting! Some of the 'entrepreneurs' have got themselves three or four cars and a female secretary. I want that too. So it makes sense that someone would be plotting against me, don't you think?" Jiansu looked over at Duoduo, whose eyes were lowered. Pursing his lips, Duoduo smashed a wine cup on the table. "Only someone from the Sui clan would dare to plot against the Zhao clan . . . Hah! I could take down whoever it is with one finger. And if it's someone from the Sui clan I wouldn't even need that." Duoduo laughed wickedly and straightened up. Jiansu looked at him uncomprehendingly.

"No, not a finger," Duoduo continued. "That thing of mine down here would be enough." He arched forward menacingly.

The blood rushed to Jiansu's head; clenching his teeth, he stole a glance at the cleaver on the windowsill.

Now that he'd smashed his cup, Duoduo no longer felt like drinking, so he took out a rusty needle from somewhere and began sewing on a button, his fleshy arm moving through the air as he sewed back and forth, causing his body to shift slightly. Jiansu's gaze was still fixed on the cleaver. When Duoduo's hand reached up next to Jiansu's head, he abruptly turned the needle in the direction of Jiansu's eye. With a yelp, Jiansu dodged to the left, clamping his right hand on the man's hand. "That was close," Duoduo said with a laugh. Jiansu, whose heart was racing, held on to the hand, a cold glint in his eyes. "Careful," Duoduo said, poking the tender area around the nail on Jiansu's index finger, producing a sharp pain. He flinched, giving Duoduo a chance to free his hand . . . The needle was back to slowly pulling the long black thread in and out. "You're still young," he said as he sewed. "Too young, in fact. You know, I learned this during the war. You've never been to war . . . your brother probably has more tricks than you."

Jiansu left Duoduo's room that night so overwrought he was shaking. He thought about heading over to the mill but didn't feel like talking to Baopu, since their argument was still fresh in his mind. Stumbling along in the chilly wind, he decided to instigate a "spoiled vat" at the factory, a thought that effectively calmed him. So he returned to his room, exhausted, but could not sleep and decided to study the accounts again. As he worked through the night, he thought about the best time to make his move; that would be shortly before daybreak, when the workers were tired. It would not be hard to create a "spoiled vat," since anything that went wrong during the process of grinding the beans, creating the sediment, changing the temperature, stirring the starch, soaking the beans, mixing in the liquid, etc. would shut them down. They would have to dump everything and start over again, a task no one appreciated. Maybe the easiest target of sabotage was the liquid.

When the roosters crowed just before the sun came up, Jiansu set out for the processing room, a black cloak over his shoulders to ward off the chill in the air.

The sedimentation pool was quiet, for the workers stationed there had gone off to rest. Jiansu stood by the pool, where the liquid had a lovely pastel green cast in the light from the gas lamp. The surface was smooth as a mirror; the starch was slumbering in the pool, the yeast cradling its offspring and sending a barely perceptible sour smell into Jiansu's nostrils. He knew this was a nearly perfect batch, the kind that nurtured the entire factory and provided the process with ideal conditions. The lamplight cast his shadow on the surface of the pool, creating an illusion that the liquid was a pair of pure, innocent, virginal eyes. Turning to look away, he searched for a ladle and a hose; everything would be brought to an end when hot water was poured into the pool, with its several ladles of dark yeast. The room next door was quiet, and even the banging of the strainer seemed weak and tired. After locating a hose and dragging it over he turned to get some yeast, when he heard a loud yawn. It was Daxi, rubbing her eyes as she came out of the next room and walked toward the pool, bleary eyed. Jiansu quickly thrust his hands inside his cloak and stood still. When Daxi saw him, her eyes lit up and all thoughts of sleep were gone. She coughed and fixed her gaze on the hot water flowing out of the hose and sending steam into the air. "Brother Jiansu!" she cried out. But he did not respond. Glumly he stepped on the hose, barely suppressing an urge to pick her up and toss her into the pool. Pushing the hose to the side with his foot, he muttered his hope that the simple girl had not seen through his plan.

As Daxi rubbed her red hands and arms against her apron, a chirping sound escaped from between her quivering lips; her full breasts were also in motion. With Jiansu's eyes on her, she backed away, squatted down, and stared at her hands. His eyes swept over her, a clear sign of exasperation, but then his heart warmed up and he walked over to hold her. As she rested her head against his arm and pressed her lips against him, Jiansu carried her over to the pool. "I'll toss you in, what do you say? You've come at a bad time."

Daxi stared at him, her eyes burning. "Don't do that."

He smiled weakly. "You're right," he said. He could feel her excitement through the loose cloak.

Though she was wrapped in his cloak, she managed to lay her hands on his chest and rest her head. He looked down at her, murmuring how she looked like a lovely, overfed cat. "I'm going to carry you over to my room like this."

"I'm yours," she moaned, "all yours. I like you a million times more than you think. I . . ." Jiansu's arms shook at the figure she'd used to express her love, for it reminded him of that other number that had him under its spell. This was no time to be cautious; he loosened the cloak and kissed her, muttering to himself, "That huge number will gradually get smaller, Daxi, but you're a very big number."

Tears streamed down her face. "I like you a million . . ." she sobbed. "Take me with you. I'll go anywhere you want. Just take me. You could kill me and I wouldn't hate you."

As he pondered her strange comment, he patted her and wrapped her in the cloak. Seeing that the room was getting brighter, he said, "One of these days, I'll do that." Then he dropped his arms and pressed her to go back to work. Reluctantly she backed out of the room.

"Poor thing," Jiansu said to himself.

For days after that, Jiansu felt badly about his morning by the pool. He regretted not moving fast enough and thereby letting Zhao Duoduo off the hook; even more he regretted missing the opportunity to take Daxi back to his room. Hot blood coursed and roiled in his young body, making it impossible to sleep or work on the accounts. The big number was now a net made of silk threads entangling him so tightly they cut deep into his flesh. It was unbearable; he rolled around on the *kang* until the mat was bloodied. He touched the blood with his finger and smelled the pungent odor; then he lay down again, only

to stare at the blackened roof beams. Sooner or later he would do
those two things; he knew it.

On the third day Duoduo sent someone for Jiansu. "The vat is
spoiled!" the man said. "It's a spoiled vat!"

With a surprised shout, Jiansu sat up and, incredulous, asked him
to repeat what he'd said. A tiny worm of happiness crawled around his
heart as he threw on some clothes and ran toward the factory, his heart
pounding.

A crowd of people stood at the door, hands hanging loose at their
sides. Duoduo was among them, his bloodshot eyes darting back and
forth. Jiansu was unbelievably happy and incredibly puzzled. The man
working the strainer kept banging on it; the sound was the same, but
no noodle threads emerged from the milky white paste, even though
he was trying so hard he was drenched in sweat. Clots of noodle starch
floated in the boiling water, like impish fish. Workers stirred the paste
in a giant vat, as always, alternating men and women, all humming a
cadence as they worked. Upset that the paste wasn't being evenly
stirred, Duoduo shouted for them to hum louder. So they did, each
shout followed by a step forward as they submerged their arms in the
paste up to their elbows. When Jiansu walked up to check out the
sediment pool he was greeted by the smell of vinegar. Tiny starchy bits
floated in the sediment beakers on the cement ledge. The pool surface
too was no longer a pastel green but had turned muddy, with bubbles
forming and popping. A giant bubble in the center remained there a
long moment before bursting and disappearing. Before he'd even entered the room, Jiansu had detected a stench that quickened his heart-
beat, for experience told him that this was serious. He squatted down
and lit a cigarette to get a closer look.

The odor was so strong that Naonao, who was supposed to be
straining the noodles, ran off holding her nose. Duoduo stopped her
before she reached the window for fresh air and snarled, "Get back to
work! I don't want to see any goddamned one of you slack off today!"
Jiansu was amused. It felt to him as if an invisible hand had draped a

solemn veil over the faces around him. No one dared laugh or say a word. He glanced at Daxi, who was calm and unperturbed, even sneaking a look at him. To his surprise, she had a remarkably bewitching appearance.

Having quickly exhausted himself, Duoduo looked around for Jiansu and grimaced when he saw him. "It's your show now," he barked. "You're the expert. As they say, a soldier is fed for a thousand days just so he'll be useful in a battle." Jiansu exhaled a mouthful of smoke and said, "Yes, and that's why I'm crouching here, so I can figure out what to do. An expert would know that a spoiled vat is always a possibility."

"I expect you to get things back on track!" Duoduo screamed. "And if you can't, then go get your brother."

Jiansu smiled and walked over to the sedimentation pool, where, under Duoduo's gaze, he stirred the paste, a meaningless gesture. Then he moved to the large vat and told the workers to stop stirring. After testing the temperature of the water soaking the beans he told them to change it. "Give it five days and we'll see what happens." Duoduo could only grunt in response.

The smell of vinegar permeated the factory the second day, and on the third day a pungent, charred odor emerged from the pool. On the fourth day, all other odors were overpowered by a stench that got worse by the minute. People thought the end had arrived. Party Secretary Li Yuming arrived from Gaoding Street, looking perplexed, and Director Luan Chunji was critical of the repair efforts. So Duoduo went to seek Baopu's help. Assuming his brother would not come, Jiansu was shocked to see him walk in with Duoduo. He cast his brother a searing look, but Baopu seemed not to notice. His back hunched over and his nostrils flared, he went straight to the sedimentation pool as Duoduo was tying a red cloth to the door frame for good luck before walking over to the Wali Emporium to invite Zhang-Wang to the factory. She'd put on a padded vest—it wasn't a cold day—which made her belly look bigger than ever. As she walked into .

the processing room, her hands covering her abdomen, she stopped and looked around, a watchful look on her face. Then she shut her eyes after sitting in an armchair Duoduo had provided.

After crouching in a corner for about half an hour, Baopu took off his shirt and began to stir the pasty mix. He then moved to the soaking pool and starch cooler. Every day for two weeks he repeated the procedure, only leaving the room to use the toilet. He roasted chunks of bean starch to stave off his hunger and slept against the wall. Even when Jiansu came to see him, he was unresponsive. His face turned dark and lusterless, his eyes were bloodshot, and he was so hoarse he could only converse with his hands.

Zhang-Wang attracted a lot of people. Her dust-covered nose kept flaring and her Adam's apple moved up and down, though she didn't say a word. Finally she waved for Duoduo to get the gawkers out and recited in a calm voice, "The enmity has no cause and the debt has no debtors, but rain falls from a cloudless sky. Watch out for petty people on the seventh and the ninth days, for the loach will squirm and muddy the water."

"Are the petty people surnamed 'Sui'?" Duoduo asked in a panicky voice.

She shook her head. "All the petty people are women, for there are cracks in their hearts." Stumped, he asked her to elaborate. She tightened the corners of her lips and exposed her short, blackened teeth. "Let me say a prayer for you." Closing her eyes and crossing her legs on the chair, she muttered something unintelligible. Duoduo crouched wordlessly beside her, his forehead beaded with sweat. Zhang-Wang had a remarkable capacity for sitting, and she sat there until daybreak. Her voice got weaker until she was completely quiet, but it rose again at midnight, so startling the girls by the paste vat and water basins that they ran up to her chair. Although she remained motionless she added "Don't you dare" to her prayers, sending the girls back.

Baopu continued spending his nights by the pool until everything was back to normal; he returned to his mill when the processing room was once again bathed in a fresh fragrance. The ladle could be heard banging and Naonao was straining the noodles again. Zhao Duoduo came down with a splitting headache; a treatment of moxibustion left three purple marks on his forehead. Mired in confusion, he couldn't be sure if it was Zhang-Wang or Baopu who had saved the vat.

Not until two days after his brother had returned to the mill did Jiansu go to see him. He was not intimidated by the glare that met him as he entered; he simply returned the look. Baopu tightened his jaw, which made the muscles on his cheeks quiver. The look in his eyes was surprisingly cold. "What did I do now?" Jiansu asked.

Baopu snorted, "You know."

"No, I don't."

Baopu roared, "You wasted ten thousand *jin* of mung beans."

As he vehemently denied the allegation, Jiansu's face turned steely gray and his lips twitched as he explained emotionally. In the end he said, smiling coldly, "I wanted to, but I couldn't find the right moment to do it. It was truly heaven's will."

Baopu seemed not to have heard him. "I know what you're like. How could I not? As I sat here, I thought that something like that would happen. You were really—"

"I tell you I didn't do it," Jiansu cut him off angrily. "It wasn't me. I'm glad it happened, but I was as surprised as anyone. I ran over there convinced it was heaven's will."

As he stood up to spread some beans, Baopu turned to look at his brother, his wooden ladle in midair. "Why would I lie to you?" Jiansu pleaded. "Didn't I just say I wanted to do it? But it wasn't me."

Baopu bit his lip and continued spreading the beans. When he finally sat down to light a cigarette he stared at the small window in the wall and mumbled, "It doesn't make any difference. I've already placed the blame on the Sui clan. I believe you, but we're to blame. In my mind the Sui clan has committed a crime against Wali . . ." His voice died out.

"Why?" Jiansu shouted, staring at Baopu's gray-streaked hair.

"Because you would have done it if you could."

Jiansu bounded over to face his brother. "Yes, I would have," he admitted. By now his hands were shaking. "But I didn't. I'm happy it happened, because that's what Duoduo deserves. I knew he'd have to ask for your help eventually, and I wanted to see if you'd come. For days I watched this door, until you eventually walked out. Aren't you great! You've done the Sui clan quite a service by helping Duoduo repair his spoiled vat. Aren't you afraid there are people who will curse you behind your back? Be mad at me, for all I care, because I'm mad as hell at you!" Jiansu's face reddened and beads of sweat rolled down his cheeks.

Baopu stood up and brought his face so close to Jiansu's that his nose was nearly touching his brother's face. He spoke in a hoarse voice so solemn Jiansu had to back away. "Go look up the town history and you'll see that Wali has been making White Dragon Glass Noodles for hundreds of years. Generations of townspeople have been engaged in the trade. Even people outside China know White Dragon Glass Noodles; they call them 'Spring Rain Noodles.' The whole town would suffer if no one could get the vat up and running again! There's a saying in Wali: 'Getting the vat up is like putting out a fire.' "

Jiansu continued with his nightly work on the accounts, gradually making the large number smaller. First he had to subtract wages—140 yuan a month for Zhao Duoduo, 90 or a 100 for each salesman, 120 for himself . . . The average monthly wage for the 120 employees was 46.7 yuan, the annual total 62,764.8 yuan. Eleven months of leasing cost 67,996.2 yuan. The noodle factory required a large quantity of coal and water. The water, which came from the Luqing River, was free. But each *jin* of noodles required 7.3 centigrams of coal, at a cost of 83,950 yuan. Then there were taxes, overtime pay for night-shift workers, and bonuses. To this total Jiansu added the various levies and welfare payments demanded by the government. The workers themselves had decided that these demands would be met with money from their wages and from the factory. Wali had little arable land, but their farm taxes still were not exempted. Then there was the fund-raising: for the promotion of provincial physical education, for the agricultural college, for provincial women's work, for a provincial children's amusement park, a provincial education center, national defense, militia training, highway construction, city and town construction, power plant expansion, county and town education . . . Many of these overlapped at the provincial, township, and county levels and totaled twenty-three items, most of which, strictly speaking, were not true fund-raising. It was all very messy and confusing, and Jiansu found himself defeated, battered and bloody.

In the end, he could come up with only an estimate for taxes, subsidies, bonuses, and fund-raising, roughly 73,000 yuan. Then he had to compute the travel expenses for the salesmen, transportation, and the cost of gifts and entertainment inherent in the ordering process. These were even messier and impossible to pinpoint. In addition, he needed to subtract other items dictated by the leasing contract, such as the amount due the government, costs for reproduction, raw materials, and reasonable wear and tear. When all these items were subtracted from his large number, he would wind up with a net profit, after adding the revenue from by-products. But the calculation so muddled his head that he was forced to abandon the task halfway through. The next night he was unable to pick up where he'd left off and had to start all over. "I hate these goddamned accounts!" he said to himself, but he was determined not to give up.

A light often shone in Baopu's room. One night, when he could not contain his curiosity, Jiansu sneaked over to the window, through which he saw that his brother was marking up a thin book with a fountain pen. He immediately lost interest. But then he saw Baopu do the same thing on two other occasions, which convinced him it must be an intriguing book. He knocked and went in, and he spotted the cover with the title in red: *The Communist Manifesto*. He laughed.

Baopu carefully wrapped the book in cloth and put it in a drawer. After rolling a cigarette and lighting it, he said, "You laughed because you don't know a thing about that book. When Father was alive, he did his accounts day and night, till he coughed up blood and died of exhaustion. There has to be a cause for that, and for our stepmother's death, plus all the other bloodshed in this town. We of the Sui clan must not live in fear; we have to find the causes. And if you want to get to the bottom of things, you cannot avoid this book. It speaks to the town and to the suffering of the Sui clan. I've read it many times, wondering how we got to where we are and where we're going. I read it whenever I come to a critical moment in life."

Casting a perplexed glance at the cloth bundle in the drawer, Jiansu recalled seeing it years before in his brother's room. A sense of anguish rose in his mind; he knew that no one but Baopu would so stubbornly try to determine the fate of his family from a little book like that. He gently shut the drawer for his brother and walked out.

It was nearly daybreak by the time Jiansu returned to his room, and he sat at his desk, staring at the cramped figures in the account books, unable to sleep. Suddenly an overhead light flicked on, momentarily dazing him. Then he pushed back from the desk, blinded by the light and yet unable to look away, before realizing that Li Zhichang's generator was working. His head buzzed, and he could almost see lights in the factory, an electrified blower fanning the burning coal, an electric motor turning countless wheels . . . He could no longer sit still. Recalling the talk he'd had with Li Zhichang on the cement platform the night of the Midautumn Festival, he decided to go see his uncle right away, for Sui Buzhao was the only person who could stop Li. He rushed out of his room, his agitated heart racing.

The streetlights were also on, and the color of electricity could be seen in every window in town. Jiansu entered his uncle's room to the sight of the old man staring at the light. He did not look around until Jiansu called out to him and immediately told him why he was there: He wanted his uncle to convince Li Zhichang not to be in a hurry to put a generator and variable gears in Duoduo's factory.

A light flickered in Sui Buzhao's eyes. He shook his head. "I talked to him. But I knew I was wasting my time. No one can stop him now. It's all up to Zhichang himself."

Jiansu fell silent. When he sat dejectedly on the edge of the *kang*, to his surprise he noted a rolled-up blanket tied by a rope with a pair of cloth-soled shoes on top. His uncle said he was packed to go see the ancient ship. No one from Wali had gone to see it since it was taken away, but he'd been thinking about it for days, even dreaming about sitting on the bridge with Uncle Zheng He. So he'd decided to pay it a visit . . . Jiansu sighed, knowing there was nothing he could do to stop his uncle, for no one knew how to deal with this old man from the Sui clan.

Jiansu often woke up in the middle of the night. His nights were long and drab, and when he couldn't sleep, he went to work on the accounts. Sometimes he thought about his father—maybe they were going over the same accounts, the son picking up where the father had left off. It was like the old millstone, turning from one generation to the next. When the groove was worn flat, a mason was called in to carve it down so it would continue to turn. One night at midnight, as he was bent over his desk, suffering through the interminable account work, he heard a knock at the door. He quickly hid the pen and account books before opening the door. Daxi bounded in. Excited and agitated, she stared at him, rubbing her hands on her tight pant legs. "What are you doing here?" he asked in a low voice.

She closed the door behind her and said in a shaky voice, "I . . . I'm here . . . here to tell you something."

"What is it?" Jiansu was both annoyed and impatient.

Daxi was so agitated she swayed back and forth.

"It was me who spoiled the vat."

"What? Is that the truth?" He moved up closer. Her face was bright red. Covering his mouth with her hand, she whispered, "Yes. I knew what you wanted to do that morning and that you'd have to delay doing it because of me. I like you a million . . . I had to do it for you . . . no one knows."

Jiansu was shocked. He looked at Daxi closely, seeing for the first time that she had lovely long eyelashes. Holding her tightly, he kissed her. "Oh, Daxi. Good Daxi. My good Daxi." What his brother had said in the mill flashed through his mind—"I've already placed the blame on the Sui clan"—and his heart skipped a beat. It was true, Daxi had only done what he'd wanted to do. He took the trembling Daxi to his *kang,* where he leaned over and frantically began kissing her on the mouth and on her big, bright eyes.

NINE

All Wali was bathed in brightness. The elated residents now viewed Li Zhichang differently. In the past, they had exchanged mocking looks when they'd seen the young man with an electrician's knife hanging from his belt. Some had even sighed and said, "He is, after all, a member of the Li clan." No one had missed what remained unsaid: that the Li family kept producing people like him. For many years, the clan had all but become synonymous with oddity and eccentricity, and so mysterious it was difficult for people to judge them. Decades earlier it had been Li Xuantong, the monk, or Li Qisheng, who had run machinery for capitalists. Now it was Li Zhichang. In the days when electricity was installed in the town, he had run about with a dirty face and long hair, beads of sweat dotting the tip of his nose. He was often accompanied by Technician Li of the survey team and Sui Buzhao, the old wandering ghost. Someone said that Zhichang had put two lights in Sui Hanzhang's room to get her to like him, but that was proven false by someone who went to check out her room.

It was true, however, that he had not installed lights for his mentally unstable father, who was seen walking around town looking forlorn, pointing at a streetlight and cursing his son. The sight of Li Zhichang had townspeople comparing him with his father. Li Qisheng had just crawled out of the machine shop owned by a capitalist, a disgrace he'd tried hard to work off with his sweat, staying away from home in order to finish work assigned by the agricultural cooperative. Before her death, his wife had complained tearfully to their nephew, Li Yuming, about how the Li family produced only eccentrics, and that any woman who married into the family had better be prepared to live the life of a straw widow. Li Xuantong, the grandfather, had gone into the mountains to be a monk, and had Li Qisheng been born at a different time, he'd likely have become a monk as well (and how was his current life different from that of a monk, anyway?). She said she was a widow and that her son, Zhichang, was an orphan. All Li Yuming could offer was commiseration. It had been a bewitched time that had yet to fade from the town's memory.

A newspaper reported that the total number of advanced agricultural co-ops reached an all-time high that year, over 488,000 altogether. An advanced co-op normally consisted of 206 farming families, which meant more than 1,000,528,000 families, 83 percent of the population, were members of advanced co-ops. It was the year Li Qisheng returned from the northeast to join a co-op. For convenience's sake, the townspeople called him a capitalist because of the work he'd done, reflecting an old habit of being content with superficial knowledge. Shortly after his return, 1,040,000 double-wheel, double-share plows were sent to the agricultural co-ops in the country, one of them going to members of the Gaoding Street Co-op, who hitched it up with two horses and took it into the fields.

The wheels started rolling with the movement of the horses, but no one dared touch the rudimentary hand cranks. The rumble and creaks attracted many people, who quickly discovered the plow's fatal weakness: It did not cut into the ground, to their disappointment. Then someone thought of the sailor, Sui Buzhao, who'd seen a bit of the world, so he was called over. After sizing up the machine, he pointed to a hand crank and said, "That's the helm." He pushed it, and a cranking sound filled the air; the wheels stopped but the blades cut deeply into the ground. The horses whinnied in agony as their front legs were jerked into the air. Fourth Master Zhao Bing, then the head of Gaoding Street, went up to rein in the horses, while the annoyed township head, Zhou Zifu, nudged Sui Buzhao away. True to the reputation of his former employment, Li Qisheng walked up to the plow, where he grabbed the handles and shouted at the horses. The wheels started rolling again and the plow turned up waves of oily black soil, to whoops of joy and applause. Overjoyed, Zhou Zifu thumped Li Qisheng in the chest and said, "The capitalist is our man!"

And so, shortly after his return, Li Qisheng had won the town's trust, in sharp contrast to Sui Buzhao. The plow rolled on and the crowd drifted away, leaving the two men behind to stare at each other. Sui Buzhao walked up and grabbed Li's hand. "I could tell at a glance that you're a man of the world, the first in this town. I admire you. From now on you'll be my best friend. I know a little about machines, but I've spent half my life on the water and am all but useless on land. We need to work together." He was unwilling to let go of Li's hand, which drew emotional sighs from Li. From that day on, they were the best of friends.

With the arrival of the double-share plows came many things. It was an age when figures meant everything; the newspapers reported vast numbers, which occupied the minds and bodies of the Wali townspeople. A distant mountain village that had been plagued by drought dug 446 wells in a month, putting an end to their suffering. A certain county produced 660,000 *jin* of yams and 4,216 *jin* of soybeans per acre. On the 132nd morning after sowing, they fertilized the land with 5,364 scoops, or 255 buckets, of manure. Then, on the day called "the end of heat," they covered the field with 164 *jin* of ashes. The town's scribes were kept busy recording these numbers. Everything, including plants, equipment, and animals, was represented by numbers. After 3,612 attempts, Wang Dagui, a poor peasant who belonged to a certain village co-op, produced a new feed mixed with distiller's grain. Given this new feed, pigs weighing 83 *jin* grew to 192, even 230 *jin,* in 41 days. Arabic numbers were slowly taking over newspapers and books, which prompted Sui Buzhao to predict that Chinese characters would be abolished within two years.

His speculation naturally became a laughingstock two years later.

But numbers were spreading, and even planting plans were expressed in numbers. After an all-night meeting, the provincial leadership decided that each acre of land could accommodate more than 6,340 sweet potatoes, or 4,500–8,600 stalks of corn, or 48,970 bean plants. The numbers were printed in red in the provincial newspaper. At first people did not understand why they had to be in red, but they later learned that it was a remarkable omen. Red, the color of blood, foretelling the lives that would be lost over those numbers. When wheat seeding season came, an old man who had done the same thing all his life was shocked to see clumps of wheat seedlings as thick as the hair on a cow. He went to ask Fourth Master, who told him glumly to ask the town's leaders. He did, for which he was rewarded with a tongue lashing and sent back with strict orders to plant the assigned number. At first he did as he was told, despite the tears that ran down his face, but when he simply could not bring himself to continue, he secretly poured half a sack of seeds down a well. When the militia found out, he was tied up and dragged into town, where they took him to a small room on Gaoding Street and beat him all night. Ashamed, the old man roamed his field night after night, until his body was found in the well where he'd poured the wheat seeds. Now the townspeople understood why the numbers were printed in red.

When the newspaper could no longer contain all those numbers, a tall wooden platform was erected, which someone would climb each morning and each evening to announce the new figures. An agricultural co-op produced 3,452 *jin* of wheat per acre and planned to produce 8,600 *jin* the next year. Then a new number was announced by another co-op: They had already produced 8,712 *jin* of wheat per acre, 112 more than planned by the other co-op. They had launched a wheat satellite and people from all the more than 880 co-ops in the province went to see it. More than 300 of them proclaimed they would beat them. With the few that were producing only about a thousand *jin,* a discussion ensued at the provincial, municipal, and county levels. Their conclusion? They would be given a white flag and their leader would be replaced, after which a mass debate would be held. Some areas had even made little black vests, symbolizing a disregard for the leadership, for those co-op heads whose production was under 6,000 *jin*. Zhou Zifu came up with a slogan for Wali: For every acre, 20,000 *jin* of grain, 20,000 *jin* of corn, or 340,000 *jin* of sweet potatoes. Fourth Master Zhao Bing said, "That's easy." Indeed, Gaoding Street produced 21,000 *jin* of corn the following year. At a Gaoding Street meeting Zhou Zifu personally pinned a flower on Zhao Bing. "Quick, let's report this to the provincial Party branch secretary," he said. Soon after that, the number "21,000" appeared in the provincial paper. Since the number came from Wali, the town party branch secretary bought fifteen thousand copies of the paper, forcing everyone in town to stare at the number. They were quiet, for the number was also in red.

A gloom settled over Wali for several days, as the people sensed that something would come in the wake of the red number. No one said a word; they just exchanged meaningful glances, a recurrence of the days following the destruction of the temple.

They waited anxiously, and it did not take long for something bad to happen. For reporting that number, Wali was embroiled in turmoil. One morning, a group of visitors came to see their corn. Zhou Zifu, the township head, wearing a straw hat, was giving a demonstration as the townspeople stood by the road, holding cornstalks for the visitors to walk through. The newcomers gaped at the dozen or so corncobs on each stalk; at first they thought they were a special variety, but they were told it was ordinary corn. "At this rate, it'll take only two or three years for Communism to arrive," someone observed.

"Nonsense!" Zhou Zifu explained. "It won't take that long. Not at all. Generally speaking," he explained, "a stalk yields one ear, or two, one big and one small. How did these produce more than a dozen big ears? By holding a revolutionary red flag high, the people grew courageous and the land became productive. Comrade Zhao Bing from Gaoding Street plans to produce thirty thousand *jin* of corn next year." Everyone applauded, searching for Zhao Bing with their eyes. But the thirty-year-old Zhao was unmoved by the applause; rather, he was studying the co-op members who were holding the cornstalks. Just then, Li Qisheng shook the stalk in his hand and yelled that he'd discovered what was wrong. All the ears were tied to the stalk with string!

People quickly recovered from their momentary shock and gathered round him. Zhou Zifu pushed the people away and stuck his finger in Li's face. "This man is a returned capitalist from the northeast," he said. Zhao Bing smiled and walked up to Zhou. "Mr. Zhou, why trouble yourself with a madman? He's having one of his fits again. It's my fault. I brought him over because we didn't have enough people." Pointing at the dozen ears on his stalk, Li Qisheng shouted, "I'm crazy?" Without a word, Zhao Bing reached out and grabbed Li by the collar, lifting him three feet in the air before flinging him away like a tattered coat. "Go home and lie down," he shouted. Li got up and ran away without even shaking off the mud on his clothes.

People recalled the old man who'd jumped into the well and the red numbers that had appeared in the paper not long before. "Li Qisheng is done for," they said.

That was also the seventh day after Fourth Master Zhao Bing's wife had fallen ill. She had been left moaning on the *kang* that night, since Zhao was forced to stay with the visitors, who did not leave until one in the morning. But instead of sticking around to check on his wife, he called a meeting at the old temple site. The townspeople sat silently on the ground, forming a circle with a small white wooden table in the middle. A coarse earthenware bowl of hot water had been placed on the table. Zhao Bing circled the table, a purple cast to his face, but didn't say a word, even after drinking the last bit of water in the bowl. Pressure was mounting among the people, who could not help but recall the red numbers. The candle flickered, giving off a clear red glow one minute and a red glow with an inauspicious blue halo the next, as the flame continued to flicker. The young Fourth Master raised his heavy lids, coughed softly, and said, "Let me ask a question. I'm in my thirties, so shouldn't I know how many ears of corn a single stalk can yield?" No response. He picked up the bowl and smashed it on the ground before continuing in a deep voice, "Anyone who eats human food knows. If you don't, then you must have grown up on dog shit! These are strange times, and whoever has objections can step up and take charge of Gaoding Street." His eyes swept the crowd before he continued. "No one? Well, then I, Zhao Bing, remain in charge. And since I'm in charge, you should all know the difficulties I'm facing. So whoever causes trouble for Wali will himself be in big trouble." The people were breathing softly, their eyes riveted on Zhao Bing. Just as the meeting was ending, Li Qisheng's wife ran up and grabbed Zhao Bing by the lapels. "Come, quick."

"Calm down. What's wrong?" Zhao said. "Fourth Master can handle anything, even if the sky is falling."

The woman sobbed. "Earlier today my husband, Qisheng, came home, covered with mud. I asked him what happened, but he wouldn't tell me. I thought he must have gotten into a fight, but then the militia came and took him away. I begged them but they wouldn't listen. They beat him up in a little dark room. At first he was screaming, but then he stopped. I asked the township head to let him go, but he said it wasn't his business. I recognized the men; they were led by someone from the local military. Fourth Master, they hung Qisheng up from a roof beam. Please help him. You're the only one who can save him now."

Zhao Bing snorted. "Damn them!" He was taking off his coat when someone ran up, panic-stricken and panting so hard his shoulders rose and fell. "Fourth, Fourth Master, hurry up, go home. Fourth Mistress, she, she's not going to make it . . ." The news shocked the tears from Li Qisheng's wife; she could only stare at Zhao Bing in despair. Everyone on the ground stood up, ashen-faced.

Zhao Bing's hands were shaking. "Natural disasters and man-made calamities," he said, clenching his teeth. "Frost falls on ice. Maybe Wali has reached the end of its fortunes." He then looked up into the sky and called out his wife's name with tears in his eyes. "Huan'er," he called out, "you go on ahead of me. After all these years as husband and wife, I'll have to let you down now, since I must choose between family and duty. Someone from Gaoding Street is hanging from a roof beam, his life in the balance." Throwing his jacket down on the ground, he took the hand of Li Qisheng's wife and walked off.

There wasn't a dry eye among the people. They were shouting, but it was impossible to tell what they were saying. The flames on the candles turned blue, flickered, and then went out.

That night, Li Qisheng's blood covered Fourth Master's bare back as he was carried home. Huan'er died, holding one of Zhao Bing's old hats so tight they couldn't pry it out of her hands.

No one living in Wali would ever forget that day.

What happened soon after that was the attempted theft of the bricks from the city wall, when the townspeople's anger finally burst forth, with the encouragement of Zhao Bing. Fourth Master was laid up in bed and could not lead the people in the defense of their town's dignity, but he gave the order for Zhao Duoduo, the head of the militia, to break the leader's leg. And he did. Zhao Bing was recovering from a debilitating illness at home, but his reputation grew faster than leeks in the spring. Lying in bed, he took care of problems on Gaoding Street by responding to Zhao Duoduo's questions through the window. It was the first time in his life he had been bedridden, and Zhang-Wang, who gave him daily moxibustion treatments, told everyone that his condition was not improving because he missed Huan'er, his second wife; she, like his first wife, had also died in the second year of their marriage. The first had given him a son. Both women had turned sallow during the first year and then turned gray and thin in the second year before finally dying in bed.

Guo Yun came to see Zhao Bing when he first fell ill. Only in his forties at the time, Guo was already a skilled Chinese herbal doctor, having spent many years in devoted study. He sat for hours beside Zhao to observe his symptoms. After a few days he explained why both of Zhao's wives had died so young. "You represent a certain type of toxic person. Any woman having intercourse with a rare but lethal man such as you will invariably succumb to a long illness or die early."

Fourth Master's face paled from the shock; he grabbed the doctor's hand and begged for an antidote, but Guo said there was none as he walked out. Zhao Bing did not want to believe the doctor, yet doubt had him in its grip for days. When he finally recovered, he recalled what Guo Yun had said to him, though that felt like a dream. The following year he remarried, and after his wife gave him a son later that year, she died in the fall. Zhao Bing was now convinced that the diagnosis had been right and swore that he would never marry again.

The town's spirit dissipated after Fourth Master fell ill, but outside pressures remained constant, things changed daily, and new, huge numbers were announced. Now they were no longer limited to yields of grain and foodstuffs but had spread to the realms of steel and iron production, as well as scientific inventions. The old co-op member Wang Dagui invented five new farm implements with the same hands that had created new feed for pigs. Overnight, 5,846 peasant scientific innovation groups were formed in the province. Each planned to invent and develop six new scientific items a month, which meant that the province would contribute to the country 420,912 new items within a year. And in a great age like this, there was a 90 percent chance that the plan would be surpassed. "Marshal Iron and Commander Steel are raising the stakes," someone shouted along the main streets, followed by another who climbed onto the wooden platform to announce yet another giant number. In July the entire province was engaged in creating new furnaces, with the projected output reaching 684,300. One village made thirty-six crucibles by using kiln-fired bricks, sun-dried bricks, dry soil, and coke ash; in them they produced seven and a half tons of steel in just three days. Another brick kiln stopped making bricks to smelt iron, producing thirty-nine tons of steel.

The ascendancy of iron and steel also brought unprecedented artistic creativity. An old woman composed fifty poems one night while she was working the bellows to keep the crucible going. In one village, the three literate individuals wrote down all the poems composed by the village and collected them in a bag they planned to send to the provincial government office. After all these developments, people gradually realized that the great poet of the Tang, Li Bai, was mediocre at best. With the giant numbers coming at such an irresistible rate, Zhou Zifu sought out the sick Zhao Bing to form a new strategy. The one thing they could agree on was that no one in Wali, except Zhang-Wang, had any imagination, a lamentable fact that had plagued the town since its earliest days. So they had to bow out of the poetry competition but could take immediate action in iron smelting and scientific inventions. They decided to form a scientific research group, but first they had to get Li Qisheng to join.

After narrowly escaping death, Li Qisheng was a physical wreck; he had lost faith in everything. All he remembered was that he was a reactionary. When they had stripped him naked and hung him up, they had covered his eyes with a piece of black cloth and beaten him. "You dog-shit spy," they shouted. "We'll beat you to death." He pleaded with them and screamed in pain, but all in vain. Someone even touched his privates with a cigarette, making him scream in agony as if his organs were bursting. He was now covered in scars, and the one down below, in particular, made him and his wife both sad and angry. So naturally he was reminded of his humiliation when Fourth Master and Zhou Zifu came to invite him to join the research group. He said nothing, which angered his wife. "Qisheng," she said, "you're an ingrate. Fourth Master saved your life, but now he can't get you to work for him! Don't be so full of yourself." His head snapped up to look at Fourth Master; then he stood up and walked out, and that was how Li Qisheng joined the scientific research group.

The first scientific invention had to be the creation of improved crucible furnaces for smelting iron. Li added ground-up porcelain bowls to the known ingredients (kiln-fired bricks, sun-dried bricks, dry soil, and coke ash), producing crucibles that could be used twice as long, at a temperature 630 degrees higher than their predecessors. Li brought Sui Buzhao and Sui Baopu into the group. Buzhao, always following Li's orders, was in charge of making the inner lining of the crucibles, while Baopu, an introvert, was the right person to grind the porcelain bowls. Barely a month later, they had produced more than four hundred crucibles. Zhao Bing and Zhou Zifu personally rallied the town to donate bowls, jars, anything porcelain. When that was all gone, Zhou told the townspeople to keep their eyes to the ground and pick up broken pieces of porcelain when they were out walking. Even pieces at the bottom of wells were dredged up. Whenever something was seen shining in the sun, everyone assumed it was porcelain and raced to grab it. As time went on, children whose bones had yet to develop fully could no longer hold their heads up after so much searching for porcelain on the ground. Years later, when people saw someone who could not hold his head up, they'd say he must have come from Wali.

Thousands of crucibles stood by the city wall, in the fields, and at the entrances to alleys, belching dark smoke that blotted out the sun. The sounds from the bellows operated by old women drowned out the torrential flow of the Luqing River. Everything metallic in town was thrown into the crucibles. Someone realized that wooden handles could replace the metal cranks on the double-blade plows, so they were removed. Militiamen, led by Zhou Zifu, checked every household for metal objects, even prying metal rings and locks from dressers. Iron pots were taken away and marched off to the crucibles on the head of a militiaman. Pottery jars were all that were left for people to cook with. In the end, the inevitable occurred—there wasn't a single piece of metal to be found in town. But then Fourth Master parted his lapels to reveal the metal buckle on his belt, which he immediately snapped off. Later that night, more than 8,200 buckles made of iron, copper, and aluminum were collected around town. Zhou Zifu hesitated, but he finally chipped off the shiny brass buckle on his wide leather belt, which greatly inspired Zhao Duoduo, who started lifting up people's shirts to check for buckles. His favorite targets were women, many of whom lost their virginity over a belt buckle, though they were too ashamed to tell anyone about it. Soon some smart girls began walking around town with a colorful cloth sash showing under their lapels, a testimony to the lack of metal on their bodies. Many decades later, women in Wali could still be seen with sashes under their lapels, a sign that a preventive measure had developed into a folk custom.

Li Qisheng managed to come up with innovative creations owing mainly to his quiet meditation. For three days no one knew where he had gone, but he reappeared from his house with a large crucible. It was an abandoned copper crucible used by a tinsmith many years earlier. Li had transformed a piece of junk into treasure by placing a small crucible under the old one and another on top, to which he had added yet another but placed it upside down. The only difference was the hole he'd drilled in the bottom of the last one. Standing to the side, Zhou Zifu and Zhao Bing gazed at the thing with questioning eyes. Finally, Li pointed to his invention, so excited his fingers were quivering, and said, "This one can smelt alloy metals and stainless steel. An hour is all it takes." Everyone looked at him with renewed respect.

Zhou walked up to shake his hand and congratulate him. "You've redeemed all your past wrongs with your special talent and have made a great contribution. This is good, very good. If you continue with your inventions, I'm sure your contributions will overtake your misdeeds and you'll be a new person."

Li Qisheng stood up and said in a sonorous voice, "You have my word, town leader, Fourth Master, that I will become a new person. Everyone here is my witness." From that day on, Li shut himself up in the deserted room to work on more inventions.

Soon afterward, a report on Li's invention appeared on the front page of the provincial paper, calling it the most powerful iron smelting furnace in the province, which the paper credited to the "Wali Scientific Invention Group," omitting Li's name owing to his questionable reputation. Zhao Bing occupied a prominent space in the paper as someone who "once again led the masses to create miracles." Pasting the report on the wall in his room, Li buried himself in new projects. What annoyed him most was his wife calling for him outside the window, for he'd all but given up on sex now that he was devoted to practical innovations. One night his wife entered the room and fondled him throughout the night, causing his thought processes to slow down; he never quite forgave himself for that.

Another day his wife pounded on his door and said she wouldn't stop until he let her in. Suddenly on guard, he asked through the window what she wanted; that was when he learned that Communism had arrived. A communal dining hall had been set up on Gaoding Street, which meant there was no longer any need to cook or pay for food. It was an earth-shattering event, so Li opened the door and ran with his wife toward the dining hall, where a crowd had gathered.

Standing on a yard-long clay cook platform, Zhou Zifu clapped his hands to quiet the crowd and shouted, "Comrades! Comrades!" But to no avail. Li Qisheng could not hear what Zhou was saying, but he saw women in white caps walk into the dining hall carrying small, heavy buckets of water, a sight that prompted another invention to form in his head. Excited by the new idea, he fought his way through the crowd to find Sui Buzhao. "Bring some sunflower stalks to my place," he said.

"How many?"

"The more the better," Li said before heading home.

Using a hooked wire, Li cleaned out the insides of more than a hundred sunflower stalks. During that time, his wife came pounding on his door again with the same kind of urgency. "Hurry. You've got to see this. Everyone in town is there."

"What's happened this time?"

"An irrigation crew has dug up an old ship. Everything has rotted away except the keel. And there are local cannons."

Li grunted a response and sat down on the floor, ignoring her, so she went off on her own.

After not seeing Sui Buzhao for several days, Li Qisheng later learned that Sui had been entrusted by the town to report the news of the old ship to the provincial government. In the days that followed, Li scraped the sunflower stalks white before wrapping them with hemp twine and brushing on a layer of tung oil. Then he connected them to bring water into the dining hall from a tank that was kept full by a water wheel. The empty stalks made it possible to have an endless supply of fresh running water, another major innovation. Again people crowded into the dining hall when the door swung open. Asked to do a demonstration, Li pulled out the cork stopper with a shaky hand to let the water gush in. Everyone applauded, except the township head, Zhou Zifu, who, like the time before, shook Li's hand over and over. Some people fixed a jealous gaze on those two hands, thinking that Li had buried himself in his work only for that handshake. "Remember what I said last time?" Zhou asked with a smile.

Li nodded and said, "Yes, every word."

"You'll be a new person in no time," Zhou said with due seriousness.

Shortly afterward, provincial, city, and township newspapers all reported the latest important invention from Wali, a particularly noteworthy event at a time when dining halls were popping up all over the country. After careful deliberation, the town's Party committee decided to hold a meeting on the old site of the former temple. It was a unique and grand meeting that, in all fairness, deserved to be recorded in the town chronicle along with Li's inventions, for it was a special occasion to commend the peasant inventor Li Qisheng.

The townspeople began heading out to the old site at the crack of dawn, and by daybreak it was teeming with activities. A red horizontal banner had been hung over an area to mark the meeting site, under which was placed the white wooden table where Fourth Master had laid down an earthenware bowl two years before. Most of the people, instead of sitting down to face the podium, continued to move slowly around the grounds. Later old women and small children came out and merged with the flow of people, who were, for the most part, dressed in their finest. Some of the girls even had colorful sashes hanging down under their lapels. Zhao Duoduo led his sweaty-faced militiamen running back and forth, brandishing rifles to secure the area. The people continued to move, rubbing shoulders while Zhou Zifu and Fourth Master sat behind the table, with Li Qisheng seated off to the side. Zhou was frustrated as he looked out at the vast meeting ground.

Fourth Master smiled and said, "I'm afraid the people have mistaken the award meeting for a temple festival." Zhou blanched, but Fourth Master patted his arm and said, "Don't worry. It'll get better as soon as the meeting gets going."

That calmed Zhou down, but they were both shocked to see Zhang-Wang walk up with some of her homemade sweets and clay tigers. People ran over to buy the sweets, while others pressed down on the clay tigers, making the familiar "gu-gu" sound from another, distant age; the people's eyes misted. After waiting patiently for a while, Zhou Zifu finally got up and shouted, "Meeting time."

Few people heard him, so Zhao Bing, still seated, cleared his throat and shouted the same words in a resounding voice, "Meeting time!" That got their attention; they slowly turned around, some with sweets in their mouths, while others covered the mouths of the clay tigers in their hands.

The meeting was finally under way. Zhou Zifu first read from a sheet of paper, which took an hour. Then he read two provincial papers with reports about Wali. People sucked in cold air when he spread the newspaper to reveal all those huge numbers in red. They could almost see the old man turn over in the well at each sentence from Zhou's mouth. Finally he finished reading both papers and told the militiamen to "do it." One reached under Li's arms to pick him up while two others unfolded a bright red vest to put on him. The red vest derived from the reversed meaning of the black vest, with an impressive result. With the red vest on, Li's face seemed to glow and bright light shone in his eyes. He was trembling when he sat down, but he quickly stood up again to bow to the township head and Fourth Master, then to the crowd in front. He stammered, "I—I— was a capitalist—"

Zhou interrupted him impatiently, "Now you're a hero-oo." The people burst out laughing at the way Zhou said "hero." Then came the flower pinning. A militiaman pinned a huge paper flower the size of a sunflower on Li's left breast, at which moment Li began to show signs that he wasn't holding up well. His body pitched forward, the corners of his mouth twitched, and his balled fists were raised to the sides of his rib cage. After casting a glance at Li, Zhou exchanged a look with Fourth Master before shouting urgently, "The meeting is adjourned." Li, who heard it clearly, leaped up and ran home.

But the crowd did not disperse right away. The clay tigers were making those special sounds in Zhang-Wang's hands. She had put the wrapped sweets in her hair so anyone who bought them could also touch her hair. Then she placed some in the buttonholes of her blouse so her customers could feel her breasts. Jiansu bought one and reached out to touch her breast timidly. Zhang-Wang grinned and said, "I can see the little capitalist bastard knows what's what." The homemade sweets and clay tigers sold out quickly. That night, the people built a bonfire on the grounds to continue enjoying themselves; someone far away was even shouting to add to the fun. Zhang-Wang clapped her hands and sang a little ditty, "I don't want silver, I don't want gold; I just want someone to have and hold." The fire finally died down, shrouding the ground in darkness. Someone called out Zhang-Wang's nickname but got only a curse in return: "Go screw yourself." She was first to leave, with her hands over the pocket filled with money from the sales of clay tigers and sweets.

Things began to go wrong with Li Qisheng as soon as he was back in his room. First he jumped up into the air, nearly hitting his head on the roof beam. Then he started rolling around on the *kang* and reaching out to tear off half of the straw mat. Lucky for him, someone saw what was happening and sent for Guo Yun, who, after examining him for only a minute or two, pronounced that Li's problem was "madness." What kind of madness? the people asked. He refused to elaborate. Instead, he wrote out a prescription while repeating "madness" over and over. With their young son Li Zhichang in her arms, Li's wife wailed, wondering what she and her child would do now that her husband had gone mad. The room was embroiled in commotion till midnight, when Li finally calmed down after being medicated. Guo Yun came to see him a few more times, with the diagnosis that Li's illness might well be incurable but that everything should be fine so long as he didn't get agitated. People thought the doctor was right, since they often saw how happily Li donned the red vest when he was calm. He also cherished the oversized paper flower. Obviously, he was incurably mad.

TEN

Many days went by before Baopu heard the sad news that Li Qisheng was ill. He went to see Li, but the tightly shut door sent him away disappointed. Now that Li refused to leave his room, the Scientific Renovation Group was forced to disband. By this time they had enough crucibles, so there was no need for Baopu to grind any more porcelain powder. Prior to that, he'd spent each day with his mortar, the white powder turning his hair gray and giving him the appearance of an old man. His disposition, however, was well suited for this kind of work, monotonous and repetitive. He had no idea how many shards of smashed porcelain he'd ground into powder, but he once spotted a colorful piece painted with a beautiful but frail young girl who resembled Guigui from the Sui family. He wanted to send the piece to her but lacked the nerve to steal raw material for crucibles, and as he ground it into powder he felt a dull pain, as if he were grinding her into pieces. The heaviness in his chest he felt on the way back to his room each day was likely caused by inhaling too much porcelain powder, and he thought he might wind up with a "porcelain lung." What would that be like? he wondered with perverse pleasure.

Entering the empty Sui estate unnerved him, as it had gotten increasingly mysterious after the house had burned down. The town officials continued to send people over to poke and search for treasure allegedly belonging to the old and wealthy Sui family. The scary part was that they didn't always leave empty-handed. On one occasion the steel pole poked through a broken porcelain bowl, which they happily took away with them. After Fourth Master snapped off the metal buckle on his belt and shovels were added to their exploration, the situation worsened; the bean trellises were thrown to the side, and moist, freshly dug-up earth dotted the landscape. Cicada cocoons that were dug up went straight from a roasting fire into people's mouths. Then someone told the diggers to turn their attention to the side rooms. Complaining that the buildings would collapse if they did, Baopu eventually convinced them to limit their work to poking around with their poles, and it did not take long for the floors to be covered in holes, into which Jiansu and Hanzhang poured fine sand to amuse themselves.

After the dining hall opened, sparing residents the trouble of cooking, popular thought had it that taking away the cook pots to smelt into iron had been farsighted. And now that everyone had to turn over their foodstuffs, they lined up morning, noon, and night with pottery jugs that were filled by a middle-aged man with a wooden-handled gourd ladle who asked, "How many?" One scoop for each family member. Baopu never saw Li Qisheng come out for food and was told that someone took it to him. Baopu's uncle, Sui Buzhao, sometimes asked him to do the same for him. On one of those occasions he saw that his uncle was again absorbed in his ancient book on ocean travel. He'd just returned from the provincial city after reporting the discovery of the ancient ship, which had restored his seafaring passion. His memories were so powerful that his mind and body were totally absorbed in imaginary masts. Baopu sat down but said nothing.

Sui Buzhao turned the pages and stopped at a place to measure a map with his fingers. With a shake of his head, he recited, "North, south, east, west," then rattled off four of the eight diagrams from the *I Ching*. Again he shook his head and moved on to the next page, where he continued to read: "Head in the *yi mao* direction for three *geng* to reach Mount Langmu and continue eight more *geng* to reach the bay at Mount Sanbawa. Do not enter the bay. At close range, the hill to the right of the entrance resembles the gate to a fortress. The water there is shallow. To the east are two volcanoes; the easternmost has a high peak, the westernmost spews fire. The ship should enter when it approaches the fire-spewing volcano. Inside to starboard there is a welcoming bay for mooring; be sure to burn incense and offer a sacrifice if the water is fast flowing. Within the portal is a row of four or five unapproachable islands. Beware of an old sandbar to the north-east." He looked up at Baopu. "I've been to these places," he said. "Everything is as it says in this manual. Alas, the ancient ship has been removed. If Uncle Zheng He were here—he would curse me. But I was afraid they would turn it into kindling for the dining hall."

Baopu fixed his gaze on the book. This was the second time he'd seen it, taken from its hiding place inside the brick wall, protected by a metal box. Baopu recalled that his uncle had shown it to him years before and that fine dust had flown out when the box was opened.

Pointing at a spot, the old man said, "One *geng* is sixty *li*. Some say thirty, but that is nonsense. The ancient book records that a large ship sank thirty *geng* from Wali Pier, which means that it was eighteen hundred *li* distant. That is how I concluded it was not the ship that was excavated. Besides, those ships had an unusual design you cannot imagine these days. The masts were made of cassia with flags woven from citronella leaves. A jade turtledove sat atop each mast; they said it knew the directions of the wind in every season."

Baopu handed his uncle the still-warm jug so he could eat. The old man reached inside and found a soft corn cake that was so hot he had to flip it from hand to hand. "This isn't bad. Color's good too. Communism is great," the old man commented after taking a bite. He then took a marinated radish out of the other jug, and as he ate he asked Baopu the names of the women cooking in the dining hall. He was so happy he could barely keep his mouth shut when he heard who it was. "I'll go over there one of these days and teach them how to use running water." What an unusual thing to say, since Baopu was sure all they had to do for water was remove the cork plug from the sunflower pipe. But he held his tongue, picked up the jugs, and returned to his room.

Baopu and Guigui's wedding banquet was held in the dining hall, although the quality of food by then was much diminished. The mills by the river had stopped turning so the mung beans could be made into gruel; the people no longer needed to carry two jugs to the dining hall since there was only one item on the menu, a mixture of mashed bean residue, vegetable leaves, and a few mung beans. It was a salty, thirst-inducing paste, and people gulped down water as they complained about the food. They were not, however, surprised by what they were given; on the other hand, they were deeply concerned about the stoppage at the old mills, something that had rarely occurred in their memory. Elders recalled that they had continued to turn even when heads were floating in the river during the Taiping Rebellion. They had, however, stopped for slightly over a month when the Land-lord Restitution Corps fought their way back and buried forty-two people alive in an underground yam cellar. So they slurped the salty gruel while keeping track of how long the mills remained still. On the thirty-third day panic began to set in, and clever older women began collecting edible leaves, while the moldy powder around the mills disappeared overnight.

At a town meeting Zhou Zifu rallied the people to use "vegetable substitutes" as a means of getting through the hard times. He told them they'd entered a new era and that there was no need to be afraid. According to him, some families had hidden food during the collection period and were partially responsible for the current food shortage. He ordered them to turn in the food within three days to avoid serious consequences. That was followed by consoling words to the effect that, if things got worse, Wali's talent for scientific innovation would be exploited to introduce new foods for consumption. In short, there was no need to panic. Hopes were mixed with threats, and the people were unsure if they should be happy or afraid. They mulled the notions of "new era," "vegetable substitutes," and "new foods," while speculating on the families that had hidden food.

Four days later, Baopu's family was arrested and led away by armed militiamen. He, his brother, and his sister were all held separately. Baopu was relieved when they crammed him into a crowded room, for that proved that his was not the only family taken into custody.

A cadre from town walked in with a note-taker, and Baopu was the first to be interrogated.

"Did you turn in all the food in your house?"

Baopu nodded. "A long time ago, when they said the dining hall . . ."

The cadre turned to the man taking notes. "Write down every word."

"We don't have a single grain in our house," Baopu added.

The man looked him in the eye and said, "Are you absolutely sure?"

Baopu nodded solemnly. "Yes."

"Good. Write that down." The man moved to the next person, and the next, and that is how the day went.

The roomful of people, men and women, were squeezed together when they bedded down. Baopu lay awake thinking about Guigui and wondering who she was squeezed up against. He hoped it was Hanzhang. Daybreak brought a different interrogator, a more disagreeable man who lost his temper and viciously poked an old woman in the shoulder when he questioned her.

"Are you going to come clean or aren't you?" he asked Baopu.

"I already did, yesterday."

The man frowned and said sternly, "Your wife gave us a different story. Who are we supposed to believe?"

Baopu looked up at the man. "She only knows how to tell the truth, so if our stories differ, I guess you'll have to believe her." That earned Baopu a slap across the face, which stung so badly he could not hear what the cadre was cursing him for. Struggling to control himself, he clenched and unclenched his fists. More people came to question them on the third day, but this time there were no slaps.

Toward dusk, a man in his forties was beaten mercilessly by the militia, who dragged him outside. Eventually everyone in the room began to realize that while they were being detained, Zhou Zifu and Fourth Master were leading militiamen in house-to-house searches and that the people in these rooms were prime suspects. The searchers not only upended their furniture but poked the floors with steel poles and even checked the color of excrement in the toilets. They had found something in the toilet of the beaten man, which was why they had grilled him so intensely. In the end, they discovered a jug of corn buried behind his house. Everyone in the room breathed a sigh of relief at the news.

By midnight, all but Baopu and five others had been released. Suspicion still hung over these few people, who became targets of terrifying curses and threats. They were on tenterhooks, knowing that saying the wrong thing could bring far worse treatment. "You planted beans in your yard. Did you eat them yourself?" the cadre asked Baopu.

"Someone from the dining hall came to pick them, but then some of the trellises were overturned by the militiamen who dug up the ground beneath them."

"Are you telling me they didn't leave even a single bean stalk?"

Baopu tensed. "A few survived, but only a handful. Guigui is sick."

The man turned to the note-taker. "Write down every word." Then he turned and shouted, "Even a tiny handful belongs to the collective! They were not yours to take!"

Everyone was finally allowed to leave, including Guigui, who collapsed as soon as she got home. Lying in Baopu's arms, she showed him her swollen cheeks from the beatings. Baopu laid her down on the *kang,* where she sank down, along with the mat; it turned out the searchers had pried open the *kang* to look for hidden food. Jiansu and Hanzhang stayed with her, watching her breathe laboriously. Her eyes were open wide on a face devoid of color as she stared at Baopu, and Jiansu was struck by how lovely yet how pitiable his sister-in-law looked. After a while he stood up to get food from the dining hall but returned with empty containers, telling them that the dining hall was closed owing to a shortage of food. They fell silent as they looked at the ground beneath their feet. After dark, Baopu walked out into the yard, where a few dried-out beans quivered in the wind. He reached out but quickly drew his hand back; the beans posed a lethal temptation. Ignoring them, he looked down at the shriveled leaves, and after carefully brushing off the dust he filled two pockets.

Back inside, and under the gaze of Jiansu and Hanzhang, he soaked the leaves. Reminded of something by the water, Jiansu ran out of the room, after which Baopu finally mustered the courage to go pick the dried-out beans out in the yard. Hanzhang found a mortar to grind them, but Baopu took it from her and pounded as if he were grinding porcelain. He kept at it until he had turned the beans to powder, then mixed it with the leaves and steamed the mixture in a pottery jug. White steam sent a sour smell throughout the room, just as Jiansu and Sui Buzhao, who was wearing only a pair of underpants, walked in. Drenched and shaking all over, he held a few tiny fish and shrimp strung together with stalks of grass. He first tossed the fish into the jug, before holding up Guigui's head to feed her the live shrimp.

All of Wali was now engaged in a search for food. Tender weeds were quickly plucked clean, followed by leaves, and then sparrows that had starved and fallen into roadside ditches. Many people, recalling the existence of loaches, dug up the muddy riverbank. In early fall, cicadas fell from the trees, where they were picked up by lucky souls and tossed straight into their mouths. Starving birds and animals along the banks of the Luqing River were caught and eaten by people who were even hungrier than they. Old women who loved their cats like their children, and had held them in their arms for years, had no choice but to watch tearfully as their sons turned the cats into soup. No one dared laugh at Zhao Duoduo anymore, for now everyone had eaten earthworms and the like. In the past, when green moths had swarmed around lanterns, he'd swept them into a pile, sautéed them, and put them in his pocket to pop into his mouth like he was munching on peas. Now, though everyone realized the bugs' potential, they could only attract a few with their lanterns. Eventually they turned their attention to trees, stripping the bark and snapping off the tender shoots. The tender bark was nearly gone by the time the Sui clan came out to search for food, so Baopu was left with stripping off dark, tough bark to get to the white layers, which would be laid out to dry in the sun before ending up in a mortar.

To his surprise, Baopu's job of grinding porcelain had given him inspiration, as he now put all sorts of things in the mortar to improve the taste and quality of what they ate. Sweet potato leaves tasted like delicate pastries, while yellow chaff was like millet meal. The "hunger therapy" took care of some of the men's problem, making them behave. Not two years earlier, they had often stolen into the fields to grope around under the crucible fires and help the women with the bellows, interfering with the smelting of iron. "Don't be so impatient!" the women complained. "Can't you even wait for the iron to melt?" Now nothing but lonely memories remained in fields littered with piles of dark ashes. The men went out as usual, but now they were there to find handfuls of dried-up sweet potato leaves.

Guigui, gravely ill, managed to sit up three times a day for the food Baopu made for her. Sui Buzhao dove into the river several times and, to the envy of all, caught a few finger-length fish that he made into fish broth for her. Since that New Year's Day when Sui Buzhao had relieved himself under the door, Guigui had been upset at the sight of him and always turned her face when she saw him. Now her anger was washed away by the steam rising from the fish broth. She felt like crying as she watched him arch his back, with its knifelike backbone, as he made the broth. Her condition improved a bit, but she was still horribly thin. When she coughed at night, Baopu held her to warm her with his body. Weak and frail, she was like a deflated ball, her arms resting on his chest, her dark eyes blinking rapidly. She would be drenched in sweat after a fit of coughing and would nudge Baopu, saying she was not long for this world. She told him she didn't mind dying but felt that she hadn't been a deserving daughter-in-law. She told him how much she missed Sui Yingzhi and that she often dreamed of him riding the old chestnut by the mills along the river.

Baopu hated it when she talked like that and worked hard to comfort her and make her happy. Once or twice she managed to get up and take down a clay tiger from the chest by the *kang*. It had been a gift from Baopu, and she loved to look at it and stroke its surface. In his eyes, she was still a little girl who could not stop kissing her man when she was happy. Touching his gaunt body, she'd stammer, "Baopu, I . . . I want you so much." He would hold her tight, but she'd go on, "I want you so much, so very much."

Kissing her in return, Baopu would say, "I know, I know. It's all my fault. I haven't had anything to eat for two weeks and I can't do it."

Shamed, Guigui would cry, "I know. Baopu, I'm the one who should apologize. Hit me then; why don't you hit me?"

Baopu held her face to his chest and forced a smile. "I'm too weak to hit you, though sometimes I do feel like slapping your bottom, like punishing a naughty child." Sobbing, she would curl up in his arms and eventually fall asleep.

Shortly after descending into "madness" Li Qisheng actually invented another machine, an all-purpose tractor that he created by refitting the only tractor in town. By then the innovation trend was dying out, but his invention was too important for the provincial paper not to report it. The tractor's uses were too many to list; it could till the land, wheel water, cut hay, grind flour, hoe a field, sew, dig ditches, and more. Some even said it could sail in the river like a boat, though no one believed that. So the township head, Zhou Zifu, came to the testing site, where he saw with his own eyes how the machine smoothly turned its blades in the feed shed to cut hay twice as thick as that cut by human hands, but four or five times faster. Zhou had not expected Li to ever again come up with a new invention, assuming that a madman was useless. Fourth Master, on the other hand, was not surprised, saying that a talented person like Li was 70 percent genius and 30 percent madness.

A test of the tractor's ditch-digging ability was conducted that night, as a group of townspeople shouted their way into the field with the tractor. At the time, most of them slept outside the city wall, where they had set up sheds and built bonfires. The grave mounds dotting the field were a treasure, which the people covered with corn-stalks and set on fire, littering the areas with mounds of dark gray ashes. "Another eight thousand *jin* of fertilizer!" someone yelled, pointing at the ashes before shoveling them into the field. Songs were heard all around as shovels and spades danced in the air. When the tractor's motor roared to life, the people threw down their shovels and spades to watch. Under their intense gaze, the all-purpose tractor, fit-ted with ditch-digging blades, groaned its way forward, leaving a ditch more than a foot deep. While it may have been a bit too shallow to be useful, it was still a ditch, and everyone applauded. But when the ap-plause finally died down, someone blurted out, "What do we do with this ditch?" No one had an answer.

Fourth Master cast a glance at Li Qisheng as Zhou Zifu asked, "So what do we do with a ditch like this?"

"It's a ditch," Li replied. Now they realized that Li was, after all, still a madman.

Fourth Master supplied an answer: "Irrigation, tree planting, flood relief." That satisfied the people, who left the area. Li Qisheng was so overwrought that night that, instead of going home, he wandered the fields on his own and gazed at the grave-top flames; he was shaking like a leaf. Gradually he went up to where people were digging in the ground. They dug and they dug, eventually making a pit, but they didn't stop until a rotting black coffin was exposed, and Li realized that they were digging up graves. With a frightened yelp he ran all the way back to town, back to his house.

This time Li Qisheng truly shut himself up in his room, not even letting family members in. The newspaper article on his all-purpose tractor, along with two other newspapers, was pasted on his wall, and life went on, until, that is, the day he discovered that the food had become inedible. He put a ball of rice in his mouth, and it burned his lips. A closer examination revealed that the rice ball was filled with chaff, husks, and twigs; incensed, he threw it as far as his strength would allow. He knew that something was amiss when he went out on the street, where he saw bell-like eyes on the people's sallow faces. He turned and ran back home, but the rice ball he'd just thrown away was nowhere in sight; he went hungry that day. The next day he received a new assignment from the town's government: He was to develop a new strain of pastries. With no more food available, Wali residents would eat pastries if Li succeeded in his invention. Quickly, all sorts of new equipment and raw materials were shipped over, accompanied by an assistant. Li now had a wok, some rice bran, and plenty of chaff.

With expectation showing in his eyes, Zhou Zifu looked at Li Qisheng, whose face was filled with uncertainty. Cooking was a woman's job, but now all of Wali was to be fed by the madman, who put on his red vest with a sense of earnestness before starting to experiment with the bran and chaff. Pursued by his own hunger, he stirred the mixture with amazing speed, while his assistant lit a fire outside the door; the thick smoke irritated Li's eyes and he began to tear up. After five days of incessant experimenting and tasting, the improper diet made Li's belly swell up like a drum.

Then a hint of a solution surfaced on the morning of the sixth day. Making the chaff and bran stick together was the first problem; the pungent, bitter taste was the second. Li succeeded by using fermented elm leaves to bring the two ingredients together and altered the taste with powdered sweetgrass. He molded the mixture into an arm-length loaf, which he wound around the inside of the wok like a snake before steaming it over high heat. He even gave the pastry a name, calling it "sectional cake," as he had to cut it into sections, one per person. Many people came for the sectional cake, but after the first bite they looked around with red faces.

One person found a nail in his piece; it was returned to Li Qisheng. Meanwhile, workers in the now defunct dining hall were called in to learn how to make the pastry, quickly finding a new use for their abandoned woks. But none of the "cakes" turned out as fragrant and

tasty as Li's, since the ratio of sweetgrass powder to the other ingredients was wrong. When these cakes were given to the townspeople,
they fed them to the old folks and children in their families, putting
those made by Li aside for later. As time went on, the people began to
gain weight; their faces turned pale and puffy, and their movements
were sluggish. Now they were in a jocular mood, poking each other in
the face and leaving indentations that seemed to last forever. At first
that threw them into a panic, but they were put at ease after the scientific principle of sectional cake was explained to them.

After a few weeks, the ingredients had nearly run out, so the people
were given sectional cake only every other day, then once a week. No
more were made after the trees were stripped bare. Li Qisheng then
turned his attention to inventing another kind of pastry, but he could
find no suitable ingredients. Still wearing the red vest, which was now
blackened by the ingredients for sectional cake, he left his room in
search of the elusive ingredient.

One day he saw an old man grind up something and put it in his
mouth. He went over to take a closer look, surprising the old man.
Curious, he smelled the concoction and dipped his finger in it. One
taste was all he needed to realize it was lime. After a few steps the old
man stumbled and collapsed. Li ran up to help him, only to see the
corners of the old man's lips twitch as white foam formed at his mouth
and he stopped moving.

Li ran and shouted, "Help, a man has starved to death here in
Wali!"

People emerged from their homes and stared at the old man, then
exchanged glances. One of them began to wail. "Oh no! The time has
come again! It is recorded in the town's chronicle that years ago many
people died of hunger and the people were reduced to eating each
other." This lament so shocked the people that they trembled in fear
and raised wails of their own. As he ran, Li Qisheng kept screaming
that someone had starved to death. He ran and ran until he reached a
narrow building that strangely blocked his way. It took him some time
to realize that he had once lived in that house, and that realization was

followed by the sound of someone crying inside. It was his son, Li Zhichang. Li Qisheng let out a cry and stormed in, where he was met by darkness and a charred odor. Something balled-up was hiding in the dark. When he reached out to touch it, it turned into a tiny body that froze for a moment before wrapping itself around him.

"Pa, Mother is dead. From hunger."

Li Qisheng screamed and jumped to his feet, rubbing his red vest and then his eyes. He saw his wife on the *kang,* her face devoid of any sign of life, the edge of the tattered mosquito net held tightly in her mouth. He knelt on the floor and muttered something before reaching out to touch his wife's face. It was cold, like iron in the dead of night. He tried to pull the net out of her mouth, but her teeth were clamped down on the yellow cloth she'd used to patch the net. Grabbing his father's hand, Li Zhichang begged tearfully, "Don't, Papa, don't. She was so hungry she wouldn't let me take it out. I was in the yard this morning and she was lying on the *kang*. When there was no sound I came inside to see her swallowing the net. I was so scared I began to cry; I tried to pull the net out, but she clamped down and glared at me. I didn't dare pull anymore. Mother was hungry. Then she stopped breathing."

Listening to his son's tearful explanation, Li kept pulling at the net until his wife's face was twitching; he immediately loosened his grip, put his face up against hers, and began to cry. His tears rained down her face and flowed over her eyes, as if she herself were crying. A while later he got up and found a pair of scissors to cut off the part of the net that hung from her mouth. It was tough going. Throwing down the scissors, he ran out through the squat gate in his yard and shouted at the silent doors down the road, "Come look. My wife has starved to death!"

At least two dozen people took turns carrying the coffin holding Li Qisheng's wife before they reached the graveyard. By then they lacked the strength to dig a proper hole. By shoveling from dawn to dusk, they somehow managed to lay her coffin into a shallow grave. An old man and another in his forties burst out crying at the same time, kowtowing to the people around them with a plea that they be buried deep when they died so wild dogs would not get at their bodies. The plea plunged everyone into such deep sorrow that they stopped digging and began to cry. Li Qisheng put a piece of sectional cake he'd found somewhere into the grave. Then an old man brought his son over and made him kneel by the coffin to toss in handfuls of dirt. "You're all useless," the old man yelled at the crowd, "every one of you. A real man would pick up a spade and send Li Qisheng's wife on the road now." Eventually, the mourners stopped crying and took up their tools to make a grave mound, which they patted smooth. The sunset painted the grave mound red as they sat down beside the grave to catch their breath, their spades and shovels resting on their knees. Taking his son by the hand, Li Qisheng left before the others, who continued to sit there waiting for the darkness to come.

"Two years ago we had twenty-one thousand *jin* of corn per acre," someone said with a sigh, "now we don't have a single kernel."

An old man snorted. "Three hundred and four thousand sweet potatoes per acre are also gone."

Another smacked his lips and said, "I don't dare think about sweet potatoes. I'd be happy with some potato vine." That was joined by more laments.

Someone complained that they should not have spent their time guarding the crucibles while they let the corn and sweet potatoes rot in the field. "The official said, 'Communism is coming!'"

That comment stirred up a hornet's nest. More and more people were shouting, "Dear good old Communism, come quickly. Hurry up or there'll be no one to greet you in Wali."

A young man tried to explain that Communism was not a person, but he was immediately shouted down: "How dare you say that? It's reactionary." After that no one said a word. Nightfall slowly arrived. In the darkness someone recalled a small can of corn that had been ferreted out a while back. Golden corn. How wonderful it would be if they could have one kernel each. Again sobs emerged from the town, silencing them all, for they knew that someone else had died.

"Come on, let's go home." The old man stood up.

Three days later, four of those who had attended the funeral were dead from starvation; one was the old man, the other the man in his forties.

On the morning of the fourth day, the townspeople did not have time to bury the four because they were following Fourth Master to steal turnips south of town. Zhao Duoduo had heard that a load of famine-relief turnips for the people from the western bank of the river would pass through Wali soon.

When the county Party committee held an emergency relief meeting, Zhou Zifu returned empty-handed, even though the committee had allocated relief based on the severity of famine in each town. Fourth Master slapped him in front of everyone. "Listen to me, Mr. Zhou," he said. "You go back and get our portion of turnips, or I'll lead the whole town in gnawing on your head!" The people, their eyes red, raised their fists and shouted, "Gnaw your head! Gnaw your head!" Shaking from fear, Zhou Zifu backed off, spun around, and ran out of town.

The next morning, Fourth Master led the townspeople to the crossroads, where they sat waiting for the wagon, but even after the sun had risen above the treetops, there was no sight of it. Suddenly he slapped himself on the forehead and jumped to his feet. "It's a trick," he yelled. He told Zhao Duoduo to stay put with a few people, while he led the rest to the northern edge of the town, where they saw a horse cart coming toward them. It sped up as the townspeople shouted, and the dozen armed militia guards took off running.

"Stop them!" Fourth Master shouted. "Dying like this is better than starving to death."

The crowd surged ahead in disregard for their own safety. The militiamen raised their rifles and fired, stopping the raiders. "Shit!" Fourth Master cursed as he tore off his coat and ran toward the rifles.

More shots were fired, sending bullets whizzing in the air, one of them grazing his ear. He pointed a stumpy finger and screamed, "You snot-nosed runts, how dare you shoot at me!" His voice was loud, his words weighty, imposing, and overpowering at a time when no one had much strength. The hands holding the rifles shook; finally the men lowered their weapons. Fourth Master stepped in front of the cart and swung his arms. "Stop!" he commanded.

The carter did not pull the brake, nor did he try to get the horses to stop, but the animals' manes shook in response to Zhao Bing's booming voice. They raised their front hooves but refused to take another step forward. A stocky man, Zhao Bing had arms that were more muscular than those of the starving men. His face had turned gaunt but had none of the ashen, puffy look of the others; in fact, it had a purplish hue. He flared his nostrils, breathing hard, and glared at the militiamen. The crowd rushed up, but before they reached the cart, the militiamen tried to protect the turnips with their bodies. Fourth Master waved them away. "We're here, so there's no point in doing that. Let's split the load so we can save many lives." The militiamen knelt before the turnips and pleaded, "Have mercy, Fourth Master. This load represents the lives of the people west of the river, and we will lose ours if we don't bring them back."

The carter, an old man who had been leaning over the shaft, turned and shouted in a cracking voice, "Stop this nonsense and pick up your weapons."

As if suddenly awaking, the guards picked up their rifles and took aim at the raiders. With a sneer, Fourth Master said, "We are separated only by a river, so you ought to know what the people in Wali are like. I think we can work this out. You had a connection at the county office that got you a cartload of relief turnips. But four more people have just starved to death in Wali."

Putting down their rifles, the militiamen looked up at the sky and began to wail.

The Wali townspeople pounced on the cart and fought over

the turnips, making noises no one could understand. When over half of the load was gone, Fourth Master waved again to let the cart drive off.

When Zhou Zifu returned from the county office the second time, still empty-handed, he barricaded himself in his house for days. One day a cornmeal cake was pushed under his door. He stared at it in amazement before looking out through a crack in the door. He saw Zhao Bing, who was walking away with his hands behind his back. Filled with gratitude, Zhou Zifu called out to Zhao, who did not even turn to look.

Famine continued to rage all across town, where nothing green could be seen anymore. That went on for over a month before the situation improved when the county Party committee finally sent down the first load of relief dried sweet potatoes.

Li Qisheng and his son managed to stay alive, and the older man never forgot to take a portion of his sweet potatoes to his wife's grave. Not saying a word to anyone when he was out, he spent most of his time in his room. His madness flared up a few times, causing him to jump around and create a scene, but Guo Yun was always there to drive the demons away. Over the next few decades, the people in Wali pretty much forgot his existence, all but the older folks, who recalled him whenever they reminisced over the sectional cake. The young people had no idea what sectional cake was.

ELEVEN

The old mills rumbled along, rubbing time itself away. Zhao Duoduo's factory leasing contract was nearly up, requiring a Gaoding Street meeting to arrange for a new lease. Zhao remarked that he had familiarized himself with the purchase of raw materials and the marketing of the product, and that he had transformed the enterprise into a full-fledged noodle factory. He added that the equipment had either been replaced or was in need of being replaced and that there had been personnel changes, which essentially meant that the operation had become quite complex. In a word, he wanted to renew the contract for a period of ten years, just like leasing land from the government. He did not care how much it would cost. Moreover, he intended to form the "Wali Glass Noodle Production and Marketing Consortium" by joining up with all the noodle factories along the Luqing River. The town erupted in amazement when the news was released. And more was on the way, for he planned to implement the kick-the-ball management system all up and down the Luqing River area, with an emphasis on "information." He expected his employees to engage in a "high salary, high consumption" lifestyle. At first no one understood what he meant, but when asked, he gave a simple, clear answer: "When a worker earns enough in one day to buy a cow, he should spend enough in one day to consume that cow." The people were speechless. "How could anyone spend like that?" There were

even rumors that he was planning to buy a car and hire a female secretary, now that he had become an entrepreneur.

What, in fact, was a "female secretary"? After much discussion, the
townspeople decided it must mean the most beautiful woman in the
world, who would stand behind Duoduo and read in secret. This drew
apprehensive sighs, for people were only too familiar with Duoduo's
character and were sure that the female secretary would come to grief
at his hands. But then someone reminded them that Zhao Duoduo
was no longer young and that his male organ was diseased. This latest
revelation drew more apprehensive sighs, expressing an altogether different sense of regret. Rumors flew, like bats circling the city wall.

Life was now moving at an alarming speed, as one shocking story
after another was revealed in the paper and on the radio. A peasant
named Zhao Dagui and a few friends bought an airplane. In three
months, 1,842 peasants flew to Shanghai, Guangzhou, and Beijing in
Boeing and Trident airplanes. A deeply wrinkled man with his head
wrapped in a white cloth (obviously another peasant) ate a whole
roasted duck dripping in grease in one sitting and littered the counter
with ten-yuan bills when he was finished. In one village, every one of
the 982 households had a refrigerator and a color TV. Seven hundred
workers had tapestries hanging on the walls of their houses and had
implemented a cooking system with a refrigerator at the center. A
specialized farmer hired a secretary (gender unclear) at the astonishing
annual salary of eight thousand yuan. When a poet heard the news, he
could not sleep for three days, torn between remaining a poet and
becoming a secretary. His indecision cost him the opportunity, and he
fell ill from disappointment and indignation. A peasant entrepreneur
invented a new welding machine that made it into the international
market, earning him 489,000 yuan.

The old folks in Wali could not avoid being reminded of their
youth, an era of gigantic numbers, one that had been recorded in the
town's chronicles. But the chronicles neglected to mention what had
happened after the arrival of those gigantic numbers, except to brush
it off as a "natural disaster." Everyone knew what that meant. So the

old folks were frightened of big numbers. A few years before, paper plaques had marched toward town in the hands of a slogan-shouting crowd. When the old folks saw that each plaque was inscribed in red with a giant red number, they defiantly denied permission for the crowd to enter their town, so the crowd turned and went somewhere else. But this time they could not stop the gigantic numbers at the city wall, since they entered town via newspapers, radios, and word-of-mouth. Besides, the numbers were often associated with Zhao Duo-duo, so they knew it was futile to try to stop them. Better to wait and see what happened next, and do what little they could within their power to forestall calamities, such as telling their daughters that death was better than working as Zhao Duoduo's secretary. Life went on, with little of interest to the people. The old men continued to show up at the Wali Emporium for watered-down liquor, while the mills kept turning down by the river.

All but Jiansu, who quietly and resolutely carried on with his plans. At night he often felt a burning sensation in his right eye, as if it had been poked by a sharp object. Rubbing the eye, he refused to stop checking the factory accounts. The pen felt heavy in his hand, like a machete he'd use to slash the giant numbers into small pieces as he copied them out. With steely determination, he checked and re-checked each step, telling himself again and again that victory would ultimately be his. He could not recall how many times he'd looked at the singular figure that so excited him he could not stop touching it. He still had to subtract several items: travel expenses, the cost for gifts to facilitate the transportation and ordering process, and entertainment. He also needed to deduct the amount due the town, as stipulated in the leasing contract, as well as production costs, raw materials, and reasonable wear and tear, which were the most complicated and consumed most of his energy. The accounts were made even more difficult by incompetent, even dishonest bookkeeping. Most of the time he had to speculate, based on knowledge he'd accumulated over time and comparisons with what the bookkeeper inadvertently revealed as he engaged him in conversation. What he learned under these circumstances could well be more accurate than what was recorded in the account book. Travel expenses, part in kind and part in cash, allocated to each salesman came to 1,950 yuan a year, which, multiplied by seven, totaled 13,650 yuan. With the 4,400 yuan the factory kept in reserve for travel expenses, the total cost for travel came to 18,050 yuan. Gifts were mainly Maotai liquor, State Express cigarettes, sea cucumbers, and dried saltwater shrimp. The Maotai had cost only about 11,000 yuan, since more than sixty bottles of the stuff were fake, produced by Fatty Han. That saved a bit. Over 870 cartons of State Express 555 cigarettes had cost 26,190 yuan. With fluctuating market prices, 90 *jin* each of the sea cucumbers and shrimps had cost 12,000 yuan. There were also two eighteen-inch color TV sets and six tape decks, 5,500 yuan. The grand total for gifts reached 54,690 yuan.

Sweat beaded on Jiansu's forehead when he saw such a large outlay for gifts, although he knew it was an unavoidable and necessary expense if he was to take over the factory. In fact, he might even spend more than that—the more one spent on gifts, the more one got back in revenue, a paradox that would likely puzzle later generations.

Jiansu smiled bitterly as he lit his pipe, preparing himself for the next item—the head-scratching entertainment expense. He was immediately reminded of the Midautumn Festival banquet, where he'd gotten head-spinning drunk. Since the guests were all local, the food was quite bad, costing Duoduo little, though he'd feigned generosity by treating his fellow townspeople, a show that he never forgot his own in his prosperity. There were several levels of banquets at the factory; the highest level required one bottle of Maotai per table, plus two bottles of liquor from the town of Fen or Luzhou, two bottles of Zhangyu red wine, ten bottles of Tsingtao Beer, sea cucumbers, abalone, and jiaji fish. One *jin* of jiaji fish cost 25 yuan, which meant that a reasonably sized fish, say four or five *jin,* cost around 100 yuan. A banquet at this level cost 350 yuan per table and was reserved for important leaders in charge of noodle exports or important businessmen. For such a banquet, Fatty Han served as chef, with Duoduo as host. Fourth Master would be the only local resident invited.

The next-best banquet had one bottle of Xifeng liquor, a bottle of the local special brew, two bottles of white wine, ten bottles of Baotu Spring Beer, prawns, turtle soup, silver fungi, pomfrets, and so on. At a cost of 230 yuan per table, it was served to city and county dignitaries. Fatty Han would still be the chef and Duoduo the host, but Director Luan Chunji and Party Secretary Li Yuming would accompany the guests.

The third level of banquet would require only large platters of fish and pork, with an endless supply of white or red wine. Chef Fatty Han would drink a cup with the guests each time he served a dish. Zhao Duoduo or the bookkeeper would be the only company for the guests. It was rare for the bookkeeper to enjoy a banquet like this, so he'd wind up drunk, which meant he'd keep a messy account upon his return. A banquet like this cost about 130 yuan.

In thirteen months, there had been six elite banquets (with Fourth Master as company), eleven second-best (with Director Luan and Secretary Li), and more than twenty third-level banquets. The total cost for entertainment was 7,230 yuan, a rather small number. Mildly surprised, Jiansu underlined the figure and walked out of his room after casting another glace at the blue notebook crisscrossed with cramped numbers.

The stars in the night sky looked like troubled eyes, emitting weak light over the bean trellis, which was shrouded in darkness. Despite himself, he walked up to the trellis, as if waiting for someone. Of course no one would come, but he could not forget how he had once held a slender body there. It had been his first time and he would never forget it. He would recall every detail till the day he died. On this autumn night, he conjured up the image of her pretty purple-and-yellow panties. He had caressed her clumsily while she trembled, covering her breasts with her hands. What a lovely little girl! She seemed to quietly appear in his small room, in the color of soil and the fragrance of green grass. He reached out to touch the bean leaves, sending a drip of icy cold water into his eye. Where was she now?

Could she be asleep at this moment, with her arms around her children or her husband on a night like this? Would she sense that her first man would be thinking of her beneath the bean trellis after an exhausting night of accounting? She must have become a mother herself; she must have put on loose, baggy clothes and become a young mother. Jiansu reached up and felt the pounding of his restless heart.

Reluctant to return to his room, Jiansu walked out of the yard and went down a small, dark alley, until he came to the Wali Emporium. He sat down on the stone steps, feeling lost and dejected. It was a store he'd set up, but the passion was gone; he no longer cared about the inventory or the accounts, leaving them all to Zhang-Wang. Each month she would report to him in a singsong voice, but he paid little attention, for his focus now was on the noodle factory. What he cared about was that larger figure, and the rusty cleaver by Zhao Duoduo's bedside. He'd dreamed several times of the cleaver flying up and being buried in Zhao's throat. His hands itched as he wrung them nervously. Sitting on the stone steps, he could not help but hear the banging sounds from the strainer in the processing room. He could almost see the plump Daxi washing noodles in a basin, her arms turned red by the cold water. And there would be Naonao, her body swaying with the movements of her hands, as nimble as if she were disco dancing. Uneasily he stood up, walked around the front of the shop, and sat down again. Finally, he unlocked the door and went looking for the liquor vat.

Straddling a large clay tiger, he sipped cold liquor. The room seemed dusty gray as the dawn light rose outside. The liquor warmed him up as he fixed his gaze on the door, recalling the night he'd been drinking with his uncle, a quiet night like this, with all of Wali fast asleep. He kept drinking, but then he heard footsteps outside and set down his cup. At the sight of a shadow passing by the door, he jumped down off the counter and ran out to see Naonao heading west. "Naonao!" he shouted.

She stopped and, seeing it was Jiansu, asked, drawing out the words, "What do you want?"

Jiansu took a step forward. "Can I offer you a drink?" he said stiffly.

She laughed and followed him into the shop, skipping past him to leap onto the counter and sit on the clay tiger he had abandoned a moment before. "Once you're on a tiger it's hard to get off," she murmured. Surprised to hear her use such a clever, fitting phrase, Jiansu looked her over. Her hair hung past her shoulders, and she was wearing a light, clingy dress and plastic, red-soled slippers. Her eyes were bright and shiny; her face glowed.

"You didn't work the night shift, did you?"

She swung her legs and nodded with a grin. "I'm not feeling well."

Jiansu found that hard to believe. He handed her a drink; she took a sip and coughed, turning her face and her pale neck red. "I didn't feel well. I was hot all over and I couldn't sleep, so I got up early. Damn it!" He was amused to hear a pretty girl swearing at nothing in particular. "I can tell by your eyes that you haven't slept either," she continued. "But your eyes are so damned good-looking. I mean it." She laughed again. Feeling a warm current running through his heart, he took a sip. She did too, before sighing. "Your illness and mine have something in common. I couldn't sleep so I kicked the blanket away, feeling an urge to curse someone."

"Could that be me?"

Naonao flicked her wrist. "No, I wouldn't waste it on you. I left my room and went over to the gourd trellis before coming out onto the street. I want to be alone. Jiansu, don't you think that's strange? Well, sometimes people just want to be alone, to think their own thoughts, even crazy thoughts. People are interesting, don't you think? You're like that, aren't you? You don't say much, but I know. I know you. Look at your face. It's pale, almost bloodless. And your eyes are big, shiny black. You have long legs. I know I'm better off staying clear of people like you, but I'm not afraid. You're scared of me, I'm not scared of you. No one scares me. No, that's not right. Maybe there is one person I'm afraid of. I'll be scared stiff when I see the one person I fear. I only like a man I'm afraid of, afraid to do anything. He can do what he wants. What I fear is he won't want to do anything. That's what I fear. Sometimes I feel like picking up a club and sneaking up behind him to smack him on the back. How wonderful it would make me feel to knock him to the floor. But these are just crazy thoughts. As I said, I'll be scared stiff when I face the person I fear. What should I do, Jiansu? Of course you don't know; I'm just talking. You're an idiot."

It was probably the effect of the liquor that had loosened her tongue. Jiansu didn't follow everything she said, but it had quite an impact on him anyway; an uncomfortable burning sensation ran through him. "You're afraid of me, right?" he yelled.

Naonao grinned and shook her head. "No, not you. You may think I am, but I'm not. You wouldn't fight back if I slapped you. Understand? You're not afraid of many people but you're afraid of me. You're the best-looking man in Wali. Your hair is so black it'd be nice to touch it. Real nice." Jiansu looked at her, bewildered, and his eyes turned misty. With an ironic smile at the corners of her mouth, she reached out and laid her hand on his head. He felt himself begin to shake; his cheek muscles twitched. With his eyes closed, he sat quietly on the counter, while her hand stroked his head. It felt as if his heart was about to leap out of his chest, and he kept his eyes closed. Then the hand left his head. He opened his eyes, and lights flashed. Reaching out, he lifted Naonao down from the counter while hurriedly searching for her lips.

He kissed her, his hands caressing her back. The image of the young girl cutting brambles appeared before him, and he could almost smell the fragrance of green grass. He pressed his cheek to her hair, touching it strand by strand. Naonao's body went limp as her lips moved away from his and made a strange noise. Then she shuddered as her lips came to rest on his forehead, her hands gripping his arms tighter and tighter. After a moment, she let go and pushed him away. "Naonao," he called out as he wrapped his arms around her and pressed against her breasts. He touched the nape of her neck, then moved his hand down to where the skin was even softer. He was breathing hard; a low moan of desire escaped his lips. Naonao began to struggle, stepping on his toes and finally slapping him across the face. He let her go. He was covered in sweat, which dripped down from his forehead, but he didn't bother to wipe it off. Instead, he crouched down. Neither of them said a word as they watched the countertop brighten.

After a long while, Naonao said, "I'm afraid of only one man, the silent man in the old mill house. Your brother."

"What?" Jiansu blurted out.

"I said, it's your brother."

Jiansu stared at her and she returned his gaze fearlessly, telling him that she meant what she said. He looked down at his feet while Naonao explained deliberately, as if talking to the man in the distant mill house. "Day and night, that red-faced man just sits there, like a stone, when you look at him from behind. You can't see his face, with eyes that are as pretty as his brother's. But there's something profound in them, something you can't forget once you gaze into them. I think of those eyes and his broad, powerful back even when I'm sleeping. I want to jump on his back and cry as he carries me up to the heavens. I tell you, I feel like hitting him from behind, but I don't dare. I'd fall apart before his hand reached me if he tried to hit me. I'd like him to hit me with those big hands of his. He's strong, but his strength is buried inside, making it impossible for people to forget him."

"I see," Jiansu mumbled.

"No, you don't. He held me once, when the machine was first fitted at the old mill. He didn't want me to get hurt so he picked me up easily in front of all those people and then put me down gently. So easy, so gentle. He's strong. He's in his forties, yet his beard is still dark. I'm scared of him, I'm scared of that man. No wonder people say I'm 'wanton.' Jiansu, now you know what 'wanton' means, right? What does it mean to be wanton?" She giggled.

Jiansu was so absorbed in what she was saying he didn't catch her question at first, but after thinking it over he answered earnestly, "There's something unusual about you and that makes you 'wanton.' "

"Is it that unusual something that makes me afraid of Baopu?"

Jiansu shook his head, but then nodded. "It makes you shudder, like a moment ago. It also pushes you toward the mill house. You go there a lot, don't you?"

Naonao smiled and knitted her brows. "You're right. You people in the Sui clan are smart. I look at his back and his head, but he can't see me. That bachelor, that bumbling mute." Excited by what she was thinking and saying, with her hands on her hips, she arched her left leg over the crouching Jiansu's head. He cursed silently but said nothing. He wished he could see his brother now; he harbored a degree of concern and indignation on behalf of his brother but was also a bit jealous. Naonao was pacing the shop, her body writhing in agitated cheerfulness. The bright sunlight turned her body into a ball of fire, which rolled out the door of Wali Emporium, unnoticed by Jiansu, who remained crouching on the floor.

That night Jiansu kept at the account book. The biggest item to be deducted was the cost of raw materials. During the thirteen months of Zhao Duoduo's lease, the factory processed 2,980,000 *jin* of mung beans, 43 percent of which were imported at 0.48 yuan per *jin*. The remaining 57 percent, from the northeast or the Luqing River area, cost 0.43 yuan per *jin*. The total cost for raw materials—615,072 yuan for imported mung beans and 730,398 yuan for domestic beans—came to 1,345,470 yuan. He also had to subtract production costs. Zhao Duoduo leased the factory, along with the mills, the processing rooms, the drying floor, and other equipment; he received over 200,000 *jin* of beans to be processed, had 248,000 *jin* of beans stored in the warehouse, and owned sixty-three blocks of starch. All that added up to 82,000 yuan. During the first four months of the lease, the factory continued to operate at its previous rate. In the fifth month 300,000 *jin* of beans had been purchased at a cost of 13,000 yuan. In the sixth month, the sedimentation system was refitted, adding more than twenty sedimentation vats, along with the expansion of the sedimentation pool. Another 100,000 *jin* of beans was bought in the seventh month, and the mill was mechanized in the eighth. A total of 180,800 yuan was invested during those three months. Jiansu breathed a sigh of relief, now that he'd finally got the total for major deductions from the giant number; he'd soon get a good sense of the final account after subtracting the amount due the town and adding the revenue from by-products.

He lit a cigarette and leisurely flipped through the pages with figures he'd written in the past. Only he knew what those figures meant. Those tiny Arabic numbers would come to life one day and stretch out their small fuzzy claws to make Zhao Duoduo very uncomfortable. Then they would tug and tie his flabby body together before twisting and turning, making him bleed and wish he were dead!

Jiansu laughed mirthlessly and looked out the window. A light was on again in his brother's window, telling him that he was reading. He closed his door and walked over to his brother's room.

Baopu had just finished a night shift, and since he had trouble sleeping, he began reading out of habit. He unfolded the bundle and opened the book to the page where he'd left off the day before. Things he didn't understand he marked in red. He glanced up at Jiansu when he came in but immediately went back to his book. Jiansu stood behind him, not saying a word, and watched his brother read. The first line he saw was, "In other words, the less skill and strength required by manual operation, the more developed modern industry becomes, the more likely it is that male workers will be edged out by female workers." He laughed in agreement with that, knowing that most of the workers were women. The only males left were those who handled the strainers. Little strength was needed for the noodles, so the idea that the female workers would "edge out" the male workers seemed to be an accurate assessment.

Jiansu laughed again, saying to himself that it seemed to be a pretty

good book, and as Baopu turned the pages he saw red marks everywhere. "It ruthlessly cuts out all the invisible feudal shackles that bind
people to their natural leaders; it strips off all connections between
people except those related to naked interests and cold, merciless 'cash
exchange.' It submerges sacred emotional evocations such as religious
faith, chivalric ardor, and petty bourgeois sentiment in the icy water
of self-interest." Jiansu saw his brother had underlined "religious
faith," "chivalric ardor," and "petty bourgeois sentiment," and he was
about to ask about that when he spotted another red mark. "Precisely,
Russia and the United States are missing here. It was the time when
Russia constituted the last great reserve of all European reaction, when
the United States absorbed the surplus proletarian forces of Europe
through immigration. Both countries provided Europe with raw materials and were at the same time markets for the sale of its industrial
products. Both were, therefore, in one way or another, pillars of the
existing European system . . . How very different today . . . And now
Russia! . . . The only answer to that possible today is this . . ."

Jiansu felt energized by the words but was lost at the same time. He
ultimately mustered enough courage to ask, "What does all this
mean?"

Without looking up, Baopu answered in a gentle tone, though
with a somber look, "I don't understand it all that well either." He
turned a few more pages. "It's not easy to grasp. I'm prepared to keep
reading it for the rest of my life. I told you I read it whenever I come
to a critical point in life."

"But it's such a thin book," Jiansu remarked, looking puzzled.

Baopu nodded. "Maybe it was thick once, since it covered affairs of
the whole world, but it's been condensed."

"I see," Jiansu muttered, still confused. His eyes came to rest on the
lines, "Our bourgeois, not content with having wives and daughters
of their proletarians at their disposal, not to speak of common prosti-
tutes, take the greatest pleasure in seducing each other's wives." His
nose flaring, Jiansu looked at Baopu, whose face turned cold and hard
as he stared at those words and reached out for a cigarette. Jiansu put

one in his hand and said, "Explain that to me." Baopu glanced over at him but continued to turn the pages, as if he hadn't heard him. Smoke emerged from his mouth and nose. He flattened the pages as he greedily soaked up the words. From time to time he wrote something in a little notebook, the sight of which intrigued Jiansu, who let his eyes roam over the words, straining to read them. His eyes came to rest on the last two lines on the page and he all but forgot to breathe.

"For that purpose, Communists from various countries gathered in London and drafted the following manifesto that would be made known to the world in English, French, German, Italian, Flemish, and Danish."

Jiansu imagined that those lines were cast in steel. With his eyes closed, he reached out to touch the metallic words but shrank back when they came in contact with his fingers. Baopu was saying something, but he didn't hear him; he just stood behind his brother, not saying a word. Now he understood. He knew that Baopu was in the grip of a peculiar, irresistible force that emanated from that thin book. He would surely be reading it for the rest of his life. Not wanting to disturb his brother any longer, Jiansu left the room after gently closing the door behind him.

He kept at the accounts. The elaborate figures gnawed at him day and night, latching onto his skin like leeches. Hanging on him, they sucked at him and made him itch even when he left the room to go to the factory or the Wali Emporium. He shook them off, but they quickly gathered around him again. What he needed to do now was add the revenue for the by-products into the giant number. The factory produced over eight thousand *jin* of sediment and three thousand *jin* of bean milk. Fifty percent of the sediment was sold for animal feed and an ingredient for spirits. Eighty percent of that figure was sold for animal feed at 0.02 yuan per *jin*. The portion sold to distillers brought in 0.05 yuan per *jin*. In the thirteen months, over 40,000 yuan in profits came from sales of the sediment. Each day, more than a thousand *jin* of edible bean milk was collected in thirty-three barrels and sold for 0.15 yuan per barrel, totaling 1,900 yuan.

Revenue from by-products, since the beginning of the lease, came to slightly more than 41,900 yuan, which, added to the giant number, made a gross income of 2,179,400 yuan in thirteen months. Following the emergence of the gigantic number were the various figures waiting to be subtracted: the cost for raw materials, workers' wages, reproduction costs, etc. One by one they were deducted, until a shaky figure emerged: 205,815 yuan. The leasing contract stipulated that 73,000 yuan was due the town, which left 132,815 yuan. To maintain the same level of production as the first thirteen months, they would have to purchase 195,100 *jin* of mung beans, at a cost of 87,800 yuan. Over 10,000 yuan was made when counterfeit ingredients—tens of thousands of *jin* of impure starch—were added to the export noodles. In sum, the factory enjoyed a net profit of 55,000 yuan, the final fruit of their labor, which belonged to Zhao Duoduo and his group, not to the factory. Funds had to be obtained through other channels if the factory needed to add new equipment or expand.

What Jiansu found daunting was that some of the numbers could not see the light of day. As a rule, the bookkeeper was the lessee's most loyal accomplice, and the shabby-looking bookkeeper in black was no exception. Now Jiansu had a clearer picture of the man, who tried to act mysterious, with liquor dripping from the corners of his mouth, as he spewed out unreliable numbers. Now he realized why the rusty needle had come after him. He pounded the table, as if it were the bookkeeper's skull.

Jiansu slept through the night. Having shrugged off the numerical net, he breathed easily and smoothly. In his dream, he was once again sitting by a liquor vat, where the tender, fair hand of a virgin rested on his hand. He called her name and saw her roll like a ball of fire in the Sui courtyard and, eventually, into Baopu's room. "Brother," he called out in his dream, with tears in the corners of his eyes.

Jiansu went straight for the mill house when he awoke the next day. He could hear the rumbling from a distance as the door to the largest mill gradually came into view. He saw his brother's broad back, and while he was staring he noticed someone in the corner. His heart raced; it was Naonao. She was holding something behind her back; the exposed part glinted, and Jiansu could see that it was a wooden club. He recalled what she'd said at the Wali Emporium about hitting the person in the mill from behind. The blood surged in his body; he wanted to call out to his brother and rush into the room. But with his heart in his throat, he stood there trembling and had a hurried conversation with himself. "Will she do it?" "No." "Yes, she will. She's so wanton." "No, she won't. She loves him." "Look, just look, she's making her move." Jiansu held his breath and instinctively craned his neck to fix his eyes on Naonao. She was still peering in; then she cautiously moved ahead. She crossed the doorsill. She took out the club. She aimed at his head. She raised the club. Jiansu was ready to storm in to stop her when her club landed lightly on Baopu's back.

Jiansu finally exhaled. He saw Baopu turn his head in surprise and glare at Naonao with reproach in his eyes. She was holding the club, which Jiansu saw was actually a stick used to separate the noodles on the drying floor. Naonao laughed as she played with the stick, ignoring Baopu, and Jiansu knew what she had in mind when she walked over to examine the millstone and the gears. She wanted Baopu to pick her up like he had before, but this time he didn't. Instead, he tried to shoo her away from the area; she ignored him. With a laugh she kicked the base of the millstone and, after lingering awhile, left with her eyes downcast.

Baopu sat quietly the whole time she was there, hardly looking at her, it seemed to Jiansu, who wrung his hands unhappily. He looked first at Baopu and then at Naonao, who was by then outside. She was walking slowly, as if dragging the millstone behind her; after a moment she stopped to gaze at the clouds in the distant sky, her hair rustling in the wind. When she turned and ran off, Jiansu strode into the mill.

Baopu was getting up to spread the beans on the conveyor belt. Jiansu stood in the center of the room with his hands in his pants pockets, and when Baopu turned around, he asked, "What was Naonao doing here?"

Brushing off his question, Baopu said, "Just fooling around."

Jiansu shook his head. "I saw her hit you with a club."

Baopu smiled unhappily. "I never go along with her shenanigans. That girl's impossible."

Jiansu laughed. "But she never uses a club on me."

"She will," Baopu teased. "Wait and see."

"If she dares hit me, I'll wrap my arms around her and never let go, the way you hold your wooden ladle," Jiansu said loudly.

Surprised, Baopu looked at his brother. "You'd do that, I know you would."

Jiansu began to pace the room, feeling agitated as he watched the gears whirl. He spun around. "You spend all day here. Do you have any idea what's going on in town?"

"What?"

Jiansu snorted. "You don't know anything. All you know is how to help Duoduo with the spoiled vat. All you do is sit on this stool from dawn to dusk, missing out on everything outside. You suffer and you make others suffer with you. I'd have been happy if Naonao had knocked you out with her club. You can just sit there and ignore what's going on all around you. You wouldn't care if the world outside was turned upside down. You might as well be deaf. You're one of the clan's . . ."

He couldn't bring himself to finish, so Baopu asked, "I'm one of the clan's what?"

"An idiot, that's what!"

His face turning crimson, Baopu moved his lips but did not respond. After a while, Jiansu walked over to the small window and, not seeing anyone outside, returned to Baopu's side. "Duoduo wants to create a Wali glass noodle production and marketing consortium."

"I've heard," Baopu replied.

Amazed by the calm expression on his brother's face, Jiansu cried out, "So you're just going to sit here and watch it happen?" Baopu nodded. Jiansu took a step back and, cracking his knuckles, spat out one word at a time. "I told you before. I'm going to take the factory back from Duoduo. It rightfully belongs to the Sui clan." He was breathing hard; his face had paled by the time he finished.

Baopu stood up and lit a cigarette. "And I've told you it doesn't belong to the Zhao or the Sui family. You can't take it away."

"It rightfully belongs to us, and I'm going to get it."

"You don't have that power, no one does. It belongs to the town of Wali."

Jiansu was so angry he had trouble breathing. He needed a smoke. But he had no sooner taken his tobacco from his pocket than he angrily flung it to the floor. Laying his hand on his brother's chest, Jiansu cried out in a pleading tone, "Brother! Brother! Don't just sit here in this old mill house. Consider the age we're living in. Everyone in the Sui clan has been an upright citizen, and see what's happened to them all these years? You don't move when they put the millstone on your head; instead, you grit your teeth and endure it, until gray hairs sprout on your head. You spend your days here and then go home to eat cold food, with no woman to take care of you. Your courage is the size of a sesame seed. I don't know what you're afraid of losing. You've put up with everything for years and you'll keep doing it. You're so strong only a few people can overpower you. You're a good man and you've never done a single bad deed, yet you let them lord it over you. This old mill is like a coffin and you're going to let it keep you in it. Why don't you stomp your feet, run out, and start a goddamn fire? Our generation cannot afford to be worthless cowards. Yet you knit your brows, not saying a word, and swallow all the wrongs done to you. You worry about yourself and you worry about others. But look what kind of life you've lived all these years. With your talents in noodle production and your character, all you'd have to do is call out softly and a huge group of Wali people would follow you. Duoduo can bring down others, but not you. Think about it. Give it some serious thought. Opportunity doesn't come around often. If we make it, we make it. If we lose, we lose."

Jiansu's excitement rose as he spoke, his burning eyes fixed on Baopu's face. With a nod, Baopu took Jiansu's hand in his own and rubbed it. "I've heard every word you said. But I can't agree with you, not completely, because I think you overestimate my power. I don't have the power to draw a crowd of Wali people, at least not now. Zhao Duoduo's good days won't last, but you've underestimated him."

Jiansu just sneered when his brother finished.

Baopu gave him a meaningful look. Jiansu took his hand back to light his pipe and said, "I didn't tell you that I've checked the factory's accounts, and I've got some ideas. Soon it will be time for the second round of leasing, and Duoduo and I will have to fight it out. I've made up my mind; you just wait and see when the meeting is called. My mind's made up."

TWELVE

Zhang-Wang was in a very good mood. Fourth Master's fleshy back did not feel particularly thick under her massaging fingers. She was pleased, as, it seemed, was he, since he moaned contentedly. When she was done, she pulled away the white sheet covering his lower body to have a look. He had taut muscles and smooth, shiny skin; his body, like his face, had a reddish glow. A pair of thin, loose Chinese-style underpants covered his substantial buttocks. With neither belt nor sash, they were held up by folding over the extra fabric on the waistband, which was a device of hers. Instead of leaving immediately, she ran her hands over his back and slapped him on the buttocks, then went ahead and sat on him. Fourth Master preferred to lie quietly for a while after his massage to enjoy a moment of relaxation. "You've got nerve," he said, prompting her to climb off. But she continued to stroke his back. "You're just a big clay tiger." With a strict regimen of a shower every two days, his body gave off a light, fleshy fragrance. It was a smell that pleased her, exclusive to him and familiar to her over the years.

Convinced that he was Wali's only true champion, she muttered something but got no response. Fourth Master lay with his eyes closed, his nostrils flaring gently with each breath, his belly rising and falling rhythmically. As she watched him, her chin began to twitch, sending her blackened teeth clattering against each other. Annoyed by the noise, he grunted, which shut her up, and sent her over to sit on a corner of the *kang*.

After a moment, she stepped down and shuffled over to the middle of the room, where water was boiling in a kettle atop a kerosene burner; she poured the water into a vacuum bottle. Next she washed two pears and two pomelos that she took from a platter with purple flowers and placed them in a small china dish under a wire net. But she had second thoughts about the pears, so she removed one and returned it to the platter. As a man who was particular about the healthy benefits of food, Fourth Master divided fruits into three categories: neutral, humid and hot, cold and chilly. He never ate persimmons or plums when he felt heat inside, and he only ate oranges, tangerines, and bananas in the fall and winter. Recently he had sensed heat, which she could feel when she massaged his back. So she had chosen cold pears and pomelos but remained attentive to moderation, which was why she had returned one of the pears. Most of the time Fourth Master preferred oranges and tangerines for their neutral quality; he also favored fruit from the south and would not allow anyone to peel it for him. He would slowly separate the meat from the peel, which infused him with a sense of well-being. Given the geographical and climatic uniqueness of the north and south territories, he believed that his spirit would benefit greatly from fruit from the south.

Each year, when cooler weather arrived in the fall, he began a tonic regimen, eating liquor-soaked clams, stewed longans, and a turtle every week. He never overindulged, believing that food was a better tonic than herbs. He greeted every significant snowfall by slowly cooking a duck with ginseng in a clay pot. When it came to trying out new ideas, he preferred Zhang-Wang over his own daughter-in-law, based on trust established over a decade. He had two sons, one a Party secretary with the municipal committee, the other an employee at the county office. Both had wanted their father to move into town but had dropped the subject after he responded curtly, "Shortsighted." So to take care of the old man's needs, the second daughter-in-law gave up living with her husband and moved next door to Fourth Master so she could cook his meals, wash his clothes, and fetch water. With the onset of winter, she also had to get the finest charcoal for his brazier. But she could not take the place of Zhang-Wang, who came each day to make sure everything was to his liking.

Now Zhang-Wang went into the yard to water the garden, in which bees buzzed over the fragrant flowers. A pot of hydrangea was in full bloom, so she moved it inside and sprinkled it so that beads of water dangled on the petals like dew drops. She gazed at the flowers and sighed, her teeth chattering again.

For her, Naonao was the only woman in the town who could rival her younger self, but Naonao's flirtations lacked a bewitching quality. Being frail and in poor health, Zhang-Wang's husband had died early. When he was alive, he'd done little but eat and sleep and had tired easily. Fourth Master had joked, "What kind of man is he!" Zhang-Wang had noticed how powerful a body Fourth Master had when she treated him with moxibustion and massage; her own husband's physique paled in comparison, a mangy dog.

Once, in the midst of a massage, Fourth Master burst out laughing and pushed her down on the *kang;* she sat up, which upset him, and so he grabbed two handfuls of loose skin around her waist, picked her up, and dropped her. She fell painfully hard and could barely move. Pleased, he took her to bed.

Fourth Master once said, "Everything in the world is divided by yin and yang." Zhang-Wang, who took great interest in telling his fortune, told him that he had the rare good fortune to be a wealthy man but not an official. Licking his lips, he said, "That suits me just fine." Shortly after that her husband died, and her sallow face lessened his interest in her—but not as a masseuse.

Nonetheless, he bedded her a few more times. To her, his voice sounded like the roar of a tiger. She had grown familiar with his strong, muscular back and knew what he was thinking most of the time. Without having to ask, she knew which occurrences in town could be attributed to him. She knew, for instance, that he wished his wife, Huan'er, would die soon and that he had given the order to string up Li Qisheng and beat him. She knew it all but kept it to herself, kneading and mixing her secrets into clay tigers and homemade sweets. Eventually, Fourth Master stopped touching her; like a knife that had not been whetted for so long it was rusted through, she seemed covered in dust, her neck always dirty. He expected her to scrub her hands and wear a cap and sleeve covers when she cooked for him, insisting that not a speck of dirt was to be allowed into his stomach. She could picture every part of his body with her eyes closed. During the day, with thoughts of his body on her mind, she stood at the counter and busied herself with the clay tigers to while away time.

On one of those days, she imagined she could see what was inside him: pink intestines fresh like gently moving flowers. Then a dark red snake slithered inside and slowly twisted itself into a knot when it reached his stomach. She cried out; the clay tiger she was holding fell to the floor and smashed to pieces. When she saw him the next day, she said, "You have a worm in your belly."

"Nonsense."

"A long one."

"Enough!" he shouted.

She never brought it up again, believing that he was feeding the snake when he drank tea and liquor or ate his ginseng duck.

After watering the chrysanthemums she was ready to leave when Wattles Wu, principal of Wali Elementary School, walked up. He first looked down at the ground, then adjusted his glasses and noticed Zhang-Wang. "Oh, it's you, Wattles."

He merely squinted, which meant that he was actually laughing, the only person in town who laughed soundlessly. She stomped her foot, he responded with an obscene gesture, and they both left the yard with a smile, one going out, the other coming in.

By then Fourth Master had sat up and was rubbing his eyes. "Is that you, Wattles?" For that was what he called him.

"Yes," Wu replied as he picked up the red clay teapot, placed it on a green platter, and carried it over to the *kang* to make tea. He took off his shoes and climbed onto the *kang,* after moving over a short-legged table with curled ends for the tea set.

The two men sat across from each other, the aroma of the tea wafting in the air around them. Fourth Master sipped the fragrant, light green tea from a red clay cup before taking down a glass case from the windowsill. After putting on his wide-framed eyeglasses, he picked up the thread-bound book Principal Wu had brought him. Once he had found his place, he turned to take advantage of better light and read, "This one, like a newly ripe, unbroken melon in the southern garden . . ."

Wattles Wu laughed, though one would not have known that, making the delicate skin on the sides of his nose twitch.

"It's a good book," Fourth Master said. "I was having tea the other day when I recalled that the phrase I used came from it. Was it hard to find?"

Wattles nodded. "I turned my book trunk inside out but couldn't find it. So I borrowed a copy from a friend."

Fourth Master glanced at him over the top of his glasses before returning to the book. Tapping the edge of the table, he read, "For you she scrubbed her body until it was as white as silver."

Wattles Wu finally laughed out loud. "That's a wonderful passage, just wonderful. I copied it out right after I read it."

Fourth Master removed his glasses, laid down the book, and took a sip of tea. "You can't read *Golden Lotus* too often or you'll get bored. A small edition like this is best. It's filled with terrific passages like that."

Wattles nodded his agreement. "You're right. But *Golden Lotus* also does a fine job when it comes to criticizing people, using lacerating comments that never give you the feeling you need to cover your ears. The author curses so well it actually makes you feel good, like a soft little hand rubbing your heart. How nice. He's so good at criticizing you never get mad. That's a real talent."

Fourth Master laughed, put down his teacup, and patted Wattles on the leg.

Few people were welcome in Fourth Master's little courtyard. Besides Zhang-Wang, Principal Wu was the only frequent visitor, for the two men went back a long time. Fourth Master came from a poor family but had a fine mind. Wattles's father, an old friend of Fourth Master's father, had paid for the boy to attend classes with a private tutor along with Wattles. After completing his studies, Zhao Bing had turned to teaching himself, earning quite a reputation after becoming the leader of Gaoding Street at the conclusion of the land reform campaign. When troubles came, instead of waiting for people to attack him, he shut himself up in his compound to live a quiet life. "I'm just a scholar," he would say to old friends visiting from the city or the county town, "I lack what it takes to be an official during these ridiculous times, and that suits me just fine."

One of the older officials reprimanded him gently, "But as a Party member, you mustn't lose your Party spirit. Have you decided to stop making revolution?"

Zhao Bing smiled. "Not if there's something to revolt against. I stepped aside for others more talented than I, but I'll never be an onlooker when it's time for a revolution. I won't stop working until Communism arrives." The old leader raised his thumb, to which Zhao Bing responded with a wave of his hand. But he was never happy when Director Luan and Secretary Li came to ask his advice. He'd give them his opinion when he felt like it; if not, he'd just wave his hand and say, "You're in charge now, don't ask me." Only Wattles Wu's visit made him truly happy.

The two men drank tea and read erotic novels together, playing chess once in a while. Wattles was a talented calligrapher and an authority on classical essays, so Fourth Master enjoyed the time they spent together. In the winter, when a snowfall turned the world white, they'd stay put on the heated *kang*. Since Fourth Master had an aversion to coal, he used a shiny, copper, smokeless brazier filled with bright red charcoal. On a copper plate by the brazier lay a tiny pair of tongs, with which he added charcoal. The brazier had been a present from Zhao Duoduo years before, and Fourth Master never asked him how he'd obtained it. Beside the brazier were a boiling hot pot and a white ceramic dish filled with chopped ginger, green onions, and sliced meat and fish. There was also a container of white pepper shaped like a gourd.

Since both men preferred spicy food, the tips of their noses were often beaded in sweat as they sat lotus style. Usually Wattles read to Fourth Master, who listened with his eyes closed, as if asleep. "Wonderful!" he'd shout from time to time. Wattles, who considered himself to be the best-educated man in Wali, had a small collection of unusual books, including a tiny copy of *The Analects* that fit in the palm of his hand, a dainty book redolent with the fragrance of ink. Eventually it wound up in the hands of Fourth Master, who could not stop touching it. Given Wattles's talent with a writing brush, Fourth Master often asked for samples of his calligraphy and pasted the best ones up on his wall. "Poor but not toady, wealthy but not arrogant, poor and pursue the Tao, wealthy and favor propriety." "The weird begets the bizarre; the bizarre begets the transient; the transient cannot stand." "The big is not bigger than a palace and the small is not smaller than a feather." And so on. He recited the couplets as he admired them on a daily basis.

Wattles had an inscribed copper ink box and an aged ink block that shone with a purple jadelike luster and gave off a musky, minty aroma. He gave them both to Fourth Master, who knew how to appreciate good calligraphy, though he himself was not particularly good at it. He watched Wu closely as he ground the ink and put his brush in motion. As Wattles ground the ink he would relax, pushing down hard but turning the block around lightly, moving it like the old riverside mills. He seemed invigorated when he picked up the brush, for his body straightened and the veins on his arms popped out. Fourth Master would sigh admiringly. "I've heard that a good calligrapher 'grinds the ink like a sick man' but 'holds his brush like a warrior.' That is how it should be." The two men even learned a formula for good health from the books they studied, until it was second nature.

Fourth Master rose at the crack of dawn each morning. He sat up straight, his eyes closed as he gently knocked his teeth together four-teen times before swallowing three times. Then he took six shallow breaths and crouched like a wolf, with the gaze of a vulture, swaying from right to left. That he did three times before getting off the *kang* and walking into the yard, where he stood still, stamped his feet three times, and raised his arms to shoulder level twice to limber them. Since the key to this formula was persistence, he never missed a day, muttering a formula that both men appreciated and had memorized:

"Energy and essence are of utmost importance, so make sure you keep them well and never lose them. Never lose them, keep them in-side. I'll teach you the way to good health; memorizing the doggerel has great benefit. Expel evil desires and you will find tranquillity; with that you will see bright lights on your way to enlightenment. Watch the bright moon; it has a jade rabbit and the sun has a bird. The turtle and the snake intertwine; the intertwining strengthens your life. You can plant a golden lotus in the fire and accumulate the five elements to use as you please. Once achieved, you can be a Buddha or an im-mortal."

Fourth Master once said to Wattles, "We want only those things that are useful. With good health and a strong will we can make revo-lution."

Wattles laughed soundlessly and replied, "That's the truth."

Their spirits rose as they drank their tea. Wattles kept turning the pages with his slender fingers and laughing soundlessly. "Fourth Mas-ter, you must think this is strange, but for me reading is like eating, and I don't mind the greasy stuff."

Fourth Master nodded. "Every book has evil *qi* and upright *qi*. You prefer the evil."

Wattles mumbled a response as he greedily scanned the pages. After a moment he looked up and said, "Here's a good passage. Very well written. The ancients knew that energy is needed in this regard as well."

Fourth Master put on his glasses and took the book. He snorted when he read the passage.

Wattles slapped his knee. "It truly is a case of 'Jadelike faces appear in the world of books.' "

Taking off his glasses, Fourth Master snorted again. "You used that saying well," he said with a laugh.

Beside himself with glee, Wattles let his head sway from side to side. Then, clenching his teeth, which caused his chin to quiver, he said, "The widow, Xiaokui, it must be hard on her."

Fourth Master looked at him out of the corner of his eye but said nothing.

"I'm more than ten years older than her," Wattles continued. "I spend all my time reading books, and one day a term came to me."

"What was it?"

With a nasal twang, Wattles said, " 'Vicarious treat.' "

Fourth Master didn't get it at first, but then he laughed so hard he had a coughing fit. Patting Wattles's knee, he said, "Wattles, why don't you practice one of your 'vicarious treats'? Ha ha ha."

With a red face, Wattles wiped his nose and reached for the teapot. After a sip he asked, "When was the last time your foster daughter came by?"

Fourth Master stopped laughing and stared at Wattles. "Hanzhang is a filial girl," he said. "She never makes me wait. She comes on her own. I don't have to summon her."

Wattles smacked his lips and repeated, "A filial girl, that's for sure."

The mention of Hanzhang seemed to displease Fourth Master, for he put the book away. But after going outside to relieve himself, he perked up when he was back on the *kang*. He asked Wattles to find a lighter book to read, having been reminded of the novel *Flowers in the Mirror*, which he'd only heard about, when he was examining the hydrangeas Zhang-Wang had placed in the center of the room. He asked Wattles to read the passage where the Flower Fairy describes the principles of flower blooming.

So Wu dug through the chest by Fourth Master's *kang* and found the book he was looking for. He cleared his throat and read, beginning with the passage where Chang'e, the Moon Lady, suggests that Flower Fairy order all the flowers to bloom at once.

Fourth Master snorted unhappily, so Wattles moved on to recite a witty remark by the Flower Fairy. Fourth Master raised his hand to slow him down and then closed his eyes to enjoy the passage to the fullest. "Excellent!" he shouted approvingly when he heard "There is so much variety among all the peonies, of orchids in the spring and chrysanthemums in the autumn, with every leaf and every blossom determined in advance, some early, others late, according to the plan."

Thinking the praise was intended for him, Wattles redoubled his effort. He held the book in his left hand and rested his right hand on the side of the page with his index finger curled on top of the thumb as if prepared to flick something away. He held his head high, slightly lower in the back, his forehead remaining still as he moved with the rhythms of his recitation, though the back of his head swayed slightly. He was reluctant to read the last few words from the Flower Fairy too fast, and his voice got heavier as he slowly enunciated each word: "Moon Lady's words were like a declaration of war." He dragged out the last syllable as his right index finger finally got a chance to flick. Then he put down the book to wipe the sweat from his face and neck with an oversized white handkerchief until his wattles were steamy red.

Fourth Master sat quietly with his hands on his belly and his eyes shut. Opening them to look at Wattles, he coughed softly and said, "What a wonderful book. You can savor it a hundred times and get a different flavor each time. We mortals get to see what it's like to be an immortal when we read about their affairs. You see, isn't it wonderful for two old men to be drinking tea and reading books? I was just thinking that it was our great good fortune to be eating well, dressing nicely, and acting powerfully, but these are not hard to come by. These easily attainable things are what are called "coarse fortunes." What's hard is to be able to communicate with soundless objects and gain pleasure from flowers, plants, books, and music. You must have a peaceful mind and a fine temperament. These are hard to obtain and are called 'refined fortunes.' Fortune, like the grains, has both coarse and refined, and only having both can bring longevity. This is what I've been thinking: There are a thousand ways to live. Just how many do the two of us know? Over the past few decades, these are the kinds of things I've been thinking about." Wattles was moved by Fourth Master's words, and his admiration showed that he would never be Fourth Master's equal.

Fourth Master continued, "What Flower Fairy said about the flowers is actually the utmost principle of life, that is, propriety, the rule for everything. Wali exists within the rules of propriety, doesn't it? Nothing good can come from a lack of propriety. Just see what happens in the novel, where a trivial matter like flowers blooming in the right season evolves into a story of turning the cosmos upside down. So you know you must not oppose propriety and that everyone in town must attend to it as well. Zhang-Wang's job is to sell homemade sweets and clay tigers, Zhao Duoduo's is to run the noodle factory, and Guo Yun's is to take care of the sick. The Sui clan had several generations of prosperity until their fortunes ran out, which is why they have only bachelors left. These are all aspects of propriety; you get things done if you follow the rules, and you will come to no good end if you act willfully. There are yin and yang; they complement and balance each other—you know that better than I. Take the two leaders of Gaoding Street for example. Luan Chunji has a hot temper but he's very decisive, while Li Yuming is a good man, but he dithers. With the two of them in charge, it's like cooking meat with alternating high and low heat; you end up with a mushy meal. Then there's Zhao Duoduo, who is bold and daring but often goes too far and loses touch with propriety. I've talked to him about this many times, but it's useless, though with him around, there are fewer people to turn their backs on propriety, so it's actually a blessing for our town. Zhao is the only one who will suffer the consequences, since, as someone who always overdoes things, he will not come to a good end."

Fourth Master rubbed his hands and sighed with sadness over his prediction. Wattles stared at him, considering the speculation concerning Duoduo's future. Fourth Master reached for his teacup and took a sip. "Now the tea has gotten better."

Wattles poured a cup and took a sip. "Drinking tea with Fourth Master is like watching a battle with a strategist who points out only the main tactics so that nothing is ruined."

Fourth Master snorted and said, "The first round energizes, the second flavorizes. That is common sense. With this kind of tea, you must wait for the third round to get flavor at its peak." Wattles nodded as Fourth Master continued, "We must take the long view when it comes to propriety in Wali. Back to the Sui clan, who, in its heyday, was the number one family in all the river towns and could rival the most powerful families in the province. Half the boats moored at the pier were there to transport beans and noodles for them. But were they happy? No. Sui Hengde, Sui Yingzhi, and now Sui Baopu are all good at management, but no one can save the Sui clan. What the ancients said, that 'no one can hold on to a household of gold and jade,' could not be truer. Who has the talent to keep a whole house of gold and jade?" He smiled as he rubbed his shiny bald head. "It's also a matter of propriety that I do not choose to be an official. The ancients have said that the way of the world demands that one step down after the work is done. It was my job to help out when Wali was undergoing land reform and the Great Leap Forward. Now that's done and I have stepped down. Isn't that the way to go?"

Pleased by his own words, Fourth Master burst out laughing. Wattles laughed too, but soundlessly; he was thinking how rare it was to see Zhao Bing laugh like that. Still happy, Fourth Master turned around and took a copper pot from a small chest at the head of the *kang*. He asked Wu to pick out a liquor, so Wu chose two bottles of Tsingtao Beer and, moving the Maotai away, located a bottle of Shaoxing rice wine with a red satin ribbon around the neck. Fourth Master smiled and nodded his approval, so Wu heated up the pot in the center of the room before bringing it over to the table, along with some meat, minced ginger, and green onions. The two men carefully blanched the meat in the boiling liquid and cheerfully enjoyed the hot pot.

Their foreheads were beaded in sweat when they heard a noise at the gate. Without looking up, Fourth Master slapped his knee and said, "My foster daughter's here."

Wattles quickly laid down his cup and looked up. Tossing the liquor down, he put the book under his arm and stood up, just as Hanzhang walked in. She seemed to be cold, for she put her hands over the pot after glancing at Wu quietly. "Fourth Master," she called out softly, but got no response from Fourth Master, who turned and took out a pair of chopsticks and a bowl. With the book under his arm, Wattles went to one of the side rooms to read. With her head slightly lowered, Hanzhang sat down in the spot he had vacated. Fourth Master added some charcoal, sending sparks flying. "I'm here to tell you that this is my last visit," Hanzhang said. "I didn't want to tell you that, but then I thought, I've been your 'foster daughter' for two decades." She stressed the words "foster daughter." Holding his tongue, Fourth Master reached out to stir the meat with his chopsticks and picked a cooked slice to place in her dish.

"I know," he said.

"You do?"

"Yes."

Surprised, she stared at him. He took a drink and put the other cup in her hand. She took a sip. "I know everything. I'm nearly sixty, so how can I not know? I knew that my foster daughter would one day stop coming because she knows exactly what she's doing. I know I've turned my back on propriety and that I will not come to a good end. I've been afraid of the gate opening up to let you in. I'd hoped you would never show up again, for that would have brought me salvation, but now here you are again. I have taken things too far and I will not enjoy a good end. The ancients have said that one is to take measure before a problem arises. One ought to take preventive measures, but that is not going to happen now, and I have no way of avoiding disaster. Go ahead, Hanzhang, do what you came to do. I've been waiting, knowing I would come to a bad end."

As she listened, the chopsticks in her hands began to quiver and she dropped the slice of meat onto the table. "I knew it," he said, "I just knew it." Her complexion had always been nearly transparent, and now it was turning blue, as if the skin had been assaulted by the cold.

"I wasn't thinking about anything else!" she screamed. "I just don't want to be here anymore. I'm here to tell you that."

Fourth Master laughed a sinister laugh. "But you're here, and you wouldn't be here if you really hadn't wanted to come. You don't have to tell me. As I said, I know everything. You, you must have given this a lot of thought and you want it to end badly. Let me tell you. I've been thinking of this for two years, but I haven't done a thing to stop it. I just let nature take its course. I thought that heaven had come to my aid when you didn't show up for two weeks. Who could have predicted that you would come again? Now I know that I will never be able to escape. So, do what you have to do."

Hanzhang stared at him blankly, with the knowledge that she could hide nothing from those bright, insightful eyes, which were now slowly sweeping the room. He was right; she had given lots of thought to so much. She had thought of that dark night more than twenty years ago, and thought of what had happened after that, and why she was so agitated all the time. The event that Fourth Master called "the end" was a result of that night. She trembled, as she did every time she thought of that night. "That dark night! That . . . night!" she said over and over to herself. It had all started on that night.

Her older brother and Jiansu had been taken away by the rebel troops, leaving her alone in the house. The members of the Sui clan were not allowed to wear Red Guard armbands, so her brothers had put on homemade bands, which were ripped off by Red Guards dressed in khaki. She'd picked them up and smoothed them out. It was dark outside and the dogs were barking. Invincible Fighters and

Jinggangshan Army Corps, the town's two largest rebel organizations, were having a war of words via megaphones. She had no idea which group had taken her brothers. The door was kicked open just as she was smoothing out the armbands, and in rushed a group of people. "Come with us, Miss Capitalist Running Dog." They pushed and dragged her out, while others sealed off the house with strips of paper. She was taken into a basement.

Without looking up, Zhao Duoduo, who was warming himself at a brazier, asked, "Got her?"

One of the men shoved her forward. "Mission accomplished, Commander."

Duoduo waved them away before dragging the trembling Hanzhang up close and sizing her up. "You stinking capitalist. You think you're better than us, don't you?" With a sinister laugh, he reached out and pinched her breast. She screamed and ran to the door, but he easily blocked her way. Then he knocked her to the floor. She started to cry and stood up, but he knocked her down again. He sneered. "Don't even think about running away. The revolutionary masses can bring you down with ease." She was still crying. "I think of your mother whenever I see you," he continued. "She was really something. Now you must come clean." He sat down to warm himself again but kept an eye on her.

It must have been midnight when Duoduo undid his pants and faced her to relieve himself. When she turned her face, he shuffled over and shouted, "You must come clean." When she backed into a corner, he pushed up against her, nearly suffocating her and extracting an ear-splitting scream. He flung her to the floor by her hair and, muttering to himself, lay down next to her, just as the basement opened with a loud crash; it was Fourth Master. Zhao rose up into a crouch and froze. Hanzhang stood up tearfully. The muscles on Fourth Master's face twitched as he walked up and knocked Zhao to the floor. When Zhao tried to get up, Fourth Master put him down again. This time Zhao stayed down. Then Fourth Master took Hanzhang by the hand and led her out of the basement, all the way to his house.

That was how it started. He took her home, washed her face, and combed her hair with his fingers. Then he made her some soup with vegetables and meat before cleaning out a room for her, telling her to make herself at home and not to go to her own home until things calmed down outside. No one would dare touch her at his place. She was worried about her brothers, so a few days later he found a way to have them released.

In all, Hanzhang spent more than six months in that room, watering the flowers daily. She ate with Zhao Bing and was never hungry again. In six months, she'd grown into a young woman. She cried when it was time to leave, once things had calmed down in town, saying that she owed him everything and would do anything to repay his kindness. He pulled a long face and said, "What nonsense. We live in the same town and you're like my own daughter. Come see me whenever you can, especially during the holidays." That was how she became his foster daughter. She left with six yards of colorful fabric. Over the years that followed, she came to see him often, and when she came, nothing changed: She did a little work around the house and watered the flowers. On holidays she came with presents. Touching her hair and patting her on the back, he praised her. "What a good girl."

Four years after leaving Fourth Master's house, Hanzhang turned eighteen and looked almost exactly like her dead mother. With thin eyebrows, a tall figure, and a willowy waist, she turned all the young men in town into clumsy oafs when she passed by. Without a care in the world, she proudly and happily went around town, displaying her full breasts and rounded hips; sometimes, when she was in a particularly good mood, she showed up at Fourth Master's house.

Early one evening, while she was watering the flowers, he looked up from a book as he lay on the *kang* and said, "Bring in a nice vase of flowers."

Happily complying, she brought the vase in, placed it on the *kang*, took off her shoes, and set the vase on the windowsill. When she bent over, Fourth Master's hand landed on her back and found its way under her clothes, as if searching for something. It found her breast and held it. Her face was burning as she cried out in panic. He took her into his arms, all but swallowing her up with a body as big as a mountain. She was trembling uncontrollably as he touched every part of her body. The mountain changed into flesh and fell on her, nearly suffocating her. "Fourth Master," she pleaded, "let me go. You're my foster father. Please let me go."

With a steady voice he said, "You're a good girl. You've always been a good girl."

It started on that dark night; without it, she would not have lived in his house and would not have had a foster father. Her eighteenth birthday had passed. What kind of day had it been? She had been shocked by the sight of Fourth Master's bare bottom. Her heart was bleeding. With her eyes closed, she endured the pain and the suffering, and seemed to see her blood turning the world red and flowing into the Luqing River. She later learned that Fourth Master had been secretly protecting her family for years. Without him, her brothers would have been struggled against till they died, and she'd have lost her virginity even earlier. She understood everything now. Did she hate her family's protector? Did she love him? She cried and cried until she exhausted herself.

Hanzhang opened her eyes after Fourth Master pinched the space between her nose and lips. "Come visit your foster father when you can," he said. She dried her eyes and walked out. That is how her eighteenth birthday ended; afterward, she refused to leave the Sui compound and was terrified at the thought of going to Fourth Master's flower-filled yard. But then Zhao Duoduo brought people over to harass them again. Baopu was often roused at midnight and taken to the militia headquarters for abuse. Through the window, Hanzhang could see her brother with his bent back and felt her heart bleed again. In the end, she went back to see her foster father. And life went on, year after year. He praised her in front of other people, saying what a good girl she was. She began to lose weight and her skin turned so transparent she could see the dark green veins underneath, which startled her at first. She asked Fourth Master what was wrong with her veins; he told her it was all right, just nourishment from male essence, which convinced her. As she grew more lethargic, she finally realized she was sick.

On moonlit nights she sat at the window, staring at the shadowy streets. Sometimes she heard Baopu pacing in the yard and thought he might be aware of her problem and worry about her. She did not dare look him in the eyes. Lying in bed quietly, she felt her heart rent by an insufferable pain. How she wished she could lock herself up in the house and see no one. Sometimes, when she left the drying floor, she felt lost, and at those moments it seemed that Fourth Master's house was the only place for her. He may have been a demon, but he was a man whose powerful limbs and neck, rough hands, even his broad hips, all displayed an invincible masculine beauty. Endowed with boundless energy, and not one to lose his composure, he exploited her to the fullest. Silently counting her days in his room, her heart was assaulted by a range of lacerating emotions: humiliation, thirst, longing, hatred, compulsion, anger, and desire.

Fourth Master had ruined her, leaving her with nothing but a pitiful hint of sexual desire. She had brought the final disgrace to the Sui clan—a humiliating thought. She clenched her teeth and waited, without knowing what she was waiting for. One day she felt the urge to see Fourth Master, but she paced her room, unable to leave. She was looking for something; finally her gaze landed on a small pair of scissors she used for weaving braids from cornstalk tassels. Her eyes lit up as she grabbed them—they felt like ice in her hand. She cried out and the scissors fell to the floor, but instead of picking them up, she just stared at them for a moment and then walked out of the room empty-handed. But from that moment on, she knew what she was waiting for: to kill the patriarch of the Zhao clan. When the idea sprouted, it took on a life of its own. Several times she held the scissors in her hand, but they invariably fell to the floor before she left the room.

Fourth Master's large eyes were glued to her as he took another sip. "I know what you're thinking. The end is near."

Despite herself, Hanzhang trembled, but she kept murmuring, "That dark night. That . . . night." A wishful thought emerged during her murmuring, that Fourth Master meant something else by "the end." Or maybe he had not guessed what she was thinking. "What is . . . 'the end'?" she asked.

Fourth Master crossed his arms and his body shrank back in on itself. "You'll kill me," he replied.

She shrieked, threw herself to the table, and began to cry, rolling her head in her arms, writhing, her shoulders heaving violently. "Hanzhang," he called to her, but she kept crying. It's over, she was thinking, it's all over. He knows everything; he's thought of everything. Her cries turned to wails; she was wailing for herself and for the whole Sui clan. Her wails, which seemed about to bring the house down, eventually drew the attention of Wattles Wu in the other room. He stuck his head in through the window but quickly pulled it back. Hanzhang was still crying, her body sliding down from the table to the *kang;* tears drenched her hair and crisscrossed the nearly transparent skin of her face before flowing down her neck.

Fourth Master finally could take it no longer and reached out to hold her. He sighed as he looked into a cold, beautiful face, washed clean by her tears. After drying her tears with his fingers, he wiped them on his shirt until she finally stopped crying. In measured tones, he said, "Child, I know why you're crying. But while you're crying on the outside, I'm sobbing on the inside, anticipating the end. I've been waiting for it for years, knowing it is what I deserve. Sometimes I look back to that year, when you were eighteen, truly like a fresh flower or fine jade, and I was in my forties, still full of vitality. It may not have been right for either of us, but at least the yin and yang matched and violated no law of nature. But now here I am, in my sixties, and at this rate, it has nearly become a perversion. When you take things to an extreme, you abandon all claims of propriety. Confucius once said that you can do whatever you please so long as you don't transgress. That's what I mean. The problem is, I still have so much vitality and male essence; how could it end well? But I have no reason to complain. I'm a contented man. Who am I anyway? A dirt-poor Wali bachelor. And you, you're a young woman of the Sui clan, the town's beauty. I will die with no regrets, and am waiting for the end to arrive. I was glad when you didn't come. I thought you'd hardened your feelings and decided to stay away. But I would have gotten off too easily that way. And then the door opened and you were here again. Now I realize that I cannot escape; it's a matter of when, not if. But I want to talk with you more before the end arrives. Don't think I'm lying; a dying man does not lie. I treat you like a treasure, the only one in my life. I cherish you. That's all I have to say."

He fondled and patted her as he talked, and when he finished, he held her face in his hands to kiss her. As he caressed her, he said softly, "Hanzhang." She stirred weakly in his arms. "Hanzhang, I should have told you earlier that the end had arrived. We don't have much time left. Don't be afraid. It will be just like before. Now sit up and have a drink. The hot pot is just right." He helped her up and drew the curtains before going over to latch the door. Feeling thirsty from all that crying, she dipped her spoon into the soup. She drank the boiling soup carefully and began to sweat. Fourth Master snorted and pushed the table away, grabbed her buttocks, and lifted her over to his side. With a satisfied moan, he smoothed her hair, moving up closer before gently laying her down and making a series of happy, cooing moans, as if playing with a kitten. As he sat there looking at her, he ran his big hand down her neck, steamy heat rising from his bare chest.

They heard Wattles Wu's loud, confident recitation beyond the window. "Indistinct and hazy, it cannot be pictured. Hazy and indistinct, it cannot be bent. Dark and gloomy, it has no shape; deep and cavernous, it does not move. It spreads and unfolds with the rough and the gentle, falling and rising with the yin and the yang."

Ignoring the recitation, Fourth Master bent over to study the dark blue veins on Hanzhang's skin; he didn't move.

Wattles Wu's voice rose and fell rhythmically, reaching a crescendo. "It is minute and deep, so it can see tiny things. It extends endlessly, so it is wondrous. Its height can reach the sky and its vastness can cover the four corners of the earth. It is bright as the sun and the moon; it is fast as lightning. It sparkles quickly and the sight is gone; it floats like meteorites; it flickers like water in a deep chasm; it mists up and floats on the clouds."

Fourth Master pressed down on two of Hanzhang's dark veins, watching them bulge under the skin. When he let go, the blood quickly flowed away. He bent down and kissed her body.

THIRTEEN

The first person to see Sui Buzhao return to Wali was the eccentric Shi Dixin, who was carrying a manure basket on his hoe at the foot of the town wall. Horse carts did not pass by here, and out of respect for the ancient wall, people never relieved themselves within a hundred meters of it. And so the old eccentric's manure basket was invariably empty. He had conjured up a new thought after Sui Buzhao went to the city to see the ancient ship: Sui Buzhao would die soon. It was not a crazy idea, since owing to tradition, one does not leave home in old age. For if an old man dies far from home his bones will be buried in an alien place. Now that there were more people and animals on the road, Sui Buzhao, bedroll on his back, would keep getting his legs all tangled up, and he would be lucky to return alive. So as to verify his premonition, the old eccentric either lingered in the area around the wall or climbed on top to keep his eyes peeled.

On this particular late afternoon, as he looked directly into the sunset, he saw Sui Buzhao stumbling toward him. "Oh, no! The man with the bad karma still lives." Shi Dixin jumped down off the wall, struggling to keep from shouting.

Sui Buzhao came up to the man, who threw down his manure basket and stood there holding his hoe threateningly. The wall was bathed in sunset colors; no one else was in sight, just sweaty Sui Buzhao, who looked up abruptly and spotted Shi and his hoe, glinting in the sun's dying rays. The sweat poured down Buzhao's face. Two pairs of eyes were locked on each other. The old eccentric bit his lower lip as he slowly raised the hoe over his head. Buzhao stuck out his neck and stared at it, like a rooster in midcrow. The hoe shook a time or two and then arced quickly down, bit into the ground, and kicked up a chunk of dirt. Releasing his lip from between his teeth, Shi cursed, "A . . . traitor!"

Then the old eccentric fell in behind Sui Buzhao as he walked into town, figuring that Sui must be bringing lots of outlandish things home, like that earlier time, when he'd returned from sailing the seas. What bothered him was why the heavens hadn't wiped him off the face of the earth. There had been plenty of opportunities.

Sui Buzhao quickly drew a crowd; the questions virtually flew at him. With a hearty laugh and an unintelligible shout, he jumped up onto a raised earthen platform, where he announced: "You people will never guess where they've put that old ship or what it looks like. They're calling it a treasure and they've put it in a big building in the provincial capital. They've replaced all the boards that rotted away and set it up on an impressive painted metal stand inside a chained-off area to keep people away. On a white wooden plaque they spell out when, where, and how the keel was found and excavated, and what dynasty it belonged to. It's been on display for more than twenty years already, and people still stream in to look at it. All those bearded foreigners try to take pictures of it, but they're stopped by the handsome young guides whose job it is to protect it. It underwent numerous chemical treatments after being moved to the capital, so the offensive odor we smelled when it was first dug up is gone and has been replaced by a fresh scent."

The crowd encircled Sui Buzhao, surprised, but generally pleased, by what he was telling them. Then he pointed at them and said, "Our ship is in the provincial capital, where even foreigners go to see it. But not the people from where it was found. More than twenty years. The person in charge said that it moans in the middle of the night, obviously homesick. In more than twenty years nobody from here has gone to see it. We're unworthy of that ship. So I got down on my knees and kowtowed to it. Then I talked the man in charge into letting me go up and touch it, the first time he'd let anyone do that. It shuddered as soon as my finger got close to it, and it shook when I touched it. I broke down and cried. 'Old ship,' I said, 'you have to accept that the people who live in Wali are disloyal and unfilial. But they haven't had the time to do anything about that. First, it was all that work involved in innovations and backyard furnaces to smelt iron; after that came the famine, and no one could travel. Not long after the people managed to eat well enough to get on the road, the Red Guards came to power, and they installed machine guns on the town wall.' When the people around me heard my tragic tale they cried along with me. Even the foreigners, whose tears were green. 'But that's all in the past,' I said. 'Now that the people of Wali can breathe easier, it's time for me to take you home, where you belong. Uncle Zheng He is no longer with us, so I'll take care of you, even if I am just a common sailor. After I die, Zhichang can watch over you.' 'We can't let you do that,' the people in charge said, so I left, still shedding tears."

The crowd voiced their astonishment; foreigners' tears and ship's moans in the middle of the night had them scratching their heads. One of the younger ones could not keep silent: "What else is new and interesting in the city?" he asked.

"All sorts of things," Sui Buzhao replied, casting off his gloom. "The young men and women wear tight-fitting jeans; neon lights flash in the dance halls, where they go to jump around and dance without touching each other. For two jiao you can see an erotic film that's a hundred times better than those peep shows we've seen. They've got martial arts movies with great fights. The man can't beat the woman, and the women lose to strange old guys. One time, instead of fighting, a naked man came out . . ." The crowd laughed. But then someone spat loudly, and when people turned to look, there was the old eccentric, glaring hatefully at Sui Buzhao.

Jiansu, who was in the crowd, came up to take his uncle's arm and relieve him of the bundle on his back. Nothing interested Jiansu more than what was happening in the city, so he couldn't wait to get his uncle home. Slowly the crowd dispersed, but the old eccentric never took his eyes off the two men; the hoe in his hand quivered in the fading sunset.

Li Zhichang, unwilling to be seen in public at the time, did not go to see Sui Buzhao. His face was seared by the flames of passion. Buzhao had not been gone long when Li Qisheng's madness struck again, and Zhichang was kept so busy going for the doctor and buying medicine that he was spent. His father finally lay quietly on the *kang,* the skin on his face hanging slack. Li Zhichang was so involved in nursing his father back to health he had no time for thoughts of Hanzhang; but then he took a break from his duties, and the flames burned anew. He was forced to go see Baopu in the mill, who could do nothing but point at the variable gears and bring up the issue of mechanization of the noodle factory. And so, instead of having the fires of love quenched, a new type of flame began to burn. At night he saw a series of golden gears whirling in the air and the beautiful Hanzhang spinning them with her slender fingers, one after the other, as they began to slow down. In a matter of days, Zhichang's hair fell out in clumps and what little he had left was lusterless. His eyes were as big as bells; his cheekbones protruded sharply. Baopu tried to console him, but nothing seemed to work, and their conversations invariably returned to the subject of Hanzhang.

Li Zhichang said that Hanzhang was waiting for him, he was sure of that. So he would keep waiting for her, never waver. That surprised Baopu, who wondered if his sister had made a promise or given some indication of her feelings. He decided to get to the bottom of this. And what he learned was there had been neither a promise nor a sign, nothing at all. Disappointed, he sighed. Thoughts of his sister's marital situation always depressed him. He was capable of accepting whatever befell him, but he could not accept anything bad happening to the youngest member of the Sui clan.

Then, in a tremulous voice, Li Zhichang revealed his dream. One night, he said, he dreamed that a tall, slim, beautiful girl was imprisoned in an abandoned fortresslike mill, never seeing the light of day, the color fading from her cheeks. Green moss grew on the ground all around where she sat, rising up over her knees. He looked in through a crack in the doorway, and she seemed familiar and unfamiliar at the same time. Her cold gaze never wavered, but when he was about to leave, she looked right at him. It was this look that told him who she was. "Hanzhang!" he shouted at the top of his lungs. A white mist swallowed up everything. The sun was out.

Baopu pondered the dream. "You went to see Hanzhang right after you woke up, didn't you?" he asked.

Li Zhichang nodded. "I called her name, but she wouldn't answer. I actually thought about smashing her window with my fist . . ."

Baopu looked at him with alarm but said nothing. He was thinking about that stormy night when lightning had struck the tree of heaven, when Xiaokui had held his feverish hand in hers; his neck felt hot. "Don't think like that," he muttered, "don't . . . it was a dream."

"So what am I supposed to do, just try to bear it? Well, I can't, not another day."

Baopu shook his head. "No," he said, "you should hurry up and work on the gears. There are so many important things for you to do. Go see Technician Li of the surveyor team. You once said you can't stop. Have you forgotten?"

When he heard that, he couldn't help himself. "I don't want to stop," he insisted. "I think about those gears day and night! Somebody else is forcing me to stop!"

"Who's forcing you?" Baopu demanded.

Zhichang's lips quivered as he blurted out, "The Sui clan!"

Baopu could hardly believe his ears. So Li Zhichang told him what Jiansu had said that midautumn night as he stood on the concrete platform on the noodle-drying ground, and of Sui Buzhao's ambiguous words. Holding his head in his hands, he said, "Suddenly I realized that I was working for Zhao Duoduo, but in light of all the Sui clan has done for me, I ought to listen to you. You know, I don't think I could keep on living if I had to stop working on my gears, and I say a silent prayer that the noodle factory will change ownership and the Sui clan will be in charge again. I say that prayer a lot."

With a look of indifference, Baopu turned and spread the beans with his ladle, then sat on his stool and lit a cigarette. "Don't be like that," he said. "The noodle factory belongs neither to Zhao Duoduo nor to the Sui clan; you should know that. As an intelligent man, you need to take the long view and keep one thing in mind: You must keep working on the gears."

With a blank look in his eyes as he gazed at this member of the Sui clan, Li Zhichang pondered what had been said to him as he walked out of the mill. It was, he felt, time to visit Sui Buzhao again and see what he had to say. When he reached the old man's room, he peeked in through the window and saw Sui reading aloud from his copy of the ancient *Classic of the Waterway.* "There are three or four oxtail reefs just below the hull, so don't sail over them; better to sail between them."

Li Zhichang decided not to call out to him. Instead, he leaned up against the window and listened to the old man recite his baffling phrases.

✐

In the wake of the disastrous spoiled vat, Zhao Duoduo often woke with a start in the middle of the night and reached out to touch the cleaver on his windowsill. He spent many nights roaming the processing room, carefully examining every corner. He could hardly contain himself when he thought about the machinery for the noodle production line. Once the marketing company was created, mass production would be the goal, but only if the machinery was up and running. He was well aware that Crackpot was a key individual but someone he despised. So he went to see Li Zhichang, who always equivocated. Then one day, he kept his feelings in check and went to the surveying team to find Crackpot, who told him that Comrade Zhichang was in charge and all he could do was lend his support. So Duoduo went back and tried to get Zhichang moving.

Li Zhichang, eyes bloodshot, mouth dry, tongue-tied, took out a sheet of paper and a pencil as he looked at Duoduo.

"Where do things stand with the gears?" Duoduo asked, an angry edge to his voice.

Li Zhichang responded by drawing a single line on the paper.

"Will they be installed this year?"

Li Zhichang added two circles to the paper.

"Are those supposed to be gears?" Duoduo asked as he pointed to the circles.

Li Zhichang nodded.

"What's wrong, can't you talk?" Duoduo asked angrily.

"I can," Li replied, "but a drawing works better."

"The Li clan produces only freaks," Duoduo said as he turned to leave. "I don't care how much it costs, just get it done! The factory will pay for it."

Without a word, Li Zhichang crumpled the paper and tossed it into the corner.

Night after night, Li Zhichang kept Sui Buzhao company, often with Baopu and Technician Li, who asked Buzhao about the old ship and about the city. After repeating himself many times, Buzhao was getting tired of all the questions and was running out of answers. But when Technician Li asked him about the ancient country of Donglaizi, he perked up. According to the man in charge of the ship exhibit, he told them, Donglaizi had had a great many warships, and it was possible that the pier at Wali had once been one of their eastern naval ports. But as fewer battles were fought, military affairs shifted to the west and this naval port was transformed into a commercial one.

"Was the excavated ship one of Donglaizi's?" Baopu asked.

"No." The old man shook his head. "It's from a much later period. This is one that Uncle Zheng He and I sailed . . ." When the conversation reached this point it was time to quit. But Sui Buzhao wasn't finished. "The best person to ask about Donglaizi is Guo Yun the healer. We're all from Donglaizi. There's one thing in the town's history that needs to be corrected, and that is, everyone in Wali is a citizen of Donglaizi. Ah, when Li Xuantong died, that left only Guo Yun who could talk of the ancient past."

"What about the school principal, Wattles Wu?" Zhichang said. "He can talk about it too."

With a snort, Sui Buzhao said, "Him? His is a heretical past."

Silence set in, and before long, the strains of Gimpy's flute came through the night, so piercing it sounded like someone raising forsaken cries into the cold air. Baopu looked up and listened closely. The corners of his mouth twitched.

Sui Buzhao pointed to the window. "Gimpy is playing the bachelor's song. The sound of his flute will change the day he gets married."

Baopu shook his head. "Him? Married? I don't think so."

Sui Buzhao laughed. "Everyone has a trick up his sleeve. He can have whatever he wants, thanks to that flute of his. And that includes a wife."

Li Zhichang listened quietly to the conversation, his mind wandering back to his golden wheels and to Hanzhang, who reached out with her slender fingers to spin the wheels. She and the wheels merged until they were inseparable. Zhichang dreamed of wrapping his arms around them and holding them tight. In the end, with the other three men as his audience, he repeated how Jiansu had given him that order during the Midautumn Festival, direct and unfeeling: He must wait. That was the night he realized the seriousness of what confronted him. It was a critical moment for the Li clan; the time had come to choose between the two contenders for power, either the Zhao or the Sui. What was he to do? What could he do? He spread his hands in a gesture of frustration. Sui Buzhao glanced over at Baopu but said nothing. Technician Li lit a cigarette and paced the floor, stopping occasionally at the window. Then, unexpectedly, he strode to the center of the room and announced emotionally, "The time has come, we must get moving with the gears!"

The others' heads shot up as Technician Li reached out to Li Zhichang and said, "Did people wait to make the first telephone? The first atomic bomb? The first man-made satellite? No! Not for any of those! So why should people wait to work on something so small as a set of gears? Comrade Zhichang, you must boldly fulfill your responsibility to science. Science is truth, and truth is light. Darkness fears the light. What in the world are you afraid of? Face the future and move forward."

Technician Li lowered his arm and shoved his hand into his pocket. Li Zhichang cast a questioning glance at Sui Buzhao, who said, "Like sailing a ship, you must keep moving forward."

Notes from the bachelor's song on the flute bounced in on the night air, creating a mixture of nostalgia and fear in the listeners. Gimpy's hair was a mess, his face gray with a purple tinge as he sat on the floodplain playing his flute. The melody was there some of the time and gone some of the time, a sign that it would live or die with the town of Wali. The four men in the room had stopped talking as they concentrated on the strains of the flute and drew their bodies inward, as if the music made the night air colder.

"The sound of that flute reminds me of Dahu," Li Zhichang said. "I saw his mother burning spirit money by the wall a couple of days ago. There were also some snacks, including sorghum candy."

"How many of the 'seventh days' did she burn the spirit money?" Baopu asked. "I should probably buy more for her."

Li Zhichang shook his head.

"We need to wait for official word that he was killed in battle," Technician Li said. "So far all we have is unreliable word of mouth. Some people even deny that it's true."

"Do you mean Dahu isn't dead?" Li Zhichang asked, stunned by the news.

"No, he's dead, all right," Technician Li said with a wave of his hand. "But the latest report has it that he died less than two weeks ago, which is not what we heard at first."

Sui Buzhao fell weakly onto the *kang*. The mere mention of Sui Dahu was more than he could take. His was a grievous loss for the Sui clan. Not all that many years before, Dahu might have gone to sea with Buzhao, who had asked everyone he could how Dahu had died. But they were so far from the front that any news they received was in an occasional letter that had made so many stops along the way it could not be considered reliable. The one thing everyone agreed on was that Dahu had died, which nearly broke Sui Buzhao's heart. If the Sui clan was to lose someone, it should have been him, with his old bones, not a young man who couldn't even grow a beard. Dahu had rushed to the end of his life before he'd had a chance to do so many things. He had died before he'd had a chance to know a woman, but maybe the latest news was inaccurate. If Dahu were still alive, Sui Buzhao was thinking, the youngster would have much to tell him. After seeing Dahu off, the town had paid no more attention to him, like seeing a ship sail away. Tears glistened in the old man's eyes as he lay there spent.

Li Zhichang chose this time to once again bring up Star Wars. He asked Crackpot to explain the difference between NATO and the Warsaw Pact. Then he listened intently to everything Technician Li said, interrupting from time to time to ask a question. Baopu, his eyes fixed on the darkened window, sat there smoking, seeming to want to snag every note from the flute that came his way. Sui Buzhao was too caught up in recalling Dahu's smiling face to hear a word of what was being said. He conjured up a picture of the young man holding his rifle and speaking to him from the other side of the window. "I'm leaving, Uncle," the youngster said. "I'm going up to the front and I might not be coming back. I'm willing to die for my country, and that keeps me from being afraid. But when I think about Wali, the place where I lived for a short eighteen years . . ." Sui Buzhao got up, walked to the window, and said: "You'll be back. When you miss home, just find a place where you can hear the rumble of the millstone by the riverbank. The old folks all say that when people leave home and travel far, the only news from home they receive is the turning of the mill-stones." Dahu nodded and stuck his nose up to the window. Sui Buzhao tried to touch his face through the glass but could not. Dahu shouldered his rifle and walked off.

After Dahu reached the front, he actually did listen for the rumble of the millstone. And he heard it. He said he did, and his company commander, Fang Ge, smiled and tweaked his ear. Everyone knew that was the sound of distant artillery. Now that the front line had been extended, guns from the far end made dull thudding noises when they were fired. Each battle was fought bitterly, with the hill they were standing on already claimed and reclaimed nine times. Fang Ge's men had just relieved another company that had suffered terrible casualties. The enemy was probably preparing for a tenth assault on the hill. As soon as they had relieved the other company, the soldiers were shocked by the sight of enemy bodies strewn across the base of the hill; none of them had ever seen so many dead in one place at one time. Some were nearly naked, an ugly sight in the bright sun. Dahu asked why they weren't wearing clothes. Fang Ge told him they were advance troops and that at night, not wearing clothes made their skin particularly sensitive, which kept them from setting off land mines.

The bloated, foul bodies made eating a problem. "There are so many of them!" Dahu exclaimed. "How many years did it take to produce that many?"

Some of Dahu's comrades laughed at his naïveté. "People are like leeks," one of them said. "Cut one out of the ground and another grows to take its place."

"Am I one of those?" Dahu asked out of bewilderment.

"How could you be? You're no more than a tiny leaf on a leek stalk."

Dahu shook his head. "The enemy are the leeks," he said. "We cannot be cut down!"

"No," the other man said, turning serious. "Everyone's the same in war. Whoever cuts down the other is the winner, for a while at least."

"We'll never let the enemy be the winner!" Dahu said.

The other man nodded. "I hope you're right . . ."

The corpses at the base of the hill were swelling fast and creating a terrible stench. Fang Ge asked command center how to deal with what lay before them and was given instructions to announce to the enemy through a bullhorn that they could retrieve their dead under a white flag. The response was immediate: They would not raise a white flag to retrieve their dead, since that would be a sign of surrender. They said they would do it under a Red Cross flag. Fang Ge reported this to command center, and after much deliberation, they agreed.

Enemy soldiers came to retrieve their dead but left the ones closest to the hill where they lay, so Fang Ge and his men went down and buried those left behind. Now what lay before them was an empty stretch of land, which afforded them a clear view of the front. Off to their left lay an open field where nothing grew, artillery shells having destroyed every trace of green. Two strategic friendly posts lay half a kilometer away, both in caves and both under Fang Ge's jurisdiction. They were manned by a rotation of soldiers, each responsible for both posts. Dahu and his comrades had been assigned to the posts during the month the enemy retrieved their dead and were relieved at the end of the month. The commander of the company who relieved them was the man who had spoken to Dahu about cutting down leeks. He and his men were on duty for less than a week when they were attacked by an elite enemy squad and wiped out. When command center heard that the posts had fallen into enemy hands, they sent a regiment of reinforcements with orders to retake them at all costs.

"In 1983 the American president delivered his Stars War speech. He outlined one hell of a big plan. My uncle dissected that plan, dividing it into three segments. Militarily, the US wants to tip the balance of power in its favor; politically, they want to force the opposition to make concessions at the negotiation table; and technologically, they want to open up outer space in order to spur economic growth in America. The old man is, after all, an expert, and he rattled these off with precision."

"Details, I need more details," Li Zhichang interrupted. "Exactly how do they plan to block an enemy launch?"

Technician Li nodded. "That's what I asked my uncle. He said that if you create a defense system with three tiers, the first utilizes missiles that can shoot down enemy missiles as soon as they're launched. That will take only four or five minutes. The second tier utilizes chemical and laser rays to neutralize warheads that get through. The third tier utilizes surface particle-beam weapons systems to blow up any that somehow get through both tiers. That's their last chance, and to be effective, they must bring down every missile within a couple of minutes . . ."

"Then why don't they have more tiers?"

"I'll tell you why," Crackpot said with a little laugh. "Each tier presents new problems. It's like getting dressed. By wearing only a single jacket see how much trouble you've saved."

They all laughed.

"There were people who recommended seven tiers, or five, but that would require a net of hundreds, maybe even thousands of satellites, like a sieve—the smaller the holes, the finer the flour."

Baopu listened quietly. Li Zhichang turned to him. "That doesn't sound like anything could go wrong."

Technician Li shook his head. "There's always a chance that something could go wrong." They turned back to him. "Just think," he said, "how do you guarantee that no missiles could get through all three levels? Let's say you knock down eighty or ninety percent at each tier. If they launched ten thousand missiles, at least a dozen would hit their American targets, wouldn't they?"

"What a catastrophe that would be if they landed on farmland!" Zhichang said.

With a smile, Technician Li patted him on the shoulder. "Who knows, some could even fall on our old mill and blow it to pieces." While the others enjoyed a good laugh over that, Baopu kept staring off into the distance.

"That's the situation in America," Technician Li continued. "How about the Soviet Union? You just know they've got their own set of plans. They're not amateurs where putting things into space is concerned. They were the first to put a man-made satellite in orbit, and my uncle told me that in the years since they've installed a network of self-defense satellites that perform reconnaissance, communications, navigational, early-warning, and meteorological functions. At the same time they've made the development of air-to-air, air-to-ground, and ground-to-air weapons systems a high priority. They've produced interceptor satellites and interceptor missiles, they're working on space shuttles, a space station that will remain permanently in orbit, and they have the ability to build a comprehensive space defense system. No small order, wouldn't you say?"

Li Zhichang snorted in astonishment. "What about NATO and the Warsaw Pact?"

Technician Li just shook his head. "Neither of those is a true bloc, since not all the member states are aligned with either the US or the USSR. They have their own self-interests to worry about. Take France, for instance. In response to the American Strategic Defense Initiative, they proposed their so-called Eureka Plan.

"Then there's England, which has its own nuclear arsenal, having developed an A-bomb more than thirty years ago. In addition to the two superpowers, France also has its sea, air, and land nuclear arsenal. Their sixth nuclear-armed submarine is already in operation and will be followed within a few years by the seventh. The plan is for countries in Europe to jointly build a worldwide net of satellites within a decade. Those satellites are not to be taken lightly, my uncle said. One geostationary survey satellite can tell when the enemy has ignited a missile."

Everyone exhaled in awe.

"Taking the long view," Crackpot said, "a mighty economic and technological struggle, involving America, the Soviet Union, Europe, and Japan, will erupt in space one day."

Technician Li stopped and looked at the people around him. It was quiet in the room, except for the distant sounds of the flute and the rumblings of the mills.

Snubbing out his cigarette, Baopu broke the silence. "I'm not sure I understand everything you're saying, but these things cost a lot of money, don't they? What happens to their economies? What I mean is, how will the people live?"

Li nodded. "I asked my uncle the same question. That, of course, is also very important . . ."

The battle to take back the two posts was about to begin, but the key was the open space. There weren't many enemy soldiers at the posts, and they had a limited supply of ammunition, but the open space was their ally, along with the artillery that would end the battle. Fang Ge, Dahu, and everyone else knew that there would be bloodshed. But the posts were so important to the overall battle plan that the command center appeared to have no choice but to take them back, no matter what the cost. The first assault was sent out at three in the morning; it was a unit from a battalion that had just arrived, whose commander was a heavily bearded soldier who waited quietly with his men in a camouflaged passageway. One of the soldiers looked familiar to Dahu, so he walked over to get a better look. It was Li Yulong, from his hometown; they had attended the same high school. After a friendly embrace, they asked about letters from home. Li said he'd received a letter from his father, who told him not to think about home and to follow orders. He added that his wife—actually his girlfriend—also wrote and sent a photograph. Dahu took out a tinted black-and-white photo from Li's pocket, a pretty girl with big eyes and hair that reached her earlobes. He handed it back. "We might be able to take care of the problem with this first assault, but even if that doesn't happen, three assault teams will certainly be enough. You're in the fourth team, so make sure to get word to my family if I don't make it back." He laughed.

The time had come, and Li leaped out of the camouflaged area. Soon gunfire was heard from the open space, with artillery fire lighting up the sky. It was as they'd predicted; the artillery barrage was concentrated on the open space, and no one in the first assault team was spared. The shooting stopped and the second team went up. Fang Ge found the battalion commander and asked him to stop the attack, but the answer was no, so he called command center to report the situation. He was arguing with the division commander when the battalion commander walked up and said, "Company Commander Fang, it's your turn." Throwing down the phone, Fang Ge shouted, "I'm not afraid to die, but—" His voice was drowned out by the rumble of artillery. He sat down, his right hand mechanically undoing the first button of his uniform. Some time passed before he whispered to Dahu, "Let's go." The fourth team jumped out of their cover.

"An arms race is big business, and the weapons will only get more expensive. I heard that a fighter plane cost less than a million US dollars during World War Two, but now you need more than two hundred million."

"Everything in the world is getting more expensive," Li Zhichang cut in. "Now five yuan won't buy as many eggs as we used to get for one."

"I agree! Armaments are costly, but on the other hand, they spur developments in technology. Take SDI, for example. It involves countless new technologies, and the demands on these technologies are ten times, no, a hundred times greater than those on the current ones. That could easily move technology forward several generations. My uncle was worried about this, saying this is what many countries will face: They'll lag behind the technologically advanced nations, they won't understand new technologies or new products developed by those technologies, and they won't be able to afford to obtain them through normal technology transfers. He once read me what an expert said in the paper: Just as sea dominance determined a country's status in the sixteenth century, one of the determining factors in the reshuffling of countries in the twenty-first century will be the opening up of space."

Li was quiet for a moment, before adding softly, "That day my uncle and I talked late into the night. He was very emotional, and as he stared at the stars in the sky, he asked someone, or maybe himself, 'Will the world continue to develop in this polarized fashion? Maybe not. As an independent power, China has stepped onto the stage of international politics. Will she become the third major power? Her rise would turn the polarized power structure into a triangular relationship and stabilize the world. China must be strong, for she is destined to be the third most powerful country in the world, with her abundant resources, strategic location, ever-growing economic and military power, a huge population, and a long and far-reaching cultural background and social structure. She could play a mediating role to stop wars from breaking out. Her balancing function in the strategic power structure is getting more prominent by the day.' The old man was really emotional that night."

The fourth squad entered the open space; the artillery barrage had wrought havoc on the soil, as the light of dawn made clear, and fresh blood had muddied the road. Stepping over dead comrades' bodies, the soldiers fell and got up again. Dahu's hands and eyes were stained with blood, but he didn't smell it or the gunpowder; he just heard Li Yulong shouting in the distance. He knew Li was dead, but he still heard his voice. The gunfire was growing more intense; a bullet whizzed by his ear and another lodged in his left arm, splashing his blood in the soil beneath him. It didn't hurt, as he thought it would, and he rushed forward, oblivious of everything else. Under Fang Ge's command, the team crossed the half kilometer or so of open space. Fang told the soldiers to spread out and zigzag toward the objective. But artillery fire finally began to howl in the air, followed by a powerful explosion. Every soldier lay on the ground, motionless. Fang Ge jumped up and pounced forward. He was hit. Dahu crawled toward him, but the moment he moved, his head shook violently, while something warm began to flow down. He wiped it off with his hand, but the blood flowed into his eyes. He tried to find Fang Ge but could see nothing; the world had turned red and then black. He groped his way ahead in the darkness, propelled by an unknown power. All of a sudden he was seeing red again. Fang Ge was gasping for breath. He was missing a leg. Dahu wanted to call out to his commander, but an ear-piercing shrillness paralyzed him.

An artillery shell exploded right next to him, leaving only a gaping hole after the smoke dissipated. The shell had turned over new soil.

Sui Buzhao jumped up from the *kang* and shouted, "Dahu, my beloved Dahu!" The others were stunned as they watched Buzhao run to the door. Baopu tried to pull him back, but Buzhao knocked his hand away.

Notes from the flute on the floodplain rose again. Sui Buzhao stumbled toward the source, leaving Li Zhichang, Sui Baopu, and Technician Li to stand by the door and silently watch him disappear into the darkness.

U nder normal circumstances, Zhao Duoduo did not dare bother Fourth Master. But one day, while ice-fishing in the river during a snowstorm, he caught a live catfish and, thinking it would make a fine soup, took it over to Fourth Master's house. Through the window, he saw Fourth Master reading by the fire in a leather jacket with snow-white fleece. Zhao held up the fish and shouted to Fourth Master, who turned slowly, removed his glasses, and replied unhappily, "Is that supposed to be some sort of rare treasure?" Obviously, the fish was not to Fourth Master's liking, so Duoduo dropped it and walked off. Two weeks later, when he came to see Fourth Master on an urgent matter, he noticed the fish was still there, dry as a board.

This time he'd come to see Fourth Master because both Li Yuming and Luan Chunji had told him to. Zhou Zifu, the county head, had phoned Li Yuming about a problem with the White Dragon Glass Noodle exports. In order to protect the brand reputation in the international market, the export division needed to strengthen quality control. During a spot check, the provincial export department had found impure starch in some of the noodles and had formed a team to investigate processing plants. Being a major producer, the Wali Glass Noodle Factory would surely be on their agenda. Li Yuming was aware that, since leasing the factory, Duoduo had added large quantities of impure starch to the mix, so he was understandably nervous when the call came. "Don't worry about it," the county head said. "I don't see a problem at your factory. I know all about Zhao Duoduo. He's a decent 'entrepreneur,' but still, you need to remind him to avoid being arrogant or overeager." The comment eased Li's concerns, for it was obvious that Zhou Zifu knew about the use of impure starch and, apparently, felt that it showed ingenuity. So as soon as he hung up, he called Luan Chunji and Zhao Duoduo together to figure out how to deal with the investigation team, which, according to Zhao, was due to arrive the following day. In the midst of their anxiety, the two officials thought first of Fourth Master.

After separating the peel from an orange before wiping his fingers on a white handkerchief, Fourth Master responded to Zhao Duoduo's question—"So what do we do?"—by merely cleaning his fingers and putting the handkerchief away.

"I've sealed up the chunks of starch," Zhao said.

Fourth Master looked up. "Can you seal up the mouths of all the people in town?"

Zhao licked his moustache nervously.

Fourth Master picked up a slice of orange, put it in his mouth, and said as he chewed, "You don't know how to stop when you're well off. I've said you won't come to a good end, but I meant in the future. This is a small matter, at most a fine, something none of us can avoid. Just try to keep it as low as possible."

Pleased by this response, Zhao clapped his hands and said, "I'll just change the dates on the starch and increase the inventory on paper. They won't weigh everything anyway."

Fourth Master moved the red clay teapot closer.

"I'll have Fatty prepare a banquet for tomorrow when the team comes to town," Zhao added.

Fourth Master waved him away. "Go back to work. I'll see you at the banquet." Zhao was about to leave when the gate opened and Luan Chunji walked in, grumbling about Zhao's bad information regarding the makeup of the investigating team. He'd just gotten off the phone and had been told that while the team members were mainly from the city, there were two officials from the provincial city, one of whom was a deputy bureau chief. Although the news greatly upset Duoduo, Fourth Master simply put down his teacup and sat up straight to consider the situation. "Duoduo," he said, "Fatty Han's cooking is passable for visitors from the city, but now that we have a deputy bureau chief, he won't do."

"Who else is there?" Luan asked.

"Zhang-Wang," Fourth Master said with a nod.

News of the visit spread quickly, but the town's residents, not privy to the details, were unaware that the newcomers were members of an investigation team. While it was normal to welcome visitors with a banquet, people were surprised to learn that the chef this time would be Zhang-Wang. Rumor had it that she calmly laid down the clay tiger she was working on when Zhao Duoduo informed her of the task at hand, exchanged a few words with him, and then shut her door to begin the preparations.

Since the team would not arrive until the afternoon, they would be guests at an evening meal, which meant that the town had the whole day to prepare. Duoduo started things off by taking Naonao and Daxi out of the processing room to be Zhang-Wang's assistants, entrusted with the job of preparing the ingredients. They worked all morning, but Zhang-Wang had yet to show her face. In the afternoon a crowd of onlookers gathered outside the kitchen, mostly male workers on their way home from the factory. Naonao, who had changed into new clothes and an apron, busied herself in the kitchen, while Daxi, dressed the same, sat on a rush mat, tending the fire. The gawking young men critiqued the pretty girls' natural attributes, especially Naonao, who had fair skin, which the men said was nourished by the bean milk. As for Daxi, the most frequently heard comment was, "Look how big she is."

And still the major figure in the drama was absent. A few nosy old men from town came over with folding stools and sat down to watch. For a change, the Wali Emporium was closed for the day, so they had no place to drink. Hearing that Zhang-Wang would be the chef, they knew that these were no ordinary visitors. So, with their arms folded, they sighed and smacked their lips. Even knowing that they would be excluded this time, they were happy to have a chance to see Zhang-Wang show off her skills and to enjoy the aroma of her concoctions.

The older residents' admiration for Zhang-Wang had a long history, and her influence on their daily lives was evident in many areas, of which soy sauce and noodle sauce were two. Instead of buying the kitchen essentials from the store, Wali women were expected to make them themselves at the appropriate time. The aroma of homemade soy and noodle sauces brought back warm, distant memories, and if the young daughters-in-law or their daughters missed a step in making the sauces, the old men would glare at them and say, "No, that's not right."

Here is how it was supposed to be: Soon after coming to Wali as a bride, Zhang-Wang taught the townspeople to be meticulous and frugal by making their own soy and noodle sauces. Since these were consumed in great quantity, they were anything but trivial or insignificant. Old women and young brides went to learn from Zhang-Wang, soon joined by unmarried young women, even little girls. In the end, men, pretending to be looking for the women in their families, showed up in front of Zhang-Wang's sauce containers. Barely twenty that year, she was in the habit of powdering her face, penciling her brows, and wearing colorful clothes. After exhausting the ingredients in her house for the earliest demonstrations, people brought their own to her yard, where her husband had set up a wok, so she could make soy sauce day and night. The dense smoke from burning chaff made her husband cough and tear up so much she could hear him from outside the house. To those who came to learn, she explained each step in the process, often staying up all night. Since seasons of the year were a factor in the production of soy and noodle sauces, it was necessary for the women to master the appropriate skill in the limited time given them in each season. They yawned a lot, while their menfolk lay down lazily and watched.

Never one to let an opportunity pass, Zhang-Wang used one of the reclining men as a chair, sitting on his back as her hands were kept busy in a blackened pottery bowl. Precision, she told the women, was the key in her method. In the past, they had used the best wheat and corn to make their sauces, but the results were unsatisfactory, and the finished products actually smelled bad. Obviously, the old ways did not work. So she first had them cut down the ingredients, using only chaff from the wheat and bits of corn, to be mixed in water on the second day of the second lunar month, the day the dragon raises its head. The mixture must not be too sticky, just viscous enough so that the women can see the impressions made by their fingers when they take their hands out of the mixture. If they can distinguish between where the thumb and pinkie had been, they have the perfect mold. The chaff mixture is then pressed into a black pottery bowl and taken to the head of the *kang*, where that year's wheat stalks have been laid out. With a quick, deft movement, the molded mixture is emptied onto the wheat stalks. Now the oldest woman in the family covers the rounded mold with a hempen sack and lays a handful of wheat stalks over it before tossing a bramble switch and a sprig of artemisia on top. It is important to face the mold while sleeping, and no nonsense is to be uttered near it; that thing that men and women like to do is to be avoided at all costs. To be safe, men should be invited to sleep in an-other room. Now everyone waits, impatiently, for forty-nine days, when gray-green fuzz appears on the seams of the sack. When touched, it is as warm as a child's head; two more days of waiting are required, when it no longer feels warm. Then it is broken into pieces, which are stirred into water boiled with bits of corn. After adding 2.4 ounces of salt for each *jin* of mixture, it is put into a porcelain jar, which is sealed and left to dry in the early spring sun. That is when the earth starts to warm up, the apricot flowers begin to fall, and peach and pear flowers bloom. The spring grass is two inches high, the yellow birds sing their lovely songs, and you can ignore the noise coming from the jar as wil-low branches brush against its sealed opening. The jar must be placed far from the eaves to prevent geckoes from peeing on it. You must then wait till the fruits turn red in the autumn and the fragrance of grain permeates the earth before the jar can be opened to reveal six months' secrets. The contents are now an inky black, flickering with salt crystals and a strange, fishy aroma that spreads through your lungs when you breathe it in. Yet at this point the soy sauce is only half done, and you must wait to finish the second part.

Zhang-Wang taught the people how to knead the lumps of chaff in the pottery bowl. First she balled up her fist loosely and raised her wrist slightly when reaching into the bowl, making the heel of the hand hard as steel. As she slowly kneaded the lumps, the heel heated up, so she quickened the pace until it was numb. The lumpy mixture had to turn powdery before it could be mixed into the jar. This was the key. When asked if that could be put off till later, she replied, "When second-month sauce is delayed too long, the old man shows up on his daughter-in-law's *kang*." Someone laughed derisively before swishing his sleeves and walking off. Later the man's family made the soy sauce in the third month and salacious rumors began to spread.

The head of that family was in his fifties. On a moonlit summer night he stumbled home, dead drunk, and spotted his daughter-in-law, who had fallen asleep at a table in the yard. Seeing her body glow in the moonlight, he staggered over and stared at her for about twenty minutes before sprawling atop the table and puckering up, waking the young woman, who began to cry and curse, calling him an old mule. Ignoring her, he stayed put. "So what if I'm a mule?" he muttered. There were rumors that a neighbor overheard everything, but the family, of course, denied it all. Later, when the man appeared on the street, people noticed he was missing an eye and assumed that was his son's doing.

Everyone was duly impressed by Zhang-Wang, who just smiled and said dismissively, "You cannot make soy sauce in the third month." As she sat on a reclining man's back, she kept kneading the chaff, her body moving up and down, nicely coordinated with the breathing of the man, whose wife was too eager to learn to object. When she turned her head, Zhang-Wang quickly kissed the back of the man's head, drawing gales of laughter, while she kept working at the chaff.

In the fall, when the dark contents were emptied out of the jar, the mixture turned into something strange and mysterious. All eyes were on Zhang-Wang as she directed the men to boil water in an oversized wok and pour it over the blackened chaff; the water turned black at once. She put the black water in another wok and told the men to turn up the heat. Crouching by the wok, she tossed in more than twenty items: anise seeds, the white ends of green onions, beans, peanuts, cloves of garlic, cucumbers, cinnamon bark, pigskin, chicken feet, orange peels, apples, pears, and chili peppers. People said that a big green grasshopper once happened to hop by while she was adding the ingredients, and in it went. When asked if that was true, she said, "Yes, good soy sauce takes on the aroma of wild things."

Someone else asked, "What about a sparrow?"

"Yes."

"How about pheasant?"

"Sure."

"A big-headed fish?"

"Of course."

"A rabbit?"

"Rabbit is gamy!" she said, stomping her foot in anger.

Everything boiled in the black water for several hours; salt was added twice, and then the wok was removed from the fire. A fine sieve eliminated the impurities, and what remained was soy sauce, an irreplaceable condiment that added a variety of flavors to any dish.

～

Naonao brought out a large porcelain jar, which was immediately identified by the onlookers as Zhang-Wang's own soy sauce jar. They gasped, realizing that she was not going to use any old homemade sauce, but her own. One observer claimed to have tried her soy sauce and said it was indescribably delicious. That could only mean that she had not revealed her secret formula in her instructions to others. More people gathered at the kitchen door, only to see the assistants, Naonao and Daxi, hard at work. As the sun slanted westward, they were getting increasingly anxious when they spotted her ambling toward them, cane in hand. As they made room for her to pass, they were shocked by what they saw. The dusty, grayish pallor was gone from her face and her neck; now she glowed with a fetching allure. She had trimmed her nails, put on clean white sleeve covers, and gathered her hair under a tall, soft white cap. Her lightly powdered face was pink. With a solemn, kindly look, she walked with light, gentle steps, her cane making a loud, crisp sound as it tapped the ground. There was not a trace of filth about her; in fact, she had become the embodiment of hygiene. Obviously she had bathed, for a strong fragrance wafted as she walked through the crowd. Taking in deep breaths, the people discerned the true aromatic essence of tea rose, not face powder or perfume. Now, they all knew that she had an old tea rose tree in her yard, but how she had managed to gather the fragrance from the flowers to her bosom was a mystery. By then she had entered the room, laid down her cane, and walked up to the stove as if on springs.

Naonao and Daxi stopped what they had been doing to await her instructions. First she went to a corner and picked up a paper box that made a rustling sound; she handed it to Naonao. "Wash these carefully and make sure you don't kill them. Save the legs." Then, pointing to a pottery jar, she said to Daxi, "Put on a pair of leather gloves and cut those open. Wash them clean and keep the liver and gallbladder."

The girls busied themselves at the sink as Zhang-Wang took out a gleaming paring knife from under her clothes, spread melons and vegetables out on the cutting board, and counted them with her index finger, putting aside the surplus pieces. Then she laid a cucumber in her palm, her pinkie hooking onto the stem while she used the knife in her right hand to begin peeling. The glint from the knife dazzled as the green skin was deftly removed from the cucumber; it looked like a green sash, which she draped over her shoulder before throwing the pulp away. Having saved the skin and discarded the cucumber, she then hollowed out four small melons, carefully cutting off the top section of each and discarding the meat and the seeds. By then Naonao and Daxi had finished their assignments. Naonao's job had been to wash some live cicadas, which were now, shiny and wet, crawling in a platter. Daxi had gutted and cleaned two large porcupines, the carcasses of which lay on the cutting board, looking alive with their quills jutting out.

The onlookers gasped in amazement, anticipating something quite unusual to happen next. The young men, rubbing their hands in excitement, called out, "Daxi, did you get pricked by the porcupine quills?" The old men began to smoke, their eyes sparkling as Zhang-Wang instructed the girls to prepare the following ingredients: minced ginger, chopped scallions, sliced meat, cubed meat, ground meat, mashed garlic, minced coriander, sliced fish, ground fish, fish chunks, fruit fillings, bean curd, shredded bamboo, sliced bamboo, strings of beef tendon, ground beef tendon, strings of pepper, shredded chicken breast, shredded mushrooms, shredded wood-ear fungi, egg skins, glass noodles, sliced ham, sliced chestnuts, diced chestnuts, green peas, shredded winter melons, winter melon slices, shredded peas, shallot powder, shallot slices, sliced asparagus, ground lotus seeds, shelled and soaked gingko, chestnuts, walnuts, peanuts, oranges, fresh peaches, pineapples, bananas, lotus seeds, and long-grained rice. She laid out a row of small bowls filled with brewed rice wine, distilled liquor, sesame oil, bean oil, lard, chili pepper powder, rice vinegar, monosodium glutamate, white chili pepper powder, oyster oil, shrimp oil, curry oil, starch powder, sugar, salad oil, *mantou* powder, and tomato sauce. When everything was lined up, she told Daxi to be on the lookout for the guests in the eastern reception room and let her know the minute they arrived.

After sending Daxi away, Zhang-Wang sat down on a wooden stool to smoke a long-filtered cigarette, which elicited envy from the young men outside. As she smoked, she directed Naonao to make dumpling fillings. But when the girl couldn't get the hang of it, Zhang-Wang stood up, stuck her index finger into the soupy fillings, and swirled it at top speed. A few quick swirls and the filling was ready. She sat down under the gaze of an impressed audience. Then Daxi, steaming with sweat, ran in to say that the guests had arrived!

"Calm down," she said to the girls as she stood up again. "We're right on time."

Zhang-Wang put on the leather gloves Daxi had worn and laid a porcupine upside down, pried open its empty abdomen, and quickly filled it with cubed chestnuts, oyster oil, rice vinegar, shallots, monosodium glutamate, ground tendon, and white pepper powder. She finished it off with a small spoonful of bean oil before carefully sewing it up. Then she scooped up some clay to cover the porcupine, turning it into a big mud ball. She repeated the procedure with the second porcupine and told Daxi to start a fire to bake the mud balls. Now it was time to heat the oil. Zhang-Wang added sea urchins to the balled fillings Naonao had made and put them in bowls for the clean cicadas to crawl onto. In the meantime, she filled a copper ladle with boiling oil and, when she saw one of the cicadas land in the right spot, poured the oil over it, locking its dead legs onto the sea urchins. The cicadas used up all the heated oil, and the surface of the work was coated with a film of oil, so she fried a thick starch cake and laid it out on the cutting board, spreading mashed garlic and coriander over it. She added bamboo shoots, peas, sliced ham, ground pork, shredded chicken breast, white pepper powder, long-grained rice, monosodium glutamate, and some salt. Last to go in were the sea urchins clutched by the cicadas. She wrapped everything in the starch cake, turning it into the shape of a long melon, and sealed up the opening with glass noodles soaked in water. By then Naonao had made another batch of filling. Zhang-Wang threw in some salad oil and rice wine after sniffing the filling, then added several dozen ingredients, mostly meat and condiments, such as ground pork, shredded wood-ear fungi, minced ginger, and shallot powder. After mixing it well, she scooped a spoonful into each of the hollowed melons and covered and sealed the tops with small sticks. Steamers were placed over a small pot of water nearby that had just begun to boil; melons and filled starch cake were laid out to steam on different levels.

While the steaming got under way, Zhang-Wang brought over a rectangular platter, into which she placed chopped sections of cucum-

ber peels from the sash she took off her shoulder. Soon a vine with
green leaves and yellow flowers appeared on the platter. She sprinkled
the vine with monosodium glutamate, rice vinegar, salt, and shrimp
oil. A delectable aroma rose from the steamer. "It's done," she announced, and told Naonao to remove the contents. The small filled
melons were quickly plunged into cold water before being placed on
a platter to resemble melons on the vine. "This dish is called Melons
on the Vine," Zhang-Wang said. Then, pointing at the melon-shaped
starch cake, she said, "And that is called a Monkey Pouch." The mud
balls were splitting in Daxi's oven, emitting an aroma that made the
onlookers' mouths water. Zhang-Wang took out the mud balls,
brushed off the ashes, and placed them on a plate. "This is called
Muddle-Fuddle Eggs," she announced.

Someone stuck his head in through the kitchen window. "Serve the
dinner," he said. Zhang-Wang nodded. Daxi and Naonao quickly
went for the plates. Daxi picked up Melons on the Vine and started to
walk out but was stopped by Zhang-Wang, who said, "Naonao serves
that one. You'll follow her with the Muddle-Fuddle Eggs." The onlookers laughed. As her face reddened, Daxi put down the plate, and
Naonao picked it up. But before she left, Zhang-Wang instructed her,
"Take the smallest steps you can manage." Naonao wrinkled her nose
but did as she was told. She cut a lovely figure, with her slender physique, carrying the melons over green leaves. She was told to call out
the name of the dish before serving.

"The esteemed leaders have come a long way and must be tired.
Please have a melon to relieve the fatigue."

She returned with a glowing face. Daxi got up to leave, but Zhang-
Wang pulled her back; five minutes later, she told her to go. Daxi tried
to imitate Naonao's mincing steps but was so plump she appeared to
be twirling in place. The mud balls rolled around on the plate, increas-
ing the mouth-watering aroma.

As soon as Daxi left, Zhang-Wang ran her hands over the row of
tiny bowls on the cutting board, picking up a pinch of the contents as
her hands moved over each of them. She repeated the step, her eyes

slitted; like a concert pianist, she did not actually have to see what she was doing. Tossing the ingredients into a tiny sifter, she sat down beside a big bowl with a broad rim and ran boiling water over the sifter, not stopping until the water dripping from the sifter had filled half the bowl. When Daxi returned, she told the girls, "This is called Oddly-flavored Soup." Daxi took a look at the clear soup and knew this would not be hers to serve, so she picked up the steaming Monkey Pouch. Zhang-Wang, who was smoking on her stool, sized the girl up and said to herself that she might appear big and clumsy on the outside but was detail oriented.

Out in the reception room there were six guests, with Luan Chunji, Li Yuming, and Zhao Duoduo as hosts. Everyone but the deputy bureau chief, a clean-shaven man with a bald head and an icy expression, was smoking a State Express cigarette. When Duoduo offered him a cigarette, he merely pushed it away with his hand. But when Melons on the Vine was announced and served by Naonao he lowered his eyes and rubbed his hands anxiously, looking up at her as she turned to leave. The others put out their cigarettes but left their chopsticks where they lay. One of the guests stared at the melons and sighed with appreciation; the others followed suit, but still no one touched his chopsticks.

"What's going on with Fourth Master?" Li Yuming muttered. That was a sign for Zhao Duoduo to stir. He picked up his chopsticks and poked a hole in one of the melons, permeating the room with an aroma that was quickly identified by the guests as the fragrance of melon. Li Yuming invited the deputy bureau chief to start; he responded with a grunt before reluctantly picking up his chopsticks.

Without warning, Luan Chunji and Zhao Duoduo laid down their chopsticks and stood up. Everyone looked up to see Fourth Master entering the room. The others stood up, the deputy chief being the last to rise. Fourth Master was dressed in a light-colored, loose Chinese-style pantsuit. Leaning on a cane with a carved dragon, he walked slowly and smiled apologetically yet offered no spoken apology. The diners stirred, almost as if preparing to leave, so he walked up and offered everyone his hand, including Duoduo. He shook the deputy chief's hand with special vigor. Then they all sat down and he laid his cane aside. The deputy chief neither smiled nor said anything for a long moment before asking, "How old is the esteemed gentleman?"

Fourth Master laughed heartily. "You are too polite. I'm withering before my age. I'm not even sixty." The deputy chief breathed softly, as if loosening up a bit, just as the Muddle-Fuddle Eggs were served. The guests stared at the jiggling eggs, not quite knowing what to do with them. So Fourth Master lifted off the bamboo strips, held down an egg with one hand, and plunged a strip into it. By twisting the bamboo strip, he exposed the red meat inside and released such a strong aroma that some of the guests actually shuddered. Fourth Master quietly picked up the first, large piece of meat and placed it on the plate in front of the deputy chief, who jumped to his feet.

"Thank you, thank you. Fourth Master, I'll help myself." The words "Fourth Master" sounded awkward in his mouth. Fourth Master stood up but then sat back down and raised his cup in a toast before emptying his glass.

Li Yuming turned to the deputy chief. "Fourth Master is in a fine mood today. We don't normally have the honor of his company. When he heard you were coming he said he ought to join us." The deputy chief smiled and nodded at Fourth Master to show his appreciation and was rewarded with a smile in return. Luan Chunji followed with a description of Fourth Master's past, how he had been a cadre in Wali since the early days and was now the most senior person in the Zhao clan, well respected by everyone in town. With a wave of his hand, Fourth Master interrupted with a sigh, "I'm just an ordinary citizen, 'not searching for the happiness of officialdom, with eyes only for a simple, carefree life,' as the saying goes. I know how trite that sounds. Recently I've had to remind myself that I was one of the town's early Party members."

At that point, he turned to look out the window. The people around the table went quiet, as if deep in thought. The deputy chief looked at Fourth Master with a respectful, if slightly surprised, gaze.

The first and second dishes set the tone for that day's banquet, which continued with Oddly-flavored Soup, Monkey Pouch, Hen Laying Eggs, Stuffed Duck, and more. The soup looked like water but produced a hundred flavors as it slid down the throat; it was impossible to tell the flavors apart, except for a slight tingling on the tip of the tongue and a strong aftertaste. Hen Laying Eggs turned out to be a glistening yellow chicken lying head down on a bed of golden yellow and tender green leaves, surrounded by white eggs. The eggs had neither yolk nor white, but were filled with delicious ingredients. With Stuffed Duck, it was not the duck but the contents in its belly that were the focal point. The shapes and flavors of chestnuts, walnuts, millet, peanuts, and lotus seeds changed after being mixed with the duck's innards and were mouth-watering. Two plates of refreshing cold dishes arrived just as the guests were sated with heavy food. One was of ordinary greens, but with a special flavor, for somehow the chef had managed to add a bitter taste. It was appropriately called Bitter Daily Greens. The other was composed exclusively of wild greens that first had a strong sour taste but turned sweet when chewed. It was, not surprisingly, called Sweet Wild Greens. The two dishes so impressed the guests that they could no longer hold back their praise, but before they finished expressing their appreciation, the final two dishes arrived: Mountains and Sea Classics, and Hanging Gourds.

The first consisted of delicacies from the sea (fresh abalone, scallops, and sea urchins) and precious ingredients from the mountains (lily flowers and mushrooms of the highest quality). The final dish came on a plate with an unripe, fuzz-covered, green gourd. One of the men reached out to touch it and was surprised by how hot it was. Fourth Master twisted the stem to open the gourd, which had been cleverly transformed into a tureen filled with milky white soup. When the deputy chief stirred the soup, the tender meat of the gourd floated to the surface like puffs of cotton; he stirred it again, and dark red pieces of tortoise rose up. He took a sip of the soup and sweat slid down his cheeks.

FIFTEEN

Everyone was aware that the leasing contract for the glass noodle factory was about to expire, and the regulation stipulated that a Gaoding Street meeting must be held within a week to discuss the next contract. The old mills by the river continued to rumble while the banging sounds went on as usual in the processing rooms. Sui Jiansu walked quickly down the street, staring straight ahead. He'd been to see Li Yuming about the bidding and was told that it had to be put off owing to an internal dispute. Later Jiansu learned that Zhao Duoduo had had Wattles Wu draft a report claiming that in the space of a year the factory had shown tremendous improvement. The report also asserted that a one-year contract undermined the overall spirit of reform. Moreover, it would be impossible to turn the business over to someone else at this time, since there was still much to be done and too great an investment was involved. Zhao had asked to have his contract renewed, since the legal procedures had already been formalized, and so on.

Jiansu went immediately to see Luan Chunji to point out that altering the original agreement would be detrimental to the interests of Wali and would constitute a great injustice. Not at all pleased by the visit, Luan replied that he didn't think there could possibly be anyone else who could run the factory, and added that Zhao had earned the reputation and displayed the bold vision of a reformer with his proposal to link up all the bean factories along the Luqing River and form the Wali Glass Noodle Production and Marketing Consortium. Jiansu countered that the factory was the issue at hand and that other matters could wait. The contract period was up, and a new contract needed to be drawn up, for there were in fact others who were willing to bid, himself included.

His face darkening, Luan Chunji went quiet after saying, "I knew it."

So Jiansu visited other town leaders, including the township Party secretary Lu Jindian and township head Zou Yuquan, in order to explain the situation to them. He brought up the investigation team, providing actual numbers on the impure starch used during the production process and pointing out the serious consequence of a significant decrease in White Dragon Glass Noodle exports.

"The fine was mainly symbolic," Lu said with a frown. "Someone must have found a way to influence the investigation team. This isn't over. When a lease period is up, the contract expires. It cannot be renewed without bids, after which we can discuss the length of the lease. We need to have a meeting to break down neighborhood barriers so we can discuss a new lease and capital investment."

Jiansu shook their hands and walked out, figures swirling in his head. "Let that day come soon," he repeated to himself. "I'm ready and I'm waiting for you, Zhao Duoduo."

Jiansu often went to the old mill house, sometimes just to watch his brother work his ladle on the conveyor belt. This time he could not maintain his silence and said to his brother, "They're going to hold a meeting soon. A bold man would seize the opportunity and grab hold of the glass noodle factory."

Baopu gave him a look and said, "You're that man."

Jiansu's eyes lit up. "I've been waiting for ages. When it happens, I'm also going to form a consortium to control production and sales all up and down the Luqing River region. I'm not bragging, but I have everything planned out. Opportunities like this don't come around often, but when you seize one everything works out fine."

"You have the guts, but, as I said before, you don't have the power." Baopu stood up and walked over to his younger brother.

Jiansu nodded. "Yes, you did say that. To be honest, I have some qualms too, even now, but I have no choice but to give it a try." Growing animated, he took a few puffs of his pipe before tossing it aside and grabbing his brother's arm. "We don't have much time. I can make it as long as you're with me. Even if we don't get it, we can edge Zhao Duoduo out by raising our own capital and starting over. I'm not powerful enough by myself, but we can combine our strength . . ."

Baopu hesitated. "It's not about strength and we can't combine it. I've said what I needed to say, so now you think it over."

Jiansu was quiet, his face darkening from the forced silence. He stood there staring at Baopu. "I don't have to think it over," he said at last, "and I won't come ask for your help again. You can sit here and watch the mill for the rest of your life, if you want." He stormed out. Unable to control his agitation, he roamed the willow grove by the floodplain, constantly stopping to stare off into the distance. Then he returned to the factory, where, despite himself, he walked into Duoduo's office. Zhao wasn't there, but his cleaver was, on the windowsill, and it caught Jiansu's eye the moment he walked in. A burning sensation began to spread in his right eye. He rubbed the eye but still felt the glint from the cleaver's edge. He reached out to grab it but was stopped by his own question: "What do you want that for? Why do your hands itch every time you see it? They're twitching in your pocket, and sooner or later they'll cause trouble." His heart pounded; he held his breath. Finally he managed to avert his gaze, but then it fell on Duoduo's pillow and the ugly indentation made by a human head on the mulberry-purple cover. He imagined how it would be dripping wet if the cleaver fell on that spot in the middle of the night.

As he stood there fantasizing, he detected a strange but familiar odor and felt as if a knife had pierced his heart. He spun around to see Zhao standing there, laughing soundlessly, his lips pressed tightly together. Jiansu looked down at Zhao's hands; they hung at his sides, empty. His stumpy fingers were knobby with blackened nails. The hands slowly raised and landed on Jiansu's shoulders, the fingers clasping his shoulder blades briefly. "Have a seat," Zhao said. "I give you more than a hundred yuan every month to be a technician, so I ought to exchange some 'information' with you."

Several strands of black hair fell over Jiansu's bloodless face; he shook his head and flipped them back.

"Your hair reminds me of a horse's mane," Zhao said with a snide laugh. He took out a prickly ash pipe, clamped it between his teeth, and studied Jiansu before lighting it and recounting the situation in the factory. He said the consortium was assured of success, since many of the other glass noodle makers had already contacted him. Soon anyone who opted out of the consortium would suffer, since it would be a centralized supplier of raw materials and a unified market for the products. An independent noodle maker, like any person alone, would suffer if he tried to stand up against a consortium. He said the company needed a car and a small van, and that he was already working on getting the car. He began to laugh.

Jiansu stared at him. "What about the lease? Is it going to be renegotiated?"

Zhao clenched his teeth and said, "Yes, but the factory is like a piece of tough, stringy meat, and you need good teeth to chew it."

Jiansu shook his head. "Chewing slowly is the answer. With so many people around, there's bound to be someone with good teeth."

Zhao laughed coldly. "I know everyone who has good teeth. I already told you, I don't need to move a finger to take care of any one of them; all I need is that thing down between my legs."

Jiansu stood up, his fists balled in his pockets, but he sat down again after taking a look at Zhao's stubby hands. "You can't do it," Zhao said. "You're not as solid as your brother, so why not just work for me as a technician? Besides, we're related, you know."

A buzz went off in Jiansu's head. "How?" he demanded.

Zhao stuck his face right up to Jiansu's face and said emphatically, "The Fourth Master of the Zhao clan is Hanzhang's foster father."

That stopped Jiansu, who got up and left.

He was a few yards away when Zhao shouted that there was something he forgot to share with Jiansu. He walked up, covered Jiansu's mouth, and whispered in his ear, "I've found my female secretary, a girl in her early twenties, from west of the river, a real looker, and she smells like perfume."

Jiansu clenched his teeth and took off.

He had not gone far when Daxi flew out of the processing room and stopped three or four paces from him. He looked at her but said nothing. She looked around, crouched down, and whispered, "Jiansu, over there, by the base of the wall, come on!" She left first, bent at the waist, and when Jiansu reached the base of the wall, she threw her arms around his neck and laid her face against his cheek. "I've been looking for you," she complained. "Where have you been? Didn't you hear me when I called out to you the other day? You didn't even look. Don't you like me anymore? Don't you want me?"

Jiansu struggled to get out of her embrace and, looking her in the face, said gruffly, "I want you, Daxi, I want you more than you know, but now I have more important things to do. Please wait. In two weeks, maybe sooner, things will be less complicated."

"I know," she sobbed. "I know, Jiansu. I often dream of you fighting with Duoduo. I know how much you hate him, so I hate him too. I'll wait for you. How can I help? Tell me what I can do."

Drying her tears, Jiansu kissed her and said haltingly, "You don't have to help. I just want . . . you . . . to wait for me. You're the only person in Wali who understands me—Daxi, just a few more days, just wait for a few more days."

So he left Daxi and went back to see Luan Chunji, who remained noncommittal, saying that opening up for bids was possible, but he was worried that it might be little more than a formality.

"We have to do it, even if it's only a formality," Jiansu said stiffly before taking leave of the director, having suddenly realized that he ought to have a good handle on the town's major clans, the Li, the Sui, and the Zhao families. The Zhao clan might not want to give the factory to someone else, though they were not unanimous in their view of things, and not many of them were intent upon following Zhao Duoduo's lead. The Li clan was impossible to gauge, since they often surprised people with the unexpected. Some members of the Sui clan had gone through decades of dejection while others had moved on to other things. Sui Hengde and his immediate family had been the leaders, but this branch had begun to go downhill in the 1940s, taking the rest of the clan with them. The time when they could rally everyone around them had passed. Who would have the resolve to follow Jiansu now? He shook his head at the thought. He needed to work on the other minor families, who had been caught between the three major clans for decades. They might have had a tough life, but they may well have produced some people of worth.

Jiansu's head ached. Six months earlier, he had begun keeping tabs on the various characters in town, realizing that, as an ancient town, Wali must have its share of talent. But the first to fight their way out would have to come from the Sui clan. In any case, they would be the Zhaos' mortal enemy. Jiansu was also worried that in this struggle he might end up as a stepping-stone for some stranger, who could leap out from a corner and take everything away from him. For years he'd not dared to get close to anyone, let alone share his innermost thoughts with outsiders; he just crouched in the dark, watching, though he often quaked in an attempt to control his urges. The time to act was upon him, and he must not remain crouching any longer; it was time to leap out and pounce on his opponents. It was dark when he returned to his room, so after a quick meal, he took out his notebook, which was now filled with figures, and copied out the important ones, checking them one final time and calculating a new figure for the amount due the town. He'd had 73,000 the last time, but the actual net profits were 128,000 yuan. If there had been a 10 to 15 percent increase, then the bidding figure would be 80,000 to 84,000 yuan. It was clear that Zhao Duoduo had gotten himself a very good deal with the factory.

The problem was, since the town's residents were uninformed, these numbers could easily be exploited by Zhao and others. Agitated, he put the notebook away and walked out of the room. The light was on in his brother's room, but he knew that Baopu would be reading that book of his, and he had vowed to never ask for Baopu's help again. Hanzhang's window was dark, which meant she was either asleep or had gone to see her foster father. He harbored a hatred for everyone in the Zhao clan, including Fourth Master, who had actually come to the Sui clan's aid during difficult times. "Why did she have to take the old man as her foster dad?" he asked himself. What a nightmare! He left the yard after looking up at the sky and, his thoughts turning to his uncle, walked toward the old man's room. The light was on, so he opened the door and walked in. Sui Buzhao was in the middle of a heated conversation with Li Qisheng, who by this time was nearly senile. Unable to join the conversation, Jiansu sat off to the side.

Buzhao made a gesture for the number ten with his fingers. "How about this?"

Li stared straight ahead, his cheek muscles twitching. He shook his head and made a gesture for the number two. Sui Buzhao, as if struck by a sudden realization, looked at Li admiringly and said to his nephew, "See how smart he is?" Jiansu got up to leave. "Why is your face so red?" his uncle asked. "Your eyes too! Are you sick?"

"You're the one who's sick," Jiansu said gruffly as he walked out, and immediately felt better, thanks to a cool breeze. With a jumble of thoughts on his mind, he kept walking, knowing he would not be able to sleep, and before long, he was jogging. When he stopped he saw he'd arrived at the township Party secretary's office, so he went in and headed for Lu Jindian's office, startling Lu, who was reading. He stood up.

"Secretary Lu," Jiansu said, "if my bid falls, I want to raise capital to build a factory of my own, and I'd like the town's support."

Momentarily taken aback, Lu quickly recovered and said with a smile, "The glass noodle factory processes agricultural products, so of course you'll be supported. But you're too young to get so over-wrought."

Jiansu nodded. "Thank you, Secretary Lu. That's all I wanted." He turned to leave but hesitated, as if he had more to say. In the end he said nothing.

Jiansu rushed through the darkened alleys and ended up back in his uncle's room. Li Qisheng, whose mind had nearly shut down again, was staring into a corner, oblivious of Jiansu. "This isn't good," Sui Buzhao muttered as he took a step forward. "I think you're sick. Your eyes are getting redder and you have a dazed look."

Unable to tolerate the old man, Jiansu grunted and nearly swung at his uncle. He swayed for a moment and walked out, his uncle's gray eyes on his back as he disappeared into the night. Five or six minutes later, Buzhao too ran out of the room.

Jiansu walked on, sometimes fast, sometimes slow, until he got to his room and kicked the door open. He pulled the chain to turn on the light and sat down on the *kang*, but quickly stood up again. Pounding his fist on the table, he mumbled some curses. By then Sui Buzhao was outside Jiansu's room, where he observed his nephew for a while before running over to get Baopu. Jiansu kept cursing, savagely pulling at his hair. When he looked down at a lock of hair in his hand, he screamed and leaped onto the *kang*.

Baopu walked in with their uncle and ran up to hold his brother. "Jiansu, what's the matter? Get hold of yourself."

Jiansu stared at Baopu with a crazed look and demanded, "What are you doing here? Get out! The big ship is coming and I'm leaving now." He struggled out of Baopu's arms, jumped away, and began to tear at the mat on the *kang*. Sui Buzhao signaled Baopu with his eyes and said, "The same symptoms Li Qisheng displayed when he was young. I'll be right back."

As he held Jiansu with one arm, Baopu patted his brother's back with the other. Jiansu began to cry, but then he burst out laughing and pushed Baopu away. "Don't hold me back. The ship is sailing. I have to run!" He would have run out of the room if Baopu had not been holding on to his clothes. Finally Guo Yun arrived and immediately observed Jiansu before closing the door and telling Baopu to let go. Jiansu immediately began jumping up and down, cursing and screaming. Even Hanzhang heard the noise and ran over. Stroking his beard, Guo Yun removed a syringe from his pouch and, when Jiansu turned, walked up and jammed it into his arm; Jiansu shook briefly and then went limp. Hanzhang and Baopu carried him over to the *kang*, where Guo Yun examined his eyes and tongue and checked his pulse.

"Is it the same as Li Qisheng's problem?" Sui Buzhao asked. Guo shook his head. "There's a thick yellow coating on his tongue, meaning the yang is too strong and is disturbing his inner clarity. It's a yang-induced madness that needs to be treated by reducing the heat to lessen the agitation." He wrote a prescription and handed it to Sui Buzhao. "One dose ought to do it. If his stool is red he'll be fine." The old doctor turned to leave but spotted Hanzhang and gave her a look before walking out.

The family stayed up all night buying and then preparing the medicine. Jiansu fell asleep half an hour after taking the medicine and did not get up until noon the following day. The first thing he did was go to the toilet; Sui Buzhao helped him over and back. When he returned, surprised but pleased, he said to Baopu and Hanzhang, "It was red."

Jiansu quickly recovered and regained his sanity. He told them all to say nothing to anyone about his illness, to which they agreed. Hanzhang made a nice meal, and he ate heartily, though he was still lethargic and weak in the knees. The next day, despite objections from his family, he went out on the street again, where he saw a crowd of people at an intersection reading an announcement by Zhao Duoduo about raising capital to expand the noodle factory. In calligraphy that was clearly from the hand of Wattles Wu, it stated that a share would cost a thousand yuan and profits would be distributed based upon the number of shares at a high rate of interest. Families could join to buy shares. Seeing how fast Duoduo was moving, Jiansu ran home and wrote an announcement of his own in big, dark, inky script, explaining how he also planned to offer shares to set up a glass noodle factory, but with better, more profitable conditions for the shareholders.

That got the townspeople talking. People were saying that the Sui clan finally had a man who could hold his head up. "What's the use of holding your head up?" someone said with a laugh. "So it can be lopped off?" Jiansu heard every word.

A day passed, but neither side had found a single shareholder. Suffering another anxiety attack, Jiansu stormed out of the house. Urging his brother to visit the old doctor and thank him for his treatment, Baopu bought some cakes and snacks as gifts. Unable to bear the pressure of waiting, Jiansu decided to follow his brother's advice.

Jiansu had rarely set foot in the old doctor's yard, which was unsettingly quiet. Guo Yun invited him to sit down and accepted the gifts with alacrity before asking Jiansu about his symptoms. Receiving only a perfunctory answer, he went back to his tea and remained silent until Jiansu brought up the subject of leasing bids for the noodle factory. The old man listened without comment. "Zhao Duoduo got himself a great deal," Jiansu said. "When the leasing bid was first publicized, people in town had no idea what it was about, as if they were still half asleep. Everything was in flux, and no one had a clear picture. That was an opening for Duoduo, who obtained the factory for practically nothing. On the surface it appears that he's the only one benefiting, but in fact there's a group of people behind him who monopolize just about everything in town. I've suffered enough. Now I want to put everything I have up against them. I'm not sure how it will turn out, but I want people to know that there's at least one member of the Sui clan who can put up a fight."

Guo Yun sipped his tea while rearranging the straps on his leggings. He stopped to look at Jiansu and sighed.

Jiansu gazed back with a questioning look in his eyes. Guo took another sip of his tea and looked down at the stone table. "It is not possible to explain away complex and peculiar worldly phenomena. All my life I've believed that getting the short end of the stick is actually a blessing, that peace and safety come from fortitude, but I'm not so sure anymore. It seems to have become the rule of the game that bad people invariably get what they want. But we should not abandon the wisdom that only those who gain the trust of the people can rule the world. After all the trouble they've been put through, the towns-people have grown timid and lazy, so they are shortsighted and side with the powerful. But if you take the long view, it is best to place your faith in those who are content with their lot and are humble and hardworking. Baopu can be considered just such a person. You are hot tempered and rash. It would be easy for you to take charge, but you lack stamina. You are quite different from the rest of the townspeople."

Guo Yun stopped and looked up at Jiansu, whose face had turned red and whose lips had began to tremble. "Master Guo Yun," he said, "my brother is a good man who deserves our trust. I share your view. He cares about people in town, but he keeps to himself in that mill year after year. Is that how the Sui clan is fated to end up?"

Guo shook his head and sighed. "That is his great misfortune." After that the old man went silent, so Jiansu left with a heavy heart and lay awake all that night, turning the old man's words over in his mind.

Daybreak brought the news that a town meeting for bidding would be held at the old temple site. Jiansu, whose heart was thrown into turmoil, got up to pace his room. After considering his options, he decided to take a sleeping pill so he'd be ready to face the important moment. He fell asleep and dreamed that he was strolling along a dark blue riverbank. A solitary figure, he walked on, puzzled by the perva-sive silence. He bent down to pick up a handful of sand, only to see that every grain was dark blue. Letting the sand drop through his fingers, he continued walking and saw a tiny red dot emerge in the distance. At first he thought it was the sun, but it leaped up and got bigger; it was a red horse. His heart skipped a beat as he opened his eyes wide and discovered that it was his father's chestnut. The horse stopped before him, rubbing him with its long, smooth cheek. He cried as he wrapped his arms around its neck, then climbed onto its back. With a loud whinny, the horse took off and galloped along the boundless blue riverbank.

At some point someone knocked on the door, waking him up. The light was turned on and there stood his brother, grim-faced Baopu, who said, "You were having a pleasant dream, but I had to wake you up. The meeting is about to begin and I know how bad you'd feel if you missed it, so let's go." Jiansu quickly threw on some clothes and left with his brother, gratitude welling up inside. As they walked along, Baopu told him that even the factory workers were taking off to attend the critical meeting. Virtually everyone in town would be at the old temple site.

A sea of black greeted Jiansu and Baopu at the meeting site. A row of tables had been set up on the earthern platform. Party Secretary Lu Jindian, township head Zou Yuquan, and the Gaoding Street leadership were seated behind the tables. An empty seat next to the township head was rumored to have been prepared for Fourth Master. Luan Chunji, who presided over the meeting, told the prospective bidders to come up close to the platform. Several people quickly walked up, and there were eventually a dozen of them. Jiansu looked at his brother excitedly. "Go ahead," Baopu said.

Li Yuming, representing Gaoding Street, opened the meeting with a bumbling speech about the major accomplishments over the past year, including the leasing of all sideline industries and the distribution of public welfare funds. He then invited the leadership to speak. Lu Jindian rose and, with a few words, pointed out the major issues. He called on more people to join the bidding, characterizing the Wali Glass Noodle Factory as the town's most important enterprise, one that needed to be run by the most capable, upright person. Adding that the same went for the other industries, he extended an invitation for more able men to stand up and be counted. No one made a sound as he spoke. Then a few more people approached the platform, which pleased Zou Yuquan. "Excellent. We don't want this to be a 'moribund meeting' or 'window dressing.'" Finally the moment arrived and everyone tensed. Luan Chunji walked over to an electric lamp, where a stack of paper, a pencil, and a brush dipped in red ink had been laid out. The initial bidding would be for small factories and workshops and would begin with a starting figure announced by Luan and end when the highest number was reached within a certain length

of time, just like an auction. "Start the bidding," Luan Chunji announced as he looked at his watch. People crowded forward, craning
their necks and nervously rubbing their hands.

Dead silence filled the first few seconds, which was broken by a
tentative voice, as if the man were too shy to announce his figure.
Another figure followed, this time from a much louder voice, followed
by more numbers, like a boat rising higher and higher as water swelled
in the river. When the time was nearly up, Luan looked at his watch.
"Three seconds, two seconds . . ." *Bang!* He slapped the table, picked
up his red brush, and wrote down the winning number. On to the
next item.

They went down the list, with people backing away and others
moving up. The bidders' shadows flickered under the light, making
even the onlookers sweat. Finally the glass noodle factory came up.
Seven or eight people stood up and moved forward, all of them bidders, naturally. Zhao Duoduo took off his jacket, tossed it onto the
chair behind him, and inched forward to block Sui Jiansu with his
elbow. Jiansu shifted and took a step forward, now blocking Zhao,
who crossed his arms, his elbow only inches away from Jiansu's rib
cage.

Luan Chunji shouted, "Glass noodle factory, the opening figure is
seventy-five thousand yuan, the time limit is five minutes. Start the
bidding!"

His words still hung in the air when Zhao Duoduo shouted, "Hold
on. There's something we need to clear up first. I gave the factory a
solid foundation after leasing it for a year. I replaced equipment and
opened up sales venues, so letting me continue to lease it is the easy
solution. If management changed hands, where would I go to recoup
my investment? That has to be made clear."

"We've studied that already and will deal with it later." Luan was
also shouting. He obviously meant this for the benefit of the larger
crowd. "The lease this time will be based on a new foundation—"

"Director Luan," Duoduo countered, "I'll be petty now so we can
be gentlemen later. However complex the account might be, it must

be cleared. I don't mind if I lose out on the bidding, but the people I work with have to survive."

Luan waved him off. "I know that," he said, "I know."

Sui Jiansu took this as an opportunity to speak to the people on the platform. "I have something to say." Without waiting for permission, he turned and spoke to the people behind him. "I have something to say," he repeated. "Director Luan has just said he'll clear the account with Zhao Duoduo later, and that's fine. But if it needs to be cleared, let's make every item public. That way we don't shortchange anyone."

With a snort, Zhao Duoduo glared at him.

Ignoring him, Jiansu continued, "It's no trouble at all, as you'll see. When the processing room was first leased, there were 2,480,000 *jin* of mung beans, 63 mounds of starch, plus over 200,000 *jin* that were being processed, which all together represented 182,000 yuan. In the sixth month, the sedimentation process was refitted, and the mill was mechanized in the eighth month, making a total investment of 144,000 yuan . . . The opening bid this time is 75,000 yuan. That number is much too low. The previous yearlong lease generated a gross profit of more than 2,179,400 yuan, with a net profit of 128,000. But the amount due the town was set at 73,000. That's a huge difference." His words were quickly drowned out by the clamor from the crowd, stunned by the speed at which Jiansu had ticked off the figures. Knowing he must have proof, the people shushed and signaled each other with their eyes while repeating some of the figures. Zhao Duoduo screamed, but no one could hear what he was saying. The crowd finally calmed down when Luan Chunji stood up and gestured with his hands, followed by Lu Jindian.

Sweat poured down Luan's face. "Yelling out a bunch of numbers accomplishes nothing, since the accounts are all carefully recorded. If the opening bid is too low, then show us what you've got and raise it!"

Jiansu too was sweating. He wiped the sweat off, his eyes fixed on Luan. Sparks danced in his eyes. "I was just telling everyone what's what," he shouted. "I'm here to bid. All I'm saying is that no one is going to get it for nothing this time."

Several people on the platform called out to stop him from continuing, so he shut up and the meeting resumed. "Glass noodle factory, the opening number is seventy-five thousand yuan, the time limit is five minutes," Luan repeated in a booming voice. "Start the bidding!" He looked at his watch.

Zhao Duoduo opened the bidding: "Seventy-seven thousand." Someone else shouted, "Seventy-eight thousand." When the number crept up to eighty-five thousand, Jiansu still had said nothing. Sweat glistened on his hair, some of which was stuck to his forehead. He looked around him, searchingly, then returned his gaze to the red brush in Luan Chunji's hand. He blurted out, "One hundred and ten thousand." That was met with silence, as the people on and below the platform were stunned by the twenty-five thousand yuan difference between the two amounts.

Luan stood up but kept his head down, "Time is almost up, almost up." He raised his hand, and at that moment, Zhao Duoduo yelled out, "Add a thousand to that!"

Jiansu followed suit. "Add another thousand!"

Instead of slapping the table, Luan just rubbed his eyes. The people finally caught their breath.

Then Zhao jumped up, raised his right arm, and shouted in a hoarse voice, "Add another thousand."

Luan's hand was falling away from his eyes, and with Zhao's cry, it landed on the table with a bang. He fell backward into his chair. Jiansu slid to the ground, hugging himself as if to keep warm.

Chaos erupted as the bidders slowly left the platform area, having quieted down a bit after Li Yuming announced the outcome. When he was done, Zhao Duoduo leaned over to say something to Li, who nodded. Zhao then turned to face the crowd and began describing his grand design—creating the Wali Glass Noodle Production and Sales Consortium—and welcoming everyone in town to invest. Jiansu, still sitting on the ground, listened before slowly getting to his feet and walking up to the front.

"Zhao Duoduo snatched away the factory again, thanks to outside help. Well, I'm not finished. I invite you, young and old, to join me in my own venture if you trust me. If I can't pay you back, I'll mortgage my house, auction off my land, even sell my wife—" "You don't have a wife to sell," someone shouted in a mocking voice. "I'll have one," Jiansu retorted. "Dear neighbors, the Sui clan never goes back on its word." Lu Jindian and Zou Yuquan stood on the platform watching Jiansu, who sat down as he finished. Another commotion spread among the crowd, but the din died down abruptly when they spotted Fourth Master, aided by a cane, who had somehow materialized at the foot of the platform. Standing quietly, he surveyed the scene. Then he thumped his cane on the ground and called out, "Zhao Duoduo."

Zhao, bent at the waist, gave a panicky response before hurrying over.

Fourth Master slowly lifted his lapel and produced a red envelope from a fold in his pants. "You've muddled through half your life, but now you've finally done a good thing in setting up a company. Here's two hundred yuan. Your Fourth Master has been poor all his life, so this is just a token investment to show how I feel. Count the money now."

With the envelope in his hands, Zhao said, "No need. I don't have to count it."

"Count it now," Fourth Master said sternly.

It was midnight when the last people left the site, with some from the Sui clan among them. At first Jiansu sat on a cold rock, refusing to leave. Buzhao and Baopu helped him up, and the three of them walked back together, a hard, silent journey, even though the site was not far from their house.

Baopu took Jiansu to his room with his uncle's help before asking Hanzhang to make something for Jiansu to eat. Then they left, leaving

Hanzhang to sit at Jiansu's table and observe her brother as he sat in the dark. "Get some sleep," she said.

"Were you at the meeting, Hanzhang?"

She shook her head, "No. There were too many people for me."

As if talking to himself, Jiansu muttered, "So you don't know . . . the situation . . ."

"I do," she murmured. "I could guess . . . Second Brother, you need to sleep. Get some sleep. You're worn out."

Jiansu did not leave the house for several days. During that time, only a handful of people came to talk about raising capital to set up a factory, all from the Sui and Li clans. All their money combined amounted to a meager few hundred yuan, which was more like a consolation than an investment. They told him that Duoduo had already raised over a hundred thousand from people, not all of them local. They added that he planned to get a bank loan, which gave Jiansu an inspiration. Why not get one himself? So he talked to a banker, who spelled out the procedures for obtaining a loan. He then went to see Luan Chunji, who told him to come back after he received permission to set up a private enterprise. Afraid that he might waste his money trying to go through the back door, Jiansu decided to apply for a loan with his Wali Emporium as collateral. Li Yuming agreed to help him and went along to see Lu Jindian and Zou Yuquan. Finally a bank manager told him he could get a loan, but for no more than 5,000 yuan. Jiansu was crushed. When he heard that Zhao Duoduo had been given a 200,000 yuan loan, he asked how the difference could be so great and was told that Zhao was now a renowned entrepreneur and the bank had received a directive that people like Zhao needed special treatment, at low or no interest. Without a word, Jiansu turned and left.

That night Jiansu stood by the trellis, staring at the withered leaves on the bean stalks, when the image of the bramble-cutting girl flashed before his eyes. He shuddered and pressed down on his chest with both hands.

Back in Baopu's room, he saw the outline of his brother's shadow in the window, so he went in, only to be surprised by what he saw.

Baopu was checking accounts with an abacus. "What are you doing?" Jiansu asked.

"I'm checking the glass noodle factory account," Baopu replied calmly.

Jiansu sat down on the *kang* and sighed. "But it's too late."

"It is, but I have to do it."

Jiansu was quiet for a moment. "I already did it," he said. "I told you that."

As he flicked the abacus beads up and down, Baopu replied, "I have to do it myself. Maybe I'll get more detailed results and a larger figure. We're not looking at exactly the same records. This is going to take some time."

Lost for words, Jiansu took a look at the abacus and got up to pace the room. He opened Baopu's drawer and took out *The Communist Manifesto*, flipped through it, and then put it back. He waited for his brother to finish before telling him about the dream he'd had right before the meeting.

Jiansu described to Baopu the vast riverbank with its blue sand. Then the red horse, like the sun, came, and he rode away on it. He paused in his narrative and said, "I'm leaving Wali."

"Where are you going?" That caught Baopu by surprise.

"To the city. I don't want to live here anymore. Now that we're permitted to start a business in the city, I want to open a store or something. Zhang-Wang can take care of the shop in town for the time being."

Baopu kept his eyes on the window as he said, "This isn't something to rush into just because you're upset. You have to think it through. Life in the city isn't easy."

Puffing on his pipe, Jiansu said firmly, "My mind's made up. I've been thinking about this for a long time. My roots are here, so I'll be back. But I have to give it a try, even if it kills me. I've suffered enough over the years." He walked out, leaving Baopu to sit alone, seemingly frozen in place, for he knew that his brother would leave, just as Sui Buzhao had done years before.

Jiansu returned to his room and felt an unsettling warm current course through his body. After drinking a mug of cold water he was standing by the window to catch his breath, when he heard someone rap on the glass. He opened the door and in came Daxi. They stared at each other wordlessly at first, then Daxi threw herself into his arms and began to sob. He held her head up to look into her eyes and asked sternly, "Why haven't you come to see me the past few days?"

Daxi replied with a trembling voice, "I didn't dare. I was afraid, afraid you were dejected and wouldn't like me."

Deeply moved, Jiansu began kissing her. "Daxi, I like you. I really do. I always feel better after seeing you."

Daxi was surprised but pleased. "Really? Jiansu, I hate myself for not being able to help. I wish I could kill that Zhao Duoduo."

Jiansu was so touched his eyes moistened. He turned to close the door before laying his head on her soft breasts and keeping it there, neither moving nor responding when Daxi called out to him. She shook him but he remained silent. Anxious, she cried out and raised his head; she saw tears in the corners of his eyes. Never expecting him to be weeping, she let out a frightened cry. He laid his face on her forehead and said softly, "Daxi, are you listening to me? I'm truly grateful. I love you and I think about you all the time. I want you to marry me. Be my wife, and we'll spend the rest of our lives together. You have no idea how badly I've failed, and I ask you at a moment like this to be with me. You won't think I'm unworthy, will you?"

Daxi began to sob. Afraid that someone might hear her, he covered her mouth with his hand. Daxi began kissing him, his forehead, his eyes, his neck, and his dirty, uncombed hair.

"Let's lie down," Jiansu said, "and I'll tell you something important."

⤝⤞

After the meeting, the town of Wali began receiving peculiar news, all of which was related to Zhao Duoduo. People said he'd found someone to make a large sign for his company, that he was close to having a car shipped to town, and that he'd hired a female secretary, whose job title was changed, on her second day, to "civil servant." Jiansu stayed home the whole time, dark shadows appearing under his eyes from insomnia. His brother and uncle knew that the battle with Zhao Duoduo had sapped his energy and spirit, so they tried hard, even asking Hanzhang to make good food, to help him recover. After two weeks, the headaches returned, worse than before. Once again they sent for Guo Yun, who said this time was different but that the two episodes were connected. He informed them that Jiansu was suffering from a deficiency of both yin and yang, which resulted in a lack of energy. "Energy is the mother of the intellect; with it one enjoys the full capacity of one's mind. When the energy is impaired, the mind has no place to go and is lost. Anyone lacking energy will die, as will one whose mind is lost."

Panicking after hearing the doctor's prediction, Sui Buzhao and Baopu begged him to resort to heavy medication. But the old man shook his head. "His energy level is too low for that. Now we can only make a broth with cinnamon sticks to regulate his yin and yang, and use oysters to maintain his energy level, solidifying the yang and protecting the yin." He wrote out a prescription, telling the family they must be vigilant about having the patient take his medicine. Baopu accepted the prescription, which indicated 0.3 ounces of cinnamon sticks, 0.3 ounces of peony, three slices of raw ginger, 0.2 ounces of licorice, six large dates, and an ounce each of stewed bean stamen and stewed oysters.

SIXTEEN

Baopu went to the mill, as usual, but devoted his spare time to checking the accounts, with Jiansu's words—"It's too late"—ringing in his ears. He made frequent trips to Jiansu's room to make sure his brother took his medicine. Jiansu had not lain so quietly on the *kang* in years. Guo Yun came every few days to check on him, once bringing a vernacular version of Qu Yuan's classic text *Heavenly Questions,* which Jiansu read to pass time. Sui Buzhao, who regularly showed up to see the two brothers, laughed at Baopu for checking the accounts, saying they were the messiest thing ever devised by people to clarify things, which only ended up even more muddled. Knowing the cause of his father's death, Baopu had always stayed clear of such matters, but the bidding auction had persuaded him to take up the abacus.

One afternoon the sounds of Gimpy's flute drifted over from a distance, alerting Sui Buzhao, who said to Baopu, "The sound has changed."

Holding his breath to listen, Baopu noticed also how the tone was now different from what it had been for decades. He did not know what to make of that. The flute had always sounded shrill, bitter, lonely, and sad, but now a discernible, seemingly purloined happiness burst forth. It had been the eternal music of Wali's bachelors; the new sound would not be easy to get used to. "I'll go check it out," Sui Buzhao said, and left.

His heart beating furiously, Baopu could not concentrate, so he paced the room as anxiety welled up inside for reasons he could not begin to fathom. It was midnight when the flute went quiet and he could lie down to rest, but he still could not sleep. Dawn finally came, bringing his uncle, who called to him from outside the window, "Xiaokui has married Gimpy."

Baopu felt as if his head had exploded, leaving behind a loud buzz. He had no recollection of running out of his room, leaving the yard, and muttering to himself all the way to Zhao Family Lane. He did not stop pounding at the window until Xiaokui showed up on the other side with Leilei. Staring at her gaunt, pale face, he asked, "Is it true?"

"Yes."

"When?"

"A few days ago, when the town was caught up in the meeting."

"Ah, Xiaokui, you should have told me. You should have waited for me," Baopu shouted, holding his head in his hands.

Xiaokui bit her lips and shook her head. "I waited for you for years, and then the other day I looked at myself in the mirror and saw all the gray hair. I began to cry, so did the person in the mirror, and we told each other we wouldn't wait any longer, no more."

Grief-stricken, Baopu crouched down on the ground and murmured, "But . . . what about Leilei? Give him back to me. He's my son."

Xiaokui replied coldly, "No, he's Zhaolu's son."

As scenes from that stormy night flashed past his eyes, he raised his fists at the window but then let them drop. He got up and walked away without looking back.

Jiansu was waiting for his brother, who stood quietly in the middle of the room before putting his hand on Jiansu's bony shoulder. Jiansu could feel the violent tremors in the large hand that was now stroking his hair. Baopu still did not say a word. Jiansu looked into his brother's eyes and said, "Uncle came back but left since you weren't here."

Baopu nodded. "Left, gone. She's gone, gone for good, putting all her cares behind her. They're all gone. Aren't you leaving for the city?

The Sui clan! The Sui clan and its people." Jiansu tried to console him, telling him to get some rest since he still had to work at the mill the next day. But Baopu clasped his brother's hands and pleaded, "Please, don't leave. Stay here tonight and talk to me. I have so much to say to you that I'm suffocating. Xiaokui has left and if you leave, who will I talk to? To the old mill? To this room? Jiansu, don't just stand there, don't stare at me like that. Sit, sit down on the *kang*."

Jiansu sat down nervously, for Baopu had never acted like this before and he was worried. Wanting to console him, he didn't know what to say. Xiaokui belonged to someone else now. Jiansu knew that his brother loved this woman with all his heart, but all he could think was, "Baopu, this is what you get for putting up with so much and sitting in that old mill all day long. No one can help you now, and it's useless to feel sympathy for you."

Baopu tried to roll a cigarette with his shaky hands, producing a misshapen one, so Jiansu gave him one of his. Baopu took a couple of puffs and threw it away. "Did you call the members of the Sui family cowards?" he asked Jiansu, who just stared at him. Baopu nodded emphatically. "You did, and you were right. I let her walk into another man's arms. I tormented myself and tormented others, as if I lived only to torture people. I'm not happy and I don't want others to be happy either. What kind of freak am I? I kept everything bottled up inside for a month, a year, my whole lifetime, like making bean sauce, until everything changed color. I've never spoken my mind; I feel like the blood has frozen in my veins. I'd like to plunge an awl into my body; I want to bleed, I don't care if the pain makes me roll around on the floor and scream myself hoarse and frighten everyone away. I think about this all the time, but I've never had the guts to actually do it. I don't have the guts to do anything, so why not keep a low profile for the rest of my life? But I can't do that either. I know how to hate and to love, how to run outside when there's a rainstorm. Sometimes I feel as if boiling water is being poured over my body, and I tell myself to let it pour and make no noise, nothing. I had Xiaokui once. I was soaking wet in the rain and held her through the night. She's mine and I don't want anyone else. I don't care if I'm poor or being trampled on, I just want her. There hasn't been a single day that I haven't thought of her, and not a single day that I had the guts to see her. Ten years went by, and then twenty years, until our hair turned gray.

"What am I afraid of? Zhaolu's eyes. They glare at me in my dreams. I'm afraid of the entire Zhao clan, Xiaokui's family. I'm scared of myself and the Sui clan. No one in the Sui clan deserves to have a family or any offspring. But then we're human too, a family of men and women. Every generation of the Sui clan has stressed the importance of reputation, but when reputation became worthless, we continued to suffer over it. I've told you the things I fear, but the most important thing, which I haven't mentioned till now, is reputation. Zhaolu was alive when Xiaokui gave herself to me. She wasn't afraid of anything. I'm a poor excuse for a man. I was afraid people were going to say I stole someone's wife while he was trying to make his fortune in the northeast. I timidly did whatever I could to avoid that. Xiaokui has suffered so much. I should have brought her into our family when Zhaolu died. I'm a horrible person and I'll despise myself forever. Xiaokui is wonderful; she steeled herself and left like a man. Me, I'm like a woman. I'll be thinking about her for the rest of my life. But no, I must forget her, I must forget everything. Everything except for the fact that I'm a worthless coward."

Jiansu, who had never heard his brother submit himself to such excruciating and painful analysis, stopped him anxiously. "Stop! Please don't talk like that. You're a good man, many times better than me. It horrifies me to see you beat yourself up like that. Baopu, as the oldest in our generation you've suffered more than any of us. I know it's been hard on you. I understand you now more than at any other time."

Tiny beads of sweat oozed from Baopu's forehead and his teeth chattered as if from the cold when he said, "No, you don't. No one understands me. But that's my fault, because I think too much and reveal too little. I didn't tell Guigui everything when we were married, not because I was afraid, but because I thought so much it became impossible to explain what was on my mind. How I envy people who are worry free, or if they have worries, it's never something that eats at them. I envied Guigui, with her childlike eyes, even on the day she died. You saw those eyes, so pretty, so dark and bright. I don't think she ever hated anyone. No hatred could exist in those eyes. Do you remember when they set up the dining hall and we were interrogated separately about hoarding food? Her face was swollen from the beatings, but there was no hate in her eyes as she lay in my arms at night. I told myself how lucky I was to spend my life with a 'child,' and how my life would be so much easier if a bit of her temperament rubbed off on me. Later I realized that it was all wishful thinking, since no one could change me. I'm like a weighted object that will never again rise to the surface. So I figure I might as well resign myself to my fate and go sit in the mill, letting it grind away my life and dull my heart and my personality. It would have been perfect if it could have ground away my sanity. But even that was wishful thinking. The old mill has only made me even more sensitive.

"It's hopeless. I don't understand myself. Sometimes my self-loathing is greater than my loathing for any other person or thing. So I sit there day in and day out, having a conversation with myself the whole time. I ask myself a question and answer it myself; sometimes I just curse myself. Jiansu, you may not know this, but quiet people are actually the most talkative; they talk so much their tongue is parched and their lips turn dry. They talk to themselves, and they suffer alone. What did I ask myself? Nothing but a bunch of muddled yet common questions. Such as, why did I turn into a quiet man? Which year did I forget my birthday? Was the harvest good the year when Father died? I also thought of what happened the year my mother died, which year it was I first saw gray in my hair, and of things Uncle said. I pondered his personality, reflected on my stepmother and her death, recalled what Hanzhang looked like as a little girl and then as a teenager and her illness. I thought about the oldest and youngest members of the Sui clan, of Guigui's infertility, of what happened on the day we married, of whether I should go see Xiaokui, of what I wanted, of whether or not I have any religious beliefs, of whether or not I'm an intellectual. I asked myself why the first word I learned had come from *The Analects,* recalled how I ground ink for Father and you ground it for me, wondered how Zhao Duoduo would die and how many times Zhang-Wang saw Father and how science could be applied to the glass noodle factory, I thought about Dahu's death, about what we'd do if there were indeed aliens, about what Star Wars had to do with Wali, about how things would have been different if the cartload of turnips had arrived earlier than 1960, and so on.

"You couldn't possibly have known that I talked to myself about all these. I sat on that stool for hours examining them. I filled my heart with things I can't forget until it was about to burst, but I couldn't get rid of them. My heart overflows with things that have happened over the decades, and I can only beg the heavens to help me forget some of them. But I get no response. All I do is curse myself when I feel bad, whether it's over the annoying barking dogs at midnight or Gimpy, who won't let up on his flute. When I can't sleep I get up to pace the yard. I feel much better when a torrential rain washes over me on a rainy day. At moments like that, I feel like waking you up and telling you what's on my mind, but I never have, not once. I don't know anyone in our family who knows what it means to enjoy a good night's sleep, except maybe Uncle. I thought you were carefree, but now I know I was wrong. The factory torments you so much your eyes turn red and the look in them scares me. I'm forever on edge, afraid that something will happen to you. I envy you, I'm terrified of you, and I hate you. You have more guts than me. You're like a panther ready to pounce on its prey. You're different from the rest of us, and maybe you were created by the times we live in. When you fell ill I knew it was because you hadn't caught your prey, just as I expected. But you wouldn't listen, so you wound up cut and bleeding. Everyone in the family felt your pain, but we have so little blood we can't afford to lose any more. That grieves me. But I appreciate your courage. You're one of the clan's real men. You've grown big and strong, a hundred times better than your brother, who'd have caught all the prey he went after if he'd had your courage. Nothing would have escaped him, including

Xiaokui. But is courage a good thing? Is it? I've asked myself that question a thousand times, but I've never found the answer. Should the Sui clan have that kind of courage? Who can answer me? Who?"

Sparks seemed to fly from Jiansu's eyes. Several times during Baopu's soliloquy he'd wanted to interrupt his brother but was stopped each time by the torrent of words. Now he saw an opening. "I can!" he shouted. "I can answer you. I say people's strength is more or less the same, so courage is the key to survival. We've been trampled on for so many years we can't breathe, and when we beg them to ease off, they only increase the pressure. What did we do wrong? As for you, even when the pressure is light, you still won't stand up; you don't have the guts. Yes, I'm bleeding, but I'll lick it clean and pounce again. How many times have I asked you how Mother died? You refuse to tell me. You tear yourself up with your own claws until you're a bloody mess and yet you won't stop. Yes, Xiaokui is gone, but shouldn't she be? Shouldn't she?"

"I don't know. Maybe she should. Was she afraid to be tainted by my blood? I know I shouldn't tear myself up, but I don't want to see anyone from our family tear up others either. The people in town tear each other apart until the blood flows like a river. You want me to tell you about the past, but I can't. I don't have the guts. I told you I'm afraid of you, didn't I? You have guts, but I don't want to be like you. For me it would be enough if I could protect myself or protect good people being attacked by bad. That's the courage I need, but I don't even have that, and that's the most disgraceful thing about me. I've known all along that you and I are different. What I fear most are people who are more like beasts than humans, because they're the reason the blood flows like a river in Wali. I don't want to think about the past, because I'm afraid of suffering. Jiansu, I shudder whenever I think of these days. I pray that suffering will leave Wali soon and never return. Don't laugh at me or think I'm worrying for nothing.

"The people here have suffered too much. Earlier generations planted crops but their bellies were seldom filled with food. They were forced to eat stalks and leaves to stay alive. What happened to the grain? No one knew; it simply disappeared. We have the most honest, most uncomplicated people in our town; they quietly suffer hunger and cold, and eat grass stalks. When they lack the energy to walk, they lie down to die. You know all this, Jiansu. You saw it with your own eyes. These things keep flashing before me. Father gave the glass noodle factory away because he thought it belonged to the people, not because he was afraid. I always knew he had his reasons. He left a small processing room for the family to live on, but eventually someone made the decision to take it away from us so it could be shared by all. That, of course, was a good thing. Maybe it was because we never shared before that generations had to lead such a hard life. But life is still hard. That's what saddens me and it is why I keep reading that book. Our poor father coughed up blood and died on horseback, all because he wanted us to share. He would be overcome by grief if he knew what happened after he died; maybe he's coughing up blood in the underworld. This is what I've been thinking. It's the core issue of being human— that is, how to live. It is no one person's concern. Absolutely not. Your mistake has been to treat it as an individual's concern. The same goes for all those who suffer setbacks. You can't make life easy for yourself, because those around you will take it away from you. Have you heard the story about the group of people who were looking for gold in the mountains? The man in front found a nugget and held on to it tightly, saying it was his and his alone. The others tried to pry it out of his hands, reminding him that they had all worked together to find water to drink and to drive off wild beasts. But he would not let go of the gold, even bit the others to drive them away. So in the end, the group had no choice but to stone him to death. It's a simple story. The world has seen countless philosophies, some of which have been written in books with gilded pages and silk covers. But in the end they all talk about one thing—how to live, and live well, to live as best as one can. That's all. You've seen me read that slim book, *The Communist Manifesto*. Well, it too is a book about living, one worth reading all your life. This is related to the issue of religious faith, but I'll return to that later. Let's get back to living. I thought that suffering and bloodshed in our town would come to an end, but now I know I was just fooling myself. How can other people have a good life when there are still people like you? People like you will hold on to your gold and keep it from others. They will stone you and you'll fight back, and there'll be more bloodshed. Jiansu, are you listening to me? Do you understand? Don't forget that you're a member of the Sui clan, whose ancestors thought things through so we wouldn't have to shed our blood pointlessly. This is what I want to say, what I want to tell you. You're hurt now but you haven't shed too much blood. Come to your senses, and quickly!"

"Do you expect to me sprawl on the ground for the rest of my life? Do you mean for me to live like you, buried alive in a coffin?" With his fists clenched, Jiansu stood up. "Well, I won't do it. I've said this before. I'm in my thirties, and I want to live like a real man. I want my own family, a wife and children. I want to live like a human being."

"Well said," Baopu said gruffly. "You couldn't be any more right. What you ask is not much, but that's only half of what you really want to say. If you say it all, you'll tell me you want the glass noodle factory and you want the town of Wali behind you. You made that clear before."

"I want the glass noodle factory. Yes, I do. One thing will never change—we can't let it remain in Duoduo's hands."

"But it doesn't belong to any one person. These days, who in Wali has the power to keep it for himself for the rest of his life? No one. Duoduo is simply deceiving himself. You wait and see, if you don't believe me. Anyone who thinks like him is self-deceiving. You want the factory because you don't want Duoduo to have it. But let me ask you, Jiansu. I've seen many toothless old men and women who are reduced to eating yams mixed with chaff. When you get rich, can you guarantee that they will have food to eat and clothes to wear, that you'll treat them as if they were your parents? Can you? Answer me."

Sweat dripped from Jiansu's forehead and flowed down the sides of his nose. He muttered something incomprehensible. "Well, aren't these . . ."

Baopu gave him a stern look and said, "Answer me, and don't be evasive. You must tell the truth, even just this one time. Tell me."

Jiansu looked up. "I can't. There are too many poor people in town."

Baopu sat down and rolled a cigarette; he took a puff before saying with a sneer, "Well, you did it, you told the truth, acting like a member of the Sui clan. Now it should be clear to you that you aren't that different from Duoduo. There's a limit to your abilities and to your kindness. You cannot shoulder all those responsibilities. The glass noodle industry has always been the lifeblood of the town, and you're being greedy if you want it all to yourself. I told you I hate myself for being such a coward that I've driven away Xiaokui, ruining the second half of my life. What you don't know is that I hate myself even more for not being strong enough to take the glass noodle factory from Duoduo and give it to the people. I wish I could say to them, 'Here, take it. Hold on tight and lock it up. It belongs to everyone, and let's make sure that no selfish individual takes it away again. Be absolutely sure of that!' That's what I've been thinking. People may laugh at me, but I wouldn't be surprised if those who mock me are unkind themselves. They'll laugh at me. Peasant consciousness, they'll say. An egalitarian.

"They are ignorant of the Sui clan's history of suffering and, for that matter, the town's history of suffering. To feel good about themselves, they pretend to be open-minded and sometimes pretend to be scholars. If they could have seen how the Sui clan has struggled for years to survive in the midst of peasantlike jealousy and envy, they'd know that we hate egalitarianism more than they do. No, that's not what it is; it's just that the people of Wali have suffered so much and shed so much blood that they need a respite to heal their wounds. They won't be able to endure having any more taken from them by the strong, and they won't easily turn over what good things they have to just anyone. Don't you agree? This is the conclusion I've reached, but it is precisely where my problem lies; I've seen through the situation but lack the courage to do anything about it. I'm afraid. Will I never get an ounce of courage? That's why I said I envy you. I mean it. I wish I could get something from you—your guts and your passion. Everyone should have those, but some people have lost theirs, to their great misfortune. I am one of these unfortunate people.

"Jiansu, it's better not to have courage if it cannot be used properly. But some people feel they lack courage because they don't use it properly. You once said that I'm indecisive, that I wind up missing everything. You were right; you pinpointed my sore spot. I often consider indecision a sickness with a deep-rooted cause, which I've had since a young age. It's getting worse now. I'm a coward, never daring to say what I think. Sometimes I manage to find the courage to say something, but I stammer uncontrollably as soon as someone shouts a response. I lack the courage to walk into a crowd or to speak my piece. Whenever something happens in town and an investigation begins, I feel that I'm at fault. I walk soundlessly, because I'm afraid someone may say, 'Look, he's walking.' But who doesn't walk? That's why I choose a deserted alley, the base of a wall, or the open field—in order to avoid people.

"In my secret observations I've noticed that I'm not the only one with that sickness, though there are more in the Sui clan than in others, and the severity is greater. Take Hanzhang for example; it's been years since I last heard her laugh. Several times I've tried to cure my sickness, and once I even went to the floodplain to laugh in the dark, as loud as I could. It felt great to hear the echoes of my own laughter, so I kept at it, but after a while it felt a bit like crying. I've been sick for so long, and the cause is so complex, that I need to start from the beginning. But I earnestly believe that I'll be cured one day, strong inside and out, and that I'll enjoy self-confidence."

"Courage is something you must find." Jiansu looked at his animated brother and added, "Do I have the same sickness? It's called timidity? How do you catch it? Can't Guo Yun cure it?"

Baopu nodded. "Yes, it's timidity, and of course Guo Yun can't do anything about it. If you pay close attention, you'll see that people from out of town tend to have more courage. You don't have this sickness, you have another, whose name escapes me at the moment. But I'm sure you're sick. You and I are both sick; so is everyone in the Sui clan. For decades I've been trying to fight it, fight it off with clenched teeth, but it's tightly bound to my bad luck in marriage. I love and fear Xiaokui, though probably no one would believe me. I think about her every night, about her eyes, her mouth, her lashes, the warmth of her body. I haven't found another woman lovelier than her or with as gentle a temperament. She lies quietly in another man's arms, maybe cries a bit when she's happy. I miss her desperately. I doubt that anyone could miss a woman the way I miss her. But when the moment came I was afraid to act. I don't know if it's right for me to miss her. Should I? Who is she? What is she? With each step forward, I take another back, so now it's decades later and I'm still at the mill. It's all because of this sickness. I tell myself to put up with it the best I can. But one day I'll be stronger. You asked me how we get the sickness? I ask myself the same question all the time, but I haven't dared to answer it. I'm going to tell you everything tonight, Jiansu, so listen carefully. I need to think back to the beginning and tell you everything."

SEVENTEEN

"I know this sickness that's been tormenting me has deep roots, but I lack the courage to probe its cause. Maybe I was sick even before you were born, since I'm nine years older than you. I've told you that as far back as I can remember, Father spent all his time doing the accounts, which so wore him down that his face turned dry and sallow. He never smiled at me; in fact, I can't remember the last time he smiled. Mother was a stranger to me at first, but later on our relationship improved. Then her father, your maternal grandfather, died in Qingdao, and she cried until she hardly had any breath left. That frightened me so much I can recall the details even now. Later on, after handing over the noodle factory, Father was more relaxed, but that was the day Mother cracked her fingers on the dining table, spattering it with her blood. She quickly wiped the table clean, but I felt as if the blood still shimmered on the table and would start to flow again if I tried to pick up some food with my chopsticks at mealtimes. After Father's death, I chopped the table up for firewood. Mother flew into a rage when she found out, for she was very fond of that red lacquered table. Back then, I thought she was too greedy to part with anything, and with a personality like hers, she was doomed to die—to die the way she did." Baopu began to stammer and took a quick look at Jiansu, who fixed his eyes on him.

"How did she die? Go on, tell me."

Baopu exhaled slowly and said, "You already know. She took her own life—poison." He was sweating.

Jiansu just sneered. Baopu continued, "I was only four or five years old. By the time I was six or seven, there were meetings in town almost daily. Mountains of people congregated at the old temple site, and armed militiamen were stationed on the top of the wall and on the rooftops near the site. Landlords from in and out of the town were dragged over to the site to be struggled against to the point that every day someone died. One day Father was told to attend one of the mass meetings, but he only had to stand below the platform, not on it. Mother sent me out to check on him, but I couldn't see, so I climbed the wall. When a militiaman pointed his rifle at me, I flattened out and shut my eyes. The barrel was no longer pointing at me when I opened my eyes, and I realized he had only wanted to scare me.

"I looked at Father first, but then shifted my attention to a long-haired, middle-aged man who had just been dragged up onto the stage. He parted his hair in the middle and was wearing a white shirt that was part of some sort of uniform. We'd never seen anyone like that in the countryside. Later I learned that he was the young scion of a landlord family who had been studying in a foreign school and was caught when he came home on family business. His father had fled, so he had to take his father's place. One after another, the villagers went up on the stage to complain about his father. After she'd finished complaining and crying, an old woman in rags wiped her tears off, whipped out an awl, and lunged at the young man. But the cadres and the militiamen onstage blocked her attack. More people went up to cry and complain. At midday, a group of people swarmed up, each holding a switch, and began whipping him. I saw blood stain his shirt until it turned completely red. I could see he was screaming and writhing in agony, though I couldn't hear very clearly. Then he died. I went home, too scared to go to the meetings again.

"Jiansu, believe it or not, I can still see those red streaks as if it were yesterday. I was only six or seven, and that was nearly forty years ago.

After that, we kept hearing people discuss whether the Sui clan could be considered a liberated gentry family. The militiamen were always walking around in our house. Everyone in the family muttered silently, 'Are we or aren't we?' But we kept our voices low. I don't know why but I had a hunch that sooner or later we would not be. Jiansu, in the late summer of 1947, things began to happen in town, and it scares me just thinking about them. I never mentioned this to anyone, because no one would believe me if not for the older folks, who can bear witness, and the records in the town's history. That summer . . ."

Baopu leaned against the wall; his lips had a purplish tinge. His hand shook as he reached out to hold Jiansu's arm.

"Go on," Jiansu said, "please, go on."

Baopu nodded and looked around; he nodded again. "I will. I've already said I'm going to tell you everything tonight."

Jiansu pulled his arm free and sat on the edge of the *kang*. His brother had retreated to the corner, his face no longer visible in the darkness.

"In late summer that year, the landlord restitution corps came to town, and many people fled to the west of the river or even farther when they heard the news. Zhao Duoduo left, so did Fourth Master, as did the political instructor and cadres sent down to the village. Some people stayed, while others were caught on the run and brought back. Some of the avenging landlords were local, but most were not from Wali. They were led by locals as they went from house to house to check on personal effects and search for people. In the end, over forty men and women, old and young, were herded over to the old temple site; I was one of them. The landlords cursed us, lit a fire, and tossed one man in. He had knelt down to beg for his life, but they threw him in anyway. He crawled out, covered in ashes and his hair badly singed, but was thrown right back in. Half of the remaining people in the group were stunned into silence, while the other half were scared into wailing. A few knelt to beg for their lives. I'll never forget the smell of the fire; in fact I think about it all the time. Sometimes I'll be walking on the street and think I detect the smell. It's an illusion, of course. The man burned to death. He'd served a few days in the militia. His last words were, 'This has nothing to do with me. Heaven help me, I don't know anything.'

"One of the kids in the group tried to run but was kicked by a man with a rifle. He fell backward and the man stomped on his belly, yelling, 'How dare you run? How dare you?' With blood oozing from the corners of his mouth, the kid died, not even given a chance to cry out. To stop people from running away, they got a length of wire and ran it under everyone's collarbone. The bloodied wire came out of one man's skin and went into another man's. With knives they made holes and strung everyone, even old women and little children, together. When it was my turn, a man pushed down on my head with his bloody hand so he could cut into my skin. Suddenly someone yelled, "He's the first young master of the Sui clan; he can't be strung together with these people." So he let me go. I still don't know who it was who shouted, whether it was someone from the landlord restitution corps or from the group of forty. Two or three people pulled at each end of the wire, making the prisoners scream in agony, and that went on until daybreak, staining the ground with blood. At daybreak, they were all dragged over to a yam cellar, and they were thrown down into it. Jiansu, you didn't see the look in their eyes, but if you had, you wouldn't forget it till the day you died. They hadn't done anything wrong; they often didn't know where their next meal would come from. All they did was keep a tiny "trophy" from their struggle against the landlords. They were all pushed into the cellar and their cries rose to heaven. But the landlords threw in rocks and shoveled in dirt; some even urinated on them.

"I can't talk about it anymore, Jiansu. No more. Just try to imagine what it was like. I'd barely turned seven at the time, so I'll have fifty-three years to remember the sight if I live to be sixty. It's too much to bear. I know my life is essentially over and that I will have to live with fear from now on, but there's nothing I can do about that. Maybe you'll say, 'I heard about those forty-two people being buried alive in the yam cellar,' but Jiansu, you didn't see them. You didn't hear them cry out. That makes a huge difference. If you had, you'd never forget it and it would begin to suffocate you."

Unable to continue, Baopu pressed up against the wall. Jiansu reached into his pocket for a cigarette with a shaking hand, and when he got it, he dropped the matches. He finally managed to light a cigarette for his brother and one for himself before opening a window to look out at Hanzhang's window. He shut the window and murmured, "There are things that people cannot imagine but nothing that people will not do. Something like that happened in Wali, and yet you'd never detect it on people's faces, not even in the color of soil on the old temple ground. People! Some easily forget things like this while others remember it all their lives. People are so different. Baopu, you suffer too much. Life's hard on you, too hard. I want to help you, but what can I do? You really need someone to help. Or maybe only you can help yourself."

Baopu clasped his brother's hands tightly and said, "You and I may be different, but you know me better than anyone else. No one can help a man but himself. That's exactly right. I'm trying hard to do that. It's like holding up a boulder, and even when your arms are sore, you can't allow them to shake or wobble. You must grit your teeth and keep at it; if you wobble, you're finished. I'm trying, I'm really trying. That's right, I'm helping myself. I'm helping myself by recalling the past and by checking accounts. I often wonder how long a person can keep on going. Forever? What's most terrifying is not the sky falling in, or the earth opening up, or the mountain toppling; it's ourselves. It's true. Just look at the town's chronicles if you don't believe me. Whatever is left out of the chronicles remains in people's minds. We must try to get to the bottom of things; being afraid is not enough.

"Has the blood in Wali been shed for nothing? Do we put a period to the town's history? No, we cannot, we cannot forget so easily. We must explore the reasons for things; every one of us—man, woman, adult, or child—both the powerful and the powerless, must examine the past. And we must examine ourselves. We use our brains for other things, to design machinery or put a halter on a horse, and these are all fine things. But how do we escape suffering? What goes wrong to cause people to be so ruthless, cruel, and murderous? Let's not be in a hurry to accuse or complain; let us first think about why we lack sympathy and pity for others. When an old woman lived to the age of eighty on chaff and wild greens, it was time for us to celebrate her longevity, yet we picked up a knife to string a wire beneath her collarbone and bury her in a yam cellar. Humans! People did that! A simple, honest person, the old woman had done nothing wrong. When she found white, succulent worms in the chaff, she thought it was a waste to throw them away, so she cooked and ate them. Even if she'd done something wrong, couldn't we have forgiven an eighty-year-old woman? She'd been on her hands and knees all her life, and when she neared the end, why couldn't we raise our hands and let her crawl ahead to reach it? Jiansu, I can't bear to think about that, I just can't.

"Sometimes when I'm sitting in the mill I hear a scream. I know I'm hallucinating, but it makes me so sad I begin to cry. Who can save me? Who will save humanity? No one. We have to save each other. I hate bellicose people who tell nothing but lies, who enjoy fine clothes and love to bully others. They spread misery whenever they get the chance. What makes them hateful is not only what they've done but also what they will do. If you don't see that, you'll never feel true loathing for the suffering or ugliness of the world, and tragedy will continue to rain down on Wali. Jiansu, have you given any thought to this? Have you? If you haven't, how can you consider yourself qualified to take over the noodle factory? If you haven't, then you're not worthy of making any contribution to Wali. It's as simple as that. The more important the things you're in charge of, the more you must think about suffering and misery. You must learn to hate some people and to ruminate on the past. You must be clear on this, for if you aren't, sooner or later suffering will knock on your door. Jiansu, you must answer me tonight—no, right now—whether you've been thinking about these things, whether you hate those who spread misery. Answer me, and be honest."

Jiansu cleared his throat and said, "I . . . I don't really think about those things, but I hate Zhao Duoduo with a vengeance."

"That's no good. It's obvious you're not worthy of making a contribution to Wali. You can't do it. I was right about you. Don't think that what you're doing now is beneath you or that you're destined for something greater. You must realize that you are a dispensable person to the town and be content with that. That's all you can do. If you were to become a person of great importance, nothing good would come of it. Some people like to stress the value of intelligence, saying a great person is someone with intelligence and courage. But I want to ask: Didn't the person who thought of stringing a group of people with a wire have intelligence? Or courage? Let him make good use of his intelligence and courage! Don't underestimate those who are quick to flatter, or those who are cautious and obedient. These are the people who, years ago, did the bidding of intelligence and courage and pulled the wire. As I said, it's not what they've done but what they will do. Be careful to avoid these people; watch out for them. Stay away from their intelligence, and that'll be a blessing for the town. I know you don't like to hear these things and that you might fly into a rage, but I have to go on.

"I've digressed too far. I was going to tell you how I got sick, so let me go on with that. I'm going to tell you things that have been stewing in my heart for decades, but I'm actually afraid to reveal them. This is the first and last time I'll talk to you about the past. I don't want you to get the same kind of sickness after hearing the story I just told you and what I'm going to tell you now."

Jiansu said in a soft voice, "I won't. If that sickness didn't strike me as a child, I'm immune. Go ahead, I'm listening."

"Bottling things up all my life is killing me. Jiansu, I'm going to tell you a horror story about a woman. Don't look at me like that, and don't interrupt me. It happened in our town at around the same time. One afternoon, a few days after I went to that public meeting, a landlord who was imprisoned in the cellar escaped, and the militia blocked off every street in town to conduct a search. They checked every house but didn't find him. During the search, people asked the militia to interrogate members of the family, a daughter and a son who had been locked up at another place. The landlord, a local bully, had raped two girls washing noodles in the processing room when he was in his forties. One of the girls got pregnant and hanged herself. The girl's brother was one of those who tortured the landlord's children to locate their father. I heard he beat them on their backs and buttocks with the butt of a rifle, over and over.

"When night came, the militiamen argued over who would guard the prisoners, but the dead girl's brother told them he'd do it himself, which he did, for two nights. On the third night, it was a militiaman's turn, and not long after that the girl died. The militiamen buried her on the floodplain. But what horrified me was what happened one morning after that. I still regret that I left the house that morning. When I got to the west end of the street, I saw a group of people crowded around a tree, laughing and shouting. Some were even stomping their feet. So I ran over. When they saw me, someone pushed those in front aside and said, 'Hey, get out of the way and let the little guy here have a look.' Not knowing what was going on, I pushed forward and what I saw stupefied me. I couldn't believe my own eyes. The girl who had been buried a few days before was tied to the tree. With her eyes closed, she appeared to be asleep. Her naked body was covered with bruises and scars. Her nipples were missing, dark blood clots congealing on the breasts. Then I looked down. Jiansu, you won't believe what they'd done. They'd stuck a carrot up her.

"I didn't give a thought to whether someone had dug her up or the militiamen hadn't buried her. I let out a loud cry and ran home. Mother and Father looked at me, startled; scared witless, they thought something terrible had happened. I didn't tell them what I saw; I never told anyone. It's been like a bloody seed buried in my chest for years. I didn't tell Guigui. I was ashamed, ashamed for all of us. I can't explain my sense of shame and guilt. Maybe the heavens had arranged for me to see that and create a memory that would make me tremble each time I thought of it. Are these things divorced from us? No, not in the least. It's like it happened yesterday; it's still clear, crystal clear. But many people have already forgotten the incident, as if nothing ever happened and our Wali is a normal town just like any other. But no, I know that's not the case, because I saw it. I want to tell everyone that's not the case. I don't understand why they had to kill her and why they had to do what they did. I don't understand why they didn't bury her or why they dug her up after burying her. Her blood stained the yellow sand. Why didn't they cover the stains with sand? Why didn't they cover her face, her hands, her breasts and her privates, her body? Why? Weren't they content with what they'd already done? Or was she too pretty? Can you put a flower in a vase after you trample and spit on it? I've asked myself that question over and over, and it always makes me so sad I weep.

"When I slept at night with Guigui in my arms, I don't know why, but sometimes I'd think about the girl on the tree and start shaking all over, frightening Guigui, who'd ask me if I was sick. I'd tell her no and hold her tight; I'd caress her and treat her with double the tenderness. It was like, after that, every man in the world owed women something. We should all be ashamed of ourselves, because we failed in our obligation to protect women. After that year I felt that every man alive should do his best to protect women, no matter what that took. Anyone who failed had to be run out of Wali. When Guigui was sick at night, she'd cry silently and gaze at me through her tears. That always got me wondering why so much suffering is inflicted upon women. Guigui, your sister-in-law, died not long after that. I dug a deep hole to bury her. Someone said it was too deep, but I said no. I kept digging so I could bury her in the deepest hole possible."

Unable to bear what he was hearing, Jiansu laid his head on his brother's knees and wept pitifully.

Baopu reached down to raise Jiansu's head, but he refused to look up. After weeping awhile, he looked up and dried his own tears. He gazed at Baopu with fire in his eyes, as if to say, "Keep going. Tell me everything. I'm listening. Go on."

Collecting himself as best he could, Baopu wiped the sweat from his forehead and continued, "The town's chronicle doesn't cover what I just told you, and that's a blemish. Never underestimate what's missing and what isn't, for that affects every generation's views of the town. Later generations will not enjoy a good life if they fail to understand the generations that came before them, for they'll try things in the mistaken view that their elders hadn't already tried them. I've wanted to ask Li Yuming and Lu Jindian to revise the town's history while those who experienced it are alive. But I lack the courage. I think too much and do too little, so all I'm good for is sitting in the old mill. Every time I think about doing something, I grow uneasy; I feel as if I fear nothing but am afraid of everything. If you're not a member of the Sui clan or a resident of Wali, you'll never understand why I feel that way. I consider it a blessing to be able to sit quietly in the mill.

"Sometimes I sit there all day, even late into the night. I come back here, wash up and eat, and then sleep or read. I read *The Communist Manifesto* over and over because I know it's so tightly bound up with our town and the misery of the Sui clan. You need to spend a lot of time reading it, and read it with your heart, not just your head. How many quiet, peaceful days have we had so far? You know what happened next, so I don't have to tell you.

"More than once, Zhao Duoduo led people to our yard and poked the ground with a steel pole; it felt as if the pole were piercing my heart. We didn't dare go out because there were rebels in town. Each time the Red Guards came to search our house, I hid Father's books by putting them in a coffin and sifting dirt with a sieve to cover the coffin. When you and I were tied up and paraded on the street, they pasted Father's picture on our foreheads. Someone watching us shouted, 'What the hell's that on their heads?' Someone shouted a reply: 'It's the old geezer's picture.' They laughed and laughed, then went back to shouting slogans.

"I went in to cook dinner after we got back home. Your face was ashen and you said nothing. You reminded me of Mother the time she hurt her hand by banging it on the table. I was afraid for you. Jiansu, that was how we got through those days, one after the other. We never had a good laugh. Hell, we didn't know how it felt to laugh anymore. We stayed in the house, avoiding everyone; we walked on tiptoes even in our own yard. Back then, I was afraid of noise, any noise. If I dropped the lid of a pot while I was cooking, I'd look over my shoulder. Once I was crossing the river and ran into Zhao Duoduo on that narrow willow bridge. As we passed each other, he spat and muttered, 'I'm going to kill you.' His words sent a chill through my heart. Jiansu, for many years I've felt like I'm just waiting to be killed. I've led a cautious, soundless life, afraid that someone might remember me and kill me."

Jiansu was breathing hard as he nervously got up and sat down again, rubbing his knees. "I don't know why but my hands itch every time I see Duoduo. The business end of a knife is what his purple Adam's apple needs. I don't know why, but every part of his body is a potential target for my knife. That's why I'd never, ever let the factory remain in his hands without a struggle. I'm not like you. A force has been building inside me and taking charge of everything I do. Now I'm beginning to understand you, Baopu. You don't have that force. It's as simple as that."

Baopu shook his head. "No, it's not. I don't have that force? Of course I do, but I don't hate just one person. I hate all suffering and cruelty. I'm on edge day and night, worrying about these things. I can't figure them out but I can't make myself stop thinking about them either. I despise people who want only to grab things, because what they take away actually belongs to everyone. If they continue to grab things, Wali will never be rid of its misery, and there will be no end to hatred. Just think, Jiansu, do you have more talent than older members of the Sui clan, like Father, Granddad, or Great-Granddad? They guarded the factory and made it prosper, spreading its reputation overseas, but in the end they were unable to keep it. What makes you think you can? Are you powerful enough to do that? Give that some thought. Father thought through some of this, but it was too late for him. He'd be sadly disappointed to see you now. As I said, an individual should never treat his livelihood as a personal matter, because that will make him fight for himself alone, and blood will once again be shed in Wali. The Sui clan has suffered a great deal, but we mustn't live just for ourselves anymore. It's important to think about what is recorded in the town's chronicles and what isn't, for these things do not belong to the distant past.

"The people of Wali have suffered too much and too much blood has been shed. When there was famine, the people ate leaves and grass, even clay and lime. Older people remember things such as how Li Qisheng's wife was buried still clenching a rag in her mouth. Everyone should be thinking up ways to have a decent life; people should not be so lazy that they place their hopes in others. We can no longer dither and drag our feet, sitting in a mill like a zombie. I beat myself up and am constantly urging myself to stand up straight and leave the mill. Maybe I will one day, but I'll never abandon the people in town or snatch things out of their hands. Many of them have been left with only the clothes on their backs. All I can do is join them in trying to find a good way to live. You know I've been reading *The Communist Manifesto*. Basically, it has exerted more influence on Wali over the years than anything else. It's not an easy book to read, but if you work at it, you can see the eyes of the authors and then their meaning slowly becomes clear. They saw more misery than anyone. How else could they have written such a book? Why has it been translated into all the languages in the world—English, French, German, Italian, Flemish, Danish? Why? Because they, along with people all over the world, were trying to figure out how to have a better life.

"I often cry when I read the book. The authors are highly moral philosophers with hearts as big as the ocean. They were devoted to a search for the truth, with no time for small-mindedness; they were good fathers, good husbands, and good men. They had much to say, but, as you know, nothing is more powerful than brevity, so they presented their ideas in small segments, deliberate and forceful. They were amazingly confident individuals. I was touched as soon as I read the first line in the little book, 'A specter is haunting Europe—the

specter of communism.' I pictured that haunting specter and imagined how it drifted over the Luqing River to arrive in Wali in darkness.
Jiansu, use your imagination to picture the specter by listening to the
wind blow through leaves or looking at the darkness outside your
window, as instructed by these two great searchers for truth. Kind,
determined, and completely selfless, they thought only about the great
humanity of people and how to help them escape from suffering.
Small-minded people can think only of small solutions for their small
problems, not a grand solution like theirs. A small-minded person
trying to explain a grand solution is a blueprint for disaster.

"So, Jiansu, I only read it in times of peace and quiet, when my
mind is at its clearest, because I want to be unbiased and inspired by
the truth. Jiansu, you ought to read it, so you can experience unique
happiness. You should have read it long ago."

"What if I don't understand it?"

"Read it carefully."

"I'm not like you. You're better educated than me."

"Try."

"Guo Yun gave me a copy of *Heavenly Questions*."

"Then start with that."

Jiansu's eyes opened wide. "Have you read it?"

Baopu nodded. "Yes. I also borrowed Guo Yun's copy." He lit another cigarette and had a coughing fit. "Have you started it?"

Jiansu shook his head.

"Go ahead, read it. That too is something you have to read with
care. You can only handle the vernacular version, since you won't understand the ancient text. Father used to have a copy with both versions printed side by side, a gift from a teacher in town. You'll be
moved by what you read in that book. It'll make you realize how nearsighted people are these days, and how people in the past were so
much better at pondering problems and issues. Qu Yuan asked over a
hundred and seventy questions in one breath. 'At the beginning of
remote antiquity, who was there to transmit the tale? When above and
below had not yet taken shape, by what means could they be exam-

ined? When darkness and light were obscured, who could fathom them?' See how he went to the core right at the beginning? His questions are mostly about fundamental issues. These days people think of nothing but what's happening right in front of them, so they become increasingly narrow-minded. That's pitiful. Have you heard Technician Li talk about extraterrestrial visitors? When I heard him once, I looked up at the stars in the sky and wondered what the aliens would look like if there were inhabited planets in any of those galaxies. How would they view the disputes in Wali? What would they think about the fighting and shouting during the bidding? Who knows? Are they mortals? When one of them dies, do they use cremation and do they cry? Do they have so much to eat they'll never run out of food? Do they hold struggle sessions, do they string people through their collarbones? What if all those things are true? No, I simply cannot imagine that they could be as cruel as the people in Wali. Otherwise, the stars would not sparkle at night.

"One evening I saw a blind man by the city wall. He had a tattered cloth bundle on his back and walked with a bamboo staff. He was old, had gunk oozing from his eyes, and could only take small steps. I asked where he was going so late in the day, and he said he was going to a distant place. I invited him to stay for the night and have something to eat, but he shook his head, insisting that he wanted to go to a distant place. Watching him move forward one small step at a time, I wondered where his family was and when he might reach his destination. How could we, including myself, let him walk on by himself? Couldn't we have some transportation for people like him and food for him to eat? Wouldn't it be wonderful if we could do that? Don't we have the power to do that? Are there many blind people like him? If so, why haven't I seen another one in all the years since seeing him? I can't believe the whole town of Wali could not relieve a blind man's suffering once a year.

"Another time I went to the city for something, and around midnight I saw an old woman scavenging in a trash can. Obviously unable to move much, she was grunting as she reached in to rummage through the contents. All of a sudden, she pricked her finger. She shrieked and withdrew her hand, but then removed whatever was stuck in her finger and continued to rummage. Finally she bundled up some papers and pieces of rope before dragging it all away. I saw her several nights in a row. She came and went at the same time. The sight of her sent pangs through my heart.

"I had the feeling she was my mother. What happened? How could we lack even the power to help an old woman? I don't know. I only know, and with certainty, that we have no reason to brag about how wonderful our country and our lives are if we can stand by and watch an old woman live like that, even if there's only one like her. Someone might say that's easier said than done, that another woman would take this one's place if we helped her. That the more we help, the more who will come. My answer would be: Yes, and we'll continue to help them, no matter how many appear. So long as the whole city doesn't live on garbage, how can we stand by and watch a dying old woman live on it? Aren't those in charge of the city, like those in charge of our town, always talking about how fair and incorruptible they are? They may say they haven't ever seen an old woman like that, but how could I, someone from the countryside, meet one on my first visit in years? If they really haven't, they ought to crouch down by a trash heap at midnight. On the first night you help her pick scraps, and on the second night you let her stay in a well-heated house."

Baopu's voice was getting louder. He didn't stop until Jiansu called out to him. "You think too much and in too much detail," Jiansu said. "You should think about the Sui clan and about yourself. You want to be broad-minded and take the long view, so you suffer. Xiaokui is gone; the one you love is gone. Everything has come to that, so you should be thinking about what I've said. Everything will be fine if you can get rid of your sickness. Baopu, you're in your forties and I'm in my thirties, so we're still young. It's not too late to do something."

With his head in his hands, Baopu murmured, "Xiaokui is gone."

"Yes, she's gone, and I'm leaving too. I told you I want to go to the city. So, take care of yourself."

Baopu looked up, "You can't leave. You have to stay in Wali. Not another member of the Sui clan should be out wandering. In our generation there are only three of us left. I'm the oldest, and you are supposed to listen to me. I'll worry about you if you go by yourself."

Jiansu stared at the window, shaking his head repeatedly. "No. I've made up my mind. There's no place in Wali for Sui Jiansu, so I have to strike out on my own. In the past I couldn't have gone even if I'd wanted to, but now we're encouraged to do business in the city. Uncle left home, wandered half his life, and ended up doing better than Father. I'll return someday and put down roots here. Besides, I'll come visit."

Baopu wanted to say more, but the strains of a flute drifted over before he had a chance. It was the same sort of melody, with a tone of happiness bursting through. He sat there, transfixed, his head raised high.

Dawn was slowly arriving outside.

EIGHTEEN

The people in Wali were always on edge when it rained or was overcast for days on end. "It's like that other year," they'd mutter. During the spring of that earlier year the people did not see the sun for two straight weeks. Water ran noisily in ditches that had gone dry the past winter, and the fields were nearly knee-deep in water. Weeds grew at a maddening speed. The unprecedented, nonstop rain put them in a state of bewilderment. Later that summer more than forty people died a horrible death, all at the same time. "The sky wept," the people said with a sense of sudden enlightenment. The streets turned treacherously slippery a week or so after the rain began.

Zhang-Wang, who was still a new bride from another town, walked out on the street dressed in red and promptly fell down. Zhao Duo-duo, a rifle over his shoulder, came out of an alley, helped her up, and groped her as he wiped the mud from her clothes.

"A damned Zhao clan mutt!" she cursed. He was nearly twenty at the time, with a bit of fuzz above his purple upper lip.

"Don't go cursing me," he whispered. "Come here. I've got a treat for you." When she walked over, he took a ring from his pocket and flashed it in front of her before handing it over. She knew it was loot he'd gotten by guarding and struggling against the landlords. There was plenty more where that came from.

She smiled sweetly and asked, "Which deflowered girl did you take this off of? The times have been good for you lately. I tell you, these days people hide these things instead of wearing them out in the open." Zhao groped her again, and she cursed again, but she did not run away. She continued, "Don't do anything you'll be sorry for or you could be struck by lightning."

Zhao snorted as he took a glance around and said, "Someone will get to them sooner or later. The smart ones just suffer less. Hell, Secretary Wang of the work team said he'd have me shot if I was one of his soldiers." Zhang-Wang laughed with visible mirth.

A beard seemed to have sprouted overnight on Duoduo's face. In the town's memory, he was still the pitiful orphan sleeping in straw at night and roaming the street in the day like a ghost. Even the Zhao clan didn't pay much attention to him, so he grew up on food of uncommon sources and ate plenty of grasshoppers. Timid by nature, he could not stand the sight of a pig being slaughtered, but he could turn whatever was tossed away by the butchers into a delicious meal. One of the landlords often butchered pigs in his yard, so Zhao would run over whenever he heard a pig squeal. But if he tried to touch the dirty bristles, the landlord's old yellow dog would pounce on him, so most of the time he got nothing but bloody dog bites.

"It bit you, so go eat it." A member of the Sui clan taught him how to turn the tables on the dog: Place some food on a barbed hook attached to a rope, and when the dog bites down on the food, drag it over to the floodplain. Duoduo did as he was told, but when he caught the dog, it rolled and yelped as it tried to get free of the hook. It kept twisting the rope, its blood dripping to the ground. Watching it struggle, Duoduo's hands shook, and eventually he screamed, let go of the rope, and ran away. He nearly starved several times that year. Then one snowy day, someone gave him two copper coins to kill the dog; Duoduo was too hungry to turn down the offer, so he caught the dog again. But this time no matter how pitifully the dog yelped and rolled around, he dragged it down to the floodplain. He later learned that the man was a bandit who stole into the dog's owner's house that same night, kidnapped him, and took him out into the wilds, where he burned his captive with cigarettes and cut off one of his ears.

That episode bolstered Zhao Duoduo's courage, and he began catching cats and dogs. When he couldn't eat a whole dog, he'd bury the leftovers, reluctant to throw them away even if they rotted and stank. But after joining the militia, starvation became a distant memory, since he could now shoot domestic animals. When the militia tied up the landlords at night, he yanked the rope harder than anyone; when they tortured the landlords to get information, he burned them with cigarettes. The foul meats he'd consumed had made him bigger and stronger, had even given him facial hair before he was old enough. It was during that cloudy, rainy spring that he became leader of the self-defense corps.

People said that meetings would be held again at the old temple site as soon as the rain stopped. They'd had a few meetings before the sky opened up, and they'd been good ones, since the belongings of the landlords and rich peasants were brought out and recorded by Wattles Wu. Eventually, he had to stop recording, for there were too many items, and they were simply piled up in rooms at the farmers' association. Later on they were passed out among the people, a chest going to one family, a ceramic vat to another. Women could not stop feeling the clothes and bolts of fabric. A bachelor who picked out a pair of flowery pants could not bear to part with them. He kept muttering to himself, "What's in a pair of pants after all?"

As the handouts continued, the recipients ran around singing a medley of songs. First it was the inanimate objects that were passed out, followed by the living loot—divvy up, divvy up, divvy up! That went on until midnight, when some families secretly returned the objects to their original owners. After the doors opened, they'd whisper, "I could see that this chest belonged to you, Second Uncle, so I'm returning it. It's how things are these days, please don't be upset with me." Luan Chunji's father, Bearded Luan, director of the farmers' association, was first to discover what was going on, and he wasted no time in reporting it to the work team. So Secretary Wang had everything removed from the landlords' and rich peasants' houses again and redistributed, but people returned the items anyway. Zhao Bing, then a local teacher, had stopped going to school to busy himself with recording the loot along with Wattles Wu.

"Whoever receives returned goods should be put in the cellar," Zhao Bing suggested to Bearded Luan. "That way no one can find them to give their stuff back." The plan was adopted and people were locked in cellars, men away from women, family members separated. But people still insisted upon returning the items by piling them up at the doors of the original owners. So Secretary Wang called a meeting of the cadres, indicating the importance of mobilizing the masses. "This is no simple matter. It's much more complicated than we expected. Fear, their habit of following the strong, and family factors are in play here. We need to ease their concerns and bolster their courage. There's a lot of work ahead of us."

The cadres were asked to involve themselves with the people, each going from door to door, paying special attention to encouraging active participants to mobilize the masses. They were to open their hearts and show how they were striving to join them in wresting power from the oppressors and destroying the evil system of exploitation. No one can sit idly by and wait for victory to arrive, it was stressed. It must be won by everyone, through force. The Communist Party is the leader, and the poor must rely upon the Eighth Route Army. Secretary Wang also recommended that they release those who were imprisoned, which displeased Bearded Luan.

Then something totally unexpected occurred: The daughter of a landlord slept with a village political instructor, who was relieved of his post by the self-defense corps. The landlord fled with his valuables but was caught and brought back. The scandal was exposed and the political instructor lost his job. Bearded Luan was so angry his eyes turned red; he cursed everyone in sight and said they should not have let anyone go in the first place. Since Zhao Duoduo was in one of the first groups of active elements who had joined the militia, he hung around Bearded Luan and frequently went down into the cellar, where he took off his belt and whipped the runaway landlord, cursing him with each lashing. Zhao Bing told him that the landlord had set a beauty trap, so Duoduo yelled as he whipped the man, "How dare you set a beauty trap! How dare you!" He lit a handful of incense and burned the landlord's armpit, sending the latter jumping and howling. The man bloodied himself after ramming his head against the wall.

When Secretary Wang heard that, he gave Duoduo a tongue lashing, even using him as a negative example for the self-defense corps and banning cruel punishments. Bearded Luan, who strongly disagreed, argued that Zhao Duoduo had suffered bitterly for years, and that the old landlords were much crueler when they were in charge. Wang countered that as Communists they were better than their enemy. Now Bearded Luan was beside himself. "We were told to mobilize the masses and now that we've done that, you're afraid."

Wang had a stern comeback. "We mobilize class consciousness in the masses, not the animal nature in some of them." Luan fell silent, but his bushy beard continued to quiver.

That night, sitting on the Farmers' Association director's *kang*, Secretary Wang reflected on his earlier aggressive attitude but refused to relent on matters of principle. He expressed a desire for both sides to take the long view as they carried out land reform. They were to tell the masses they must not act rashly and violently for temporary gratification, that they had to uproot the source of exploitation in order to build a new society. Bearded Luan responded frankly, "You're my superior, so I'll do as you say."

The mass mobilization work got increasingly thorough, thanks to the Women's Salvation Association and the militia. The work team also made up some songs about land reform for the children to sing. From one end of an alley to the far end of a street everyone was talking about land reform, including those who ordinarily shut themselves in. Meetings were held on the temple site, where active elements would jump on the stage, followed by waves of people complaining about their suffering and ill treatment. The meetings heated up, and when the people shouted slogans, they were as loud and clear as thundering mountain floods. Wali was finally ignited by the flames of anger and would soon be consumed by a violent fire.

The rain continued to fall, changing from a drizzle to a downpour, the large drops of rainwater falling slowly to the ground. Secretary Wang, Bearded Luan, and the new village political instructor were called in for a meeting at district headquarters, where all three were severely criticized for their right-leaning line, that is, the rich peasant line that commonly existed in land-reform work. Wali was singled out as a place where land reform was "too gentle." Secretary Wang, excoriated by the district inspection team, returned to Wali worried and listless. Bearded Luan chain-smoked, clenching and unclenching his fists. Zhao Duoduo, on the other hand, was all smiles.

That night he and several militiamen stripped the prisoners they most disliked and put them out on an earthen mound to freeze. As they trembled from the cold, Zhao asked them, "Would you like a fire?"

They knelt down to beg him, "Commander Zhao, please have mercy and light a fire." Smiling broadly, he touched their private parts with a cigarette, shouting, "There's the fire." The prisoners screamed and covered their bodies. For some at least it was a night of great enjoyment. At dawn Bearded Luan went to see Zhao and tell him that Landlord Pockmark was rumored to have hidden a jar of silver coins. "Leave it to me," Zhao replied. He had Pockmark bound tightly into a ball before putting him on a table and demanding, "Where's the jar of jingly stuff?" Pockmark said, "I don't have one." A militiaman got on the table and kicked him to the floor. Another militiaman picked him up and put him back on the table.

Zhao asked again, "Where's the jingly stuff?" He got the same answer, and Pockmark received the same treatment, blood now dripping from his nose and mouth. When Zhao Bing heard what was happening, he told the militiamen to stop and to go outside, as he wanted to have a talk with Pockmark. After Duoduo led the militiamen out, Zhao Bing sighed as he untied Pockmark. An educated man, he said, "Even the country has changed color, so what's the point of keeping a jar of silver coins?"

Pockmark ground his teeth before finally responding, "I don't care about the silver; I'm just filled with hate."

Zhao Bing sighed again. "The common people's lives are like weeds. What good does it do to hate? Listen to me and don't take this so hard. They're just some stinking coins."

That went on for a while until Pockmark finally said, "Very well then." He blinked and told Zhao Bing where the silver was. When Zhao Duoduo returned with his men, Zhao Bing told them to let Pockmark go. "What's the hurry?" Duoduo said. "I'll have a cigarette with Pockmark first." After Zhao Bing left, Duoduo lit a cigarette and touched Pockmark with it after each puff. The landlord rolled around but did not cry out. So Duoduo tossed his cigarette away and said, "Quite a smoking habit, I take it. We'll have more later." That night he came back alone and, with a happy smile, said, "Let's have a smoke." Pockmark looked at him but said nothing. Then without warning he lunged at Duoduo and gouged his eye. Ignoring the pain, Duoduo took out his cleaver and with one swipe lopped off Pockmark's hand, leaving him quivering on the floor. Rubbing his eye, Duoduo walked up to Pockmark and stepped on his face. He looked and mumbled, "It's so dark I can't see very well." Then he brought his cleaver down on Pockmark's face, chopping his head in two. It was the second man Zhao Duoduo had killed.

The rain kept falling, covering the town like a net of water. Zhang-Wang tripped and fell; so did Bearded Luan, Shi Dixin, even Sui Yingzhi on one of his infrequent trips out of the house. A rumor had been spreading in town for days: Things were not looking good, as new instructions had been sent down to start the killing. The situation turned ugly, as the militia, protected by rush-woven rain gear, patrolled the streets day and night. Sometimes gunshots were heard at midnight, followed by silence. Dogs barked and children wailed. The old folks stood by their windows to smoke and converse in hushed tones. "The killing has begun." But that was just a rumor, since no one was actually killed, although they began to see more and more people with bloodshot eyes walking silently with their arms folded. People said they'd be the first to pick up a knife when killing time arrived.

One of those red-eyed people saw Zhao Duoduo and whispered, "Well?"

Zhao hurried along and without stopping, he tossed off a quick answer: "Soon." The residents came out onto the streets, where they talked about the prisoners, coming up with all sorts of wild ideas. "I'm afraid Flour-face won't make it this time." "No, he won't," everyone agreed. "Flour-face" was the nickname of a landlord with a white, puffy face. When the people recalled some of the things he'd done, they spat angrily. One year, a maid ran away from his household, refusing to go back even in the face of death. When asked why, she said she had to do everything in the house, including dressing Flour-face. Shocked, the people asked, "Did you even have to pull on his pants for him?" She blushed and nodded. Now Flour-face was doomed. "Braying Donkey won't make it either," someone said. "No, he won't," others agreed. Braying Donkey had a long, dark face, a wife and a concubine. After the concubine slept with one of his household workers, he branded the worker's forehead, leaving a scar the size of an apricot. He also had someone cut off one of the man's testicles; the worker died a few weeks later, his pants soaked in bloody puss. Now Braying Donkey's days were numbered. Someone mentioned a rich peasant nicknamed Melon, saying he was a good man and should be released. An honest, simple man, he made yams, melons, pumpkins, and gourds the main staple of his family meals, considering grain too great a luxury. "Melons aren't bad," he often said. "They're soft and easy to swallow."

The townspeople analyzed nearly every one of the prisoners, man and woman, reaching the conclusion that a few of them would have to die. But after they were killed, a few more might have to go as well. Among the prisoners were several pretty young women who would surely lose their virginity, so the residents felt they should be married off quickly to guarantee them a better life. The people talked on, but all they really knew was that the meeting would be held as soon as the rain stopped and then they'd learn the fates of these prisoners.

It took another ten days for the rain to stop. The meeting was held, but the results were not exactly as the residents had predicted. Non-stop meetings and unending rain had left an indelible impression on their minds; Wali was like a pot of boiling water, its steam permeating the ancient city wall. When the heat of summer arrived, the people finally realized that the rain had been the tears of heaven.

The townspeople cursed the fact that not enough had been killed during the spring meeting, which led to disappointment in the meeting held after the rains. In late summer, the landlords returned, their eyes red with the heat of vengeance. Most of the active elements and land-reform cadres had fled by then, but the landlords managed to nab a few, whose fate would be worse than falling into a pot of boiling water. Bearded Luan, who had fled a few days earlier, had sneaked back into town with a grenade tucked in his belt and was caught jumping over a wall. The landlords spent the night trying to decide how to deal with him. Some suggested "setting off firecrackers"—driving a long nail down the top of his head and then pulling it quickly to send blood gushing in all directions. Someone else recommended opening up his belly; another urged giving him the slicing death; one suggested "lighting a lamp"—piling his hair on top of his head and pouring kerosene or bean oil over it before setting it on fire so they could admire the red flames flickering with a tinge of blue. Someone urged "death by five oxen"—tying an ox to each of his limbs and his head and driving the oxen ahead to tear him apart. This was the one they adopted, and since it required a large space, the temple site was the logical choice.

It was a bright, sunny morning when, under the gaze of the town's residents, the trussed-up Bearded Luan was tied to five black oxen. He cursed while others shouted slogans and five men whipped the oxen. The animals raised their heads and cried out but refused to take a step. So they were whipped harder and cried out louder. That went on for a long time before the oxen lowered their heads and slowly moved forward. Bearded Luan's cursing came to an abrupt halt and was followed by popping sounds. His blood gushed far and wide, even staining the oxen, which immediately stopped walking. That night the landlords picked the liver out of the bloody mess and stir-fried it to go with their drink. They ate and drank, saying that human liver would bolster their courage. To prove the theory, one of them went out and brought back a village woman, raped her in front of everyone, then cut off her breasts and plunged the knife up her vagina, laughing the whole time. Once they were good and drunk, the landlords decided they ought to "take care of" the four dozen men and women prisoners by stringing them together with wire and burying them alive in the yam cellar.

The plan proceeded smoothly. The last one left was the director of the Women's Salvation Association, whom they kept back on purpose. They tied her hands and feet, stripped off her clothes, and laid her out on a door plank. Before daybreak, one of them took out a pocket watch and urged everyone, "Hurry up." They then took turns raping her. When an old man with a reddish beard climbed on top, all he could do was laugh, for which he was rewarded with hoots from the others. Angry and ashamed, he bit off one of her nipples. They then went to bed and did not get up until midmorning, when the first thing they did was raise the door plank for her to witness what was about to happen. They tied her child's legs to the knockers of two closed doors, then kicked the doors open, tearing the child into two. Her head twisted to the side; when they slapped her face, they saw she had passed out.

The avenging landlords ravaged the town for two weeks and then left. The town's residents washed away the fresh blood on their streets with their tears. Clenching their teeth, they could not stop from crying out in shock; crushed by remorse, they buried one body after another, all the while regretting not having killed more of those people after the rains. But the meetings were done with. Would there ever be any more? Recalling the details to lessen their regret and anger, some of those who had been hesitant hung their heads in shame, wishing they could have the meetings over again.

They recalled how the meeting had started as soon as the rain stopped. Rifles were stacked around the site, where Flour-face was the first to be struggled against. Secretary Wang presided, assisted by Bearded Luan, the director of the Farmers' Association, the director of the Women's Salvation Association, and the town's political instructor. Zhao Duoduo stood to the side with several of his armed militiamen. On the other side, Zhao Bing and Wattles Wu took notes. When two militiamen brought up Flour-face, the director of the Women's Salvation Association got everyone to shout slogans. His hands trembling at his sides, Flour-face hung his head, not daring to look anyone in the face. His puffy face had turned ashen after a few weeks in the cellar. After the slogan shouting, Secretary Wang and Bearded Luan took turns giving mobilizing speeches, followed by the venting of complaints by individual peasants.

As they gave detailed accounts of the man's crimes, the tone of the meeting turned solemn. Then people jumped onto the stage to beat Flour-face. A weak and frail old woman, lacking the strength to hit him, bit him. Secretary Wang shouted for the militia to stop the violence from getting out of hand, but Zhao Duoduo went up with his men to hold Flour-face down so the peasants could kick, hit, and bite to their hearts' content. As he knelt on the stage, he banged his head on the ground for forgiveness, but the people below shouted, "No, we won't let you go!" A rock flew up with the shouts. Afraid that the cadres on the stage might be hurt, Zhao Duoduo took Flour-face to the side, where a wooden stake was planted. The militiamen bound him and lifted him up to the top of the stake.

Now the people had to look up to vent their anger, still in thundering voices. An old man walked up with a scythe and hacked the rope off. Flour-face dropped to the ground, blood gushing from every orifice. People ran up to kick him but were blocked by the scythe-wielding old man, who said to the cadres on the stage, "My son worked for this man for five years and injured his back; now he's laid up in bed. So I'm going to cut off a piece of flesh to make medicine for my son. Is that too much to ask?" Before the cadres had time to respond, the crowd yelled out, "Hurry up, do it." So the old man looked down and, amid piercing cries of pain, cut off a palm-sized piece of flesh, which he raised above his head, and shouted to the stage, "That evens the account." He left.

Secretary Wang banged his hand down on the table, shouted something, and rushed down off the stage, followed by Bearded Luan. "We're going to eat his flesh today," Luan shouted. "Who are you trying to protect?"

Wang roared, "I'm protecting the policy of our superiors! We are soldiers of the Communist Party's Eighth Route Army, not a band of brigands! As a Party member, you should know you need the approval of a traveling court to kill someone!" While they were screaming at each other, more people came up with scythes, making it necessary to try to stop them. During the melee, Wang was hit on the arm; fresh blood stained his gaunt frame. As Bearded Luan shouted for a bandage, Wang ignored the wound and fixed his eyes on Luan. "Do not forget that you are a Communist Party member."

The meeting ended. Secretary Wang called an all-night meeting of the cadres, where it was decided that he would report to his superiors and that struggle sessions would be halted temporarily. No unwarranted beatings or killings were allowed.

It was two in the morning when the meeting was adjourned, but Wang chose not to rest. Tucking a pistol in his belt with his good hand, he got on the road. Daybreak brought a deadly silence to the town. Bearded Luan, unable to stomach the dressing down from Wang, was laid up in bed. The following day unrest broke out again. "The masses are revolting again," Zhao Duoduo reported to Luan. "What do we do?"

"Tell them to go home," Luan replied unhappily. But the crowd surged into the streets and the meeting site, and it was no longer possible to drive them back home. They started their own meeting, with a young man from a wealthy family as their first victim. They beat him to death. Next was a plump old man whose wife came up to protect him and refused to leave once the struggle got under way. So they were tied together, shoved to the ground, and beaten until there were no more shouts. Finally it was Braying Donkey whom Zhao Duoduo decided to punish before putting him on the stage.

"How come you have two wives, you bastard?" Zhao fixed his eyes on the man and kicked him in the crotch. Braying Donkey fell to the ground screaming in pain, his lips turning black.

He was pushed onto the stage, and before he steadied his feet, the mother of the dead worker, wailing and screaming, stormed up. Seeing she was overwrought, Zhao Bing went up to steady her and told her to vent her anger out loud. She stood fast, slapped her knees, and screamed, "My son—" and passed out. People rushed up to revive her by pinching the spot between her nose and lip, while others crowded around Braying Donkey, sending a chorus of pummeling, yelling, cursing, and screaming people around the stage. The old woman finally came to, and the crowd stopped the beating. "Granny," they said, "we vented your anger for you." She crawled over to the bloodied Braying Donkey and, shaking her graying head, said, "No. I'll do it myself. I don't need anyone to do it for me." She eyed a spot on his neck and bit down ferociously.

The remaining landlords and rich peasants were brought onto the stage on the third day; those who had made enemies were doomed.

Melon had a pretty daughter. Two years earlier, Zhao Duoduo had jumped their wall and broken into her room; he was caught by Melon, who, instead of having him beaten, merely gave him a tongue lashing. Now, Zhao, a rifle over the shoulder, ambled back and forth in front of Melon, shaking his head, as he held a rod wound with untanned pigskin. When Zhao stopped he sent the man to the ground with a crushing blow against the head; the man wound up with a mouthful of dirt as he clawed at the ground. Zhao bent down to check on him before adding three more blows to the back of the old man's head, finishing him off.

The meeting continued, with the crowd surging like waves on the old temple site. Secretary Wang returned on the fourth day, along with comrades from the People's Traveling Court. Stricken with a fever from overexertion and the infection from his wound, Wang had been carried back to town on a stretcher, but he refused to be sent to a nearby medical unit halfway through the journey; instead, he pointed his bony finger in the direction of Wali. The meeting was under way when they entered town, and Wang asked the comrades from the People's Traveling Court to carry him up to the stage, the sight of which silenced the crowd. He immediately asked someone to get Bearded Luan, and when he was told that Luan was ill, he said, "Bring him even if you have to carry him over. He must be present at the meeting."

Then, asking to be taken off the stretcher, Wang leaned against an old door to wait. Soon Bearded Luan was carried over; his beard had turned gray in a matter of days, and that sent a shock wave through the crowd. The People's Traveling Court demanded to read the minutes of the meetings taken by Zhao Bing and Wattles Wu. The sufferers' complaints filled three notebooks, which, if it were all proven true, meant that no more than five of the accused would be given the death sentence. But, to the astonishment of the visiting comrades, over a dozen had already been killed. They made their stance known in a firm and unambiguous manner: The town had seriously violated government policy by failing to follow legal procedures, and someone must take responsibility for the illegal beatings and killings.

When the comrade was finished with his comments, people below the stage began shouting slogans: Knock down the rich peasant line, knock down this, knock down that. At that point, Secretary Wang asked to be helped up. He swept the crowd with his eyes to quiet them down before speaking in a voice so feeble it was nearly inaudible, although his resolute tone of voice was familiar to the townspeople. "If you want to knock down anyone, start with me. That will be easy, now that my arm is injured. But as long as I'm standing, no beating or killing will be tolerated. I'll arrest anyone who uses land reform as an excuse to kill, since that will sabotage our efforts. If you have complaints, vent your anger. But why have a court if you can kill anyone you want? That is not the policy of the Eighth Route Army." He swayed as he talked; people rushed up to steady him. The site was quiet.

~

The summer of blood and tears was finally over, and the incident in which forty-two people were buried alive in a yam cellar was entered into the town's chronicle by Wattles Wu, who made a point of recording the unending cloudy and rainy spring days. But they would be erased with a red brush in a mere ten years. On the heels of the summer came a fall that was shrouded in grief and indignation, a time when an unprecedented large-scale military enlistment campaign got under way. No one relished the possibility of being buried in a yam cellar, so meetings were held again on the old temple site, and since Secretary Wang had been transferred and Bearded Wang had died a hero's death, the town's political instructor and Zhao Duoduo, commander of the self-defense forces, convened the meetings. Shortly after that Zhao Bing joined the Party, which automatically accorded him the right to preside. His refined demeanor and seniority in his family gave him great rallying authority, which in turn emboldened the Zhao clan, who had performed so well during the land-reform reexamination; it seemed as if the clan was again in the ascension.

At the meetings, Zhao Bing often gave impassioned speeches to instruct the masses, winning them over with reason; his speeches were usually followed by shouted slogans as tears streamed down the people's faces. Zhao Duoduo and his militiamen then took the lead: "Hurry up and enlist. Hurry up and get the honor. Even betrothed girls want to see their future husbands off." Fervor and passion overflowed at the site, where people joined up on the spot. Red flowers were pinned on the chests of enlistees, who then mounted horses and rode around town, surrounded by crowds. They were then sent to the county seat. One group left, followed by another and another, until few young men were seen walking proudly on the streets. The town's political instructor urged Zhao Bing to enlist, saying that young men like him would make rapid progress in the army. Zhao said that he'd been contemplating that for weeks but that he'd been too busy. Now it was time to answer the call. The political instructor was delighted.

The next day a drunken Zhao Duoduo, his face purple from alcohol, grabbed the instructor by the lapel and bellowed, "Goddamn you. If Fourth Master leaves, then the rest of us will have to, and with us all gone, you'll be the local overlord. You don't think that sooner or later someone will take you down? Well, someone will, later if not sooner." Duoduo patted the cleaver resting on his hip. The instructor struggled free and backed away, stammering. The very next day he fell ill, and when he recovered, his superiors looked into his case; that struck fear in him.

Wattles Wu and Zhao Duoduo spent the day in whispered conversations, after which Wattles wrote three petitions. "He may be the political instructor," Zhao told the investigators, "but he escaped unscathed, while Bearded Luan and the director of the Women's Salvation Association died. How can anyone deny the obvious—collusion with the enemy? Someone even saw him run into town when the landlord restitution corps arrived."

A week later, the unsuspecting political instructor was arrested and sent in shackles to the county office. Zhao and his militiamen escorted the prisoner for a large portion of the journey. At one point he said to the instructor, "Believe me now? Lucky for you, they got you while we were still in town. You'd have been a goner if we'd left." The political instructor did not respond, except to grind his teeth in anger. He never returned to Wali, and soon afterward, Zhao Bing was appointed Gaoding Street political instructor.

Since the beginning of the rainy days, Zhao Duoduo had been troubled by a nagging feeling that he'd neglected some important matters that deserved his attention, including the Sui clan, which remained a constant worry. Once the most powerful family in Wali, the Suis had held sway over both the Li and the Zhao clans for decades. But Duoduo had discovered that the powerful clan's foundation was loosening up, and he eventually found the courage to take people into the Sui compound. His hands itched as he gazed at the main building's vermillion columns and the maids lingering around them. He was standing in the yard one day when he commented to an old man and a girl working on some Chinese roses, "I'll get rid of them one day."

The old man, who was hard of hearing, put down his spade and looked up, "Get rid of these . . . flowers?"

Zhao Duoduo tapped both their foreheads before raising his hand to sweep the main building and the side wings. "I mean all of that." The startled old man gaped at him just as Zhao spotted Huizi and Sui Yingzhi walking past the door of the main building; he watched them for a moment before muttering to himself, "Yes, it's best to get rid of them." He then swaggered out of the yard.

Back then, Secretary Wang, who was still stationed in Wali, had called meetings for the cadres to engage in discussions regarding the Sui clan, stressing that Yingzhi, being an enlightened local gentry man, should be protected. As founders of the glass noodle industry in the Luqing River region, they enjoyed a fine reputation in several big cities. Besides, they had donated several noodle processing rooms to the town, so they deserved to be protected. Their personal safety was to be guaranteed during the second round of land reform. When Wang conveyed the government's instructions to the town, Duoduo and several others were both disappointed and disheartened.

"The struggle sessions won't be worth a damn if we're not allowed to touch the biggest family in town," someone said.

"Instructions from the government?" Zhao mocked. "That's pure bullshit!"

On and on they talked, but no one in the Sui family was dragged up onto the stage. Then the work team left, ending the struggle sessions. But Zhao Duoduo and his allies were not about to let the matter rest. "Why don't we just get rid of them?" Zhao said to the political instructor, who just waved him off. But following the arrest of the political instructor, leaving Gaoding Street in a leaderless state, Zhao Duoduo called a meeting of his own. He had, by then, entered the Sui compound several times, searching out Huizi, who had clawed and scratched him bloody. So he brought Sui Yingzhi up onto the stage, where it was debated whether or not he ought to be considered a member of the enlightened local gentry. If he was, then he'd have slipped through the net. The meeting proceeded in a lackluster manner until Sui Yingzhi passed out midway . . .

But then, when Zhao Bing became the political instructor, he told Duoduo to stop what he was doing. "The Suis' days are numbered," Fourth Master said, "so the Zhao clan need not do a thing except wait for them to rot on their own."

Soon afterward, Sui Yingzhi died in the sorghum field.

"One rotten Sui down," Duoduo commented.

Fourth Master smiled faintly. "Don't worry. Just wait."

All the Sui processing rooms in other cities changed ownership, and in the end, even the last one in Wali had to be given up. Idlers no longer lingered at the Sui estate; bustling activity there became a thing of the past. Over time, fewer horses and wagons appeared at the gate, until finally there were no more. The gate was locked day and night. On one occasion, Sui Buzhao, who lived in a room outside the courtyard, came knocking at the door but got no response. He left, cursing indignantly, "The Sui clan is doomed." He was overheard by someone who said that the Sui clan must truly be doomed, since the prediction had come from one of its own.

By contrast, the Zhao clan was growing in importance by the day. Zhao Bing was often invited to discuss town matters with the new town head, while Zhao Duoduo was in charge of weapons, which were far more advanced than before. On holidays the militiamen, dressed in old army uniforms, were given live ammunition and set up guard posts on the street; since the country had only recently gained

stability, violent class struggle was still a possibility. When Fourth
Master left his house on cloudy days or in the dark of night, he was
often accompanied by armed militiamen.

Any time Duoduo walked by the Sui compound, he kicked the
bricks in the wall and said, "There are more inside." He never clarified
exactly what that "more" meant, but it sounded more ominous than
mysterious. Fourth Master would only grunt in response. Before long,
a certain member of the provincial leadership was found guilty of
committing serious errors, all of which were listed in the provincial
paper, one related to Wali: The man, it seemed, had protected the
town's biggest capitalist while working for the city committee, and
that capitalist turned out to be Sui Yingzhi. After reading the paper,
Duoduo went to see Fourth Master and said, "Let's search the
house."

Zhao Bing, who was reading the article at the time, said, "You have
to call a meeting first. Then we can do it. Things are different now. We
cannot be arbitrary."

"The time has come to get rid of them," Duoduo said.

But Zhao Bing shook his head. "Confiscating their property and
driving them out of the house is enough. Don't overdo it."

So a meeting was called, after which Duoduo led a group of noisy
militiamen into the Sui estate. The search and confiscation began,
with Wattles Wu recording each item taken. Huizi was holding Hanzhang's hand, with Baopu, Jiansu, and Guigui, her last remaining
maid, crowded around her. Her face was ashen gray, her graceful
brows tightly knitted; she was biting down on her red, moist lower lip.
But she did not make a sound during the entire process. Hanzhang
was crying and so was Jiansu, but she ignored them. The two children
cried until dusk, when they lost their voices. Since the ransacking was
not yet finished, a few militiamen stayed behind to guard the house,
spreading wool blankets in the yard. They got little sleep. They resumed their work at dawn and did not finish until that afternoon.
Everything was carted away. Before Duoduo left, he announced that

the family could keep the side rooms, but the main building now belonged to the people; they had three days to move their belongings out before the building was sealed off. He left.

"Let's all move into the side rooms, Mother," Baopu said to Huizi.

Without a word, she gathered up the children's blankets and bedding and took them over to the side rooms. Then she returned to the main building, where she lay down on a *kang* padded with thick blankets and stared at the ceiling. She refused to move when Baopu took his brother and sister to see her. Finally she sat up and took Baopu's hand in her own. "Baopu, you're the oldest," she said, "so listen carefully. Your father left this house to me. It is all that's left of the Sui clan. So I am going to guard it for your father with my life." Realizing that she'd never leave the place, he led his younger siblings back to the side rooms.

Sui Buzhao no longer dared to set foot in the main building, avoiding Huizi, who cursed him whenever she saw him, saying that he had ill intentions and that his brother was waiting to even the score in the underworld. The light went out in Sui Buzhao's gray eyes as he walked out the last time, his head down, his legs getting tangled up more than usual. Three days went by and the militiamen came to seal up the house. Huizi told them to seal her inside, so they backed off, telling her she had three more days and after that it would not be up to her anymore. That night she walked around the house with a candle, touching the carvings on the windowsills and the vermillion lacquered columns in the long veranda under the eaves. When morning came, she told Baopu to take his siblings to their uncle's place so she could have a good, quiet sleep. Baopu did as she asked but returned immediately, bothered by a worrisome premonition the minute he entered his uncle's room. When he got home, he touched his sweaty forehead to the window. Seeing Huizi lying quietly on the *kang,* he went back to his room.

Huizi got up and changed into her favorite silk clothes. She painted her brows and her lips, after which she gazed at her reflection in the mirror for a long time without moving. Then she took a ceramic bowl from a corner of the room and ate and drank from it before going back to the mirror to wipe off the water on her lips. After shutting the door and windows, she set fires in several places where she had carefully doused bean oil the night before. The flames leaped up as she lay back down on the *kang* and closed her eyes to wait, her lovely face a picture of tranquillity.

Baopu detected an odd odor and heard popping sounds, and when he looked up he saw a ball of fire drop from the eaves of the main house. With a cry, he ran out of his room, his mind a confused jumble, and banged on the door and windows madly, as red flames kept falling from the eaves. Smoke billowed inside.

Huizi remained quiet on the *kang,* but her fingertips bled from digging into the mat.

Frantically Baopu climbed onto the windowsill and broke the glass panes but still could not crawl into the room. By then people with axes, spades, and buckets were rushing into the yard. Flames licked at the corner of an eave, which crumpled to the ground, spreading red sparks over to the wall and the columns before the wind blew them into the air. People ran looking for the well, while others flung dirt onto the roof.

"Mother, my mother is inside!" Baopu shouted.

No one heard him, for everyone, gripped by panic, was also shouting. Spotting an ax in someone's hand, he snatched it away to hack at the door but promptly got it stuck in the wood. Someone came up behind him, pulled out the ax, and hacked the door open with one swing. It was Zhao Duoduo, who walked into the room with two militiamen and looked around before going up and standing by the *kang.*

"Mother!" Baopu called out as he threw himself onto the *kang* and reached out to shake his mother. But instead of opening her eyes, Huizi pushed her head against the *kang,* her neck raised in a painful arc.

"Mother!" the boy wailed as he pleaded with the three men with his eyes.

Zhao Duoduo looked on. He put a cigarette in his mouth but tossed it away after a single puff.

Huizi's neck continued to arc upward, seemingly on the point of snapping. Then her head relaxed abruptly, her body fell back to the *kang,* and her neck flattened out. Her hands were dug into the mat until it was tattered and stained by her blood. She was writhing. Duoduo stormed around the room.

"Please, please, save my mother!" Baopu screamed as he tried to pick her up.

Duoduo fixed his eyes on the two militiamen. "A stubborn reactionary, that's what she is! She took poison, but before dying, she sets the fucking house on fire." Rolling up his sleeves, he signaled for the two men to restrain Baopu before he walked up to Huizi. "I'm not going to let you take a single pretty dress with you," he said as he began to strip the silk robe off Huizi, who was twisting more violently now. Her clothes were stuck to her body, but Duoduo's hands kept at it, cursing and hitting her in the head.

Baopu stopped crying and, with his eyes open wide, stared, as if in a daze.

Failing to strip the clothes off Huizi, Duoduo found a pair of rusty scissors and stuck them under her clothes to cut the fabric. Still writhing, Huizi made a grunting noise each time the scissors cut through her flesh and stained Duoduo's hand with her blood. She calmed down once the fabric was cut free. As Duoduo peeled away the last thread of fabric from her body, he cursed and shook his hand when it stuck to his fingers.

Huizi finally stopped moving. She lay naked on the *kang,* the blood congealing in the spots cut by Duoduo's scissors. Baopu's eyes were still wide open. Cursing loudly, Duoduo took a careful look at Huizi's body before he clenched his teeth and released even more obscenities as he slowly undid the sash around his waist.

Using both hands in a spraying motion, Duoduo pissed all over Huizi's body.

Darkness fell before Baopu's eyes. They dragged him out just before the roof caved in. Out in the yard, Fourth Master Zhao Bing stood with his hands on his hips as he solemnly watched the house go up in flames.

NINETEEN

Jiansu was sitting in a corner drinking an orange liquid through a straw. He sucked up a big mouthful but found it awkward to keep the straw in his mouth and swallow. He felt like throwing the straw away, but on second thought he kept it in the glass, as he stared uneasily at the elevator to the top floor. Dressed in a dark green suit, he unbuttoned his coat to reveal a black pinstriped tie, an outfit he'd gotten used to without feeling any sense of discomfort. Six months earlier, when first coming to the city, he'd had no trouble changing into suits, and he believed it was in Sui blood to adapt easily. He quickly got used to drinking the orange liquid through a straw and frequenting the six-story World Hotel, the most elegant building in this midsize city. He was in the first-floor lobby. The sixth floor had a dance hall, and the person he was waiting for would soon be coming down in the elevator. A man named Xiaofan had brought Jiansu here, ordered a soft drink from the lobby bar for him, and gone up to find that person. A slurping noise rose from the straw, and now that he'd finished the drink, he wished he'd taken it more slowly. He glanced over at the bar and figured he ought to at least be brave enough to order another, so he walked over. A pretty waitress with red lipstick and dangling earrings came up after a fleeting, questioning look at him. He liked that look, and he'd remember it.

He hesitated for just a second. "One more, please, comrade." The look on her face turned frosty as she reluctantly picked up a glass and held up a finger. Jiansu knew that meant money, but how much, 0.10 yuan or one yuan? He thought he'd better give her one yuan, and that turned out to be the right decision. When she took the money, he noticed the name card on her breast. It had a color photo, some foreign writing, and Chinese characters that said "Miss Zhou Yanyan." He was a bit smarter when he walked away with his drink. "Thank you, Miss Zhou." The frosty look gave way to a faint smile. On his way back to the table to continue the battle with the straw, he slowed down when he passed a column inlaid with mirrors so he could check himself out. His face was pale, but the suit fit perfectly on his tall, slender body. The man in the mirror looked relaxed and carefree but somewhat untamed, which enhanced the harmony between him and the hotel atmosphere. He returned to his table, confident that no member of the Sui clan should ever look uncomfortable, no matter where he was. The straw no longer felt awkward in his mouth.

No sign of the man. Jiansu knew he had to be patient, that everything required patience, including coming from Wali to this city and to the World Hotel lobby. In the beginning patience was needed to shake off the shackles of Wali little by little. Sui Buzhao was the only family member who had not objected to his decision to leave to make a name for himself. Daxi had sobbed the whole time. It seemed to him that before he left he was making endless promises to everyone in town, telling Baopu he'd never do anything outrageous or immoral, telling Daxi he wouldn't abandon her, telling Li Yuming that his departure for the city did not violate any regulations, and so on. He'd spent two weeks dealing with all sorts of arcane procedures and another month or more of the same after reaching the city. He'd planned to open a small shop with the hope of getting some help from Wali, but that had proved to be a fantasy. His first obstacle was finding the right location—they were all either too far from downtown or too expensive. Over the first ten days, he lost several hundred yuan in his dealings with personnel in the commerce and taxes departments; later he lost even more when the public security bureau got involved.

Several times he decided to return to Wali and never come back to the city, but he forced himself to stay. Devoting all his time to searching for opportunities, he slept no more than four or five hours in the hotel basement, feeling like one of the characters he'd read about in novels—a lone individual out to strike it rich in the big city. The only difference was he had a motley assortment of IDs and documents, plus some cash from the Wali Emporium.

At night he roamed the streets, looking at the flashing neon lights and surging flow of bicycles. There were so many people. He kept to the sidewalks, thinking about the things he'd tried since his arrival: watching videos, watching people dance, eating at vegetarian restaurants, watching people skate on man-made ice. One time he watched a 3-D movie and was impressed. The streets bustled with vendors selling melon seeds, jeans, watches, and eyeglasses. The watches, all imports, cost only a few yuan and felt light as peach stones. Eyeglasses came in various colors: red, black, blue, orange, and rose. Jiansu would have liked to have bought one of each, but he exercised forbearance. On one occasion a sickly young man pointed a pistol-like object at him and shouted, "Fifty fen for a peep." Jiansu calmly produced fifty fen and took a look inside, where he saw people kissing and fondling each other until a fox flew out and twirled around the people's necks. He laughed, for that reminded him of Wali in the old folks' memory and the "Western peep shows" that had long disappeared in the dust of history. Late at night he often went to diners for some food and strong liquor, and plenty of gossip. On one of those nights he met a shop owner who had fallen on hard times. The man had lost money in a fabric deal and could not stock any more merchandise. Jiansu treated the man to some food and drink and walked him home after he was drunk. He wanted to see the man's shop for himself.

The shop, it turned out, was also where the man lived with his wife, who ran the business. Its location in a relatively busy area of the city was highly desirable, and the idea of partnership occurred to Jiansu right off; he couldn't sleep that night, thinking about the details. After finally getting some sleep during the day, he found the shop owner that night in a small tavern. They drank and talked till midnight, with

Jiansu raising the issue of partnership and showing the man his documents and certificates, stressing how his strong financial backing
would expand the business. The owner was swayed, telling Jiansu he'd
talk it over with his wife, but by the next day he'd had a change of
heart. Jiansu stopped himself from slugging the man and offered to
order drinks instead. This time the shop owner turned him down, saying he planned to take a bath. Jiansu managed to get him to down one
drink before following him to a bathhouse.

Located in a small alley, the bathhouse was filthy and crowded.
After inquiring into the services, Jiansu decided to spend a bit more
money and took the man to a nicer, smaller pool, where there were
fewer people. After checking their clothes, they received wooden tags
they looped around their wrists and went into the bath. The shop
owner was a skinny man with a surprisingly noticeable potbelly. They
decided to scrub each other's backs; when Jiansu was done with the
shop owner's back, he moved on to his belly, getting a look from the
man, who thought Jiansu was in a joking mood. But the look told
him that was not the case. Then, aided by the buoyancy of the water,
he picked the man up and sat him on a cement platform, so he could
have his back scrubbed. Wrapping a towel around his hand, the shop
owner scrubbed Jiansu's back, admiring his skin and physique. Jiansu
responded coldly, "I'm your backer." The hand stopped and Jiansu
said, as if issuing a command, "Don't stop. Keeping scrubbing."

The hand resumed, as its owner asked tentatively, "What you
mean is . . ."

Jiansu nonchalantly lathered himself up and painstakingly washed
his lower body, before responding casually, "I own a glass noodle company in Wali, with branches in other places. I don't need your shop to
make money; I just want to have a place where I can stay so I can
enjoy myself in the city."

He did not consider this a lie, for he retained the vague belief that
the noodle company indeed belonged to him. "Uh-huh," the shop
owner murmured, as his hand took on a gentler touch. He reached
around Jiansu and rubbed his chin softly. Jiansu pushed the hand

away and stood up. Through the watery mist, he detected a covetous look on the man's sweaty face. The next day they settled the matter of partnership; on the third day, Jiansu drafted something akin to a contract and found a notary public. Light glowed in the man's and his wife's eyes, but their hands shook as they exchanged looks, unsure if they were signing for good fortune or disaster. They finally breathed a sigh of relief when Jiansu produced some money on the spot.

On the heels of his acceptance of an offer to move in with the couple, Jiansu suggested expansion by incorporating the alleyway separating their shop from the neighbor's; wanting to change the name and paint the outside, he promised to take care of all the details, so the couple had nothing to complain about.

Some days later, Jiansu hired an interior designer to give the shop a makeover. Above the door now hung a sign that read "Wali Emporium" in Chinese script above the name spelled out in pinyin. Both sides of the door were painted in bright colors, to which were added a good-looking man and woman dancing in knee-high leather boots. Two days later, the shop owner increased their inventory with money from Jiansu, who even purchased a boom box. Jiansu suggested adding a speaker on each side of the door for a stereo effect.

Thanks to the loud music, customers flocked to the shop. But Jiansu did not spend much time there, preferring to roam the streets as before. When he did show up, he busied himself with changing displays, minor adjustments that produced noticeable changes in the shop's ambience. For instance, he placed three-legged stools in one corner and a cardboard sign with "Coffee" written on it. If someone ordered coffee, the shop owner's wife brewed a cup of inferior instant coffee behind the counter. Most of the coffee drinkers were young men, who either sat on the stools or leaned against the wall, holding the cups and hungrily eyeing the female customers. A few days into the venture, Jiansu hired another designer to paint the words "Gentleman" and "Lady" in artsy purple characters beneath the drawings of the man and woman.

Now that the shop had taken on an odd appearance it attracted odd customers, the only kind willing to spend freely. Business was booming, to the delight of the shop owner. On one occasion, when Jiansu was there enjoying a leisurely smoke, the owner, who was carrying a basin of water, pranced with the beat of the music, spilling some of the water. Jiansu stood up and shouted, "Is that any way to walk?" shocking the owner, who stopped abruptly and then slowly carried the water away. The man's wife turned beet red and even Jiansu was embarrassed, sensing he should not have talked to the man like that. As he puffed away on his cigarette, he realized that that had been a familiar phrase back at the Sui estate, one their father had yelled at Baopu when he was imitating the way their uncle walked.

Jiansu often hung around small alleyway stalls run by vendors, all different, but mostly laid-off workers or peasants from the countryside. They mainly sold polyester clothing, fake leather goods, and jeans, and it took Jiansu a while to notice that the so-called imported jeans were local counterfeits. The vendors knew all the tricks of the trade, which Jiansu quickly learned after hanging out with them. He became drinking buddies with one of them, who took him down a narrow alley one day, a tentlike place where a boxing tape was playing. The audience was bored but looked up quickly when the boxers were abruptly replaced by a naked man and woman who promptly did what men and women invariably do; Jiansu felt as if he'd entered a fairy world. He watched for an hour before the images on-screen were in turn replaced by boxers.

He exhaled loudly, his back soaking wet, as he left with the vendor, not uttering a word. After that, he went back every night, and suddenly he was sleeping badly and food lost its taste. When he looked in the mirror several days later, he saw that his face had lost its glow and his eyes their focus. Reminded of the sickness he'd had before coming to the city, and suddenly bothered by the shakes, he forced himself to stay away from that place.

But he continued to hang out with the vendors and noticed a man who was doing well selling bizarre used clothing. He bought some and then resold it at a profit. Seeing how briskly it sold, he decided to try to locate the vendor's supplier, but failed. So he asked for help from his vendor friend, who just shook his head and said, "You have to get to know Xiaofan, who sells used clothes, but he's pretty much unapproachable." After asking around, Jiansu learned that Xiaofan was a clerk at Yihua Limited. It took him another two months to get the scoop on the company, which turned out to be a firm that dealt directly with foreigners and whose employees traveled extensively overseas. But no one seemed to know if it was government-run or privately owned. As if doused by a bucket of cold water, Jiansu was thrown into turmoil for several days; his head ached from his effort to find a way to deal with Xiaofan. Maybe it was only natural for Xiaofan to be unapproachable to local vendors, and it ought to be easier for someone with real connections. The hardest part, actually, would be to develop a close friendship after getting to know the man.

Now that he was looking at things from a different angle, Jiansu felt better. He had a talk with the shop owner, telling him that the road to prosperity was to run the business the way it was meant to be run. Although the owner had never been overly ambitious, eventually he agreed to let Jiansu become general manager of the Wali Emporium. The first order of business was to have business cards printed. Once that was done, the shop owner grinned when he saw his name and his title—assistant manager—printed on the cards, one side in Chinese and the other side in a foreign language.

That done, Jiansu put on a suit and strode confidently into the offices of Yihua Limited, where he found Xiaofan, handed him his card, and told him he was interested in establishing a business relationship. Xiaofan, who turned out to be a polite young man in his thirties, reacted with barely suppressed enthusiasm. Their opening conversation lasted only a few minutes before Jiansu got up to leave. Xiaofan handed him his business card, which gave off a faint yellow glow emitting from silver lines crisscrossing the surface. Jiansu had never seen a card like that. He stopped, examined the smiling face on the card, and could barely keep from ripping it up and throwing it into the gutter. His hand shook as he closed it around the card, but in the end he simply tucked it away in his inside pocket.

Jiansu's first meeting with Xiaofan must have been a great success since they met several times after that. After treating his new acquaintance to a meal at a so-so restaurant and giving him a cassette player as a gift, he was surprised when Xiaofan visited the Wali Emporium unannounced, ordering a cup of coffee and watching the door. Jiansu emerged and was startled to see Xiaofan, who smiled and took a sip of his coffee. Jiansu, his face burning, stared at Xiaofan for a moment before walking up and shaking his hand. "This place is too small, isn't it? It's not our main store."

Xiaofan patted him on the shoulder. "I know. Since we're pals, why not tell me what you need." With his hands in his pockets, Jiansu invited him into the back room.

After a long and enjoyable conversation, Xiaofan was about to leave when Jiansu asked to meet his general manager. Xiaofan smiled. "You're very ambitious, but I'm afraid that's impossible. In the year I've been there I've only had a few words with him myself. Maybe you can meet our Mr. Yu, the GM's assistant."

"That'll do," Jiansu said. All Xiaofan would tell him about the general manager was that he had an interesting background and was only nineteen years old. Jiansu was impressed by the man's youth and wanted to know more about him. "Don't ask. The answers might scare you away," Xiaofan said, and walked out.

Over the days that followed, Jiansu tried repeatedly to set up a meeting with Assistant Yu, but Xiaofan told him they had to wait for the right moment. In the meantime, he helped Jiansu pick out some new ties and had a fresh batch of business cards printed for him, adding a color photo to the text. And when all that was done the right moment arrived—Xiaofan took Jiansu to the World Hotel, where they would have a brief meeting.

Jiansu continued to drink, aware that the man he was waiting for was upstairs dancing. Miss Zhou had moved around behind the counter, and from where he sat he could see her lovely profile. He recalled the quick glance she'd given him when he went to get the second glass, a look that had made him feel as if his body were on fire, a sensation that, surprisingly, lasted several seconds. Naonao was the only other person who could make him feel that way. He took another drink, lowered his head, and looked over again. He knew that there was a great distance, a chasm even, between that fair, downy young thing and himself. He was neither a coward nor a weakling—Baopu had once called him a panther—and when the time was right he'd pounce. The problem was the great distance that separated them.

Aided by these idle thoughts, Jiansu managed to while away the time until the elevator door opened with a ping. He spotted Xiaofan among a group of people.

Xiaofan stepped out and walked toward Jiansu as some of the others headed in another direction. Jiansu assumed that the man beside Xiaofan must be Assistant Yu. He ought to stand up, he thought, but a stubborn voice inside said, "No. Don't be too eager. Sit and drink your orange drink." So he cast a casual glance at the man; in his forties, the man was clean-shaven and had a nice haircut. He was wearing a black leather jacket with a blood-red silk scarf showing beneath the turned-up collar. With a hint of a smile, he walked up on springy steps.

When they were five or six steps away, Jiansu stood up and smiled. After Xiaofan made the introductions, Assistant Yu took Jiansu's extended hand, gave it a powerful shake, and let go, and at that moment Jiansu understood that even with a handshake, one acts first or becomes the passive agent—in this case the man was in control of the time, rhythms, and force. Jiansu forced a smile and tried to sound familiar. "We can talk over there, yes, over there." Yu put his arm around Jiansu's shoulder and gestured with the other, moving across the room, with Xiaofan leading the way. Before turning in that direction, Jiansu made a small move that he would long regret—he sneaked a look at the half-full glass on the table. Following his gaze, Yu glanced at the drink and, as a smile spread at the corners of his mouth, he said, "This way, Mr. Sui."

They walked down a red-carpeted hallway to a small reception room.

It was the grandest room he'd ever seen, and he told himself he'd never have been able to conjure up a room like that if he hadn't seen it with his own eyes. But, of course, he couldn't show it. With his eyes half-closed, he took in every corner of the room, acting as if he didn't much care for it. The floor was covered by a plush, pastel blue carpet on which was arranged a row of overstuffed brown sofas. He could not tell if the yellow material on the wall, with its intricate yet simple design, was paper or silk. The oversized windows were fronted by two curtains, one made of gauze, the other of thick velour. When Xiaofan pulled a cord to open the half-drawn curtain, the tiny pulleys made a pleasant gliding sound. The facing wall was hung with a giant seashell etching of a miniature Penglai fairy tower. Off in a corner, away from the etching, stood a flower stand carved out of a tree trunk whose roots intertwined around the stand. A potted landscape in gold and silver was in full bloom, permeating the room with its fragrance.

While Jiansu was examining the potted plant, a "young miss" came in with a ceramic tray and, after a pleasant welcome, handed everyone a towel with bamboo tongs. As they wiped their faces and their hands, Jiansu detected a fragrance much stronger than honeysuckle. The young miss left with a smile, and in walked another, this time with a platter of drinks, oranges, bananas, and cigarettes. She also smiled as she left. Taking another look around the room, Jiansu now saw that all the tea tables were pastel yellow with curved lines in the spots where the legs met the tabletops. They were quite pretty and reminded Jiansu of the shoulders of the girl who was cutting brambles. His throat felt hot, so he rubbed his eyes and looked back at the sofas again. This time they no longer looked so bulky to him, but sturdy and solid, as if they could not possibly be moved off of that carpet. The sight gave him a strange feeling that no one in the room, including Assistant Yu, of course, quite belonged on one of those sofas. Who did belong? Fourth Master Zhao of Wali. Yu pointed at the drinks, but Jiansu smiled and nodded, then picked up an orange. It was Xiaofan who got the conversation started by saying some complimentary things about Mr. Sui.

The meeting lasted only thirteen minutes, but according to Xiaofan, Assistant Yu rarely spent that much time at such meetings, since at Yihua Limited time was money. Jiansu wasted no time in presenting his plan to set up a special Yihua counter in the Wali Emporium with the hope of future cooperation and support from the company. Yu smiled and nodded but gave away nothing, except to tell Mr. Sui that he could go over the details with Xiaofan. After Yu left, Xiaofan and Jiansu went into the lobby, where Xiaofan ordered a drink and, in a somewhat dejected tone, told Jiansu he wished he had more authority. All he could give the shop was some imported clothes. Jiansu smiled nonchalantly, and Xiaofan never would understand what lay behind that smile.

To Jiansu it had been a resounding victory. The Sui clan had been in decline since the 1930s and '40s, withdrawing from the cities first and, in the end, losing even the Luqing River area. Now Jiansu had taken his first step forward, gaining a foothold once again in a city; a member of the Sui clan had stepped on the carpet of a fancy reception room for the first time in decades.

Suppressing his excitement, he engaged in small talk with Xiaofan but could not stop glancing at Miss Zhou every once in a while. When he looked up to see her give him a fleeting glance, he lit a cigarette and fell silent, lowering his head to suck hard on his straw. He looked up at Xiaofan. "Let's have another."

Xiaofan headed over to the counter, where he gestured and joked with Miss Zhou until Jiansu walked up and, with one hand in his pocket, thumped Xiaofan on the shoulder with the other. His new friend turned and smiled, and then introduced him to Zhou Yanyan. Zhou looked at Jiansu with questioning eyes, then at Xiaofan. Jiansu took out a business card and handed it to her. She looked and, raising her voice, said, "Oh, Manager Sui, welcome," as she extended her small, fair hand. Jiansu looked down at the hand and held it gently.

Once they were outside, Xiaofan said, "She's pretty, but too old."

That was a shock. "How old is she?"

Xiaofan smiled. "Twenty-four, not all that old, you probably think. But in this city that's a sensitive age. She's the oldest girl working at the hotel."

Jiansu mumbled a response, trying not to change the subject. Xiaofan told him that Zhou Yanyan had once worked in a county guesthouse. Her uncle was a county head by the name of Zhou Zifu. She had quit the guesthouse and gotten a job in the city, thanks probably to her uncle's connections, or those of a distant relative who was a section chief on the city committee. Finding a job in a fancy hotel or restaurant these days was hard for any girl. Jiansu listened, without showing how surprised he was to learn that Zhou Yanyan had also come from the Luqing River area. All of a sudden, she didn't seem so unreachable; the chasm between them had vanished.

TWENTY

The Wali Emporium was the only shop on the street with a laser ear-piercing service, thanks to Yihua Limited, which was the first to sell one of the devices to a privately run store. A giant sign hung in front of the door, on which the excellent features of the device were described in the most succinct language. It also stated that the store sold twenty-four karat gold-plated earrings from the US, just like the ones on the painting of the blond model on the sign. Amid blaring music, customers surged into the shop, leaving shy girls to pace the sidewalk, wishing the crowd would thin out. With the explosive increase in the number of young men coming for coffee, the owner's wife had trouble keeping up, so she raised the price by ten fen. Her husband was in charge of ear piercing, but, given his poor eyesight, he produced four or five off-center holes each day.

When Jiansu was in a good mood, he'd emerge to assist the female customers. He handled the laser with such care that the girls preferred having him pierce their ears, with the hope that he would, at the same time, beam romantic love into their lives. After touching so many earlobes, he began to feel much more at ease and confident around girls. Dressed in his dark suit, but with a different tie each time, he and Xiaofan were frequent guests at the World Hotel, where the amiable Zhou Yanyan would bring their drinks to them. On his way out Jiansu would speak to her, but only to say thank you, as he gently shook her hand. In time, he started coming by himself. As before, Miss Zhou would bring him his drink and return immediately to the bar.

Sipping whatever she'd brought him, he'd look around the lobby casually, and when he sensed a fleeting glance in his direction, he'd say to himself, "There you go!" One day he handed her a pair of twenty-four-karat-gold earrings. Blushing, she tossed them back and forth as if they burned her hands. She seemed about to say something, probably to thank him, but her lips closed almost as soon as they parted. Jiansu looked at her with blazing eyes, thinking that those lips were perfect for kissing; but he quickly recovered and gave her a faint smile before turning to leave.

As he tossed and turned that night, he recalled the first time he'd seen Zhou Yanyan, then the second time, and the third . . . He knew that a woman could be lonely even if she were being pursued by many men. Zhou had arrived in the city alone and must have been intimidated by all the unfamiliar things she encountered, though her fears were masked by vanity. Pleased with his judgment, he sensed that he was inching irreversibly in a certain direction, and when he neared his prey, he would pounce without a second's delay. Each generation of the Sui clan had produced someone like him, as if God, in His balancing scheme, had given the honest, slow-acting clan someone who knew how to exact revenge.

By then he had all but forgotten Daxi, her warm, voluptuous, and fragrant body, except at night, before falling asleep. The first thing she'd said to him when she tearfully saw him off was for him not to fall for another girl. She knew what kind of man he was, but that did nothing to lessen her love for him. That was unfortunate. Jiansu closed his eyes and mumbled to himself, "Everyone in the Sui clan thinks too much about others." He rolled over and went to sleep.

Xiaofan proved to be a true friend, for he quickly delivered a batch of imported, odd-looking secondhand clothes. Jiansu raised the price by 14 percent, and they sold out quickly. Enormously pleased, he and the shop owner decided to use 20 percent of the profit to host a banquet for Xiaofan and Assistant Yu. Xiaofan recommended the World

Hotel, and, in addition to Assistant Yu and himself, they could use the occasion to introduce their shop to the business world by inviting a few important players, advice Jiansu was happy to follow, in part out of respect for Xiaofan.

Although the dinner guests had never heard of the Wali Emporium, they knew that only a significant enterprise could afford a banquet at the World Hotel. There was little talk of business around the table. One of the guests told them he'd attended a memorial service for a martyr, which led to talk of war and reminded Jiansu of Dahu.

"It's bad out there," the guest said as he scratched his head and took a sip of his drink, "far worse than any past wars. My nephew was wounded in the leg by a land mine and is now studying at some school. He told me a lot about what was happening up at the front. He said that only one man returned after a pitched battle over some guard posts, and that he too died eventually. He was from our province and actually shared a family name with Mr. Sui here."

The liquor splashed in Jiansu's glass. "What was his name?"

"My nephew told me so much I can't remember it all. Besides, the soldier's dead anyway."

Jiansu wanted to know more, but Xiaofan held up his glass and said, "Let's not talk about that now. Here, a toast, everyone."

Jiansu clinked glasses along with everyone else and then tossed down his drink, but he didn't really taste it. His head was buzzing. "It must have been a son of the Sui clan," he muttered. Yu glanced at him and made an unintelligible sound.

After dinner they all went up to the sixth-floor dance hall.

Jiansu was captivated by the extravagant, lively ambience. Not sure where to look first, he fixed his gaze on his feet and cautiously followed the man in front. The spongy brown carpet had a deeper plush than any he'd stepped on before. When members of his party sat down, he picked out a velour-covered easy chair facing a fancy round swivel table. Two stemmed glasses had been placed on the table, one filled with pink ice cream, the other with a light green drink. There was also a platter filled with preserved fruit, fruit-filled pastries, oranges, and bananas. A red pitted cherry caught Jiansu's eye, and he reached out for it, when he recalled that he was not alone. He looked up and saw Xiaofan sitting across from him, while Assistant Yu was nowhere to be seen. The man sitting next to him, who covered his nose with a handkerchief, turned out to be the one talking about the war and reminding Jiansu of Sui Dahu. He lowered his eyes, and when he looked up again, he saw Yu sitting on a sofa to his left, talking to a girl wearing a necklace; they talked and laughed, their heads bobbing up and down.

With painted eyebrows, lipstick, and false eyelashes, the girl seemed pretty enough, but Jiansu could not tell whether her beauty was natural or artificial. Xiaofan was applauding something, so Jiansu turned to see what it was. Xiaofan was watching people out on the dance floor, in particular a potbellied man in his fifties who was twirling a short, slim girl in a red skirt. A lovely girl with short hair. A large band supplied the music, including a silver-haired elderly man playing a clarinet. He had the refined look of someone whose whole life had been wrapped up in music, and as Jiansu stared at him, he wondered if that was a profession worthy of a man's lifetime. The look on the man's face led him to conclude that it probably was.

The dance floor was crowded; after each selection some couples returned to their seats, while others walked up to take their place and wait for the music to begin again. Jiansu looked over at the potbellied man, who was panting hard, hitching his shoulders with each breath. But he refused to let go of the girl's hand. A bad man, in Jiansu's opinion, since he wouldn't let the girl dance with anyone else. The music started up again, but this time a singer stood in front of the band. With each line, she cocked her head, as if drawing a circle; she was the picture of innocent youth. But Jiansu could tell that she was in her forties, roughly the same age as Xiaokui back in Wali. About that time, Assistant Yu and Xiaofan went out onto the dance floor; Xiaofan's partner was Zhou Yanyan.

As his heart raced, Jiansu shifted uneasily; he spotted Yanyan's gold earrings and wished she knew who was watching her at that moment.

Assistant Yu was dancing with a girl with false eyelashes; they were such good dancers that they quickly drew the attention of many in the room. In one of their moves, the girl swung her booted leg over the head of Yu, who bent down and twisted his body. But Jiansu wasn't watching them; his eyes were glued on Zhou Yanyan. Finally she saw him and gave him a faint smile that only he could see. He was thrilled.

Assistant Yu and False Eyelash pulled out all the stops, showing off new dance steps, forcing other couples to slow down and eventually stop dancing, leaving the dance floor and returning to their seats. Even Jiansu was distracted, shifting his gaze from Zhou Yanyan to the sole couple left on the dance floor. They came together, moved apart and spun, then held hands and spun together. They would bend one leg and smile at each other while rolling their shoulders rhythmically. Suddenly they were dancing back to back, and when they turned around, they waggled their thumbs in front of each other's face. What amazed Jiansu was how well they matched their moves to the rhythms of the music. Admiring sighs rose and fell throughout the room. At that moment a peculiar song rose from somewhere in a voice that could have been male and could have been female. Where was the singer? The music played on, a sweet, enchanting melody, though the lyrics were unintelligible.

Jiansu searched with his eyes, certain that the owner of that voice was hiding somewhere. Checking the lips of the people onstage one by one, he finally located the singer—it was the silver-haired clarinet-ist. With his instrument lying across his knees, he sang with a peaceful look on his face and arms folded across his chest. Jiansu sighed softly.

It was quite late when they left the dance hall, and Jiansu saw that most of the people left in private cars. The man who had spoken about the war returned to the lobby, saying his car hadn't arrived, so he'd have to wait. Jiansu sat down with him.

The music kept playing in Jiansu's head. The other man took out a cigarette, knocked it against the table, and, remembering Jiansu, took one out for him. They smoked silently for a while before the man turned to Jiansu and asked, "How many employees do you have?" Jiansu responded with a question of his own: "When was your nephew sent up to the front?"

The man blew out a mouthful of smoke. "Two years ago, I guess. He spent some of that time in training."

Since Dahu had been sent up at about the same time, Jiansu was convinced that the soldier was Dahu. As sadness set in, he recalled drinking with his uncle late at night after learning of Dahu's death. He decided to talk to the man about the front, in hopes that he could determine exactly how that son of the Sui clan had died. The man's face was red, obviously still feeling the effects of the liquor, but he didn't seem to mind talking about the war, since, as he told Jiansu, he'd been a soldier himself twenty years ago, although, regrettably, there'd been no war at the time.

"But my nephew and his buddies are in it all the way. Half his leg was blown off by a land mine. There are so many of the things it'll take years to clear them away after the war. Many of our troops have suffered land mine injuries, but not the enemy, since they know where they are. My nephew and others had to dig in. Nights were the worst, because they couldn't sleep. When they heard rustling sounds they knew it must be enemy soldiers, so they tossed grenades at the noises, which stopped after the explosions. But in the light of day they found nothing, which meant they hadn't killed anyone. Except for one time, when they found the body of an enemy soldier, a rail-thin teenager with long hair and boots with soles that were as hard as steel plate.

"What is digging in? Man-made holes in the hill, some barely big enough for two men to hide in. They squat there day and night, cradling their rifles. Their biggest fear is that the enemy might cut off their supply routes and they'd be done for. But everyone, including my nephew, knew that sooner or later that would happen. But they have no choice but to stay in those caves—the soldiers called them 'foxholes.' Well, they were stuck in those for two months, surviving on army rations. At first, they punched a hole in the can to sip the liquid, then they scooped out the grease little by little. Eventually that was all gone. What did they eat and drink then? The tender grass around the foxholes. When that was gone, they chewed on the thick grass stalks like gnawing on sugarcane. When the seats of their pants wore through, they turned the pants around, front to back. When the front was also worn through, there was nothing they could do. The elbows, sleeves, and shoulders were also worn through, exposing skin that would be scraped and become infected. The wounds festered, leaving gaping holes, but never got better. That's what happened during the first two months, with endless days to come. If that had been us, we'd have found a way to kill ourselves."

Jiansu held his breath as he listened. He smoked when the man paused.

"But they didn't; all they cared about was to stay alive and defend their foxholes. Some of the infected wounds stank terribly. They needed to be cleaned with water, but there was none. Men ran high fevers and hallucinated. Those who could move would pick leaves, chew them up, and rub the paste on their buddies' lips, but a lot of them died anyway. That's how it was. Some of them actually turned on cassette players, trying to fend off hunger with music. When they could no longer fight off their hunger, they crawled out to search for anything green to eat. They never knew when the enemy would fire their big guns. Some of the shells would land in foxholes and bury the soldiers inside alive. Just think, they survived that for two months. There was barely a breath in their bodies when they were relieved. Their faces were too hideous to look at. Their hair, yellow and brittle, snapped off when it was brushed, as if they'd been buried underground for years. Their uniforms were rags, like nets thrown over their bodies. It was a horrible war, impossible to imagine without seeing it yourself. My nephew survived it, so maybe he'll live to be a hundred. He's studying medicine now, so he can save people who shouldn't die. No one can save those who are doomed."

Jiansu stubbed out his cigarette savagely. "What about the Sui soldier? Was he stuck there for two months?"

"No, not quite two months. They were on different hills, so my nephew didn't know how he was doing. He heard about it later."

"How did he die?"

"His company was guarding an outpost and got stuck there when the battle turned ugly. The outpost had lost its strategic importance, so the company tried to make its way back to the front. Half of them died in the mountains in a period of six weeks or so, including the company commander, who was killed during the first two weeks. Many were killed by land mines, and that's why I said the land mines were terrible. I heard that the Sui kid was quite young, brave and very smart, which was why he survived as long as he did. I don't know who took the place of the company commander; no one will ever know, I guess. Maybe the Sui kid was fighting all by himself. Just think, a hot, humid place, the vegetation so dense and tall it made walking hard.

"Someone found a scrap of paper in his pocket after his death; it was filled with numbers and symbols, which turned out to be the dates and places of his comrades' deaths.

"A triangle was placed on a number marking the fifteenth day, so that was likely when the company commander died. The Sui kid's body had scars from knife wounds, scratches, and bite marks. What a kid! Imagine how many enemy soldiers he killed before he died. A great soldier, I'd say. He didn't die from hunger, battle, or thirst, and the enemy couldn't bite him to death either. He kept moving toward friendly territory, even if that meant death. He must have been hit by something when he was close, and he lost his legs. So he clawed his way back, using his arms to move an inch at a time. His fingers dug into the soil and between the cracks of the rocks, dragging his bloody stumps along. But he was blocked by the damned trees and tall grass, and no one spotted him when he was a mere hundred yards away. His voice was gone from thirst, so he couldn't call out for help. He was about fifty yards away when someone finally saw him. A group of soldiers ran up, rifle at the ready, in case he was an enemy agent. When they realized he was one of their own they picked him up. By then his fingers were nothing but bones, blunt white bones. He died soon after they carried him back, shedding the last drop of his blood, but at least he died on our soil. The soldier was a Sui."

Jiansu slammed his fist on the table, surprising the people at neighboring tables, who turned to look.

Sounds of a car engine were heard outside, and a driver walked in. The man got up and shook hands with Jiansu, who sat back down after he left and lit another cigarette, smoking as he watched the crowd thin out in the lobby. When he looked up, Zhou Yanyan was standing by his table. He nodded. She asked him if something was wrong, but he shook his head. They were silent for a moment, then Jiansu got up, said good-bye, and trudged out of the World Hotel.

Over the next few days the shop owner and his wife lowered their conversations to a whisper, afraid to annoy Sui Jiansu, who seemed to be in a terrible mood. The man quietly busied himself with ear piercing, and if the girls giggled, he frightened them by saying their ears would get infected. When a particularly pretty girl came in, he'd turn the machine over to Jiansu, saying, "I have to go to the toilet." Jiansu's mood improved after piercing the ears of a dozen beautiful girls, and his legs began keeping the beat of the music. When weekends arrived, he eagerly awaited the arrival of Xiaofan, who had taught him so much over the past few months, things he could never learn in Wali, such as how to use a knife and fork to eat a Western meal. Not in Wali, and not without Xiaofan. One weekend the two of them went to the World Hotel. Zhou Yanyan was nowhere to be seen, so they went up to the dance hall, where they sat and watched people dance.

Jiansu kept glancing at the silver-haired clarinetist, waiting for him to sing. Both he and Xiaofan were disappointed not to see Zhou Yanyan on the dance floor. When the music ended and the dancers stopped to wipe their sweaty foreheads, some of the musicians got up, indicating a change of some sort. The music started again, this time startling the audience as they realized they knew the song: the Cultural Revolution Peking opera *Surprise Attack on the White Tiger Corps*. As everyone knew would happen, a man stepped out and began singing rousing lyrics. A few couples got up to dance the disco, including

Zhou Yanyan, who was wearing jeans and a fiery red blouse. Her dance partner was a thin young man who looked a little wild. Just as Jiansu was about to point the man out, Xiaofan let out a surprised cry and whispered in Jiansu's ears, "General manager."

Confused, Jiansu just looked at him.

"The one dancing with Zhou Yanyan is our general manager."

Jiansu almost jumped to his feet. "That skinny guy?"

Xiaofan nodded. With his eyes glued to the dance floor, he said, "Our general manager doesn't usually come to places like this, so he's probably interested in her."

"Her?"

Xiaofan smiled. "Zhou Yanyan. She's quite something, actually getting hooked up with our general manager."

Jiansu fell silent, his eyes glued to the skinny young man, who appeared to be a good dancer; but all Jiansu could think was how he'd like to break the guy's neck. He took a sip of orange juice but couldn't taste it. After a while, the music ended, and the dancers returned to their seats, where the skinny guy draped a coat over his shoulders. He wore a cold expression, smiling only occasionally when Zhou Yanyan whispered in his ear.

The gold-plated earrings dangled from Yanyan's ears as she followed the skinny guy out. Jiansu jumped to his feet. "Let's go," he said. Outside, Xiaofan pushed him into a second elevator, and they arrived at the bottom in time to see Zhou Yanyan walk toward the hotel exit arm in arm with the skinny general manager. A brawny, middle-aged man opened the door with a slight bow before following them outside. Jiansu glanced at Xiaofan, walked out, and saw a Japanese Crown vehicle roar away. Xiaofan walked up and explained, "The guy who opened the door is his driver. He's a brute." Staring at the place where the car had disappeared, Jiansu seemed not to have heard him. A while later he asked, "How old is your general manager?"

"I already told you, he's nineteen."

"Not a good match," Jiansu said, shaking his head.

Xiaofan laughed and slapped him on the shoulder. "Our Mr. Sui is too naïve."

Jiansu shoved his hands in his pockets and smiled bitterly. They went drinking, and Jiansu wound up very drunk.

Business was so good at the Wali Emporium that they hired two sales-clerks. Both were girls in their late teens and very pretty in their sky-blue uniforms. For the owner's wife, it was a bitter pill to swallow, but they'd been chosen by Jiansu. After the first day they knew how to make the awful instant coffee, and after the second, they knew how to measure out fabric and keep a few inches behind, which pleased the owner's wife. The laser ear-piercing machine brought in pretty girls, who in turn attracted young men, who came in for the coffee. The girls were not disinterested in the young men, and the ultimate effect of that mutual attraction was a packed shop. Some of the men took advantage of the crowded conditions to grope the girls, who screamed in protest.

Inevitably, a fight broke out one day and two fine coffee mugs were smashed. The owner's wife decided to mediate but had barely taken a step forward when she was hit in the chest. Chaos ensued as she wailed in pain. It was two hours before the customers were willing to stop and leave, leaving the floor littered with clumps of hair, spit, and bloodstains.

Jiansu got everyone together to clean up, all but the owner's wife, who went inside to rest, claiming her breasts were painfully swollen. Jiansu and the owner both knew it was time to expand. To the right of the shop was a public toilet that had seldom been used in years but still served for emergencies. The owner and his wife had gotten used to the stench, but Jiansu and the two new girls could hardly stand it. So Jiansu decided to take it down both to free up room for the shop expansion and to get rid of the smell once and for all. For over a month he ran around town, wearing himself out, before he finally realized that he needed some mighty force to help him get rid of the reeking toilet. But what? He thought and thought till his head ached before he was reminded of Assistant Yu. With Xiaofan's help, Assistant Yu finally agreed to write a few notes of introduction for Jiansu but refused to alert the general manager.

With those notes, Jiansu looked up several individuals, each of whom contributed to his success, which ended up costing him two or three automatic cameras and several cartons of State Express cigarettes. During that period, he met a section chief who, it occurred to him when he ran into Zhou Yanyan at the man's house, was a distant relative of Yanyan. Unaware that the two youngsters knew each other, the section chief introduced them. With a look at Yanyan, he mumbled, "It's a pleasure to meet you," and reached out to shake her hand.

Startled and feeling a bit awkward, she glanced at the section chief before giving her hand to Jiansu, who looked into her eyes and gave it a vigorous shake.

They both stayed for dinner at the section chief's house that night but turned down his offer to get them a car and left together.

In silence, they walked down the sidewalk. When Jiansu stopped to light a cigarette, Yanyan kept walking, giving him a chance to admire her back. He admitted to himself that he'd been right; she was captivating. Leaving a fragrance behind her, she walked slowly enough for him to catch up. Up ahead a man was scrounging in a pair of trash cans, a sight that broke the tranquillity of the moment. Yanyan walked up and saw the man stuff something into his mouth and crunch away. She stood stock still. Jiansu walked up. "What are you eating?" he asked. "Are you that hungry?" Ignoring them, the man kept rummaging and crunching. They stood there silently for a while before walking off.

Yanyan leaned up against a French plane tree and called out softly, "Mr. Sui."

Jiansu's heart was pounding, but he forced himself not to show it.

"I haven't seen you for days. You were having such a good time with that general manager that I didn't want to bother you—"

"Mr. Sui," she cut him off, this time more urgently.

Jiansu fell silent. When she began to sob, he just stood there. After a while she said, "He lied to me."

Jiansu said coldly, "And you'll be lied to again."

That startled her. "By whom?"

"Me."

Letting out a little cry, she covered her face and sobbed some more. "No, you wouldn't lie to me. I knew you wouldn't the first time I saw you. I wish things were different." She shook her head.

His heart no longer pounding, Jiansu tossed away his cigarette and stamped it out before going up and putting his arms around her. She stopped crying and pressed her face against his chest, and when he turned her head to kiss her forehead, his heart was pounding again. "You've completed the first stage. A job well done," he told himself as he was kissing her.

After walking Yanyan back to her room, Jiansu announced that he'd spend the night. She wouldn't have it and threatened him with a paring knife. With a laugh, he started making up the bed. When she dashed for the door, he easily grabbed her and, ignoring her struggles, kept kissing her till she quietly closed her eyes.

Jiansu went to see her every night after that, and on their first weekend together, they decided to go dancing at the World Hotel. She looped her arm through his along the way and kept stopping to kiss him. "You're wonderful," she said.

❦

After the toilet was torn down, the Wali Emporium interior was considerably larger. The workers even dug a few feet down to remove soil that had been fouled by years of seepage from the toilet above. Gravel was laid on the foundation and a cement floor was added once the expansion was completed. Brightly colored roses adorned the new counter to ensure that everyone would forget the shop's former incarnation. Yihua Limited was unusually generous, supplying the shop with a huge inventory of imported clothes at an unprecedented discount. In the meantime, after making a deal with a fabric merchant from Wuxi, Jiansu traveled south to buy a large order of cheap goods, with an estimated profit of thirty to forty thousand yuan.

The trip to Wuxi took about two weeks, and the first thing Jiansu did when he returned from the exhausting journey was look up Yanyan.

She opened the window a crack. "Go on back to your big store. I figured you out while you were gone. I'll never speak to you again."

Stunned, Jiansu stood stock still. His face turned dark and his lips quivered as he called out, "Open the door, Yanyan. Please, let me explain." He knocked softly, as if to caress the door, but it remained shut. His eyes reddened as he bit his lip and paced the hallway before stopping again to pound on the door. He called her name.

No response. He recommenced his pacing. Then he stopped, backed away, and, with loathing in his eyes, glared at the door. He backed up a few more steps before sprinting ahead and ramming his shoulder against the door. *Ka-boom.* The latch on the door flew off, and he crashed into the room along with the door.

Yanyan screamed in terror and cowered in a corner. Jiansu's arm was bleeding, but he ignored it and stared at her. In a hoarse voice, he said, "So you figured me out, did you? You know everything, do you? That I'm a poor slob from Wali, a member of the down-and-out Sui clan? That before I came to the city I lost my chance to bid on a lease? My, you're so quiet, you must know everything. Is there anything I can add?"

Yanyan was hugging the wall, trembling, but she shook her head, not knowing what else to do.

Jiansu threw his balled fists down violently and paced the room as his voice grew louder. "You know everything, so you should be proud of yourself. It's great that you know everything—just goddamn great. This is what I am. It's your good fortune to meet someone like me, who can pick you up and put you in his arms, press you close to his heart, conquer you completely, even kill you. You'll never meet anyone like me again. No, you won't. You're a coward. A fledgling who has yet to see the world, unfaithful, disloyal, and fickle. You don't care how much I missed you while I was away, and now you're going to toss me out just like that. Well, I finally understand. Girls like you were born for the general manager of Yihua Limited, for those sons of bitches.

"What are you glaring at? I'm too vulgar for you, is that it? Yes. But that's the only way you'll ever understand me. You think I lied to you, because I have no connections, no money, and I'm just a ruffian, a sad sack from the countryside. Yes, that's who I am, but I've never tried to cover it up. Did I deceive you with my title, my business card, my suit, and my manner? Who says people like me shouldn't have that kind of title, shouldn't print nice business cards, wear good clothes, or behave like an educated man? Who? Is it you, or stupid people like you? Who are you anyway? Didn't you quit a job in the country to come here? Are you better than me? You think you are, but I think the Sui clan is better. Go check the town chronicles and you'll know that the man standing before you is from a clan that used to own businesses in several big cities, whose influence reached all the way overseas. It was a glorious family for many generations, and it's only been in recent years that it's been reduced and confined to a small town.

"Make your comparison and you'll see. But what I want you to know is, that kind of comparison is fucking pointless! Standing before you is a lonely man with no friends or family, but all you have to do is look at him carefully. Look into my eyes and you'll know that nothing can hide from them. They see the road clearly on cloudy days or dark nights and will take you to a good place. Look at my arms and my hands. They're so strong no one can get the better of them. They'll fight to have a place for you. This man came to the city with nothing but his courage and his strength. Are these the hands of a worthless man? You're so shortsighted you see only what's in front of you. You'll never understand someone from the Sui clan.

"The Sui clan has suffered so much we don't open our hearts to women easily. But now I've opened mine to you, but you can't hurt it anymore. Do you really think you can hurt someone from the Sui clan that easily? If so, you're sadly mistaken. You're mine, don't you know that? You're vain and you're stupid, so any son of a bitch can hurt you and make you cry. But I never abandoned you, because we're both wanderers from the countryside and we share the same fate. I thought I'd protect you, make you pretty, and pamper you for the rest of your life. I can do that, but others can't, not even that son of a bitch. He's depraved, and that's why he's so skinny. How can he have any claim to strength? But I do. Now you want to leave me, and before you leave, you have to insult me. You're cruel. Your pretty face can make men surrender to you, but you bully them, not caring how much blood your captives shed. The best match for a woman like you would be a heartless man who pretends to surrender, then kills you and spits on you before walking away. But I can't do that, because I love you. I've only loved two women in my life, Naonao—of course you don't know her—and you. If you point a knife at me I'll snap it in two, but I'll never hurt you."

As he raged on, he got closer and closer to Yanyan, who saw that he was sweating. Several times she screamed and raised her hands, as if to surrender, and then crossed them over her chest; she was gasping for air, and her shoulders were heaving, when she suddenly cried out:

"Stop it, Jiansu!"

Raising her hands again, she jumped up and draped her arms around his neck and began kissing him. Her tears soaked his neck before flowing back into her mouth.

Jiansu did not stop her, though he did shift his bleeding arm a bit. Then he stroked her hair before pushing her away. "Don't be so quick to change. Take some time to think things over, while I go see to the shop. I haven't set foot in it since my return. I'll wait for you there, but don't come to see me if you think it's better that we break up. I won't be coming here for the time being. Oh, but first I need to repair your door."

The Wali Emporium was jubilant. The new inventory from Yihua had sent sales soaring. Jiansu's vendor friends swarmed into the shop and purchased large batches of imported used clothes. The shop owner and his wife called Jiansu "our manager." He was too preoccupied with the possible appearance of Yanyan to react to their praise. The owner often whispered in the salesclerks' ears, making them blush and laugh. And when his wife wasn't around, he even gave them some spending money. One day he told Jiansu excitedly that a speech contest was being held on the street and the top prize was several hundred yuan. He encouraged Jiansu to give it a try, but Jiansu just smiled as he anxiously continued to wait for Yanyan to appear.

One morning a group of strangers stormed into the shop, some wearing broad-rimmed hats, and chased away the customers while demanding to see the manager and the account books. Everyone, including Jiansu, was shocked. Quickly, however, they learned that the strangers were there to confiscate the imported clothes, claiming they were illegal goods that had been traced from the vendors back to the shop. The clothes would be burned and the Wali Emporium would be heavily fined. "This is all wrong!" the owner's wife screamed. She fainted.

The shop was turned upside down as the two clerks exchanged glances, not knowing what to do. Jiansu tried to explain, but the stern-faced strangers ignored him. Desperate, Jiansu went to see Xiaofan, who told him he'd been fired. Finally realizing that he'd been taken in, Jiansu sat down on the ground and stared blankly at the dirt at his feet.

Everything changed overnight. Even the start-up capital was gone. For days Jiansu walked silently back and forth in the shop. "I've been sucker-punched," he said to himself. "Sucker-punched." Between bouts of tearful remonstrations and loud nose-blowing, the owner and his wife blamed Jiansu for the disastrous turn of events. When he was leaving one night, the owner grabbed him by the lapel, eyes still red, and said, "You can't run away and leave us just like that. You've ruined my nice little shop."

Jiansu grabbed the man's wrist and threw him to the floor. "You stupid pig! Our partnership was notarized, so where do you think I can go? You stupid pig." He walked out, brushing his palms as if they'd been soiled.

It was late; stars sparkled in the sky above. Jiansu avoided busy spots as he walked on, fighting the urge to go see Yanyan. Without realizing it, he arrived at the French plane tree where he had first kissed her. He stood there, eyes closed, and muttered, "They sucker-punched me." A dark shadow slinked over—it was the man they'd seen that earlier time. He leaned over to rummage through the trash can, and before long he was crunching away, drawing Jiansu closer. He watched the man eat, and touching his fist, he asked, "How do I strike back?"

The shadow's chomping grew louder, as if in answer to that question. Jiansu turned to walk away, but this time he headed toward the commercial district, where he watched with cold detachment the vendors hawking jeans, melon seeds and sugared chestnuts, and fifty-fen peep shows. He soon found himself standing in a crowded square, where a red banner proclaimed "Modern Era Speech Contest." Seeing a sweaty man at a podium giving a speech, he stuck around to listen to a few of the speeches.

As a warm current of blood surged in his chest, his anxiety and his anger were transformed into an impulsive desire to fight and, if necessary, kill. He quickly saw through the essence of the contest: The winner would be the one who used the latest vocabulary more than anyone else. So he filled out a simple form and paid the required fee of five yuan before waiting quietly for his turn, which came after three more speeches.

Up at the podium, Jiansu first swept the audience with his intense eyes, after which he posed a string of questions with all the new terms he'd learned since arriving in the city. He used them nearly twelve hundred times and angrily tossed out even more terms that weren't currently in use but might become popular in the future. When his twenty minutes were up, he stepped down from behind the podium, drenched in sweat. Someone with a calculator announced the results: Sui Jiansu was crowned champion, having used new terms more than eleven hundred times in twenty minutes, six hundred of those with the term "information" alone.

The crowd applauded the champion, who calmly accepted the prize money—three hundred yuan tied in a red ribbon—and left, feeling totally spent.

Back at the Wali Emporium, Yanyan was waiting for Jiansu, who stopped in his tracks when he saw her, the three hundred yuan dropping from his hand.

Locked in a tight embrace, they kissed in front of everyone. The two girls backed away to hide behind a pot of roses, while the owner and his wife looked down at the floor, unable to tear their burning eyes from the beribboned three hundred yuan.

TWENTY-ONE

Wali had been in turmoil since the bidding auction, starting with Zhao Duoduo, who bought a car that raced about town like a short-legged pig, surprising the people with pleasure and alarm. Then a "civil servant" appeared—she was hired from west of the river by Zhao—and people found her strange way of dressing unsettling. Moreover, the geological survey team lost a lead canister, which was said to contain a tiny amount of radioactive radium, a critical component of the survey work. The survey team notified the public security department and requested assistance from the local government, which posted a notice warning of the lethal nature of the canister. If an unsuspecting person decided to keep it for the lead, the ensuing radiation sickness could result in generations of deformed babies. At a town meeting, county Party secretary Ma and town Party secretary Lu Jindian rallied the townspeople to get busy locating and turning in the canister.

Technician Li gave a full description of the canister and told the people that tossing it down a well, burying it, or hiding it in a haystack would be useless. The radiation effects would be felt in Wali for a long time, causing strange illnesses and producing deformed children. But even after the notice went up and the meeting was over, the canister did not turn up. Concern and worry hung over the town like dark clouds, giving rise to public complaints and heavy sighs. The person affected the most was Li Zhichang, who, after a long period of hesitation, had started up on the gears again. The golden wheels that had been swirling in his head first appeared on paper, then turned into smooth wooden ones before eventually transforming themselves into green cast-iron wheels. Technician Li and Sui Buzhao helped during the process, but the complex assembly and installation work had to be postponed after the disappearance of the canister. Sui and Li, no longer able to lend a hand with the wheels, spent days looking for the missing item; Sui cursed whoever was hiding the canister. Then Li Qisheng fell ill, and Li Zhichang put everything aside to take care of his father.

Sui Baopu stayed with his old job of tending the mill for the Wali Glass Noodle Production and Marketing Consortium. In addition to sharing a feeling of unease with the other town residents, he was worried about Jiansu, who, shortly after arriving in the city, had sent a brief letter saying he was doing well and would return soon, and for everyone to take care. But months had passed, and no more letters came, nor did he return for a visit. Before Jiansu left, Baopu had repeatedly cautioned him not to take any risks, to which Jiansu had given his promise. Thinking back now, Baopu was afraid that Jiansu might have been humoring him. The noodle factory had changed its name, but the mill remained the same; so did the noodle-processing room. Major changes included Zhao Duoduo's new car and the growing number of visitors to the factory, along with all the banquets hosted for them. The empty lot next to the original factory could be used for expansion, so Duoduo got another loan of several hundred thousand yuan.

Zhao's driver was originally on loan from someone else, but he hired the man away by giving him more money. During his free moments, Zhao had the man teach him how to drive, saying that a "big-time entrepreneur" should know how to drive a car. One day, Baopu walked by when the car was circling the old temple site, and Zhao called him over and invited him to hop in. Zhao told him he'd be honored to be the young master's chauffeur and would not be unhappy to die with him if there was a crash. The car proceeded to lurch through the open area, with the ashen-faced driver yelling instructions from outside. Clenching his teeth, Zhao clawed at the steering wheel and some levers, and shrieked when the car headed straight for a crumbling wall. Baopu was feeling dizzy, but the car leaped up and groaned to a sudden stop when Zhao stomped down with both legs. They were only a couple of yards from the wall. With a nervous laugh, Zhao said, "I'll kill it if it doesn't behave." Bean-sized drops of sweat dripped from his forehead. Looking over at Baopu, who was staring calmly at the wall, he said, "You're a lot harder to deal with than your brother."

Lumps of impure starch usually showed up in the processing room at midnight. Baopu knew that in the wake of the visit from the investigation team, Zhao Duoduo had become even more reckless about mixing in impure starch. The thought pained Baopu, as he was worried that the reputation of White Dragon Glass Noodles would deteriorate until it was unsalvageable. After some time, he could no longer hold back and went to see Party Secretary Lu Jindian, who grasped Sui's hand and told him that he didn't recall ever seeing Baopu in the town committee office.

"Maybe that's because I'm from the Sui clan, but I'm worried that the noodle industry will go under in these people's hands. I'm here today not because I've suddenly found a pool of courage, but because I'm worried."

Lu's face darkened as he stared into the distance before finally replying, "The town committee has tried repeatedly to stop Zhao Duoduo, but it hasn't worked, since someone high up is backing him. When county Party Secretary Ma came a while ago, we told him everything. He said we had to hold firm, and it didn't matter if Zhao had a backer, either at the city or the county level. We must not relent, he said, because it's crucial to our international reputation. He told us to put a dossier together." Li stopped and pounded the desk. "Some of these bastards must be blind. So what if it's a county head? Or a deputy bureau chief? They don't scare me. As long as I'm a Communist Party member, I won't stop fighting those bastards! I refuse to believe there's no one willing to take them on!"

Sui Baopu spent most of his free time on the accounts, tirelessly moving the beads on the abacus. He was coming around to his brother's view that he'd waited too long to do this. Gimpy's flute was the only thing that could take him away from his desk and out into the yard, where he looked around, unwilling to return to his room. By now, the melody carried an unmasked happiness, even a hint of debauchery; Baopu wished he could run over and smash the man's flute. He could sense from the melody that Xiaokui was probably wasting away, with dark circles under her eyes, and that Leilei, underdressed, was running around barefoot. On nights like that, he simply could not work and could not sleep, and in the mornings, what he wanted most was to see Xiaokui and Leilei. He'd roam all the places they might be found but was invariably disappointed. A long time passed before he finally saw them, and they looked just as he'd imagined. She was almost emaciated, her long hair a tangled mess, and Leilei, whose eyes were devoid of light, seemed to have gotten smaller. She was buying candy for the boy, and when she saw Baopu she turned and walked away. He stopped her. "Let me take a look at Leilei."

"His daddy is waiting for him at home," she said.

"You've lost weight," he said, but she smiled coldly and walked off with the boy.

Sui Buzhao talked of nothing but the lead canister when he saw Baopu, telling him that the longer it remained missing, the harder it would be to ever find it, and it'd be a decade or more before anyone would know its whereabouts, when someone gave birth to a deformed baby. As the oldest member of the Sui clan, he would not live to see that, so he urged his nephew to remember that no matter which family had a baby, he was to take a look at it. After exhausting the topic of the canister, Sui Buzhao moved on to his friend Li Qisheng. "He's not going to make it this time," he said with a sigh. "That's Guo Yun's prognosis. It's the same old problem, but in the past he'd jump up onto the *kang* and tear at the mat. Now he can only roll around on the *kang*. I know he's just about used up all his strength, like a candle burning to the end. When a man suffering from a madness illness can't even act mad, he's reached the end. The last hero of Wali is leaving us."

After talking about Li Qisheng, Sui Buzhao lost interest in everything else and only livened up when Baopu mentioned Jiansu. "Any news?" he asked. "No? Well, that's okay. I never wrote home when I went to sea. You go out on your own and make a name for yourself before coming back to see your friends and family. That's how you gain respect. I've been to that city. Lots of snack vendors and lots of pretty girls. You can also see people engaged in swordplay for money at an intersection. I knew a pretty girl in her twenties with big hands and big feet. Very nice. I still recall what she looked like, but not her name, though it might have been Chu'er."

Baopu cut off his uncle, who stroked his beard and said, his gray eyes blinking, "Have you seen Zhao Duoduo's 'public servant'? You have to admire the man's taste. How else could he find a cute little thing with such dainty white hands and feet? She sort of wiggles when she walks. And those legs, those long legs. I tell you, if I were ten or twenty years younger I'd be on her trail."

At this point Baopu stood up and asked his uncle to go with him to visit Li Qisheng.

∾

Zhao Duoduo had his "civil servant" in tow whenever he made his rounds in the processing room; she would be panting softly as she trailed behind him, all eyes on her. Wearing a red silk blouse tucked into a pair of tight denim pants, she gave anyone who saw her plenty to think about. Zhao would reach out to touch the hanging noodles and ask the workers how many starch lumps their shift had made or inquire into the quality of the bean milk. When he had his answer, he'd turn and say something to the civil servant behind him. Once, the swarthy man banging the strainer saw her and yelled out, "Hey! Hey! Hey! Hey!" Zhao looked up and growled, "You got a problem? Why don't I burn you with the fire tongs?" That made everyone roar with laughter, and when the girl asked why, Zhao said, "They're laughing about burning his worm." She was standing next to Daxi, who elbowed her while washing the noodles.

Then the girl walked up next to Naonao, who was working silently by a warm-water basin. As soon as she saw the girl turn her back to the basin, she splashed some water on her taut rear end. The girl stormed out of the room with Duoduo. They were barely out the door when she began to complain, but all he said was, "Ignore them, they're a bunch of scoundrels." They walked on and came to the millhouse; Baopu was inside, but he didn't get up. "This is the first young master of the Sui clan," Zhao said.

The girl offered her hand, and Baopu shook it. She smiled. "I can see why he's called a young master," she said to Duoduo. "He's so much more civilized."

"That's something he's good at." Zhao walked up to the conveyer belt and rubbed some of the mung beans between his fingers. Baopu's attention was caught by the girl's wet behind when they walked out.

That night, as Baopu flicked the beads on the abacus, he experienced an unprecedented sense of anxiety. It was a complicated account, and as he went at it, it dawned on him that he was using his father's abacus. The two sets of accounts seemed to be linked. He got up and stood there dully, beady sweat oozing from his forehead. As the night deepened he felt weary, so, as usual, he smoked a cigarette and sat down to read the little book wrapped in oilcloth. By now the edges were worn and the pages filled with notations he'd made in red, passages he hadn't understood the first time through. After reading them twice, he often realized he'd gotten different interpretations each time and that he'd misunderstood parts the first time.

There was one passage he'd read three times over the past month but wanted to read it once more. "The bourgeoisie, during its rule of scarce one hundred years, has created more massive and more colossal productive forces than have all preceding generations together. Subjection of nature's forces to man, the adoption of machinery, application of chemistry to industry and agriculture, steam navigation, railways, electric telegraphs, clearing of whole continents for cultivation, canalization or rivers, whole populations conjured out of the ground—what earlier century had even a presentiment that such productive forces slumbered in the lap of social labor?" As before, Baopu found the passage stirring.

Contrasting "scarce one hundred years" with "all preceding generations together," he sensed that the two authors were able to make important comparisons and calculations. He could see that hidden in this passage was an even more important and more complicated account. Stirred by the thought, he pushed his abacus to the side and thought about the subjugation of nature's forces and its application to Wali. As for the "adoption of machinery," he knew that it had been barely two years since the old mill was mechanized. Wali could lay no claims to the application of chemistry to industry; if you took away the "steam" in "steam navigation," Wali could claim extensive use in the past; the town obviously had no connection with railways, since no more than four people in town had ever seen a train; and Wali lacked access to the telegraph because the post office was not equipped for it. To him, these should have been in place long ago but were not, and they were thus difficult to grasp completely. This was Baopu's dilemma: It was all so complicated he had to accept the possibility that he'd never figure it out, though he was determined to keep trying. He picked up a match with trembling hands to relight a cigarette that had gone out. Then, turning to another page, he searched for a passage that he had read and understood: "Nothing is easier than to give Christian asceticism a socialist tinge. Has not Christianity declaimed against private property, against marriage, against the state? Has it not preached in the place of these charity and poverty, celibacy and mortification of the flesh, monastic life and Mother Church?"

He stared blankly at the passage, his usual reaction each time he reached this part of the text. He asked himself repeatedly, wasn't he strongly opposed to private property? Yes, he was. What about his attitude toward marriage and the state? Hard to say. Had any thoughts of charity and poverty, celibacy and mortification of the flesh, monastic life and Mother Church occurred to him? Yes or no? Had he or hadn't he given them a passing thought? Had he overemphasized the external hue so much that he had diluted or altered the essence? What's the answer?

Baopu examined these questions with a sense of detachment, but sweat beaded his forehead when he couldn't find any answers. He felt a searing pain in the chest when he probed his thoughts, for the questions had touched the deepest part of his soul, forcing him to confront pain, worry, and pleasure. He needed to examine everything, including the basis of behavior and all the many processes. He was reminded of the long talk he'd had with Jiansu the night before his brother left for the city; it had involved recollection, self-affirmation, self-criticism, as well as incomprehension and fear. Life went on and that night's talk would be continued . . .

When his head began to throb he closed the book and walked outside, where his first sensation was the coolness of the pleasant night breezes; then he looked up at Hanzhang's lit window just as she was opening it to gaze up at the stars. He wanted to talk with his sister on a night like this but decided against it.

〜

Zhang-Wang's business had fallen on hard times. For some reason, people in town seemed to have lost interest in the Wali Emporium, where the liquor vat had not been refilled in weeks. She doubled the amount of orange peels but that didn't help. The old men, who had shown up punctually at the aroma of the liquor in the past, had stopped coming, and she wondered if there was any need to open at the usual time, since she spent an hour behind the counter for nothing.

Sui Buzhao, her only regular customer, came at times like this and earned her undying gratitude. She'd share a drink with him, adding sparkle to his tiny gray eyes. Once they closed the door and put up a sign that said "Closed for Inventory" so they could drink without interruption. She poked him on the forehead and said, "Are you still good at it?"

"I'm okay, but no match for Fourth Master."

"I can attest to that. But he seems to have lost interest," she said with a giggle.

Before he left, she gave him five sweets to show her gratitude. He ate three on the spot, lamenting over how the taste wasn't as good as he remembered, which did not please her. No one had complained about her sweets when she was young and pretty. Wishing he hadn't spoken so truthfully, Buzhao apologized and told her not to close up the shop, that business had fallen off mainly because of the damned canister. Besides, Zhao Duoduo and his automobile and oddly clad civil servant had put everyone on edge, but that too would pass. He let on that he'd heard the survey team had received some detection gadgets from the city, and it was only a matter of time before they found the canister and the person who'd stolen it. He pointed both index fingers at her like pistols.

"Those things are like pistols. When you sweep the area, they make a *dee-dee* sound. When they locate the canister, they start clicking like a rabbit, *jii-jii-jii, jii-jii-jii,* faster and faster, until the muzzles point at the canister's hiding place."

The new search started the day after the shop's "inventory," stirring up the town, as the lost canister incident reached a climatic moment. Everyone came out to watch, clogging the streets and making it impossible for Zhao Duoduo's car to pass. He had no choice but to walk down the street with the little civil servant, drawing everyone's gaze to the girl behind him. Technician Li from the survey team walked around with some men holding Geiger counters, followed by Sui Buzhao. Li Zhichang, whose father was gravely ill, missed out on the event. When Technician Li and the others were unable to break free of the gaping crowd, Sui told them to take advantage of the appearance of the civil servant to get away. It worked, but when the crowd turned back to look for the team, they were disappointed to see that Technician Li and the others were gone; growing unruly, they started moving in all directions, until Luan Chunji showed up with Erhuai, who guarded the pier, and told the people to go home. Luan put Erhuai in charge of keeping order, but it took considerable urging from both of them before the crowd slowly dispersed.

Luan Chunji had been worried sick for days, following a heated debate with the town committee regarding the impure starch at the noodle factory; now there was the incident with the canister, which could endanger the lives of future generations if not found. He went to see Fourth Master for advice but was told not to worry, since it would take a generation or more for the destructive or beneficial effects of the object to appear. It was pointless to worry. He told Luan to devote his energy to the noodle factory. Luan left Fourth Master's yard feeling somewhat mollified, but the anxiety surged up again, so he went to see Li Yuming. The two men decided to ask Zhang-Wang to use her powers of divination. That was when the Geiger counters arrived, and they could breathe a sigh of relief.

Technician Li and his team arrived at the base of the city wall, where they decided to divide the town into grids and search each one methodically, starting with the streets and moving on to people's houses. Each man held up his pistol-like gadget and swept the area around him, as if firing bullets. *Dee-dee.* The sound rose up all around. Sui Buzhao, looking quite solemn, studied the gadgets individually, gritting his teeth and making grunting noises, as if in chorus with them. No *jii-jii* sounded in the first grid, so they moved toward the center of town.

Buzhao followed along, his feet getting tangled from the excitement. "All things that have a spirit spin when you use them. When I was a sailor, the compass we used moved like that. You can't sail without one. It spun in the center of a circle with marks for all the directions. Seafaring books teach you how to use a compass. 'When the needle points south, you must start with the Qian position, which is the first of the twenty-four directional points. Qian represents the nature of the sky, so it must be the first. Following the compass will always keep the ship from danger.' " Sui Buzhao recited the compass instructions as if it were a chant before asking Technician Li, "Do you want me to go get that book? You must start with the Qian position, since that is the first of the twenty-four directional points."

Li smiled and declined his offer. "Yours is a seafaring book and has nothing to do with what we're doing."

People emerged from their houses to watch the team approach, and when the gadgets pointed at their house they were on edge until they heard a *dee-dee*. Sui Buzhao scrutinized the people's faces and, from time to time, shouted, "Check it again." The team usually followed his advice, but always with the same result. Disappointed, they moved on, slowly attracting a large following, which Erhuai chased away with his rifle. Forced to the side of the road, they stared at the gadgets that incorporated a power to determine the town's fate. The team continued their sweep, moving farther into the town and trailing *dee-dee* sounds as they went. As that continued throughout the morning, Sui Buzhao began to believe that the gadgets weren't as effective as they were reputed to be. The men wielding the gadgets were looking tired, all but Technician Li, who remained focused. When they neared Sui Buzhao's room, he perked up; his heart was in his throat when the "muzzle" was pointed at his room. He was, of course, afraid of hearing *jii-jii*.

He held his breath until he heard the slow, languid *dee-dee*.

The day was nearly over when the gadgets came together to make one final sweep in the fading sunlight. Erhuai could no longer handle the gathering crowds; many eyes were fixed on the black "muzzles," but no one spoke.

Dee-dee-dee . . .

Always the same languid sound. Tired and disappointed, Technician Li, whose energy had been concentrated on the search all day, now slumped to the floor.

As a chorus of discussion erupted amid the crowd, Sui Buzhao walked around the gadgets, rubbing his hands, and with sweat dripping from his face, he clapped his hands, looked at the crowd, and shouted, "Quiet down. Listen to me. I have something important to say, so shut up and listen."

Silence descended. Sui cast a fearful glance at the gadgets and shouted, "Have you all taken a good look at these? Well, we've searched all over town for that canister, and nothing has turned up. It's lost in Wali, well hidden somewhere by someone. So I want all of you to remember that in this month of this year, a tiny object disappeared in Wali. From now on we must be vigilant. Starting today, don't be surprised if someone in town comes down with a strange illness or an odd-looking baby is born. You must understand that it will have been caused by that tiny object lurking in a corner of Wali. Be vigilant and do not panic. Adults must alert their children and those children must alert their children, from one generation to the next." He was shouting as if he'd already witnessed the calamity of which he spoke. His face was covered in sorrow, his eyes brimming with tears. No one said a word as the people exchanged glances. Then someone cried out in a mournful voice, "Wali! Our beloved Wali! When will we see the end of tragedy?"

Half the people did not sleep that night.

Around daybreak Li Qisheng breathed his last, plunging the town into different sorrow when the news spread.

One by one they stood in their doorways and looked silently in the direction of the Li house. Given the public knowledge that he was deathly ill, no one was surprised by the news, but they felt an oppressive sadness nonetheless. Older residents recalled the taste of Li's section cakes during the famine. Another old friend was gone, someone who had played a special role in the town's history for decades. Supported by their canes, they lifted their heads as tears streamed down their faces, overcome by remorse for not having visited Li during his last days, caught up in the drama of the lost canister and leaving the Li family to take care of him all on their own. While they waited in agony for the sun to set, they visited each other to share sorrow and memories of Li. They had not expected that the town would seem so much emptier by his sudden departure, even though Li had been bed-ridden for years. A void had been created in Wali by the death of Li Qisheng.

"The last hero of Wali has left us!" Sui Buzhao repeated as he stumbled his way down the street.

His words were heartbreaking. Even the young stopped their happy chattering. If people were bewildered by Zhao Duoduo's car and his civil servant, and worried about the disappearance of the canister, then they were deeply saddened by Li's death. The cadre from the township committee personally inquired if Li Zhichang needed any help with the funeral, while Li Yuming took charge of the arrangements. After hearing Sui Buzhao's shouted comment, Zhang-Wang closed the Wali Emporium and rushed over to Li's house to supervise the rites. When she asked Li Zhichang, who had been weeping silently, about details of his father's last moments, he broke down completely, but she ordered him not to cry or talk too loudly during the first eight hours. After telling him to close the door, she began to chant. It was nearly dark, eight hours later, when they washed Li Qisheng before changing his clothes. Li Zhichang turned on the light, but Zhang-Wang quickly turned it off and replaced it with a thumb-sized candle and then removed Li Qisheng's clothes.

That night, groups of people came to pay their last respects to Li Qisheng, who could not have imagined that he was loved by so many people. The guests brought incense and so much spirit paper it was piled as high as a table. The old men and old women were more grief-stricken than the others; they would bend over and wail before they even laid down the spirit paper. If Li were alive, they felt, the past would live on in their memories. There had been tears and blood in that past, but there had also been laughter and happiness, and now Li had taken those memories with him. He'd left a hole in their hearts, and even the young were beginning to sense the gravity of the situation from the sad faces of the old folks. Who, they asked, would create section cake for them in the next famine, now that Li was dead? Their questions and their concerns turned to sobs.

Supported by their children and grandchildren, more and more old men and women arrived at Li's house. There were so many they could only spend a few minutes inside to light a stick of incense and kowtow before they had to back out. A member of the Li clan was keeping track of the spirit paper brought by guests. Meanwhile, Zhang-Wang sat on a rush mat and, with her eyes partially shut, chanted. Flickering candlelight brightened her face one moment and darkened it the next. Li Zhichang received the guests, conversing with them in a hoarse voice. Just when the crowd was thinning out Fourth Master walked up with a cane and some spirit paper. His arrival touched everyone's heart, just as his earlier visit to Dahu's bier had. Those in the room sighed as they fixed their gaze on Fourth Master, who bowed three times before Li's body after lighting a stick of incense. He then shook hands with each member of the Li clan and left. After him, Zhao Duoduo showed up with some spirit paper. With a gloomy look, his hands in his pockets, he looked around the room. People were surprised to see him dressed in a neatly pressed suit.

Zhao's civil servant arrived shortly after his departure. The people were outraged by the way she was dressed, but she had, after all, come to pay her respects to the dead. Or so they thought. But then they realized that she hadn't even brought spirit paper. The outlines of her breasts were clearly visible through her thin blouse, which was tucked into a metallic belt, accentuating her small, round buttocks. She had no sooner stepped inside than she said, "Is Manager Zhao here? He has a phone call." No one responded, so she asked the taciturn mourners around her, "Have you seen him?" Still, no one said a word.

Zhang-Wang stood up and gave her two resounding slaps. "Slut!"

The confused girl was about to say something when two men from the Li clan walked over, picked her up, and tossed her into the darkness outside.

The townspeople could not believe that the lewd woman had come in to seduce the spirit of the dead man. For them that was a first.

Zhang-Wang redoubled her chanting effort as Sui Buzhao walked in with his niece and nephew. Baopu and Hanzhang knelt behind their uncle, who spoke to the dead man with tears rolling down his face.

On the following day a tent was set up next to the house. The same musicians Zhang-Wang had hired for Dahu's funeral played one beautiful song after another. The only difference was the absence of that devilish flute, and that enhanced the emotional impact of the music. On the day of interment, the whole town came out. Someone later remarked that it was the most magnificent funeral in years and deserved to be recorded in the town's chronicle.

Zhang-Wang served as the undisputed funeral director; she chose the site, checked the feng shui, and determined the hour for burial. Only she could keep track of all the complicated rituals. She even picked the pallbearers, taught them how to tie the ropes around the coffin, and determined which end should be lifted up first. Before the procession set out, she sent someone to walk the route and arranged for people to burn spirit money by the city wall. They were to keep watch over the funeral route, making sure that no vehicle was allowed to pass, especially Zhao Duoduo's sedan.

Once the procession was set to start out, Sui Buzhao suggested that they inter everything in Li's room to keep him company. Zhang-Wang discussed his suggestion with the Li clan elders, who were reluctant at first. They finally gave in when Buzhao pointed out how the objects in that room had kept the lonely Li Qisheng company for years. He was forceful and the auspicious hour for burial was drawing near, so in the end they acquiesced.

With a shout from Zhang-Wang, someone raised a black pottery platter and smashed it on the floor. Wailing erupted as the coffin was lifted up, and the procession set out. Li Zhichang was so overcome by grief he collapsed on the dusty road, dirtying his white mourning clothes. He had to be helped along. Everyone from the Li clan was there, some in mourning clothes, some not, depending on how close they'd been to Li Qisheng. Little by little, townspeople joined the procession and formed a long line of grieving humanity. Wailing sounds erupted when the coffin approached the city wall, seemingly able to rock heaven and earth, stirring up dust and sending it flying over the wall like dark clouds. Someone saw the wall shudder under the tearful assaults. The procession stopped at the foot of the wall, as if frozen. The crying grew louder, like a flash flood gushing down the mountains and thudding against the wall.

And that was how Li Qisheng was buried that autumn.

All Wali spent that autumn in sorrow and fear. The canister had still not been found, meaning that the seeds of disaster were hidden in some unknown corner. With the arrival of the long, cold winter came several heavy snows that covered the city wall. The expansion of the glass noodle company was progressing so slowly that investors were getting suspicious. The Wali Emporium no longer opened its doors on time, since Zhang-Wang had lost interest; commodities had gotten so expensive that she had to add more water to the liquor to break even. Li Zhichang was still grieving, unable to focus on his gears. Sui Buzhao and Baopu were worried sick about not hearing from Jiansu. The incident at the funeral had left an apricot-sized scar on the civil servant's face, which displeased Zhao Duoduo, who was thinking about firing her.

TWENTY-TWO

Snow that had accumulated over the winter was melting slowly. The narrow Luqing River was crusted with a shell of ice hard enough for the people to cross from one bank to the other. The geological survey team moved their derrick to the floodplain, where the rumble of a drill overpowered sound from the old mill. Melting snow flowed down along the floodplain and tiny buds exploded onto willow branches.

About six weeks later, the survey team revealed a secret: Another river was flowing as much as a hundred meters beneath the Luqing River.

The team had discovered the secret river quite by chance, and the revelation shook the town. People spread the news and rushed to the floodplain, even though there was nothing to see, since the second river was deep underground. Yet they sketched a picture of the river in their heads. The greatest achievement of the discovery was that a puzzle that had vexed generations of Wali townspeople had finally been solved—why had the river narrowed to the point of drying up, driving ships away from town and deserting the famous Wali pier? Wali had lost its prominence, along with the pride that had been passed down from generation to generation. It became a quiet place, slowly retreating from the world like the water in the river. And now everything had cleared up. The water had run underground and become another river. It hadn't abandoned the town. The old folks, their faces flushed as if from drink, congregated at the floodplain to exchange looks of surprise and happiness. The sorrow and worries that had tormented them over the past year seemed to have disappeared. They forgot Li Qisheng, forgot the canister, as they were now preoccupied by the burning question of how to utilize the underground river.

For the first time in six months, Sui Buzhao was able to drink happily and worry-free. He swayed as he tottered down the street, singing seafaring ditties. For him, the vanished river was about to return and Wali would soon see its river crowded with ships again. "Uncle Zheng He!" he yelled out, to the amusement of the people in town. For days, he'd been reading his seafaring book, singing "The Sun Locating Song" and "The Four Seasons Song."

"I really miss the ancient ship," he said to Baopu one day. "It belongs to Uncle Zheng He and me, but it's now in the provincial capital. I think we ought to get it back and enshrine it in Wali. Yes, we must get it back one of these days. It belongs to us."

Buzhao invited Baopu to his room at night, where he told his nephew about how he had once battled the wind and the waves on the ocean. As he talked, he took his book out from the brick wall and began to read.

"I may never have a chance to sail the ocean again," he said. "But you can. This book will be yours when I die. You must protect it with your life, for it will be useful to generations of people. You may be lucky enough to set sail one day."

Baopu, who hadn't really wanted to be in his uncle's room, had come because he didn't want the old man to be alone and die like Li Qisheng. Sharing his uncle's excitement over the new river, he had decided that the new river ought to be called Luqing.

Jiansu returned one spring morning when Wali was waking up to immerse itself in the happiness and excitement of the season. Daxi was first to see him. She had gone to the river, and as her eyes wandered over the scenery, she spotted him on the bridge and cried out in surprise. But then she stared at him blankly and stomped her feet; with a loud wail she ran back the way she came, madly, crying as if all

were lost. No one dared stop her; dreading a disaster, they looked behind her in fear. But there was nothing. What had she seen?

It was Sui Jiansu, and he was walking across the bridge hand-in-
hand with a pretty girl.

They were greeted in town by confusion. People froze and stared at
Jiansu, who was wearing a suit, and the girl, who was dressed like the
civil servant. With his head held high and his chest thrust out, Jiansu
nodded to people with a smile as he strode along. He was carrying a
fancy brown leather case, something new to the people, who were unable to tear their eyes away from the couple until they disappeared
into an alley. Speculation arose at once, waiting to be verified. The
topics of conversation in Wali changed that day; before the excitement of discovering the new river had died down, something even
more extraordinary had happened in the Sui clan.

Someone went to the Sui house to check things out but returned
empty-handed. The doors and windows were all tightly shut, and everything seemed normal at Jiansu's old room. The next day someone
went to the mill and encountered a somber Baopu, whose eyes were
bloodshot. Then someone else saw Sui Buzhao summon his nephew
to his room, leaving the pretty girl to pace outside his door. Finally
someone received the news that the girl was Zhou Zifu's niece. The
town erupted in surprise, as people remarked that the Sui clan might
well rise again, now that it had formed a relationship with the county
head. Others made the connection between the underground river
and the Sui clan, saying that the Wali pier always buzzed with activity
when the Sui clan prospered. So now, after decades of decline, they
might be thriving once again. Rumors spread, elating some and disap-
pointing others. Soon people saw the Wali Emporium open all day for
business, sometimes tended jointly by the girl, Zhou Yanyan, and
Zhang-Wang. The old men resumed their old drinking habits, while
children were back asking for clay tigers. Zhao Duoduo was angered
to see workers from his noodle company patronize the business during work hours.

Baopu was immensely disappointed in his brother, but in spite of that, he asked about Jiansu's life in the city, especially his shop. After struggling for a year, Jiansu had been unable to make his fortune, but he lied to his brother, telling him that the business was thriving. Taking out his business cards, he told Baopu that he was managing two stores and had come home both to see his family and also to straighten out the shop in town. Baopu looked at the fancy business card and returned it.

"What I want to see are the accounts—revenue and expenses."

Jiansu replied that those were minor accounts and that his brother ought to be more concerned with the big one—the pretty girl he'd brought back with him. Baopu's face reddened as he reproached Jiansu for abandoning Daxi.

Jiansu fell silent, not responding to his brother. But then he said, "There's nothing I can do about that. I'm not in love with Daxi."

Jiansu had brought some fancy clothes home for his sister and made a point of asking Yanyan to give them to Hanzhang. Laying the clothes on her knees, Hanzhang caressed the material and put them aside. She then asked Yanyan to leave the room so she could talk to her brother in private. As soon as Yanyan left, she looked Jiansu in the eye, her pale, nearly transparent face twisted with anger. Jiansu averted his gaze, but she would not relent. In the end she said, "Daxi will never forgive you."

More shocking news came the day after Hanzhang's confrontation with her brother. In despair, Daxi had taken poison, stunning the whole town. Lacking the nerve to leave the house, Jiansu begged Baopu to go see the girl.

Daxi's house was submerged in tears as Guo Yun worked up a sweat trying to save the girl. Upon seeing Baopu, Daxi's mother pounded her knees and cursed the Sui clan, asking that the family be struck down by lightning. Baopu was so ashamed his lips quivered, but he held his tongue. Guo Yun told them to hold Daxi as he forced medicine down her throat, not stopping even after she spat it out. After

Baopu went up to help, she threw up, soiling Guo Yun's clothes. "Good," the old doctor said, "she'll be fine now," easing everyone's concerns.

Daxi's mother knelt on the *kang* and cried, "My beloved child, you can't die, you must live to see how lightning strikes the Sui family."

Baopu looked down at the girl, whose face was a waxy yellow. She had lost weight. Moving her eyes sluggishly, she saw Baopu and said, "Jiansu!"

Baopu cried and so did the girl's mother, who said, "You little tramp, how can you still be thinking about that heartless man at a moment like this?" Daxi reached out from under the blanket with trembling hands to touch Baopu's hands. "Jiansu." Baopu's tears rained down on the mat as he bit his lips and said, "Jiansu isn't worth a single hair on your head."

Baopu spent the night out in the yard keeping a vigil for Daxi, feeling as if he did not have the right to sit inside. Neither did he apologize—he was too ashamed over the unforgivable crime committed by a member of the Sui clan for that. When he left, Daxi was asleep, obviously out of danger, so he went out and bought some refreshments, which he laid on Daxi's *kang*. When her mother saw the gifts, she wordlessly gathered them up and tossed them into the pigsty.

Jiansu was waiting for Baopu when he returned home. "Where is she?" Baopu demanded.

"I sent her over to Zhang-Wang's. I knew you'd be home soon."

Baopu lit a cigarette and inhaled deeply before grinding it out. He looked down at his own feet, not saying a word.

"Go ahead, Baopu," Jiansu said. "Say what you want, and get it over with. I've been waiting for your scolding."

Baopu looked up and said, "I won't scold you. You don't deserve it. You scare me, and you shame me. And you call yourself a Sui? How dare you tell people you're from the Sui clan? You didn't have the courage to go see Daxi, because you were afraid they'd tear you apart. You should see how she was writhing on the *kang*." He began to pound his knees. "Years ago, a woman from the Sui clan was driven to take poison, and now the Sui clan has done that to another woman. Has that sunk in, Jiansu, has it?"

Jiansu sat down hard, his lips quivering, unable to say a word. Then he began to tear up, the tears falling faster than he could wipe them off. He stood up and held his brother by the arms. "I didn't want to come back to Wali, but I couldn't help it. So here I am. I'm from the Sui clan and my roots are here in Wali. I know what I've done, but I don't regret it. I feel bad about Daxi, and if she dies, her blood will be on my hands, and I won't be able to wash it off. I know all that. But I can't live without Yanyan; I truly love her. I can't stay here; I have to go back to the city. I'll visit more often in the future, once this is behind us. I am a member of the Sui clan, Baopu. We are from the same clan, and no one can renounce it."

Soon after that, Jiansu quietly disappeared from Wali.

Daxi recovered and returned to work making noodles. She was different, with a glum look in her deep-set eyes; she had lost quite a bit of weight. Now nearly as thin as Naonao, she was no longer the chatterbox she'd once been.

After Jiansu's departure, a car came from the county town to unload some cargo at the Wali Emporium. It was goods Jiansu had brought to the city from the south, but he hadn't had time to deliver them to Wali because of Daxi's attempted suicide. From then on, exotic objects kept appearing in the shop, including jeans that hung from a rope, brightly colored acrylic knitwear piled high on the shelves, lipstick, depilatories, antifreckle lotion, whitening lotions, false eyelashes, perm kits, and more, so many new things the customers could hardly take them all in.

An old man took down a pair of jeans with his cane and muttered, "Do people actually wear these?" Zhang-Wang demonstrated the new products by putting on lipstick and using depilatory to remove the fine hairs from the back of her hand. Men and women from the noodle factory swarmed to the shop, ignoring and obliterating Zhao Duoduo's management method. At first they just looked without buying, but their eagerness to try the new objects quickly won them

over. Naonao bought a pair of jeans and changed into them in the
shop, with Zhang-Wang serving as a shield. When she walked outside,
people turned to look at her, their eyes glued to her back. Pretending
to study the new fashion, young men took their own sweet time admiring Naonao's nice buttocks and long legs. Even Daxi visited the
shop a time or two but she never bought anything; the sight of the
jeans always reminded her of the woman who had stolen Jiansu from
her, and disgust and hatred filled her eyes.

Within a week, the streets of Wali were swarming with girls in
jeans. Townspeople looked on with surprise, unsure if that was good
or bad. But it was clear that the boys loved seeing Naonao and the
other girls walking around proudly in their jeans; their moral recti-
tude was being severely tested. Tantalized by buttocks tightly wrapped
in jeans, they could not sleep at night and their faces took on a dark
sheen. A week went by with no untoward occurrence, and by the second week everyone had gotten used to the sight; once again the men
and women were getting along. The young men could talk and laugh
naturally.

When a batch of larger jeans arrived, the boys put them on, and
this time it was the girls whose moral strength was being tested. The
crazy old man, Shi Dixin, clenched his teeth at the sight of young
people in jeans as he walked around town with a manure basket on his
back. The young residents avoided the squat old man like the plague.

Jiansu and Yanyan returned to town but did not attract the same
shocked attention. They arrived in a small van and stayed in the Sui
house, where they listened to music day and night.

One night, at around midnight, Erhuai, who guarded the pier,
came to knock on their door, his rifle slung on his back. Jiansu and
Yanyan were sleeping. Jiansu, noticeably upset by the interruption,
got dressed and opened the door.

"Do you have a marriage certificate?" Erhuai asked.

Jiansu swallowed and said, "Yes, we do. Come in, I'll show you."
Erhuai had barely taken a step before Jiansu knocked him to the floor

and kicked him. Erhuai unwisely got to his feet and was promptly given a sound beating. "I'll get you, you wait and see," he threatened as he was leaving.

Jiansu waited but saw nothing, as it turned out. Erhuai had gone to see Luan Chunji to have them arrested. Luan yelled at him, "Are you crazy? Don't you know who County Head Zhou Zifu is?"

When Jiansu and Yanyan went out in public they walked arm in arm, to the envy of the young men in town. Some, but not all, of them said that Yanyan was prettier than Naonao. But they all agreed that the civil servant was no comparison, now that her face was scarred; these days she wasn't even the equal of Daxi.

Zhou Yanyan spent half her time tending the counter with Zhang-Wang, rearranging the display and redecorating the shop interior. Jiansu hired a painter to give the storefront some color, added a mural, and set up two speakers. He also placed coffee cups at the end of the counter but had to change to selling tea since the town had yet to learn to drink coffee. Customers doubled amid the blasting music, drawing complaints from the old men, who now had no place to sit and drink. Overwhelmed by work, Zhang-Wang took advantage of the situation to seal off the liquor vat. That occurred around the time the civil servant was fired from the noodle company. Zhao Duoduo had dithered for a long time, but Zhou Yanyan's arrival made the woman's scarred face even uglier, prompting him to fire her. When Jiansu spotted her sobbing on the street, he hired her as Zhang-Wang's helper. Brimming with gratitude, the girl redoubled her complaints against Zhao Duoduo.

While business was booming at the Wali Emporium, the noodle company suffered a series of setbacks, starting with the several hundred thousand *jin* of noodles that were stopped at the border by the Export Department. Then the expansion money ran out before the job was completed and a bank loan was not approved. The only option was to sell the noodles at a reduced price to domestic consumers, which translated into a substantial loss. The unfinished work on the factory expansion was the most worrisome, since no loan could be obtained and no capital raised. The original investors were now on edge, repeatedly requesting to have their money back.

The fired civil servant gloated over all these misfortunes. "No man can stand up to a woman's curse. I've cursed Zhao Duoduo every single day, and see the trouble he's in now." Her customers were convinced of her mysterious power, for a rumor had been circulating that another investigation team would soon arrive in Wali. The people heard that the man in charge of the previous investigation team had been punished. As predicted, another team came two weeks later, and Lu Jindian, the town's Party secretary, was among them.

Clearly Sui Jiansu was on edge. He went out several times a day and had become uncommunicative; most of the time his brows were knitted in a frown. One night, after the civil servant and Yanyan had left the shop, he climbed up onto the counter and crouched down—a habit he'd long since outgrown—just as Zhang-Wang came in and closed the door behind her. Jiansu gave her a guarded look. She held her head straight, but her recessed chin was twitching; she smirked as she kept her eyes on Jiansu, who coughed uneasily.

"You—" Her chin kept trembling. "You think you can hide from me? You're just a wet-behind-the-ears kid." She slapped him on the behind.

Climbing down off the counter, he gave her a wary look. She rubbed the loose skin under her chin and said, "You're a youngster who doesn't know his place. With those hawklike eyes of yours, you've spotted your prey, now that the noodle factory seems to be in trouble. Am I right?"

He lit a cigarette and blew the smoke in her face. "So what if you are?"

She waved away the smoke with her hand and whispered, "Fourth Master has high hopes for you. He's always singing your praise."

Jiansu's heart began to race, but he wasn't sure where this was going. "Fourth Master says Zhao Duoduo is an old fool," she continued,

"and only Sui Jiansu can make the noodle business profitable again."
Her eyes were fixed on Jiansu's face.

Now he understood. Zhao Duoduo was not going to last long, and
Fourth Master was trying to find a stand-in to pick up the pieces.
With a smirk of his own, he said, "I must thank Fourth Master for
thinking so highly of me."

She laughed, "I was right. You're a smart kid. Anyone who wants to
do something in Wali has to have Fourth Master's backing. So don't
ever forget Fourth Master." Jiansu nodded his agreement, but at that
moment the woman filled him with disgust, a feeling he'd never had
before. He grinned and made an obscene gesture. She shivered with
excitement.

Jiansu and Yanyan had to return to the city, since she was only on
a leave of absence. The next time they came back, he brought along
the laser ear-piercing machine. Given their experience with the jeans,
the girls in town had no trouble enjoying the new machine's benefits.
In short order all the girls in the noodle room, except for Naonao and
Daxi, had pierced ears. Daxi often gazed in the direction of the Wali
Emporium, thinking of the man inside. Knowing that he would have
to touch her earlobes if she had her ears pierced, and unsure how she
could act at a moment like that, she forced herself to stay clear of the
machine.

Naonao, on the other hand, was dying to be the first to wear earrings, but when she overheard Baopu talking about Jiansu with their
uncle, she learned that Baopu was virulently opposed to the machine,
and she lost interest in it. In the noodle room, she sighed constantly
as she worked the starchy paste with her fair arms. The other girls
found the sight of Naonao without earrings unimaginable, so they
frequently reached out to touch her lobes, which so upset her she
pushed their hands away and took deep breaths. Sometimes she
walked out alone to the drying ground, where she picked up a drying
pole and carried it over to the mill. There, as a prank, she made as if
to swing it down on Baopu's broad back. When he jerked his head

around, she quickly put the pole behind her and started leaping and jumping around the mill, a sort of disco step she'd learned. Baopu would just smoke his pipe.

"They all have their ears pierced," she said to him once.

"Oh," Baopu replied simply.

"Putting holes in your ears, I don't like it."

"Good."

"Men smoke too much," she said earnestly. "You smoke too much." Baopu didn't respond, so she gave him an angry look and walked out, heading to the floodplain. After running for a while, she lay down among the willow trees and picked branches that she then broke into pieces. She wanted to take a bath, but the water was too cold, so she just washed her face.

Naonao would loathe that autumn for the rest of her life.

It was a pleasant afternoon. The floodplain was bathed in lazy warmth, with sunlight glinting off the white sand. Wanting to get away from the watery mist in the processing room, she'd come out to the floodplain alone. She ran, jumping up and down on the sandy soil, like a vibrant little mare. The blue jeans made her appear even more slender, more charming. Her beige blouse was tucked inside a belt, accentuating her full breasts and a tiny waist that elongated into straight, strong, and long legs. She bent down to pick up pebbles— pretty round pebbles that she held in her palm for a while before throwing them into the river. She was looking for something on that vast floodplain, but she knew she wouldn't find it. Autumn had come so quickly, and soon it would be winter, when the water would turn to glistening ice in the severe cold.

Naonao looked around, but all she could see anywhere were willow saplings. She wondered why they never grew into tall trees and yet swayed so gently in the wind.

As her thoughts wandered, Erhuai, rifle still slung over his shoulder, walked out of the willow groves. He was chewing something, a sight she found almost comical. She felt like cursing him but stopped herself and began walking back to work. Erhuai shifted his rifle to the other shoulder and waved for her to stop, so she did. He was grinning as he walked toward her; she stuffed her hands in her pants pockets. "You're damned ugly," she said.

"All the same," he replied.

That puzzled and irritated her at the same time. "What do you mean?"

He laid down his rifle and sat down. "All the same."

She laughed and cursed him.

A brightly colored snake slithered toward them.

Erhuai jumped up and caught the snake, which he held by the tail and shook. Naonao screamed. "Unmarried girls are afraid of these things," he said with a look she found to be both strange and terrifying. He tossed the snake to the side and took a step toward her. "There's nothing I'm afraid to pick up."

She nodded, having recalled seeing him play with a big toad, which had left a white secretion all over his hand. The memory frightened her. His eyes were fixed on her lower body, and she was tempted to throw sand in his eyes. But when she bent down, he grabbed her from behind. She thrust her elbows backward but failed to loosen his grip.

"Let go of me," she said as she turned her head. Then she planted her feet in the sand and, holding her breath, struggled with all her might. But Erhuai pushed back, his arms tightening around her like a chain. She cursed and she pushed but could not break his grip. He just waited till she'd used up all her strength and then easily pushed her to the ground. As she lay on her back, she looked up at him; she was panting hard and sweat was streaming down her face, which was now red as flowers. She was biding her time. When she had gathered enough strength, she kicked out violently, landing a kick on his mouth, and as he wiped the blood from the corner of his mouth, she sat up and crashed into him like a crazed lioness. She pulled his hair and bit him, making him scream as he tried to dodge her hands and teeth. Eventually he found an opening and smacked her in the face. Blood spurted; she fell back down. He straddled her and looked down. She was quiet, but before long she tried to sit up again.

Another, heavier, punch in the face stopped her.

She spent the rest of that afternoon wiping her once pretty, now soiled jeans. She went down to the river to wash her hands and face. What an autumn! What an afternoon! She kept washing her hands and her face, till she burst out crying. She cried and cried till the sun set, staining the water a bright red.

With obvious difficulty she walked along the floodplain till she found the noodle pole she'd dropped in the sand earlier. Using it as a sort of crutch, she resumed walking and arrived at the mill, where she leaned against the door frame, breathing hard.

When Baopu heard the panting sounds, he turned and asked in a voice that betrayed his surprise, "What are you doing here?"

She didn't move, she just pressed her body up against the door frame. Again he asked what she was up to. "I came to hit you," she screeched, "to break your head open! I want to kill you!" Tears ran down her face as she screamed and raised the pole, but it fell to the floor.

Baopu finally noticed the bruises on her face and jumped to his feet. "Naonao, what happened? Tell me. What happened? Who did this to you? Why do you want to hit me, what did I do? Tell me!"

"I hate you. I hate you. Who did this to me? It's you, it was your brother. Yes, it was your brother who did this to me. I'm here to settle accounts with the Sui clan, and you're one of them." She was sobbing now, her head pushing up against the door frame and writhing in agony.

Baopu was confused and startled, as if someone had smacked him in the head. "Jiansu," he cried out in his mind, and began to tremble.

He went immediately to the Wali Emporium to find Jiansu, but he wasn't there, so then he went to his room, where he found his brother smoking a cigar. Jiansu picked up a package wrapped in newspaper and removed a suit of clothes, which he held out to Baopu. Ignoring the clothes, Baopu gripped his arm and yelled, "Did you hit Naonao and give her all those bruises?"

"What are you talking about?" Jiansu stared at him blankly as he jerked his arm free. So Baopu told him what had happened, and a chill settled on Jiansu's face. Baopu asked him again if he'd hurt Naonao, but Jiansu just kept puffing on his cigar. Then he tossed the cigar away and said, "She likes you. She's in love with you, Baopu."

Baopu stepped back and sat down gingerly. Exhaling deeply, he muttered, "Who did it then? Who did this to her?"

"You did," Jiansu said angrily, "you hurt her feelings. You wait and see. She's going to be another Xiaokui. I may not have treated Daxi right, but you sure haven't treated Naonao any better. Now you and I are alike." He closed the window and turned to stare at his brother. Finally he blurted out, "Zhao Duoduo is going down. The noodle factory is changing ownership."

Baopu stood up and fixed his bright eyes on Jiansu. "To whom?"

"The Sui clan."

Baopu shook his head, but Jiansu just smirked. "I know you're going to say I don't have it in me to take over. Well, Sui Jiansu is not backing down this time. Go ahead, shake your head, but take a look around and tell me who else could come forward to take care of the mess." Baopu slowly rolled a cigarette, took a puff, and nodded at his brother.

"Maybe I'll walk out of the mill and say to everyone that Baopu is here to take charge of the noodle factory for you. I'll tell them to hold on tight, so it won't be snatched away by any other greedy person. I will. Believe me. I'll tell them that."

Jiansu's lips were quivering; dark veins bulged on his forehead. He looked to the side and muttered, as if to himself, "It's over. The Sui clan is truly finished this time. Someone from the Sui family is shaking his fist at one of his own, and brothers are fighting each other." He turned to the window and shouted, "Daxi, Xiaokui, Naonao. You're all blind. How could you have fallen for such worthless men?" He threw himself onto the *kang* and began to sob.

TWENTY-THREE

Jiansu pounded the *kang* as he sobbed, more heartbroken than Baopu had ever seen. The sound alone told him all he needed to know about his brother's despair. Several times he stood up to comfort him but sat back down again, with a clear sense that the two brothers might well part company on this autumn evening. And what a tragedy that would be. His gaze fell on the suit, a gift for him from Jiansu, who had brought it from the distant city. Reaching out to pick it up, he spotted the newspaper wrapping his brother had torn away. It was so dark in the room he had to bend over to see it clearly.

His hands began to quake. Gripping the paper, a scream burst from his throat, startling Jiansu, who was shocked to see beaded sweat on his brother's forehead and cheeks. "Where did you get this paper?" Baopu shouted.

Bewildered and surprised, Jiansu looked at him and said, "It's just an old newspaper I used to wrap the suit." Then, snatching it from his brother, he read the first few lines of a story, the contents of which so stunned him that he sank to the floor.

" . . . murders that occurred during the Cultural Revolution. In August 1966, a large-scale killing of the representatives of the 'Four Bad Elements'—landlords, rich peasants, counterrevolutionaries, and local criminals—and their families occurred in X city in X county, as armed struggle and random killing increased in frequency and ferocity. A production brigade would kill one or two people, then two or three, ultimately killing a dozen or several dozens of people. They began by killing the 'Four Bad Elements' themselves but ended up indiscriminately killing wives and children . . . wiping out whole families. From August 27 to September 1, forty-eight production brigades from thirteen communes killed three hundred twenty-five people, the oldest aged eighty, the youngest merely thirty-eight days old. In all twenty-two families were eliminated . . ." Jiansu cried out, his face drained of color, like a choking man.

"How did this newspaper wind up in my hands?" he asked as he undid his collar button. Baopu, who was gazing out through the darkening window, did not turn to look at Jiansu, who grabbed him by the shoulders and shook him. "What's wrong, Baopu? Say something." Baopu gave him a cold look, so frightening Jiansu that he pulled his hands back. He saw the stars in the sky through the window. Dogs were barking in town; someone was calling out. Outside by the window a dark shadow jumped; Jiansu pressed his face on the window to see that it was only a small tree bending in the wind. He sat back down; his brother was still silent. Although the room was now pitch black, he did not turn on the light. Such a dark night, no different than that earlier, terrifying night. Jiansu's ears rang with chaotic footsteps, shouts, dog barks, and terrified screams. On that night, the three children of the Sui clan had sat in the dark, panic-stricken, waiting for daybreak.

Jiansu softly called out to his brother but still no response. Ripping sounds filled the silence; his brother was shredding the newspaper. Then silence for a moment, followed by the sound of someone groping in the dark. He quickly turned on the light to see his brother squatting on the floor, carefully picking up pieces of newsprint and laboriously putting them together to form a palm-size piece.

It was barely daybreak when the first of the rebels smashed an old stone monument on the temple site, a temple of the earth god outside the city wall, and the word "fortune" painted on the walls of everyone's house. Wattles Wu, who came out to watch the fighting, told everyone that the round diagrams on the tiles forming the old-style eaves were actually misshapen characters for "happiness." The Red Guards then spent half a day defacing all the old-style houses, followed by more intense searches. Starting with the base of the city wall, they went from house to house to look for "the four olds—old thoughts, old cultures, old habits, and old customs"—as well as "feudalists, capitalists, and revisionists." They destroyed everything, smashing anything that could be smashed and burning anything that could be burned, including flowerpots, platters and utensils painted with ancient people, old paintings, water pipes for smoking, carved ink stones. After entering a government-owned shop, they ran straight to the cosmetic counter, destroying all "bourgeois trinkets" such as face cream and perfume.

When the manager tried to stop them, he was knocked off his feet by a muscular fellow wearing an armband. A youngster in his late teens barged into the dorm for female workers, where, amid screams from the girls, he smashed their jars of rouge and face powder before he shook out a sanitary pad. Surprised, he wondered why the strange-looking pad needed to be placed in a pretty little paper box, but he was certain it was another one of those "bourgeois trinkets" and tore it apart. The girls were sobbing by the time the search team left for Fourth Master Zhao Bing's little courtyard. When they were hesitant to enter, someone said, "To rebel is right; why do we have to worry about those big shots?" He proceeded to knock on the door, which opened to reveal Fourth Master, who said, "Oh, you're here to rebel, is that right? Come in, come in." He pointed at the young man at the front. "Little Ma San," he said, calling the fellow by his nickname. "Bring them in to rebel." Bushy black eyebrows were dancing on his glum face as he disrupted the orderly search team. They left, and with a sigh, he closed the door.

After the town was ransacked, the team split up and fanned out to focus on individual families. Thinking that it was a reexamination for land reform, a rich peasant put all his clothing in a porcelain vat and buried it in the ground, but it was easily unearthed with a steel pole by experienced members of the search team. He and his family were taken to the old temple site and struggled against, the same as before, except that fewer people came up to vent their anger and complaints. "It's happening again. It's starting all over," Wali residents muttered as they showed up at the site. People on the stage shouted and whipped their victims with switches and leather belts, sending them howling and rolling on the stage. That went on for a while before they bound the hands of the rich peasant and his family and paraded them on the street. After that, the search team used a steel pole on every family, who would be bound and paraded whether anything was found at their house or not.

By this time, the Sui clan, no longer able to claim the title of enlightened gentry, had their compound poked and dug in for three days; Baopu and Jiansu were bound and paraded on the street. When one of the rebels found Sui Yingzhi's photographs during the search, he had a stroke of genius and pasted one on each brother's forehead. All those arrested were bound together with thick ropes and led out onto the street flanked by Red Guards carrying red-tasseled muskets and 38 rifles. When they reached an intersection, using the "three-eight" work style developed by Mao, four Red Guards took charge of each "bad element" and pushed their heads down, while those around them shouted slogans and others urged the Red Guards to "show what they've got." So that's what they did: Pushing down on their heads while kneeing the victims from behind, they flipped them backward, eliciting applause from onlookers. As the parading continued, people finally understood what it meant to rebel. A plaque was hung around the necks of the bad elements; women had dark circles drawn on their brows. Although Zhao Duoduo had put on his armband much later than everyone else, he managed to stand out. "Hey," he shouted, "the good times for the revolutionary masses are here again!" Never without his cleaver, he showed up wherever a bad element was found and dressed down the woman whose husband was arrested, not leaving the house till midnight.

Those were times when nights were no different from days, for the popular sentiments ran particularly high after sunset. Bright gas lamps were lit on the temple site, where struggle sessions were held and then followed by plays performed by neighborhood propaganda teams. The plays all began the same way: A girl in yellow clothes and a yellow hat stood in front of the others and, bending one knee, balled up her fists and shouted, "Wali Propaganda Team for Mao Zedong Thought, begin the battle!" "Begin-begin-begin! Battle-battle-battle!" shouted the line of actors behind her, and the stock performances of "Two Old Men Learning Mao's Work" or "Four Old Women Learning Mao's Work" began. For the first, two old men with white towels around their heads stood back to back and swayed from side to side. The greater the swaying movement the better.

One time Sui Buzhao performed "An Old Man Learning Mao's Work," during which he shook and swayed, earning a great reputation for getting up after falling down when his feet got tangled up. Inspired by his act, those in charge mobilized the oldest men and women in town, put makeup on their faces, and sent them up onto the stage. With thick powder caked on their deeply wrinkled faces, they presented an unsettling sight that led to failed performances. One play, "Children Who Could Be Taught Well," with its exposure and criticism, left a deep impression on everyone. The children of those struggled against denounced their parents' crimes by singing or talking fast with a clapper, or by performing a comic monologue. They were a sad sight to behold; shamed by their parents, they were eager to make a clean break, while trying to achieve at least a minimum of artistry. The best performance came from the children of a rich peasant, Ma Laohuo, who did a fast-talk duet. In pursuit of rhythm, they called themselves "teachable children": "Ai, Ai, our bamboo clappers reach the sky / Dear comrades listen to us try / Mao Laohuo, don't be sly / We teachable children won't let you fly / Never never let you fly."

Throngs of rebels surged through town, filling the walls with comic drawings and big-character posters whose contents varied, exposing a thief, a reactionary, or a cadre who had taken the side of someone with a bad background. Nearly all of them had one phrase in common: "How venal!" New targets of public criticism began to appear: town committee members, especially the township head, Zhou Zifu. Posters listed his crimes over the years, his outrageous behavior during the backyard furnace campaign, which had caused so many to die of starvation. How he'd had the town's armed militia illegally tie up the masses. Problems with tax revenue. Apportioning. Labor conscription. Appropriations. Military draft. Interrogations surged onto the streets. Rebels appeared even within the town committee, for someone had pasted up posters exposing things unknown to the public: Zhou Zifu had once harassed a female typist, who had then reported him, but nothing was done. The townspeople were outraged.

An ingenious comic drawing appeared one day: A male organ several feet long was spiraling down on Zhou Zifu, who looked like a pig, surrounded by a group of panic-stricken women. Second and third drawings quickly followed. Then someone asked Wattles Wu to write a large slogan with oversized characters: "Down with the Capitalist Powermonger Zhou Zifu." Then came another: "Down with the Town Party Committee." Old folks who knew how to read blinked their lifeless eyes and whispered, "They really are rebelling; they're even going after the yamen." They also predicted that soldiers would soon be sent into town, and they were right. A brigade of soldiers came, but their leaders said, "We firmly stand together and enjoy victory with the revolutionary masses." That befuddled the old folks, some of whom got together and said, "Why don't we rebel too!"

After the streets were saturated with posters targeting the town Party committee and Zhou Zifu, new ones appeared naming Fourth Master Zhao Bing, exposing the way he lorded it over Gaoding Street, calling him Wali's tyrant. They placed the blame for beating up the masses on him, and he was said to have colluded with Zhou Zifu in abusing the town's residents. Another poster asked why the people had turned a blind eye to Zhao's evil influence during the Great Leap Forward, the Socialist Education Movement, and the Four Clean-ups. Was he responsible for the people who starved to death, those who died an unjust death, or those who committed suicide? There was only one poster like that, but it drew crowds, who went up to read but said nothing. It was torn down the same night it went up and replaced shortly afterward by a comic drawing of Fourth Master with his prominent buttocks as the center of attention.

As the crowd gathered to look at the drawing, someone came with a bucket of paste to put up another poster, also about Fourth Master, the sole difference being that his name was written in reverse. The crowd quickly abandoned the first poster to gawk at the new one. Someone yelled that he couldn't recognize one of the characters and dragged the man to the wall, saying, "This one, this one here." The man dropped his bucket and went up so close that his head was almost against the wall. "Which one?" he asked. Someone shoved him from behind. "This one." The man's head crashed into the wall, bloodying his nose.

All sorts of "combat units" and "rebel brigades" emerged in Wali, with so many different names that even the cleverest people were confused. Wattles kept busy writing "battle banners" for these organizations, for which he was given a "Great Leader" memorial badge as a reward. The badge was the size of a button but got larger as time went by, until it was as big as a plate. Some of the names of the organizations, such as Jinggangshan Corps or Invincible Battle Brigade, were easy to understand, but others, like Fierce Third-Rate Battle Brigade or True Blood Revolutionary United Headquarters, were impossible to comprehend. When a member joined one, he swore to defend it with his life; endless debates and verbal abuses were flung back and forth among organizations. In the end, nearly everyone belonged to one or another of the groups, embroiling every corner of the town in never-ending debates and verbal insults. When a couple belonged to different organizations, they argued before bedtime and quarreled during meals. Reminded that their spouses were in different organizations, they lost interest in sex, and it was common for couples to live separately. Even a child in middle school was free to put a poster on his father's back.

Zhang-Wang belonged to Revolutionary Headquarters, but her skinny husband joined the Fierce Third-Rate Battle Brigade. Never particularly fond of him, she now found new reasons to loathe him, to the point that on a chilly night she pushed the naked man off the heated *kang;* he caught cold, fell seriously ill, and died. Out on the street, old men sunning themselves sat in groups based on their "viewpoint" and would pick up their stools and leave if they discovered they were in different organizations with different "viewpoints." Pedestrians were often stopped every few yards, not for their money but for their "viewpoints." "What's your viewpoint?" A wrong answer would bring verbal abuse if he was lucky, and physical abuse if not. And even the correct viewpoint might not save him the next time he was stopped, since he might be ordered to "recite a section from Chairman Mao's 'In Memory of Norman Bethune.' "

Sui Buzhao stood out for his ever-changing viewpoints. In a single month he joined two dozen organizations. He said he'd tasted everything new because each organization had its own flavor, but he managed to escape serious beatings as a result of the friends he'd made in each organization. He regaled them with his seafaring adventures and awed his audiences by explaining the meaning of the lyric "The helmsman is the guide when sailing the open sea."

Ultimately, Jinggangshan Corps and Invincible Battle Brigade became the most powerful organizations. Zhao Duoduo took over as commander of Invincible, transforming a cellar into his headquarters.

The situation grew increasingly complex and tense, while terrifying but unverifiable rumors flew. Some said the town would be realigned based on viewpoints, and some of the families, such as Ma Laohuo's and the Sui clan, might be "swept out" and have their property confiscated. People said that the movement would continue to develop further and that the revolutionary rebels planned to implement a dictatorship. Others said that people in villages outside of town were being arrested at night and never seen again, while people in town treated the capitalist roaders with "gentle winds and fine rain," but within the concept of "revolution is an insurrection," not "painting or embroidery." There were other rumors, some of which came true. Eventually, people actually began disappearing in the dark of night, and some began clamoring for a struggle against capitalist roaders. Most of those who disappeared at night returned, however, filled with complaints. One complained that he had been hung up and beaten, and that he was stripped to have his privates patiently whipped with a willow switch. His organization put up a poster that said, "No one can escape the crime of oppressing the revolutionary masses." If it was a girl, after returning with a puffy face, she would not reveal how she was mistreated.

The demand to root out and struggle against the capitalist roaders grew stronger, drawing more and more complaints at meetings. During that period, the townspeople were most impressed by a red-faced young man in his twenties who wore an armband and an army cap while giving a six-hour speech on crimes committed by Zhou Zifu and Zhao Bing, supported by materials he'd spent countless hours examining. When he spoke of the oppressed, suffering, and struggling Wali people, his audience shouted slogans nonstop, their faces awash in tears. Many were outraged at the thought of the famines and all they had suffered through the years. "To rebel is right! Down with the unrepentant capitalist roaders!" they shouted. "Let the enemy die if they will not surrender."

The young man went on with his speech: "I'd let myself be cut to pieces in order to pull the emperor off his horse. My revolutionary comrades, let us shed our blood to turn the world red. My revolutionary comrades, let us unite and fight. Fight!" With tears rolling down his cheeks, he thrust his fist into the air. Below the stage were many girls who, their teary eyes wide open, could not take their eyes off the red-faced young man.

The day after the speech, several battle brigades stormed the town committee compound to grab Zhou Zifu, who had gotten wind of the impending arrest and fled, but was caught two days later. Some went for Fourth Master but were stopped by the Invincible Battle Brigade. With his hands on his hips, Zhao Duoduo screamed, "Who

among you has the guts to step forward? Do it and you'll answer to
me, damn you! Fourth Master has devoted his life fighting Zhou Zifu's
counterrevolutionary line. If not for him, we'd all have suffered griev-
ously. I curse the ancestor of anyone who has forgotten that and lost
his conscience." He rested his right hand on the leather sheath of his
cleaver as he talked. After some whispered remarks among themselves,
they left. Duoduo posted a guard outside Fourth Master's home.

As for Zhou Zifu, a paper placard was hung around his neck before
he was dragged up onto the stage and struggled against several times,
then paraded out in the street. Nearly everyone came out to watch
Zhou Zifu and the Red Guards, shouting slogans so loudly no one
heard Zhou's confessions to a variety of crimes. After a few days, interest waned, so someone fetched a costume from an amateur drama
troupe and made Zhou, whose face was painted, wear it. Interest was
quickly rekindled. Then when the appeal of that died out, someone
came up with a staggering idea: since Zhou was a notorious braggart,
engaging in what they called "blowing a cow's cunt," why not remove
that part of a cow and fasten it around his mouth? Given that his
boasting at times seemed about to bring the sky down around the
town, the idea was met with raucous laughter and unanimous approval. One of them went out and cut one off a cow.

"I've got it!" he said, holding the gory item high. "Here it is." While
a few of the men pulled tightly on Zhou's hair, others tied the cow's
organ around his mouth. A gong was sounded for the parade to re-
commence. With tears streaming down his face, Zhou stumbled
along, bloody water mingled with saliva wetting his chest. The crowd
followed, some laughing uproariously, some shouting slogans. And so
it went, from main streets to small alleys. Only during mealtimes was
Zhou allowed to take the thing off. A couple of older Red Guards,
who had tailed the procession and dashed around town all day, returned home feeling sore all over. "Too bad for the animal. A really
good cow, gave birth to a pink little calf just last year." They thumped
each other's backs as they talked.

More posters appeared on the wall outside the town's elementary school, all of which were well written but perfunctory and lacking passion. One exposed a cook at the dining hall who had looked all around before swallowing a whole egg on the sly. One criticized a teacher who had used facial cream, spreading the perfumed breeze and poisonous fog of the bourgeoisie. Yet another focused on the marital situation of a female teacher who had a high opinion of herself because she was the only one who had a degree from the normal college. The poster castigated her, a woman in her forties, for defying the masses by not getting married. With a salary of over eighty yuan, she had the highest wage among the teachers, which meant she had sucked more blood and sweat from the working masses. On the upper right corner was a drawing of her face, her cheeks tinted red alongside the comment, "I'm a young mistress." The poster quickly sharpened the focus of struggles, directing most of the subsequent posters at her.

Now people showed an unprecedented degree of interest in the teacher's marital status. According to one posted analysis, she was overly cautious and seldom smiled or talked, which proved she was suppressing sexual desire. How venal it was for her to put her pink underpants out to dry by her door! She paid special attention to older male students, and when one of them had a low-grade fever, she took advantage of his illness to hold him and was reluctant to let him go. Other posters concentrated on her intolerably high salary, questioning why she could be given so much even though she wasn't strong enough to carry a load or work with her hands. Incredible! She must pay back her debt of blood and sweat, they demanded. She must spit out all the delicacies she has indulged in. Later a poster linked her to Zhou Zifu, claiming that she had the support and protection of the town's biggest capitalist roader. Someone reported seeing Zhou beam as he spoke to her during a school visit. That resulted in another comic sketch in which she and Zhou were wearing a single pair of pants, giving rise to all sorts of fantasies. "How dare they wear the same pair of pants!" people cried out in alarm. The reasons for her unwillingness to get married would soon be revealed, which meant that a struggle session and parade were unavoidable. One afternoon, the Rebel Corps dragged the trembling female teacher out and bound her together with Zhou Zifu, hanging a string of stinky old shoes—the sign of promiscuity—around her neck.

When the parade reached its high point, with throngs of spectators blocking traffic, old folks thought it was a definite improvement over temple festivals of yore.

Fourth Master remained untouched, drawing the ire of many. A few of the smaller combat units tried to drag him out but were stopped each time. Indignant, the red-faced young man who had given the tearful speech said, "We can drag an emperor off a horse, so why not a Zhao Bing? The most urgent moment for the masses has arrived. Follow me, revolutionary comrades!" He led a swarm of Red Guards, who marched shoulder to shoulder and sang battle songs all the way up to Fourth Master's courtyard. Members of the Invincible Battle Brigade were already there. Zhao Duoduo stood on a block of stone by the gate. "Are you blind?" he shouted, glaring at the Red Guards.

"We will give our lives to safeguard the revolutionary line! We will wage a bloody war with the capitalist roaders! Charge!" With a thrust of his hand, the red-faced young man stormed the enemy redoubt.

A fight broke out in front of the gate, sending broken clubs flying into the air. The red-faced young man screamed as the fighting turned increasingly violent, covering his face and falling to the ground. His comrades stopped to pull him up, and when one of them pushed his hands away from his face, they saw that something had pierced his eyes. He kept rubbing his eyes, making them bleed.

Many were injured during the fight, including the young man. Blinded, he disappeared from public view for a dozen years before there was any news of him. It was said that he had studied hard and that his blindness had helped with his clarity of mind, enabling him to compose several poems on any given day. He had become the nation's most famous blind poet.

Fourth Master opened his door and walked outside after the crowd had left. He stood wordlessly gazing at the broken clubs, clumps of hair, and bloodstains, looking older than his years. Zhao Duoduo called out to him but received no response. Duoduo ran off when he heard a clamor in the distance. He soon returned to say, "It's nothing, just the teacher. She hanged herself."

No one who had experienced the bizarre incidents would ever forget them, even though they were not entered into the town's chronicle. In barely two months, the town had fallen under the control of two dozen groups, beginning with Jinggangshan Corps, then Invincible Battle Brigade, and on to Fierce Third-Rate Battle Brigade, True Blood Revolutionary United Headquarters, Five Two Three One United Headquarters, and more. Each seized power by occupying the town committee compound and planting its flag. Later it was said that occupying the compound did not amount to seizing power, that the key to power was controlling the account books, documents, and name lists—in a word, the files. With the files came real power and control.

Yet a different view was proposed, replacing the files with the chop, the town's circular seal, the real symbol of power. This latest revelation created pangs of regret among organizations that had earlier taken control, for they now realized that what they had gotten was an empty shell. "What is power?" the uninformed town's residents asked one another. "It's the town Party committee," some said. "What's the town Party committee then?" "It's a circular thing," one of them said, forming a circle with his hands. But no one had ever seen the circular thing. So the various committee clerks were subjected to repeated torture and interrogation over the hiding place of the "town Party committee" by whichever group controlled the compound at the moment.

In the end, the leader of one group got his hands on the seal, which lent him true control of the town. With the "power" in his hands, he ran back and forth in the hallway, not even resting at night; three days later he blacked out and collapsed on the floor, foaming at the mouth. The seal fell into the hands of his second-in-command, who, having learned from the leader's experience, decided not to go out at night and to sleep with the seal. It worked, for a week later he still held power. But on the tenth night he had second thoughts about simultaneously being the owner of a town and the husband of an ugly woman. So he drew up a divorce paper, stamped it with the seal, and divorced his wife the same day. He woke up the following day, however, to find the seal gone, which threw everyone into a panic. During the search, a guard said that he seemed to recall seeing a dark shadow cast against the wall around midnight.

Who was the dark shadow? No one would likely ever know.

But what everyone did know was that the "town Party committee" had evaporated, along with power and control. Even a decade later, when people recalled the incident, they could not help sighing over how the second-in-command had lost power along with the "town Party committee." He should never have been so happy over the divorce that he lost the seal. No one would ever forgive him.

As power in town went through a succession of changes, someone had his eyes on control of Gaoding Street, but everyone knew that the real power was held by Fourth Master. After what happened to the red-faced young man, few, if any, people dared to storm into that yard again, yet control of Gaoding Street gained importance after the town Party committee was lost. While everyone knew that Fourth Master held that power, the big question was, who would dare try to take it away from him? Some people merely talked about it, others were eager to try.

Over the prolonged struggle, the Invincible Battle Brigade had made enemies, creating an incentive for Jinggangshan Corps and the other organizations to join forces. Three days and nights of negotiating led to an agreement that they would form an alliance to attack the last reactionary bastion of Gaoding Street and wrench power from the hands of capitalist roaders. A member who had some artistic talent was ordered to create a detailed military map of Gaoding Street to hang on the wall. All night long the leaders consumed an unknown amount of cigarettes as they studied the maps and devised a strategic deployment, arguing over the numbers and locations of troop placement and guard posts. One individual, who had read a few lines of Sun Zi's *Art of War,* kept saying, "According to Sun Zi . . . ," finally enraging the others. "To hell with your goddamn turtle spawn Sun!" they said. In the end they reached a consensus to adopt strategies that were the exact opposite of what Sun Zi would have recommended. That took two days.

The third day was overcast with cool breezes. People with strange expressions were appearing on the streets, the sight of which prompted experienced older folks to bring their children home and bolt the doors. Sui Buzhao was the only exception, for he roamed the streets, tangling his feet and stumbling along as he chatted up people in the various organizations. When someone warned him not to die as collateral damage, he merely laughed and said, "Two battling forces never kill the messenger." Then he responded to a snide retort regarding his lack of qualifications as a messenger by saying, "I've been sent by Uncle Zheng He. Our ships are moored at the pier and will fire our cannons on his orders. Have you seen the excavated old ship? Well, all our ships this time are bigger. So *you* had better watch out. Heh-heh." He stumbled away, trailing the smell of alcohol, which made people wonder where he'd gotten the alcohol now that the distilleries had all been shut down.

When everything was carried out according to plan, a group of people with clubs showed up at Fourth Master's gate. A small number of Zhao Duoduo's loyalists, rifles in hand, remained in the yard leaning across the wall, while others circled the area and closed in on the enemy. More members of the alliance arrived to surround the Zhao troops and were in turn surrounded by them. They all glared hatefully at each other, but were not prepared to make the first move. Eventually confusion set in, with no one able to tell friend from foe, as their hatred-filled eyes roamed the area blankly before finally resting on their own comrades, who cursed them in return. By noon, as stomachs began to grumble, someone yelled, "Let's get it over with!" Zhao Duoduo, dressed only in shorts, climbed up onto the wall, raised his rifle, and fired a shot. "Bullets have no eyes." Chaos followed the sound of gunfire. "Charge!" someone shouted from the back. "Charge . . ." That was as far as he got, probably after getting a slap across the face. A young female comrade raised her arm and shouted crisply, "Revolutionary comrades, Zhao Bing won't surrender, destroy him!" Slogans filled the air. From a distance, Zhao Duoduo pointed his finger at the girl and hurled obscenities at her. Then he pulled down his shorts. "Come on. I know what your problem is." Loud guffaws were quickly drowned out by shouts of "Death to the hooligan!" More chaos ensued as the crowd surged forward with terrifying screams. Zhao fired his rifle again, just as the door creaked open.

Fourth Master's large figure emerged on the steps outside his door.

A hush fell over the crowd.

Zhao Bing coughed softly and said, "Dear townspeople, I, Zhao Bing, have come too late. I know all about the recent fights and squabbles. There have been rumors about me, but instead of defending myself I shall wait for things clear up on their own. What I want to say today is, I am an ordinary man who is ill equipped to be in charge of Gaoding Street. My years of hard work seem to have become an impediment to your future, so I am glad you're here to seize power. I've long wanted to remove myself from that position so I can enjoy a carefree life. Today I am returning the power to the people. I've said my piece, so come on, take it." He turned back his lapel, snapped a leather ring from his belt, and removed a dark red wooden seal. He raised it high over his head and shouted with an air of solemnity, "Once it leaves my hand, it will never return. So watch carefully, fellow citizens."

He took half a step backward, drew his hand back, and rushed forward, flinging the seal into the air.

Zhao Duoduo yelled out in despair, for which he received a slap on the face from Fourth Master.

When the seal fell to the ground, people scampered out of the way but then quickly ran up to fight over it. The lucky winner raised it high over his head and walked off, flanked by all the others. Zhao Duoduo was about to give chase with his own people, but Fourth Master stopped him with a shout.

While all this was going on, the situation at the Sui compound alternated between frenetic activity and total silence. Rebel organizations came to make trouble, repeating their demands or poking the ground with a steel pole, for no self-respecting organization would miss out on the Sui clan, the once illustrious family. The three siblings would be lined up to be yelled at and poked in the chest by the leader. They especially enjoyed poking Hanzhang. "A real cutie," they'd say, gazing at her profile. Once, when Baopu tried to block one of those fingers with his arm, he was hit in the face; the blood from his nose soaked through several layers of clothes. The man's fist was in mid-recoil when Jiansu pounced like a panther and bit down on his arm, not letting go even as other people pounded and kicked him in the head and rib cage. Screaming for dear life, his victim finally fell to the floor, taking Jiansu with him. Someone stepped on Jiansu's head and pried open his mouth with a steel pole.

The two brothers were taken away that night, stripped naked, and hung up to be whipped with willow switches. At first they howled in pain, but after two days they could no longer squeeze any sound from their throats. On the third day, Sui Buzhao bribed one of the leaders with two bottles of liquor and took his nephews home. Seeing what bad shape they were in, he went out late at night to get Guo Yun, who smeared an ointment with a rusty smell all over the young men's bruised and cut bodies.

The rebels' successful search for the town seal brought peace and quiet to the Sui compound, where the siblings walked on tiptoes and whispered, sometimes resorting to mere gestures. Only Sui Buzhao never bothered to lower his voice when he walked out into the courtyard, sometimes reeking of alcohol. How he managed to get liquor remained a mystery to Baopu and Jiansu until one day, when he smugly revealed that Zhang-Wang was the secret distiller of a strong brew with a slight vinegary taste.

Buzhao had discovered this the day he went to buy some sweets and spotted a porcelain vat with a blue design. When he opened the lid the aroma of liquor permeated the place, although Zhang-Wang insisted that it was brine, not alcohol. He looked at her and said she was looking younger by the day, to which she responded with a charming smile and an invitation to fondle her. She also admitted that it was indeed liquor but would not let him taste it. Anxious and impatient, he stopped fondling long enough to flick his finger on her thin, dusty neck. He did not get to taste the liquor that day. Later he learned that she belonged to Revolutionary United Headquarters, and he managed to join the faction before going back to see her. She giggled and poked him. "Go on, drink till your belly bursts, you old sot." That is exactly what he did: He got so drunk he fell into a deep sleep, and when he woke up, the room, now empty, was locked from the outside and his hands were tied over his abdomen. Unable to move, he waited patiently for her to return, when they both started drinking again, using liquor to cure his hangover.

For a long time, Buzhao traveled between Zhang-Wang's place and the Sui compound, dividing his time between family ties and the lure of alcohol. Later, the three siblings were arrested again, but Hanzhang was saved by a protector and the two brothers returned safely. By then the situation had gotten increasingly tense, as a revolutionary committee was formed in the provincial city and a letter sent to Beijing with an opening that said, "To our dear, dear, dear great leader." Similar committees were also formed in other provinces, with even longer strings of "dear" in the address. Meanwhile, Sui Buzhao continued to frequent Zhang-Wang's place. Once he held up a cup to drink, but she snatched it away, scolding him, "Have you done the 'first of all'?" She then taught him how to stand, hold up the little red book, and shout his wishes of long life to the great leader and good health to the leader's closest comrade-in-arms.

"Is this doing the 'first of all'?" he asked.

She nodded. "From now on, we have to do the 'first of all' before meetings and before we eat."

Sui Buzhao considered her response and said, "Got it. My seafaring book says we must pray when we launch the ship. 'Prostrate and infuse with sacred smoke; pray with sincerity from the heart.' The only difference is the words."

"Come do the 'first of all' with me," Buzhao said to his nephews and niece after receiving copies of the little red book from somewhere and teaching it to the youngsters. He even told Baopu how to lead the others if he wasn't home.

One day after putting food out on the table, he called the two younger siblings over to do the "first of all" before the food got cold. They stood up, but Baopu had barely begun when their gate was kicked open and several people stormed in, apparently outraged. "What do you think you're doing?" they demanded of the trembling siblings.

"We're doing the 'first of all,' " Baopu replied.

One of the intruders slapped him and screeched, "How dare you, you mongrels! You're not worthy!" One of the others yelled, "Don't think we don't know what's going on with you. The eyes of the revolutionary masses are open wide." As they screamed at the siblings they took all the little red books before swaggering out the door. Hanzhang was in tears, while Jiansu reached out for a piece of corn bread. Baopu stopped him. "Not yet. Do the 'first of all' in your heart."

Sui Buzhao was beside himself with anger and indignation when he heard about the incident, wondering why the three youngsters were not allowed to show their loyalty and how the rebels could have found out about it. After considering the mystery from all angles, he said to Baopu, "They must have binoculars."

His speculation soon proved to be accurate.

When Flour-face was killed during the reexamination for land reform, he was survived by a wrinkly faced wife and three daughters, who rarely left their house and were soon forgotten by everyone. But one day, the leader of an organization climbed up onto a watchtower and, through his binoculars, spotted the wrinkly "landlord's wife" burying a pottery vat under a peach tree in a corner of the yard. He'd had the binoculars for six months and from them had gained endless pleasure, for they made him virtually omniscient. "I know everything!" he'd say to others enigmatically. He ordered his second-in-command to take some people and dig up the vat. His second-in-command left and returned quickly with a trembling woman with bound feet, along with the vat and its contents—several old stock certificates and a blackened account book that no one could read. "This is a landlord's comeback account book," the leader announced. His second-in-command looked at him with astonishment. "How did you know it was buried under a peach tree?" "I know everything!" was the response.

This development energized the rebel organizations, whose members spent the night drafting a report while one of them was sent to the watchtower with a megaphone to inform the town. The town was abuzz. "They found a comeback account book." The leader was the envy of all his peers. "Fuck!" one of them cursed. "All he has is a stinking pair of binoculars." But nearly everyone showed up for the struggle meeting.

That particular leader took to wearing his binoculars around his neck as he swaggered around town, hands behind his back, the picture of self-satisfaction. Burning with jealousy, the other leaders could only fantasize about taking him down and ripping the binoculars off his neck. One day the second-in-command saw the landlord's daughter delivering food to her mother; on the way she stopped at the leader's room and did not emerge for a long time. Puzzled, he eventually arrested the landlord's daughters and got the truth from them after hard questioning.

The leader had threatened the girls that he would execute their mother. When they got down on their knees to beg for her life, he proceeded to deflower them, one at a time. The second-in-command exhaled deeply as he realized that he could not deal with his leader by himself, so he made a secret pact with two other groups and arrested the leader one night, hanging the binoculars around his own neck the following day.

A solemn criticism session drew nearly everyone in town. Taking turns to preside, the other leaders ordered the girls to repeat their story in detail, while the bound leader was made to stand on the stage. After two days, the place swarmed with people, turning the meeting into a form of popular education. When one of the girls reached a critical point in her narrative, a leader would walk up and yell at the offending leader, "Is this what happened?" When the meeting was over, the three girls were locked up to await a further decision, but the oldest one, seeing that the other two were asleep, hanged herself from a windowsill that night.

A pair of binoculars had helped cement the alliance of several rebel groups, which, along with the changing situation in the provinces, gave Wali the ideal conditions to create a revolutionary committee. A few weeks of heated debate and negotiations ushered the committee into existence. Several strong men were chosen as drum beaters on the day the announcement was made, and a ten-yard-long string of firecrackers was lit off. Zhang-Wang was given the task of training some women in their fifties to perform on stilts. Since they had all been performers for temple festivals, it was a roaring success, with the celebratory procession slithering through main streets and small alleys like a python. One section beat drums, another lit firecrackers, but the finest of all was Zhang-Wang's stilt team.

On stilts the women seemed nimbler than when they walked on the ground, and no one worried they might fall and break something. Twisting their bodies and rolling their shoulders, they were intent upon making the old men laugh; but the men puffed on their pipes and commented in loud voices that things just weren't as good as before. The skill of the stilt-walkers wasn't bad, they said, but they lacked the seductive quality that had once driven the men wild with desire. In the past, watching the stilt performance had been a true pleasure, for the men and women would push and shove each other but they never fell. How wonderful it had been to see men and women grope each other on stilts. The old men sighed and smoked, dabbing at the corners of their eyes with sleeves adorned with red armbands.

The celebratory parade continued on late into the night, with torches and lanterns lighting the way. By then, shredded paper from the string of exploded firecrackers littered the ground, and the stilt-walkers were limp from exhaustion. The drums had been quiet for some time, and only scattered slogans could be heard. The sluggish procession was still roaming the streets when, without warning, someone on a rooftop poured a foul mixture of excrement and urine down onto the street, overpowering the celebratory atmosphere with a nauseous stink; with startled yells the crowd dispersed. Everyone later learned that several sections of the procession had been splattered with the stink at the same time, which meant it had to be the handiwork of saboteurs. Finding the culprits became the first task for the Revolutionary Committee after it had assumed powerless control (the seal had been stolen by a strange shadow) of Wali, but in the end they failed, even though they adopted the "from the masses to the masses" line of investigation. Someone made the observation that it boded ill for the Revolutionary Committee to be splashed by night soil on the first day of its existence.

Wattles Wu, who still smelled bad, despite several showers, was entrusted with the arduous task of drafting a respectful greeting to Beijing. Disdainful of the addresses that had come before, he vowed to spare no effort and compose a letter that would shock the world. He began with the usual series of "most"s, but his true ingenuity was displayed in how he used "most" seven times in each of three rows, followed by elegant traditional writing and filling the gaps with emotional sighs. Unwilling to casually accept the address, the secretary of the Revolutionary Committee asked his first-in-command to read it.

The latter, being illiterate, looked at Wu's tidy calligraphy, found it to his liking, and said, "Good!"

"I see the leader's consciousness is very high," Wu said smugly to the secretary. "Did you think this was petty scribbling? For your information, I adopted the sentence structure of the famous Preface to 'Essay on Tengwang Pavilion': 'The setting sun soars with the lone heron / The autumn water shares a color with the endless sky.' You can recite it or you can sing it. Its flavor lasts as long as aged liquor. Addresses from other places can be bland as water, with no literary qualities, but Wali, with its proud history, demands from us great care." What could the secretary say to that?

Wu struggled with the contents and word usage for a week before producing a final draft. Using an old fragrant ink stick, he copied every word in neat calligraphy, but people at the committee agreed that it could not possibly be sent to the capital, for it emitted the hint of a foul smell. It took the puzzled people a while to realize that the odor came not from the ink but from Wu, who had been splattered. Someone suggested airing the letter to give the odor a chance to dissipate, but it lingered even after several days, throwing the committee members into a panic. Finally, someone thought of Zhang-Wang. After sniffing the paper, she gathered some mugwort and dried flower petals, which she burned to smoke the paper. An hour later, the white smoke was gone, and the letter was so fragrant the people could not put it down.

That year the town's residents participated in countless parades. Their days were filled with the racket of drumbeats and shouts and their nights were frequently restless. Even when they somehow managed to fall asleep, from outside would come the popping of firecrackers, rousing them from their beds to join a parade, either because a "treasured book" had been brought back from the provincial town or the "latest instruction" from Chairman Mao was broadcast, neither of which could wait till the next day. One night, after finally falling asleep, Sui

Buzhao was awakened by the beating of a drum, so he quickly put on his pants and ran outside. The streets were filled with noisy people who formed lines and moved forward; they walked for some time before he heard that they had received the "latest instruction," but he could not tell what it was owing to the crowd noise. Not until midnight, when he was about to leave the procession, did he finally hear something: ". . . not a minor good." After following the procession in the cold all he'd gotten was "not a minor good." He sighed over the bad bargain.

Trouble had not ceased to visit the Revolutionary Committee since its first day, as predicted. It all began with a complaint about unfair power sharing by the Invincible Battle Brigade and the Revolutionary United Headquarters, followed by vicious attacks from the "support the left" troops, who claimed that the Revolutionary Committee had established a phony stronghold and vowed to get rid of them someday.

Then petitioners began to show up outside the committee's yard; at first they came in the morning and left in the evening, but the day came when they decided to spend the night there and stage a hunger strike. Units opposing the committee formed a loose coalition, with one group putting up a tent under which another group staged the hunger strike. The hunger strikers made endless demands, including conditions to "restructure the Revolutionary Committee." Three days after the strikers stopped eating and drinking, some panicky members of the committee agreed to a few of the minor demands, but the strikers merely ate some thin gruel before returning to the tent. After racking their brains, the anxious and fretful committee members thought of asking the aging Li Xuantong to sit with the strikers. Unhappily, the addled Li thought they were meditating in the tent, so he recited "Amita Buddha" and sat down. Closing his eyes, he crossed his legs and sat in a yoga position, and before long he was in a trance, his breathing shallow. That went on for five days, during which the hunger strikers were relieved twice. Li continued to sit, calm as ever, for another five days. The hunger strike thus broken, the strikers left, cursing Li the whole time. When he emerged from his trance and went home, there would be no peace for him, as the opposing factions kept showing up to harass him, calling him a reactionary or a member of such and such faction. This was all beyond the old man's understanding. Whatever the young men were saying was a complete puzzle to him. Then one day he discerned the word "rebel," which drained the color from his face and sent him to bed. He died three days later.

Several organizations were deeply shamed by the failed hunger strike, which had not only gained them no advantage but wound up reducing a dozen of their most resolute revolutionary comrades to skin and bones. Now they were increasingly fervent in their belief that "power grows out of the barrel of a gun." With the tent gone, the area outside the office of the Revolutionary Committee looked empty, suddenly rendering Wali quiet, which in turn filled people with suspicion and unease. The streets were deserted as people tried to avoid this terrifying silence, though not for long. A shocking piece of news exploded in the air above town: Late one night the soldiers were disarmed by a group of strangers. That threw everyone into a panic, for they knew that warfare would break out again. In the past only clubs and bricks had been used in battle. Zhao Duoduo's militia owned a few rifles, but they were mostly used to fire shots into the air or to kill dogs (nearly all of which ended up on Commander Zhao's dinner table). Now the soldiers had been disarmed, and no one knew by whom. The leader of the disarmed soldiers demanded over the loudspeaker that their weapons be returned, threatening severe punishment if they were not. The commander vowed to "fire on those who stole our firearms." But with no arms to fire, he was not convincing. Groups in the Revolutionary Committee camp and those who opposed them spent days plotting in secret.

Zhao Duoduo was now the proud owner of the large map that had been made for the attack against the Invincible Battle Brigade. Every rebel faction had a "frontline command center," which was headed by

its leader. As rumors circulated, the sense of imminent warfare intensified. Some said it would break out not only among factions in town
but also among those from out of town. Battles raged outside of Wali,
giving the arsenal a chance to show off its might; tanks were sent
out—impressive! Blood was shed in some places, and the battles never
ceased. One accurate bit of news had the rebel factions supporting
their comrades-in-arms by bringing out a tank that had been refitted
at the county tractor factory.

As the town was embroiled in rumors, someone sounded the alarm
that the biggest capitalist roader of Wali, Zhou Zifu, had escaped from
lockup and could not be found. The town shuddered at the discovery;
everyone felt that their efforts had been in vain. Outraged residents
surged into the streets, some surrounding the Revolutionary Committee, only to be immediately surrounded themselves. Communications were cut; the telephones stopped working. Before sunset the first
shot was fired, followed by endless gunfire. It was the first time people
in their twenties and thirties had heard real gunfire; it continued spo-
radically even after the moon rose into the sky. One man was running
on the roof in the hazy moonlight when a sudden bang sent him tum-
bling off the roof. Nearly every rooftop was occupied by people who
were shooting guns, tossing roof tiles, or simply yelling. They crouched
down on the eaves when the battling groups were out on the streets.
Some of the warriors had white towels wrapped around their arms;
others had them on their heads. The town was filled with the sounds
of thumping clubs and howls of anguish. Fire would break out in
one part of town, followed by an old woman calling for her son. "Get
the hooligans!" someone would shout, but the voice would come to a
sudden stop.

On these nights of bloody battles, many people sprawled on the
ground and huddled motionlessly. Sui Baopu and his siblings were
among them, as they hid under the bean trellis, trembling in fear.
There were many places like that in town, where silence reigned and
the people held their collective breath.

In a thatched shed in the northern corner of town darkness blanketed everything, for a big house had blocked the moonlight, shrouding it in perpetual darkness. It was a shed for livestock, where the owner had exhausted himself caring for one of his animals. He was now fast asleep in a corner of the shed that was occupied by an old horse, two old cows, and their offspring. For years the owner had taken meticulous care of one of the cows; he'd always talked to her before going to bed, except on this night. Even with gunfire raging outside, he was so tired he slumped to the floor and fell asleep. Someone had plunged a knife in the cow's rear end several days earlier. When her owner saw her lying on the ground in a pool of blood, he nearly passed out. He got a veterinarian and watched over the cow day and night, but to no avail, for on this night, the cow was breathing with visible difficulty, barely able to stand. She was a yellow cow, mated to a black bull to produce a yellow calf that would grow into a powerful bull.

Now the black bull and the yellow calf were kneeling by the old cow, which licked the calf's nose, showing for the last time her tender love for her offspring. A tear flowed from the corner of the bull's eye, while the yellow calf mooed softly. A light seemed to flicker in the old cow's eyes but it quickly went out. Her head slumped forward as she rolled over onto her side. With a long cry, the old black bull got to its feet.

The owner woke up.

The gunfire intensified outside.

TWENTY-FIVE

Standing behind the counter, the onetime civil servant served a variety of customers expertly, accompanied by relentless invective directed at Zhao Duoduo. Since the arrival of the investigation team, she felt smugly vindicated, and that made her increasingly dissatisfied with her usual repertoire. Now she had a jumble of epithets, which she delivered in a venomous tone, assigning Zhao a horrible early death, while adding a graphic description of how he had abused her over the past year or so. Zhang-Wang laughed as she listened, revealing her short black teeth. "Then what happened?" she asked. They had become fast friends, the slap the young woman had received at Qisheng's funeral forgotten. Zhang-Wang taught her how to cheat the customers while measuring out fabrics and how to reverse a decrease in sugar, baking soda, and pepper powder in stock. The young woman was a quick study and so impressed Zhang-Wang that she would sometimes say, "Jiansu has a good eye." The mention of Jiansu's name usually made the young woman's eyes glaze over, and she would grumble that when Zhou Yanyan, who did not deserve Jiansu, was tending the counter she detected the unmistakable odor of sweaty armpits.

Jiansu returned to town often, always bringing new merchandise. Once he brought back a movie projector, with which they showed a variety of movies, mostly martial arts films. After setting up a tent outside the Wali Emporium, Zhang-Wang and the civil servant charged moviegoers twenty fen. The films took the town by storm, attracting young and old alike. Employees of the noodle factory abandoned their work and spent hours watching the movies. Zhao Duoduo, preoccupied by the investigation, could spare no effort to get them back into the factory. By using an examination of the film's contents as an excuse, Luan Chunji managed to see the movies without paying, while Li Yuming followed the rules and never tried to see a free show. Sui Buzhao never missed a movie and paid each time, but he always sat up front to provide commentary for the audience. When he first returned from visiting the ancient ship in the city, he'd already given them a summary of these films: A young man is no match for a woman and a woman never defeats a weird old man. One time a gimpy old man appeared on-screen, drawing his undivided attention, as he cautioned other characters on-screen, "Be careful!" As expected, the old man met with no resistance. When the old men in town emerged from the tent with their stools, they had to admit that these movies were a lot more interesting than the Western peep shows of their younger days.

Relaxed and entertained by the movies, for a week or more the town's residents put the hidden danger posed by the radioactive canister and the elation brought on by the underground river out of their minds. But there were a few who, by paying close attention, noticed a new development: The Sui clan was slowly returning to prominence, while the Zhao clan, following the collapse of the glass noodle company, was once again in decline. Someone observed that Sui Baopu had not shown up for a single movie but had, instead, entered the factory several times, where, like a true owner, he tended to the bean milk and the sediment pool, even checking the temperature of the water used to soak the beans. Daxi and Naonao had not seen a movie either. Naonao's changes were more visible than Daxi's, for she hardly ever talked. Someone claimed to have seen Baopu walk past the pool and stand a few paces away to watch Naonao as she worked. Wearing odd expressions, they stared at each other for a long time before Baopu scurried away.

Jiansu, on the other hand, left town immediately after setting up the projector, leaving everything to Zhang-Wang and the young woman, who were so exhausted by their job of collecting money that they decided to show movies only on weekends. That raised a protest from the youths in town and gave the old men an excuse to ask Zhang-Wang to sell liquor again. She agreed to the old men's request but was adamant about the film schedule. By then the civil servant had learned to add water to the liquor vat, although she was less generous with the orange peels. Zhang-Wang was pleased, except for the time she saw the woman eating snacks on the sly on her return from giving Fourth Master a massage.

All the excitement made people forget Gimpy and his flute, which he had not played for some time. One night when Sui Buzhao was home he suddenly sensed that the town seemed to have emptied out. Lacking the interest to read his seafaring book, he went to see Baopu. As they spoke, the subject of Xiaokui's marriage came up, and Baopu went quiet before finally saying he felt obligated to go see them.

The following morning a panicky Sui Buzhao rushed over to see Baopu. "You said you wanted to pay them a visit, didn't you? Well, now's the time. She just had a baby."

"A baby?" Baopu cried out, his hands trembling. "She had a baby?"

"Yes. No wonder Gimpy hasn't been playing his flute lately. He's been too busy taking care of his pregnant wife. Counting back, I see she must have gotten pregnant at about the time the flute changed melodies."

"I must go see the baby, I must."

Steam was rising in Gimpy's tiny yard. Baopu pushed the gate open and walked in, sweat dripping from his forehead. Gimpy, who was squatting by a steel pot, straining to add firewood to boil some water, quickly got to his feet and blocked Baopu with his arms. "You can't go in." Baopu had to restrain himself not to push the man aside. "Not counting the midwife," Gimpy said, "the first one who goes in to see a baby is called 'the look-alike,' since the baby will take on the person's temperament. I have no quarrel with you, but you're a member of the Sui clan, and I don't want my child to have a Sui personality."

Baopu's face burned, as if he'd been slapped. He felt profoundly insulted. "Has the Sui clan really sunk so low?" The thought so enraged him that he bumped Gimpy aside and stormed into the house amid the new father's startled cries. When he heard the infant cooing in a room to the east, Baopu's heart was in his throat; taking care not to scare the baby, he tiptoed into the room, where he gently placed some brown sugar and eggs on a chest. Xiaokui, who had just fed the baby, gazed at him with a firm but unusually peaceful look in her eyes. He noticed a glow on her face that made her look young and pretty. She tugged at her blouse to cover her breasts.

Baopu bent over to look at the baby, a pink little boy who looked back with big bright eyes infused with happiness, as if he actually saw something. Baopu reached out to touch his tiny legs and the baby began to kick. Then he covered him up but kept staring at him; the baby's eyes left Baopu's face and he began to cry. Not knowing what to do about that, Baopu stood there awkwardly. The baby kicked off his blanket and wailed in a voice that sounded like water rushing through a breeched dam. Xiaokui gave the baby her nipple, but he spat it out and turned up the volume as Gimpy rushed in and, making inquiring sounds, glared at Baopu. Xiaokui signaled with her eyes for Gimpy to leave, so he did. But the baby continued to wail, a sound that seemed to tear Baopu's insides to shreds. He paced the area around the *kang* for a while before sitting down to wait for the baby to stop, which he eventually did. Xiaokui wiped him down with a soft yellow handkerchief.

All the while Baopu was in the room he never managed to finish a complete sentence. The older boy, Leilei, had gone out to play and was nowhere in sight. Xiaokui lay on the *kang* content and happy, looking at Baopu and the baby calmly. Warm sunlight slanted in through the window. Detecting the fragrance of roses, Baopu searched the room with his eyes and found the flowers in an old vase sitting atop the chest.

His uncle was still there when he returned from Gimpy's house. "Is the baby all right?" he asked Baopu. "I was thinking about that canister."

Baopu shook his head. "The best baby I've ever seen. He'll grow up to be big and strong."

Jiansu had stayed away so long the shop was running out of novel merchandise and the theater had been showing the same movies over and over. Zhang-Wang kept uttering his name, and the civil servant pasted his business card on the back of her pocket mirror. The factory employees lingered at the emporium, seemingly leading a life of leisure. Their general manager, on the other hand, seemed to have lost his emotional compass following the arrival of the investigation team, for he was drunk nearly every day and kept up a constant howl in his office afterward. He insisted there was a traitor in Wali and that sooner or later he'd take care of the bastard. The situation had worsened precipitately once noodle exports were stopped, and no more loans were forthcoming. The export section had to concentrate on raising capital for the expansion of the factory.

But that expansion was going nowhere, while the investigation moved along nicely as details began to emerge. Zhou Zifu, who was himself under investigation, had no energy to spare to protect Zhao Duoduo, for both the provincial committee and the provincial disciplinary committee had looked into the case, in which even the export department deputy bureau chief was implicated. Lu Jindian was steadfast in his attitude and meticulous in his inquiries. The head of Gaoding Street, Luan Chunji, tried to block the investigation but failed miserably, while Li Yuming, a harmless man, was severely criticized for incompetence and for his unprincipled, undisciplined behavior. In the end, he decided to cooperate. Given Jiansu's long absence, charges were brought against him as well, claiming that the lewd material he brought back was harmful to the town's morality and thus a violation of the law. As further evidence they pointed out the jeans the youngsters were wearing. Wattles Wu, as it turned out, was the informer, supported enthusiastically by Shi Dixin. The local Public Security Bureau launched an investigation, prompting hundreds of young people to show up in their jeans to prove Jiansu's innocence. Even the old men testified that there was no nudity in the movies, which were far more decent than the peep shows of an earlier age. Even so, the bureau ordered that the frequency of the movie showings be cut in half, to once every two weeks. With so much going on, Sui Buzhao and Baopu were worried about Jiansu; it was not like him to neglect a booming business and not send a single letter home.

One day Zhang-Wang handed an opened telegram to Baopu; delivered to the Wali Emporium, it had only two terrifying words: "Jiansu ill." "Who sent this?" he asked.

"That's all I know."

Baopu's heart began to race as he gazed at the two words. Knowing he must go see Jiansu right away, he went looking for his uncle.

After his arrival in the city, Baopu spend most of the first day locating the Wali Emporium. From the evasive look in the eyes of the shop owner, who had sent the telegram, Baopu could see that the situation was serious. The moment the man spoke, Baopu's face paled and he fell to the floor. Helping him to a chair, the owner mumbled, "Our shop is done for. Done for. This is like a thunderclap on a clear day!"

Everyone in the shop was listening to what the owner was saying to the brother of their manager.

Baopu learned that Jiansu had suffered dizzy spells over the past six months and one day had actually fainted. Sent first to a clinic nearby, he was quickly transferred to a hospital. At first no one thought it was anything to worry about, and Zhou Yanyan and the two clerks went to see him every day, Yanyan sometimes staying the night. But when the tests were completed, the hospital asked to speak with his next of kin. That was when they knew that something was seriously wrong. Though not officially married, Jiansu and Yanyan were living as husband and wife, so the owner told her to go. She returned in tears. Jiansu had a terminal illness. Stunned by the news, they decided not to tell Jiansu before sending for his family.

By then, Zhou Yanyan had not visited the hospital for weeks, pleading a busy schedule at work. When the shop owner told Baopu how much money he had already paid the hospital his voice cracked.

"What do we do?" Baopu asked. "Transfer him to another hospital?"

"If a famous hospital can't do anything for him, no one can. It's the nature of the illness. I don't mind the expense, but I think it's better to take him home so he can eat better."

"He's only thirty-seven!" Baopu said tearfully before leaving for the hospital, where Jiansu reached up to him when he walked in the door. The brothers embraced.

"I should have come earlier, Jiansu. As eldest son I should not have let you go roaming like this. I've failed you." As he stroked his brother's disheveled hair, Baopu spoke as if the words were stuck in his throat.

"I didn't want to tell you, and I didn't want people in town to know. If I can't return walking on my own two feet, I'd rather die here. I don't want Wali to see another dying man. But I miss home. I miss Hanzhang, Uncle, and our town. I have no one here. Even Zhou Yanyan stopped coming to see me."

"We'll move you to another hospital, and we'll find a cure."

"My illness is terminal."

"There's no such thing, not in this world."

Jiansu got up and pleaded, "Baopu! I miss home, I really do. I've been wishing you'd take me home. I feel terrible. Even a healthy man would get sick feeling the way I do. I know there's no cure for me here in the city, so please take me home with you."

Baopu stared into his brother's bloodless face.

Jiansu kept pleading, pressing his brother's face against his chest.

The next day they set off for Wali.

Everyone from the Sui clan came to see Jiansu, followed by the town's leaders, Lu Jindian, Zou Yuquan, and Li Yuming. Hanzhang was sobbing when Fourth Master arrived but stopped and glared at him as he stood in the yard, an imposing figure. He turned after a moment and walked out slowly. Silence reigned in Wali, reminding people of the time Dahu died; it was as if the town itself had a terminal illness. Even those who longed to see the Sui family become the butt of ridicule had a change of heart, for a death notice had been announced. This was no time for ridicule.

Sui Buzhao stumbled and fell to the ground after leaving Jiansu's room; he lay there on the moist soil, unwilling to get up, and looked up at the sky, yelling something unintelligible. Spotting a hawk circling above, he raised his arms to the bird, as it continued to circle, observing the goings-on in the Sui courtyard. Suddenly reminded of the big bird in the sky the day the ancient ship was unearthed, he called out, "You! What did you see? Cry out to me if you saw something."

All the visitors left before night fell, leaving the three siblings in Jiansu's room. Hanzhang went in to make dinner; Jiansu ate little but commented on how tasty it was. As the night deepened, a wind began to blow, when suddenly they heard someone knock at the window. Jiansu sat up and shouted, "Daxi!"

Baopu and Hanzhang tried to stop him from climbing down off the *kang*. The door opened and in came Daxi, who sat down beside Jiansu and gazed into his eyes, as if no one else was around. As tears welled up in his eyes she took him in her arms and rested her head on his chest. Baopu dabbed at the corners of his eyes and took Hanzhang out with him, leaving just the two of them in the still room. Tears rolled off Jiansu's face onto her hair and then her face. When she reached out to wipe his tears, he took her hands and kissed them. Then he flung them away, cowered in a corner of the *kang*, and whispered in a barely audible voice, "Daxi, I'm dying."

She shook her head.

"It's true. I'm not afraid of anything now, and that's why I came back."

She kept shaking her head.

A week later the investigation team announced its decision: The glass noodle company would be fined a huge sum of money, and everyone knew that Zhao Duoduo was finished. The investors were beside themselves with anger. With the departure of the investigation team, disputes arose. Luan Chunji yelled at Li Yuming, calling him the most useless member of the Li clan. Instead of fighting back, Li shut himself up in the house to reflect upon his life, feeling as if he'd muddled through decades in a dream world. The loss this time was simply too great, and it was all of Wali, not just Zhao Duoduo, that suffered. Business fell off at the factory, and that somehow led to another spoiled vat. Zhao stayed in his office, leaving the anxious workers to their own devices.

It was obvious that the factory could no longer be saved, and this latest incident was like clubbing a dying man. Town and village leaders called people together to save the vat, with Lu Jindian yelling himself hoarse in the processing room. Three days later Li Yuming tied a red exorcism ribbon on the door, and by the morning of the fourth day, a familiar sour stink rose up from the bean milk vat and the sediment pool, attracting swarms of flies that circled the entrance. Baopu remained at Jiansu's bedside. Then Guo Yun came to check on Jiansu. The old doctor sighed and took the patient away with him, freeing Baopu to try to save the vat; it was by then the fourth day, and the stench lay heavily in the air. After telling some people to burn mugwort to chase away the flies, he told several strong young men to stir the milk vat and the pool. He tasted the milk and suffered from a bout of diarrhea the next day, followed by several days of intestinal discomfort. But he set his jaw and continued to work on the milk. For days the employees worked breathlessly, sweat dripping from their foreheads. Naonao's jeans, soiled by the milk and dirty beyond recognition, clung to her body, making her even more alluring. She worked quietly throughout the day, happily taking on the dirtiest jobs. At night she'd roast a ball of starch to share with Baopu after blowing on it to cool it off. The seventh day arrived with a pleasant aroma permeating the room. "It's working!" people shouted excitedly, and stared at Baopu's back as he walked out. Naonao returned to the milk vat, where she brushed the dripping wet noodles as usual. During that period Zhao Duoduo did not make a single appearance, showing up only after the vat had been saved, reeking of alcohol, his eyes bloodshot. He cursed, but only four words were intelligible: "Get rid of him."

Duoduo often went out driving alone, sending pedestrians scurrying out of his way. The rest of the time he closed himself up in his office to sleep, drink, pace the floor, or just curse. One day he went to see his former assistant, begging her to return to work for him. He reached out to touch her breasts but drew his hand back and made a series of bizarre gestures. Convinced that he was losing his mind, she clapped happily. That night she sneaked over to his office, where she peeped through a crack in the door and saw Zhao, dressed only in his underpants, pacing the floor, his face dark and lusterless. For some reason she assumed he was dying, which for her was a very happy thought. Then she spotted the cleaver on the windowsill and was reminded of how he had threatened her with it one night. How she would have liked to pick it up and disembowel him. However pleased she was by thoughts of his imminent death, she was obsessed by a desire to exact revenge. In the end, however, she had to be content to give his door a vicious kick before running away.

⌖

Baopu had never felt so tired. For the first time since Jiansu fell ill and the vat was spoiled, he could return to his room and sleep. He dreamed that he and a healthy Jiansu were out on the floodplain, where the sand was a vast expanse of pastel blue. Jiansu gestured in the direction of a leaping object, red as the sun and growing bigger as it drew near; it was the Sui family's old chestnut horse. Jiansu mounted the horse and so did he. With the two brothers on its back, the horse pounded its hooves on the blue sand and galloped away.

Baopu woke up, still savoring the cheerful dream, and recalled how Jiansu had told him about the horse and the blue sand. He jumped down off the *kang* and went straight to see Guo Yun. On the way he thought of how the old doctor was the only one who truly understood the Sui clan, which meant that if Guo could do nothing, then Jiansu's case was hopeless. His dream could be an auspicious omen, but it could also be the opposite.

Opening the old doctor's gate, tense with apprehension, he spotted him reading under a wisteria trellis.

Taking care not to disturb the old man, Baopu tiptoed up beside him. Guo Yun was holding a thread-bound book, his head moving slightly as he read; every few seconds he turned a page with his index finger, surprising Baopu, who had never seen anyone read that fast before. He finished the book in short order. Baopu exhaled as the old man laid the book down on a stone table and gestured to a stone stool next to him for Baopu to sit down. "Did you just read that whole book?" Baopu asked. Guo Yun nodded. Baopu stood up, then sat back down, shaking his head. "Some people read words," Guo said with a smile, "and some read sentences. I read the spirit, the *qi*."

Baopu was lost. What was *qi*? How could a book have *qi*?

The old man took a sip of tea and said, "The author poured the *qi* in his heart into his work. The *qi* follows the mind, giving the book a magical spirit. When you read, you start out slow and get faster as you read so as to capture the literary *qi* and follow it forward. If it breaks off, it is a bad book. There is nothing but the color of ink, like black ants, when you first look at the page of a book. When the *qi* begins to flow, some black ants die while others live. Your eyes pick out the living parts and ignore the dead ones. You will begin to experience the essence of the moment the author moved his brush. Otherwise, you are just wasting your time and energy, for you will touch only the surface and get no pleasure from your reading." Guo Yun glanced at Baopu as he picked up the book and put it in his pocket.

Baopu sat in a daze, unable to speak for a moment. While he did not understand the old man completely, he was convinced he had learned something important. Now he castigated himself for not having visited Guo more often instead of spending all his time in the mill. Guo pointed to the eastern room. "Jiansu is staying there. I gave him some calming broth, so he's sleeping. He must remain here. With time and care there may be a chance for him. If carefully guarded a vibrant youth full of energy ought to be able to fend off external evil." Baopu nodded and let his eyes drift toward the room under the shelter of a plane tree, feeling an urge to tell the old man how Jiansu had suffered more than anyone in his family and how he may have exhausted his youth as he trudged through life. But he resisted the urge, for he knew that Guo was the best person to care for his brother.

Baopu did not expect a miracle; all he could hope for was that his brother might find a thread of hope with Wali's wisest resident looking after him. As Baopu's eyes misted over, Guo stood up, walked around the wisteria, and looked down at his feet. "We're lucky to have time, so we will work hard. I'll watch his every move and make sure nothing goes wrong. I'll see that he takes his medicine, performs qigong exercises, and eats or drinks nothing that is not fresh. 'The five grains are the main staple, assisted by the five fruits; the five animal meats are beneficial, supplemented by five vegetables.' By getting rid of the evil, we can correct the core and strengthen the essence. I'm old, and this will be the last good deed heaven allows me."

Baopu rushed up to grab the man's arms, his lips quivering, unable to utter a word of gratitude, as the two men went inside the house. Having served as a clinic years before, it was a spacious house where Guo lived alone since the death of his wife. It was suffused with the aroma of herbs. Two tall medicine chests stood in the eastern room, while the middle room was clean and had a simple grace, with a set of fine, red-lacquered furniture and a few potted plants. The western room was Guo's bedroom and study. Baopu felt something new and unique as soon as he entered with the old man. Inside were a bed, a desk, a chair, and a bookcase that stood next to the bed for easy access. The walls were hung with scrolls, some of calligraphy, some paintings. Above the desk and on the opposite wall were round plaques that could be turned. One was called "Diagram of the Six *Qi* and Four Seasons"; the other was "Guest and Host Visiting Diagram." There were concentric circles on the plaques, each filled with arcane writing. To Baopu it was all quite incomprehensible. Seeing his knitted brows, Guo pointed to the first diagram and said, "Our illnesses correspond to the five movements and six *qi*. Wind, warmth, humidity, heat, agitation, and cold are the six *qi*, which are also divided into three yin and three yang, and influenced by seasonal changes. The six *qi* are monitored along the twenty-four solar divisions and divided by six steps that originate from the order of the five elements, each step controlling sixty days and eighty-six and a half hours."

Baopu laughed in embarrassment and shook his head. "I'm getting more confused by the minute."

Guo tugged at his beard and paused for a moment before continuing. "Jiansu did not get sick in a single day, and the basic principle for his cure is connected to what I just said, to whether we go for speed and use heavy doses of medication or take it slow with nurturing care."

Baopu spun the round plaque and tried to read its contents carefully. On the ground near the bookcase was a pair of stone weights, which he assumed were used for exercise. By the weights was a small cloth sack, which turned out to be filled with walnut-sized pebbles, with two cloth sashes fastened to the opening. Baopu knew that it too was an exercise prop, and he asked the old man how to use it. Guo shook his head. "It's better that young men like you don't know."

Baopu looked in on his brother frequently that day, but he was asleep each time. After dinner he returned and, as he entered his room, he saw Jiansu leaning against the window gazing at something. As if to embrace his brother, Jiansu took a few steps forward, but then backed away to sit down on the *kang*. Baopu touched Jiansu's forehead; he was still running a fever. "Hanzhang came by but left soon after," Jiansu said with longing in his eyes. "I've been waiting for you. Guo Yun won't let me out, so please come see me every day." Baopu nodded.

Moving the blanket around, Jiansu leaned back to stare at his brother till tears were slipping down his cheeks.

As Baopu dried his tears, Jiansu gripped his hands and said, "I have so much to tell you. I'm afraid I won't have time if I don't tell you now. I know I won't get better, no matter what anyone says. No one can cure me, not the doctors in the city and not Guo Yun."

Baopu angrily shook off his hands. "No. You must listen to Guo Yun. He'll make you as strong as before. Don't think those thoughts. I don't want to hear them."

Jiansu sat up and pounded his legs. "I'm not afraid to die," he said forcefully, "so why deceive myself? No, I won't do it." Again the tears came. Looking at the gray in Baopu's hair, he sighed and leaned back down. "All right, I'll abandon that thought. I will live . . . I will be . . . strong."

Baopu sat down on a stool to smoke.

As he gazed up at the ceiling, Jiansu said, "I thought about a lot of things when I was in the hospital. At first they came to see me, but they stopped when they realized that I was dying. Even Zhou Yanyan. But that gave me some quiet time to think about all that's happened. Like the bidding meeting, our nighttime arguments, especially the last one. I also thought about Mother and Father, about Father's death and Uncle's life, and I began to have self-doubts. I was wondering what this generation of the Sui should do. Maybe you were right. Maybe we should all be like you; maybe I shouldn't have fought with Zhao Duoduo or gone to the city. I thought so much my head hurt. The Sui clan has been fated to suffer endless hardships.

"There is so much I hid from you. When I started out in the city, business was going pretty well, but I was cheated, first by a company, then by a fabric merchant from Wuxi. The owner and I shared responsibility for the losses. When I was hospitalized, I signed an agreement with the owner, using the Wali Emporium in town as collateral. I never told you any of this. But that's nothing. What I'm about to say will really shock you. Remember the fight we had that time when I returned from the city, that night when I lamented on the *kang*? I knew you'd made up your mind to clear up the mess at the noodle factory and I was incensed. Zhang-Wang had relayed a message from Fourth Master, Zhao Bing, who wanted me to take over for Zhao Duoduo, so I'd thought I'd finally be in charge of the business. I hadn't expected that you'd show up to block me. I hated you. I really did. That was when I realized that my real foe wasn't Zhao Duoduo but you! You, my own brother!"

Baopu jumped to his feet and stared at Jiansu as if he didn't know him. "What did you say?" he shouted. "What did you just say?"

Ignoring the outburst, Jiansu hurried along. "I cried and cried in front of you, but you hadn't a clue why. I cried because the heavens were tormenting me in so many different ways, and in the end they sent an adversary to me. I was angry and bitter when I returned to the city, but did I give up? No—I'm not going to leave anything out this time. After I went back to the city, I thought things over and decided that I'd take the business back; no matter whose hands it fell into for the moment, it belonged to the Sui clan. Why? Because you repeatedly said that it didn't. So I pooled my resources, siding with Fourth Master with the help of Zhang-Wang. I was prepared to win my last battle by defeating you and taking back the factory. You see, my brother, I lost my way and actually collaborated with the Zhao clan to fight you. That thought was still on my mind only days before I was hospitalized. You can call me whatever you want. You can beat me to death, and I won't raise a finger. I had no right to think like that. Fortunately, heaven's eyes were wide open and handed down a death sentence at the critical moment. A terminal illness kept me from the last battle. It was my punishment. All the wrongs I've done to you, to Daxi, and to others are now being atoned for. But I have to tell you this so you'll know just how bad someone from the Sui clan can be."

Overcome by a fever and sweat, he fell back onto the blanket, breathing hard. As sad tears welled up in Baopu's eyes, he sat down next to Jiansu to stroke his hair and lay his head back down on the pillow. "I've heard everything you said, and I understand now," he murmured. "That's just how it is. Jiansu. Jiansu . . ." His hands were trembling, and he couldn't finish, so he looked out the window, his eyes flickering in the dark night.

Then he turned to face his brother, barely able to control his shaky hands. "I also thought things over while you were away, and I'm going to reveal everything to you tonight. I'm saddened by what you just said, but I don't blame you. I want you to know what I've been thinking and doing. When the investigation team came and the noodle company was on the verge of collapse, I realized that I'd been guilty of an unforgivable error. By this time it wasn't just the loss of the company; the whole town suffered the consequences. The investors could not bear any more injury. But I was stuck in the old mill like a dead man. I was unhappy with you and I gave you a hard time. I was dead set against you going into the city, but looking back now, I can see I've never had the fight in me that you have. You say you lost everything in the city, and I say, so what! You can do anything you put your mind to. You'll never be cheated out of what's coming to you. I envy your courage, your guts, your shrewdness, and your determination to conquer the world. Those are all things I lack.

"But you? What you just said was a denial of all that. Do you know how bad that makes me feel? What you should deny is your excessive greed. I prize my kindness and fairness too much, and now see what happened? Families invested their hard-earned money, not to mention the tens of thousands of yuan Zhao Duoduo received in loans. Now old men cry and old women weep, and that breaks my heart. If I'd gotten up there with you at the bidding meeting, maybe we could have beaten Zhao Duoduo. Am I kind? Am I fair? I curse myself—my hesitation, my cowardice, the Sui family disease. I failed to act on an opportunity and wound up being a terrible brother. Oh, I criticized myself before, but the problem was, I never turned that self-criticism into action.

"It's good and it's bad that our last competition did not occur. If you had given me the thrashing I deserved I would have gained enough remorse to last me all my life. But if you had taken over the business, sooner or later disaster would have befallen the town and I'd have had to pick myself up, wipe off the blood, and turn against you. It would have been an energizing fight, that's for sure. So now you must be strong. And if you see your brother cowering again, put him down with your fists!"

Jiansu stopped crying and looked at his brother excitedly. "No, even if I regain my health, I'll never turn on you."

Baopu shook his head and sat down wearily. "I'm still working on those accounts, and the more time I spend on them, the more trivial and the more complex they get. There seems to be no end to them. And when I'm free, I keep reading that little book. I was so tired and so disturbed all that time you were in the city; I kept thinking about Wali and the Sui clan, past and present. I've never felt such an urge to be strong, to invigorate myself, and I've never experienced such self-doubt. I was afraid I'd badly misread that book when I realized that it was written more than a hundred years ago and that what has happened in Wali is more complicated than that book. But it's a book I can't avoid, and it's closely linked to the Sui clan. How should I read it knowing what has happened in Wali over the past hundred years? I don't have an answer, and that bothers me.

"Another book I read a lot is Qu Yuan's *Heavenly Questions,* written thousands of years ago, at a time when Wali experienced great changes. Is there a connection between these two books? If so, how do I find it? If you can't avoid one, can you then avoid the other? And should we avoid books we haven't read but surely will someday in the future? Is it considered evasion if we in the Sui clan just remember the hundred and seventy questions in that one book? Is it evasion if we read only old, yellowed pages, not white, new books? What are the consequences, and who will be able to point them out? Is it sincere to say 'What happened in Wali is much more complex than what is written in books, and no book could possibly cover it all'?

"And then there's Uncle's seafaring book. Haven't we all been avoiding that book over the decades? If so, what are the consequences? Why does he hold on to that book as if his life depended on it? Is there a connection between the book that's thousands of years old and Uncle's book? How do we find that connection? Both are old, both have yellowed pages. Conversely, aren't we also avoiding the issues if we only read new books? And what are the consequences of that? And don't forget, these are all thin but important books. Are the thick ones equally important? What are the connections? Some books are simple and easy to understand, others are complicated and difficult, so which should we concentrate on in order not to come to grief? Have people in Wali listened to so many simple things that their intelligence has degenerated? Would they be fed up with questions posed by the author of a book written thousands of years ago? If so, then how do we make them keep listening? And if we ask more questions, will this weariness become the consequence of long-term evasion? I kept asking myself one question after another, but I could not find a single answer. My mind was tired but seemingly clearer than before, and I was grateful to that little book for getting me to think about so many other books. It slowly gave me strength and the courage to question myself."

Jiansu, who was more than a little surprised, gazed at his agitated brother, who stood up, suddenly realizing he'd talked far too long and that he ought to let his brother rest. Rubbing his hands together, he went over to adjust the blanket over Jiansu before leaving, but Jiansu called him back. He grabbed his brother's hands. "Are you going to tell me tonight?"

"Tell you what?"

"Tell me how my mother died."

Startled, Baopu shook his head and said, "You already know. You know it all . . . she took poison."

Jiansu replied in a cold voice, "You're hiding something from me. I know it wasn't that simple, because your expression always changes whenever I mention her. In the past I never pressed the issue, but now I'm dying, and this is my last request. You can't say no. Tonight, now, you must tell me."

The burning house, with fireballs rolling off the eaves, appeared again in Baopu's mind. Zhao Duoduo cutting off Huizi's clothes, blood streaks on her body, Zhao cursing and urinating on her. He clenched his teeth and, his chin quivering, said, "All right, I'll tell you. I'll tell you everything."

They did not say good night until midnight. Baopu could not sleep after returning to his own room.

Dawn was just breaking when Baopu heard someone bang on his window. He opened it to see Guo Yun, who, with a strange look on his face, asked if Jiansu had come home. Baopu shook his head, and the old man told him Jiansu had disappeared.

Baopu's head buzzed as he recalled how he had revealed everything to Jiansu the night before. He threw on his clothes and took off, with the old man following, heading straight for Zhao Duoduo's office.

Zhao's door was open, but the office was empty.

Startled cries came from a distance. Baopu let out a cry and ran off alone.

People were swarming toward the town Party committee compound, which was already packed. A pungent smoky smell hung in the air. Baopu elbowed his way up to a burned-out object that was still smoking. He backed away in shock when he noticed a charred body curled up near it. "Zhao Duoduo," someone said, pointing to the body. Now Baopu saw that the other object was Zhao's car. People were asking each other what happened. Slowly it became clear that Duoduo had gotten drunk before driving his car over for a showdown with Lu Jindian. When someone came out to stop him, Zhao mistook him for Lu and stepped down on the gas, crashing into the stone wall. Baopu breathed a sigh of relief.

Then he heard someone shouting in the crowd; it was Jiansu. Baopu pushed the surging people out of the way. "Let him in," he shouted. "Let him see this."

Jiansu was shaking as he crawled and clawed his way through the thick human wall.

When Baopu lifted him up and carried him over to the smoldering Zhao Duoduo, he felt a hard object at Jiansu's waist. He took it out; it was a rusty cleaver.

About a month before the consortium was formed, Li Zhichang had promised Zhao Duoduo that he would start on the variable gears, but work progressed slowly, owing partly to Jiansu's interference and partly to other reasons. When Li finally produced the first batch, the missing lead canister prevented him from fitting them to the mill. After his father's death, he stayed in the old house where his father had spent half his life, looking through his father's effects, shrouded in the smell left by the dead man. During that time, a series of major events occurred in Wali. Technician Li had forgotten all about the Star Wars debates, while he remained worried about the radioactive canister. Then the geological survey team had found an underground river, solving the puzzle of the slow disappearance of the Luqing River.

Novelty items kept turning up at the Wali Emporium at about the time Jiansu brought home a pretty girl. Then, following the second visit of an investigation team, Zhao Duoduo crashed his car out of desperation, immolating himself. The noodle company changed hands as Sui Baopu took over. Every occurrence seemed both anticipated and reasonable. The townspeople had been living in a state of trepidation since the day Zhao Duoduo took charge of the glass noodle company, and now they could finally breathe a sigh of relief. Those days were gone, new days had begun. In the midst of his hermitlike existence in the old house, Li Zhichang recalled Hanzhang's pretty eyes, and that made him restless, just as Sui Baopu, his uncle, Buzhao, and Technician Li came to see him. The first thing Sui Buzhao said to Li was, "It was I who broke down the door with an ax to get you out more than a decade ago." The others were puzzled by the comment, while Li himself was beyond shame. "Let's install those gears," Baopu said.

"It's been put off for too long, and we all know how hard it is to embark on new projects," Technician Li added.

Li Zhichang looked at them. "Let's go, then," he said at last, leading the three men over to his house, where the first batch of gears was stored.

Sui Baopu left the riverside mill for the last time after nominating himself to be general manager of the noodle company, for which he seemed better suited than anyone else in town. People from Gaoding Street and most of Wali gathered at the old temple site for a meeting, where many came with money wrapped in red paper to invest, so that the halted expansion could get under way. Baopu refused to take their money, knowing it was all they had left. When he'd first accepted a red packet from an old man, he saw it had no more than twenty yuan or so, all in small bills; his eyes misted over as he returned it to the old man. Baopu told him to save it for some liquor; the factory would continue operation and expand only when it made enough money to do so. It was not an uplifting meeting, but Baopu felt energized and, on his way back to the factory, realized how much there was to do. When he saw the hair piled up on the heads of Daxi and Naonao, he immediately abolished the "kick the ball" management system. The girls' charms returned the moment they let down their hair. Baopu's eyes met Naonao's and his heart raced; there was passion in their gazes.

Baopu walked past the pool and the drying ground, straight to the office of the general manager, a large, foul-smelling room filled with Zhao Duoduo's personal effects: several overstuffed chairs, a desk, a telephone, a back scratcher, a large *kang,* and a medium-sized stove. It took Baopu all afternoon to rip out the *kang* and the stove. After the sun had set, Sui Buzhao dropped by with a bottle, so dust-covered Baopu turned on the lights to rest. His uncle, who was not pleased about the demolition of the stove, took a drink, wiped his mouth, and told Baopu that the eccentric Shi Dixin was ill. "The old guy has been my foe all these years. He's stubborn, a loner who's never been with a woman." That reminded Baopu that he hadn't seen the old man for several days.

When he asked if Shi was being cared for and whether a doctor had been sent to see him, Buzhao said that one of Shi's relatives from west of the river was looking after him. As for doctors, Sui said, "A female doctor from the town clinic tried to give him a shot and he broke the needle. But he behaved himself when Guo Yun treated him with acupuncture. I'm still afraid he can't hold out much longer. Li Qisheng is gone, and now the old eccentric isn't long for this world. That means that most members of my generation are gone. As for the next generation"—he began counting on his fingers—"Dahu from the Sui clan was killed and Zhaolu from the Li clan died, both youngsters who were barely old enough to shave." He stopped, and Baopu knew he was thinking of Jiansu. The sadness was contagious, so Baopu clenched his teeth and stood up.

They walked back home single file, a pair of hunched backs disappearing into the deepening evening. "Hey-ya! Hey-ya!" Behind them came shouts from the man banging the strainer, and "Yee-sha-ya! Yee-sha-ya!" from the young people stirring the milky paste in the processing room. The evening shift had begun.

Hanzhang went to see her brother every day. She brought canned food, fruit, and pastries she'd bought with money earned by making straw braids. Jiansu only ate what was permitted by Guo Yun, who checked what his sister had brought and allowed him only the fresh fruit. She always brought some for Guo Yun and gave whatever he would not allow to Baopu, who in turn gave them back. So she took them to their uncle, who would say, "Hanzhang is such a good girl. These all go nicely with a few drinks."

When Hanzhang got off work at the drying ground, she braided straw. Once, as she moved along, she saw that the braid was getting thinner, which meant she'd woven it too tightly. So she cut off the spoiled portion with a pair of scissors she whetted daily. And as she sharpened the scissors, she thought of how long it had been since she'd seen Fourth Master; her hands shook so badly she dropped the scissors, which grazed her leg, the razor-sharp edge slashing her nearly transparent skin. She looked with surprise at the blood flowing down her leg and did not bandage it until the blood had formed a coin-sized pool on the mat.

Would it just keep flowing if she didn't bandage it? she wondered. Rolling up her pant leg and her sleeves, she checked the pale skin and light blue veins under it. At night she often dreamed of a giant, shiny, red, steamy body with quivering flesh. She would reach out for her scissors but never could take hold of them, and she would wake up filled with anxiety, her heart pounding as she sat up in bed. She recalled what Fourth Master had said—he knew the end—and how her hands had shaken so much she could barely hold her chopsticks when he said that.

She quietly got out of bed and went outside to pace the yard and shake off the effects of her dream. Drops of dew fell from the trellis onto the bean stalks and leaves. Hearing a rumbling from the mill, she remembered that her brother was no longer there. She also remembered that the mechanization of the mill had been accomplished by Li Zhichang, he with the tangled hair; she tried not to think about him but couldn't help herself. Yet she also knew she would never be his, because she belonged to a demon.

On nights she spent out in the yard, she sometimes spotted Baopu working at his desk in a room that seemed to stay lit much later, now that he had become the general manager. On one such night, the two siblings had a long talk.

Baopu was reading *The Communist Manifesto* and had just turned
to a page he'd marked when she knocked, came in, moved a chair to
his side, and rested her head on him. Looking at the abacus and the
book on the desk, she asked, "Why are you always checking the
accounts?"

Laying his hand on her shoulder, he answered in a soft voice, as if
talking to an innocent child, "Each account is entangled with others,
like the straw braids you make. The only way I can manage the company well is by knowing every account by heart." She smiled for the
first time in many days. How pretty she looked when she smiled, he
was thinking. He combed her hair with his fingers as she snuggled
against him.

"And you're always reading this," she said. "Is it really that interesting?"

"I read other books too, but I do spend a lot of time with this one.
Of course it's interesting, it's a book about life, and it's enough for a
lifetime. It's indispensable."

Hanzhang turned the pages and focused on the lines in red, then
began to read in a soft voice, " 'The bourgeoisie has subjected the
country to the rule of the towns. It has created enormous cities, has
greatly increased the urban population as compared with the rural,
and has thus rescued a considerable part of the population from the
idiocy of rural life. Just as it has made the country dependent on the
towns, so it has made barbarian and semibarbarian countries dependent on the civilized ones, nations of peasants on nations of bourgeois, the East on the West.' " She looked up and asked, "What does
that mean?"

Baopu smiled and said, "I'm not going to say. I might interpret it
wrong for you. What's unusual about this book is, whoever reads it
has to understand it with her heart. That's all."

She knitted her brows but they quickly smoothed out as she continued to turn pages, until she pointed out a passage to him. " 'Owing
to their historical position, it became the vocation of the aristocracies
of France and England to write pamphlets against modern bourgeois

society.' " Then: " 'Thus, the aristocracy took their revenge by singing lampoons of their new masters and whispering in their ears sinister prophesies of coming catastrophe.' "

She ran her nail over "sinister prophesies" as if analyzing the words, but Baopu paid little attention, for he was focused on the subsequent passage. He took the book to read the passage to her.

" 'In this way arose feudal socialism: half lamentation, half lampoon; half an echo of the past, half menace of the future; at times, by its bitter, witty, and incisive criticism, striking the bourgeoisie to the very heart's core, but always ludicrous in its effect, through total incapacity to comprehend the march of modern history.' "

Laying down the book, Baopu stood up to pace the room. He took a pack of cigarettes out of his pocket but quickly put it back and sat down again, facing his sister to look in her eyes. "Older Brother," she said, taking his hands in hers.

"Little Sister, you can't understand this book now," he said, "but you must have seen what happiness it's brought me."

"Yes." She nodded.

He looked over at the dark window and said, "Hanzhang, you know that the people in town have turned the noodle industry over to the Sui clan, right? Well, I'm happy about that, but I'm also worried I may not have the skill to run it properly. There's so much to do. The people of Wali cannot afford another disaster, and yet they can't seem to avoid it. They placed their hopes in the noodle company, but Zhao Duoduo meant to have it all to himself. I check the accounts so closely because I'm afraid I'll do the wrong thing. Now I understand why Father worked on the accounts and paid off his debts—that was a means of self-criticism. Every generation of the Sui family has forged ahead as best they could, trying to find its way out of suffering and evil. Jiansu and I have criticized ourselves severely, but how much of that criticism is right and how much of it is wrong we have no way of knowing. Have we misunderstood something? We're not sure, and that's where the problem lies. If someone were to come up and explain things to us, I'd probably think he was either a naïve child or a con man. Sometimes I think I have nothing to fear so long as I'm morally upright and honest. So I'll continue to search for answers among the people in town."

His eyes sparkled as he talked. Taking her hand, he stood up. "What's most important is to be on the side of the people. Hanzhang, the biggest problem the Sui clan has had over the years was living quietly in our side rooms. Now I feel nothing but resentment and disgust toward these side rooms. Why does everyone in the Sui clan live in one? You, me, Jiansu, and Uncle. Why? Because our main house was burned down. How simple and resigned of us to live in these rooms from then on. Why in the world didn't we try to build another house? The four of us, together?"

Hanzhang looked at her brother, her eyes also sparkling, unable to say anything. Then she gripped his hands tightly.

Shi Dixin finally realized that he hadn't long to live, and he did something that stunned the town before taking leave of the world. It, like the discovery of the underground river, deserved to be entered into the town's chronicle. By then, nearly everyone in town knew they lived in a place without "power," for the seal had been lost on a chaotic night over a decade earlier and had fallen into the hands of a mysterious shadow. Now Shi Dixin turned over the lost seal, an old, crude, and filthy object that nonetheless solved a decade-old mystery.

Why had he taken it? Was he afraid of bloodshed from factional battles over it? Was it greed, or had he cherished the power it gave a man? What had motivated him to risk his life to steal it? Why hadn't he given it back after things had calmed down? No one would ever know the answers.

As Shi lay unconscious, entering the last moments of his life, out on the street he and the seal were the major topic of conversation. Old folks looked at each other and said, "He's dying." "Fortunately he isn't taking the power with him." "Our town now has power again." Sui Buzhao, who placed particular importance on the matter, even went to the town committee and asked to see the seal. He stared at it and was lost in thought for a long time, his mind on the lead canister. Convinced that the disappearance of the canister had something to do with the eccentric old man, he slapped his head and reproached himself for not making the connection earlier. He jumped to his feet, yelled out something, and ran toward Shi's house.

"That canister, old man, you can't take that with you too!" Sui Buzhao shouted into the face of the man, whose eyes were tightly shut.

Shi was barely breathing. Sui Buzhao tried to send the woman caring for Shi away, saying he had something important to discuss with him.

"He can't hear or say anything now," she pleaded in a soft voice. "Please go. Let him die in peace."

Sui turned to leave but stopped after another glance at Shi. "No. I can't. This is something that concerns the whole town. Leave us alone, please. I won't be long. Please." The woman hesitated but then left. Sui pressed up close to Shi's face and said, "Open your eyes, old man. Are you on your way out? Looks like you'll die before me. Go on then. I won't be long. Since we were born to be adversaries, we can start up again on the other side. I'm just begging you to give us the canister. You can't open your mouth? Can't talk? Point with your finger then, or signal with your eyes, so I'll know where it's hidden. Come on, old man."

Shi opened his eyes just a slit when Sui stopped talking. He sneered and shut them again.

"Aiya. That was a sneer, old man. Can you hear me?" Sui was so anxious he began to pace the floor, stumbling as his legs got tangled up. The sneer reemerged at the corners of the old eccentric's mouth. When the woman came in and saw Shi exhale loudly, the wrinkles disappeared from her face and her hands began to tremble at her sides. Shi reached out to press down on the blanket, as if he wanted to sit up; the woman went to help him up but he was too heavy, so Sui Buzhao propped him up. The old man slumped in Sui's arms, his breathing shallow, but he still wore a derisive smile. Then Sui heard a startled cry from the woman and looked down to see the smile frozen on the old man's face.

Shi Dixin's funeral could not begin to compare with that of Li Qisheng or Zhao Duoduo, since the Shi clan was not one of the important families in town. Nonetheless, the townspeople displayed once again their willingness to be neighborly; nearly every family sent someone to help out with the funeral preparations or supplied spirit paper and incense. The news quickly spread all over town that Shi had died in the arms of Sui Buzhao, who was busy running around on the day of the funeral. He called Baopu and Hanzhang over, telling them, "Come kowtow to your stubborn eccentric uncle." People clicked their tongues to show their amazement at how he refused to bear a grudge. The original grave site was so close to Li Qisheng's grave that it had to be dug elsewhere, after objections from the Li family, who said that Shi was such a rare eccentric he should not be Li's neighbor.

After Shi was buried, Sui Buzhao wailed at Sui Yingzhi's grave and did not leave until it was pitch black. That night he went to Zhang-Wang's shop and got drunk, then stumbled his way home. When his feet got tangled and he fell, he crawled along, cursing the town for being ungrateful and for forgetting their ancestors, the old ship, and Uncle Zheng He. Then he began calling out sailing chants, his voice so shrill it seemed impossible that it had come from the throat of an old man. Many people, roused by his shouts, came out to see; they'd seen him drunk before and had heard his chants, but never this loud, never this insistent. "Grandpa Sui sure knows how to sing," the children said to the grown-ups. "Those are chants, not songs." Foaming at his mouth, Sui pointed at the people alongside the street and yelled, "Why don't you people go to sea?" Spittle gathered at the corners of his mouth. "Why?"

They could only stare at one another. "You goddamn worthless people!" he continued. "You're young and strong, so why cower around here, losing face for your ancestors? Hurry up, come aboard. The water in the Luqing River is rising, the wind is good, and the current is just right. Uncle Zheng He's ship already left. Ah-hei-lai-zaiyo-yo." He cursed and he yelled, all the while unable to walk properly. When word reached Baopu he came to take his uncle home.

"Are we going aboard ship?" Buzhao asked his nephew, the smell of liquor suffusing the air around him.

"Yes," Baopu replied, drawing laughter from the onlookers.

Under the constant gaze of the town's residents, Baopu took his uncle home, where he laid him down on the *kang* and gave him some water. He'd never seen his uncle this drunk, but he knew that Zhang-Wang was good at getting people to drink heavily. He wanted his uncle to rest, but the old man grabbed his shirt and asked him to stay to talk to him. Baopu sat down. His eyes nearly closed, the old man said, "You're the oldest of your generation, are you aware of that?" Baopu nodded. "Good. Then you should take your brother and sister aboard Uncle Zheng He's boat. Do you hear me?" Baopu nodded again. "Go sail the seas," the old man said excitedly, struggling to sit up. "That's what I call real living. I'm going to give you my nautical book. It means as much to me as my life." He stepped down off the *kang*, removed the metal case from the wall, and picked up the book with bamboo strips. "A wonderful book," he said as he turned the pages carefully. With a sigh, he began to read, the hint of a light shining in his gray eyes: " 'Keep adjusting course, follow the stars, record the islands, the currents, and mountains to draw a map. It is imperative to choose as navigator one who knows the compass well, who observes the stars, mountains, and islands closely, and for whom the color of the water is meaningful. Take care in deep water, study it repeatedly and do not take it lightly. In this way, there will be no problems.' "

He stared at Baopu. "You hear that? Sailing the ocean is no simple affair. 'Study it repeatedly and do not take it lightly.' " After putting the book back inside the metal case, he lay down and said, his eyes barely open, "Baopu, my generation is about to die out, and I was thinking that Wali isn't getting older, it's getting younger. There are two things I want to talk to you about, but I'm afraid you might write them off as the drunken ramblings of an old man."

"What are they?"

The old man nodded. "First, this book. It'll be yours once I'm gone and you must protect it with your life to ensure it is not misused."

"You have my word."

"The lost canister, with its bad seed, has not been found, so you must check every baby that's born. And try to find the thing."

"That I can do."

Sui Buzhao exhaled before continuing, "You should also go look at the old Donglaizi wall. People in town should not forget that Wali was once the seat of state power. And then there's the ancient ship. It's being kept in the big city, but people in town should know it's ours and ought to worship it. You must pay your respects in your heart if you can't possess the real thing."

Baopu mumbled his replies, and, for some unknown reason, his eyes were getting misty. "Worship the ancient in the heart," he repeated.

～

Daxi and Naonao often went to see Jiansu, who had by then settled in at Guo Yun's home. He took walks in the yard, sunbathed, took herbal medicine, and learned qigong from Guo Yun, who forbade him from eating anything that was not fresh. Once Daxi gave him a sugarcane, but Guo Yun snatched it away and said sternly, "How can this be fresh after being transported from the south?" When they were in his room, Daxi kissed him repeatedly, ignoring Naonao's presence. Kissing his forehead, his eyes, and his bloodless neck, she had to dry her moist eyes with the back of her hand.

"How could the wretched spirits give you an illness like this?" she cried out sadly. "You should never have gone into the city. That's what caused your illness, I just know it. Jiansu, please get well soon."

He just looked at her, not saying a word.

Naonao, who always sat nearby, sometimes flipped through his bedside copy of *Heavenly Questions*. She knew it was the only book Jiansu was allowed to read during his illness. She had lost weight and her face had turned sallow; she looked quite frail. Once she said to Jiansu, "I'm waiting for him."

"Keep waiting," Jiansu said with a nod.

The planning and production of the variable gears entered its critical stage, so Li Zhichang, Crackpot, Sui Buzhao, and the blacksmiths in town who came to help worked day and night. The curious gathered daily, aware that they were witnessing the most important innovation in Wali's noodle industry in decades. Li Zhichang's house was converted into a workshop, where the men were immersed in their work; it was a place that stimulated their desire to work and infused them with spirituality. They worked and they talked, especially Li Zhichang and Technician Li. Sui Buzhao, of course, often regaled them with seafaring stories, impressing his audience with strange tales and bizarre sights, but what he liked the most were Technician Li's stories about the universe and Star Wars. "It's good to listen to young people," he'd say. Baopu was a frequent visitor who never failed to touch the gears and axles, and as the work neared its end, he found himself getting more and more excited.

Crackpot once laid some gears out on the floor to illustrate the solar system. "Earth, Saturn, Venus, moon," he said as he pointed to the gears. Li Zhichang was captivated by the orbits of spaceships Technician Li later drew on the floor but was stymied by the concept of space walks. Everyone's interest peaked when the talk turned to flying saucers, and Sui Buzhao swore that one night more than a decade earlier Wali had been visited by a line of flying saucers that circled above the bend in the Luqing River three times before flying off. Li Zhichang, whose interest remained focused on Star Wars, expressed surprise over the circling flying saucers but turned immediately to Technician Li to ask about US and Soviet Union space travel.

Li Zhichang found the technical terms particularly difficult and impossible to keep in mind, but Crackpot could rattle them off the top of his head. Li was convinced that the technician must have a very unusual brain, as had Li's uncle. Infrared probe, laser beam, long-wave infrared probe, self-adjusting optical technology. Who could get them all straight? But strangely, the more confused he grew, the more he wanted to know, as if he were addicted. "What was that lethal thing? I forgot again."

Technician Li answered without stopping his work, "Long-wave infrared probe. It can acquire a missile warhead and conduct preliminary identification and tracking in the outer atmosphere. And the self-adjusting optical technology can ensure that it won't be affected by the atmosphere when it probes objects in the air and outer space. In terms of data collection, the Americans can process ten billion items per second."

Li Zhichang was impressed. "That's incredible."

Technician Li nodded. "Without all these in its arsenal, the Americans wouldn't dare start work on Star Wars. My uncle told me that only a tiny fraction of the plans are strategic and that the remaining ninety percent is related to cutting-edge technology. That is to say, technology is the key. The Americans are very ambitious. Their space agency once held a symposium on space activities where they claimed that by the end of the 1980s, except for Pluto, they would have sent space probes to every planet. And they'd set up a manned base on the moon."

Li Zhichang considered what he'd just heard. "What about Pluto?"

Technician told him that Pluto was too far from Earth.

"What's so important about the moon?"

"It has lots of precious heavy metals. But its main function is as a base from which to explore other planets. Some of the cutting-edge technology can only be developed in space, where, taking advantage of weightlessness, the work can be done quickly and effectively. No wonder the American president once said, 'We can produce life-saving medicines in thirty days in space that would take thirty years on Earth.' "

That piqued the interest of everyone in the room, who all looked up at Li. When they resumed work, Li Zhichang asked about the

Soviet Union. Then, without waiting for an answer, he turned to say to Sui Buzhao, " 'Missile' actually means 'miss all.' " Buzhao merely snorted in reply.

"The Soviet Union is playing catch-up in many areas," Technician Li said, "but they are more advanced than the US in others. Take space flight, for instance. A newspaper once reported that the Soviet Union spends more than double the American outlay for space flights and ten times the outlay for space launches. Last year, the Soviets launched three times more flights than the rest of the world combined, four times more than the Americans. Soviet astronauts have spent twice as much time in space as their American counterparts. The record number of days the cosmonauts spent in weightless space was two hundred and thirty-seven, while the Americans only claimed eighty-four days. Now do you see?" No one said a word. Technician Li paused for a moment before beginning again in a low voice. "When I went home last time I read an article by my uncle with this unforgettable passage: 'The inevitable result of space competition and the arms races will be the development of a new generation of weapons corresponding to the technological revolution. The material factor in determining the winners and losers in wars may well be scientific technology and the ability to control space and time; it will no longer be a nation's population, landmass, or geography.' "

No one in the room spoke until Baopu stood up and said solemnly, "Would you repeat what you just said?" Technician Li did just that.

After more than a week of intense work, the gears were fitted in the noodle processing room.

A diesel generator was set up in its own space to provide power for the entire factory. The gears, in different sizes, were held in place by shafts, some hanging from the roof beams, others buried underground. They were all connected by a mechanized belt. The test run attracted a large crowd of people, all of whom were baffled by the complex installation. Li Zhichang, Technician Li, Sui Buzhao, and the volunteers from the metal shop were covered in grease, but they all wore a solemn look. Work stopped as everyone waited quietly for the machines to rumble.

After a final round of checking, Li Zhichang shouted, "Let's go."

The machine shuddered into operation, shaking the ground as the gears began to turn, some fast, others slow. Bean milk flowed and mechanical tools stirred the paste. The onlookers wished they had more eyes to take in everything. Someone shouted, "Hey, look at the strainer." Everyone looked up at the metal strainer and realized that the dark man who had always attended it was gone. In his place was a machine that kept a measured pace as it turned. They laughed, just as a howl rose from somewhere nearby.

They turned to look, only to see Li Zhichang shaking a bloody arm while his other hand was madly tugging at something—someone was caught in the belt. They cried out when they saw it was Sui Buzhao. "Oh no!" They screamed and ran forward, all but Technician Li, who ran in the opposite direction, pushing everyone out of his way to turn off the machine.

But momentum kept the gears turning. People covered their eyes as Sui Buzhao's small body turned, the gears shredding his clothes and splashing blood in all directions. The body curled as it was taken up to the highest apex, at which point the gears stopped turning, followed by a loud thud as a mangled, bloody body plummeted to the floor.

Many of the people cried and ran off. The blood drained from the faces of those who stayed and looked on as if transfixed. Kneeling by the bloody mess was Baopu, while Li Zhichang tried to pick up the formless old man. But before his hand reached him he passed out in the old man's pooling blood.

TWENTY-SEVEN

The fortresslike old mills stood erect on the floodplain, facing the ruins of the old city wall, as if waiting for something or perhaps telling a story. The water flowed slowly in the laddered waterway, narrating the history of a river's slow decline. Without it, none of the younger generation of Wali could imagine that there had once been a bustling pier there, nor would they believe that someone from their town had set sail from the river to begin a hazardous oceanic adventure. That man's brief history was closely connected to the rise and fall of the river; he died not long after the emergence of its sister—the underground river.

That tragic yet heroic scene would be forever etched in the memory of the townspeople. The oldest, most rebellious member of the Sui clan, he had been caught in the gears trying to save Li Zhichang and had ended his life as a misshapen, bloody mess. Blood seemed to flicker in the eyes of the townspeople for days after, as if a special period had arrived in Wali, its residents given the special task of sending off its old men—Li Qisheng, Zhao Duoduo, Sui Buzhao, and Shi Dixin. As members of that older generation left town they took with them a bygone era and left behind an unnerving stillness. Sui Buzhao, despite his nautical roving and prodigal past, had added vitality to the town but had also spread promiscuity. When he was about to be lowered into the ground, those who cried their hearts out were older women who seldom left their houses. Having died saving the life of Li

Zhichang, he became the most controversial man in town, one whose vices were inevitably tangled up with his virtues.

For days, Sui Baopu looked as if he'd lost his bearings; his hair uncombed, his speech reduced to stammers and mumbles, he went to see Hanzhang and Jiansu before finally going into his uncle's room to sit. When people came to see him, he held their hands and said, "Did you see? You did, didn't you?" They were understandably confused. Naonao and Daxi, considered by the townspeople to be among the most virtuous girls in town, now had to take care of Hanzhang, spend time with Jiansu, and comfort Baopu.

As he gripped Naonao's hand, Baopu said to the trembling girl, whose face was flushed, "One brother coughed up blood on horseback, the other shed his blood in the processing room." One day after the girls left, Technician Li came to see Baopu about holding a memorial for Sui Buzhao, which the leadership of Gaoding Street and the town committee considered important. Lu Jindian and Zou Yuquan were both planning to attend. Regaining his composure, Baopu discussed the details with Li, but then Zhang-Wang, her eyes swollen from weeping, insisted on Taoist rites. Since she represented the views of his uncle's generation, Baopu was powerless to object. In the end, a ceremonial memorial, presided over by Li Yuming, was held side by side with a grand Taoist rite headed by Zhang-Wang, with Baopu moving back and forth, bridging the two generations' ways of dealing with grief.

It was the most extraordinary funeral in Wali's history. Besides the Sui family, Li Zhichang and Zhang-Wang were also deep in mourning. Li cried so hard he passed out several times, each time revived by Guo Yun pressing the spot between his nose and upper lip. "Old uncle is gone, so what am I doing here?" Li wailed.

"You mustn't say that, you have to go on," others comforted him, though tears welled up in their eyes as well. As she prayed, tears snaked down Zhang-Wang's face onto her thin neck. No one understood her prayers, but the cadence of her voice reminded them of the passing of time. On the day of interment, the whole town turned out, crowding the gravesite, which proved to Baopu that his uncle had been the most beloved and respected man in town. Everyone came up to bid farewell to the old man, seemingly forgetting how they had mocked and criticized him at one time or another.

Only at that moment did the town's residents realize that there would no longer be a guileless, carefree old man among them. He took with him all the seafaring tales, the bygone days, even the chromatic essence of town life. The younger members of the Sui clan sprinkled dirt into the grave, followed by the townspeople, who put their shovels to work, clanging as they filled the grave. Finally many could no longer contain their grief and began to lament. As she was tossing dirt into the grave, Hanzhang slumped forward and fell into the hole, to the vocalized astonishment of the people around her. It was a struggle to bring her out.

Back on level ground, she continued to cry, her wails drowning out all other sounds, and Baopu was stunned by the violence of her reaction. Her hair hung down around her shoulders, veiling her pale face and her clothes. Covered with dirt, she writhed on the ground, as if in great pain. Baopu picked her up, but she fell down again. Pounding the sandy ground, he called out to her, all the while weeping himself. He cradled his distraught sister, and he rocked her to get her to stop crying, but to no avail. He was sad and he was surprised, yet he was powerless to make her stop. "Hanzhang, what's wrong? Please stop."

After damping down the dirt on the now filled-in grave, the mourners came up to surround the brother and sister. A middle-aged woman walked up and crouched before them; she combed Hanzhang's dusty hair with her fingers and called out to her softly. Hanzhang stopped abruptly when she heard the woman's voice. "Xiaokui!" She fell into Xiaokui's arms. Watching the two women holding each other, Baopu turned in search of something. Then he spotted Leilei, who walked up to him. Baopu laid his hand on the boy's head.

The old men stopped going to Wali Emporium to drink, for the moment they neared the liquor vat they were reminded of their departed drinking comrade. With diminishing customers, the civil servant and Zhang-Wang passed the lonely time together. Zhang-Wang continued to massage Fourth Master's back, the only difference being the stronger pressure she applied. Her eyes were puffy, her expression glum; she yelled at the young clerk every day, and then she sighed, saying that life had lost its glitter, its meaning.

One afternoon Zhang-Wang went to see Jiansu, who was practicing qigong beneath Guo Yun's wisteria trellis. In a soft voice, she detailed the shop's revenues and expenses before quietly walking away. That night she bought a poisonous fish and fried the most toxic roe with eggs, which she washed down with liquor. Then she stumbled over to the cemetery, where she first lay down on Sui Buzhao's new grave before going over to lie atop her deceased husband's weedy grave. She waited, and time passed, and she felt nothing unusual. Dawn brought profound disappointment, but she remained motionless, recalling the times when her husband was still alive. When the sun's rays lit up the sky, Erhuai walked by on his patrol and spotted her. He chuckled as he looked down on her as she lay with her eyes closed. Snapping at him and calling him a no-account bastard, she ordered him to carry her to Fourth Master's house. Fourth Master was lying on the *kang,* so she took off her shoes and climbed up. After covering his slack body with a white sheet, she massaged his back. Then she watered the flowers in the yard and went home; by then the sun had climbed above the roof. She saw the fish when she walked into the kitchen. With a sigh she could tell it wasn't poisonous after all; her eyes had played tricks on her in the dark. "Well," she said, "the heavens aren't ready to let me go yet, it appears."

Baopu devoted all his efforts to seeing that the noodle factory resumed operation, making sure that the generator rumbled away, turning all the gears. Li Zhichang added protective shields around the belts and shafts. Workers manned their posts quietly. Now nearly every stage in the production was run by machines, which seemed to carry magic powers. A long strainer turned by a crankshaft sifted the dregs from the bean milk, clanging as it moved. Every sound was loud and rhythmic, vitalizing the old processing room, but the workers were quiet; no one spoke, no one laughed. Sui Buzhao's death had shaken the whole town, in much the same way that the machinery produced a shudder in the noodle processing plant.

The power of the machines quickly manifested itself in the sudden increase in productivity, followed by the expansion of the drying ground and trucks loaded with noodles roaring down the streets. People kept coming to see how machines had replaced humans, a sight that amazed them, but the visitors were muted, their expressions a mixture of sorrow and excitement. Some actually bowed at the gears hanging down from the roof beams and left.

Technician Li came to the plant often to discuss technical issues with the grease-covered Li Zhichang. Lu Jindian and Zou Yuquan also came to inquire about production and check on the quality of the noodles. They stressed the fact that since Wali was a major producer of White Dragon Glass Noodles, they must make sure not to damage their international reputation, which would affect the whole noodle export enterprise. When they came, Baopu grasped their hands but said little. He was the focus of the town, having moved into the office at a critical moment. After spending half his life in the mill, he still felt an indescribable agitation when he heard the rumbling of the stone. The swarthy man who had worked the strainer now found himself with nothing to do, so he asked to work in the mill. Baopu flew into a rage, which was rare for him, when he heard the man's request. "How dare you? You're young and strong as an ox, why do you want to work in the mill? And you call yourself a man? Damn you!"

He yelled and he cursed until he saw a look of disapproval in Naonao's eyes. With a tinge of regret and guilt, he told the man to go work on the drying ground. That night Baopu went for a walk along the floodplain, thinking about his uncle and the conversation they'd had shortly before his death.

It had certainly been an unusual conversation. He'd done the first thing the old man asked him to do, and he was sure that he'd manage the second thing as well. On the day the old man was buried, Baopu took the book from its hiding place in the wall back to his own room and told himself he'd treasure and study it. Knowing that he'd likely never sail the ocean, he thought he could at least dream about sailing by reading the book. And he vowed to find the lead canister. The geological survey team, which had found the great source of energy and the underground river, had lost the canister and left a seed of suffering for future generations. He vowed to find it.

Hanzhang fell ill after returning from the gravesite and asked for sick leave for the very first time. Baopu brewed herbal medicine for her, but she secretly poured it out. In the beginning she ate some gruel, but then she stopped eating altogether. Lying quietly on the *kang,* she looked up at the ceiling, her hair falling onto her shoulders. There was neither hate nor sorrow in her eyes. Baopu sat by her side and called out to her, and she responded in a soft voice. Sometimes he adjusted her lying position or combed her hair, but she remained motionless. When he tried to get her to eat something, she simply did not respond.

"You have to eat," he said, stamping his foot anxiously. "You can't go on like this. Please, just a little." She looked at him with tenderness in her eyes and signaled for him to sit down. He did, and she reached out to touch his stubble. He was shocked to find her hand and arm so soft, white, and seemingly boneless. Touching her hair, he tried to get her to eat again. "Have some gruel. I'll feed you, like when you were young."

She shook her head. "I don't want to eat anything. I understand now that I should not have been born and, once born, that I should have left with Mother. It's too late for that, so I'll go with Uncle. Please don't say any more; I won't listen. I've been pouring out the medicine when you aren't around." She spoke to him with a peaceful look, as if telling a story. Baopu clenched his teeth, forcing himself to keep quiet. Then he hugged her, pressing her tightly against his chest, while his arms shook violently. He looked at the window with his dry, sleep-deprived eyes, his lip quivering.

As if talking to himself or calling to someone outside, he said, "It's too late. Too late for everything. And it's all my fault. As the oldest son, I should have found a way to cure what ails you. But it's your fault too, it's the fault of the Sui clan, this damned side room, all of us in the Sui clan. What are you thinking? What's ailing you? Tell me, please. You keep everything to yourself, like me. Do you want to destroy your future? You don't want to get married, you don't want to talk, and you won't even look at Li Zhichang. You're going to ruin everything. You said you wanted to leave with Uncle. Fine, go then. We'll all leave one day. But before you go, you must tell me what you've bottled up all these years. Say something! What's going on? Oh, this family!"

He kneaded her thin, nearly transparent skin, as if trying to crumble it, until he was exhausted. When he let go, she crumpled to the *kang,* where she continued to look at him with tenderness. She shook her head and said in a weak voice, "It's not Uncle, Second Brother, or me, but you who have suffered the most. I have tainted the Sui clan's reputation and am unworthy of the name. If I said what you want me to say, I think it would be too much for you. You might even be driven to kill me. Oh, I want to tell someone, so I'll go tell Uncle." Baopu just stared at her blankly, obviously confused. After a while, she asked him to leave and go back to the office, but he refused, so she told him she wanted to take a nap. He had no choice but to get up and leave.

After he was gone, Hanzhang struggled to get out of bed and then crawled over to a stool, propping herself up to look out through the tiny window at the floodplain with its white sand and emerald-green willow saplings. Someone was walking down there, carrying something on his shoulder. The drying ground, where silver threads would be flapping in the breeze, was off to the north. As she looked, she recalled how Baopu had taken her to the floodplain when she was a little girl. Then her thoughts turned to her mother, who held her hand to pick the beans. Father was a hazy memory to her, but she recalled him galloping along the floodplain on a chestnut horse, and the red sorghum field, where drops of blood dripped from the horse's mane.

Leaning against the window, she said to herself, "I'm leaving now. I'm leaving Wali with Uncle, but I feel like crying for Second Brother, who has a terminal illness, and Older Brother, who is busy all the time. I want to cry for that person also. How wonderful if he could come now. I'd tell him I don't deserve him because not a single part of my body is clean. I'm leaving now. How I wish I could go see the old mill with its familiar rumbling. I want to say good-bye to Older Brother and to the drying ground. I don't deserve to stay in this town or this room. I know my brothers will be sad, but that won't last long. They'll have a better life without a tainted sister like me."

Taking one last look at the floodplain and the blue sky above, she left the window and searched for a rope under a chest. Her hand shook as she slowly pulled out the rope; angry at her hand, she jerked, and her scissors came out with the rope.

Confused, she sat down on the floor with a sharp cry. When had she hidden the scissors there? The scissors. She closed her eyes and her teeth began to chatter as a chill wracked her body. The scissors had been there for that certain person, the rope for herself. She thought she would only need the rope and had completely forgotten about the scissors. But now both showed up and she couldn't decide which to use. She ignored the scissors and picked up the rope, but despite herself, she picked up the scissors and cut the rope into pieces.

Fourth Master sat on his *kang*, panting slightly, after his back rub. A creak from the gate told him that Zhang-Wang was leaving after watering the flowers. When he reached out for the newly brewed tea, Wattles Wu walked in. Fourth Master's hands shook as he brought the tea up to take a sip. "I've been feeling very old the past few days."

"How can the Fourth Master get old?" Wu smiled.

Fourth Master shook his head. "I'm getting old. My hands shake, my *qi* doesn't flow smoothly, and my pulse is weak."

"Send for Guo Yun," Wu said, after looking into his face.

Fourth Master coughed softly, pushing the teacup away. "Tell Er-huai to shoot a few pigeons so I can make some pigeon stewed with cinnamon."

Wu nodded but secretly suspected that Fourth Master was indeed getting old, as he recalled how he'd seldom ever heard him sigh. At around dusk one day he'd seen Fourth Master linger at Zhao Duoduo's grave, where he'd burned some spirit paper. That was the evening Wu thought that the man might be getting old.

Wu added some water to the teapot before sitting down with his hands tucked up in his sleeves. The two men sat quietly until there was a sound at the gate, which made Fourth Master's cheek twitch. His cup crashed to the floor. "Someone from the Sui clan has come," he muttered.

Wu looked up through the window and saw Hanzhang. "I'll leave," he said, and walked out.

Hanzhang leaned against the door, breathing hard, as if she'd been running. With sweat beading her face, she stared at Zhao Bing, who remained seated with his legs crossed, motionless. "I'm waiting for that 'end,' " he said without looking up. Hanzhang moved away from the door and took a few cautious steps forward until she reached the *kang,* where they could hear each other breathing. He jerked his head up until their eyes met. Finally he sighed, reached out, and pushed a cup of cold tea toward her. She followed the movement of that hand with her eyes before leaning over to grab it, twist it, and squeeze it. With a muffled cry, she pounced on him and wrapped her hands around his neck. He reacted by shaking his head and twisting his body, but he remained seated, not moving an inch. Hanzhang ripped his clothes and scratched his chest with her fingernails. His nostrils flared as he snorted and, finally getting agitated, sent her stumbling all the way to the far side of the room. When she stood up, blood oozed from the corners of her mouth.

She pounced again. "Did I hit you too hard?" he said. The words were barely out when she whipped out the scissors and plunged them into his belly.

With blood splattered onto her arms, she screeched, as if burned by boiling water, and let go of the scissors, which remained stuck in him.

Fourth Master fell on top of the blankets, his eyes still on her, while he pursed his lips and bit down. "Hurry and twist the scissors. Twist them, and I'll be finished. Hurry."

She backed away, shaking her head. With his head on the blanket, he looked up at her. "Very well then. You're a child after all; you can't do it. I could kill you with two fingers, but I won't. I've badly mistreated the Sui clan, and this is what I deserve." The scissors jiggled as he spoke; blood from the wound was turning the color of soy sauce.

Hanzhang screamed as she jumped off the *kang*, pushed the door open, and ran out.

Wattles Wu rushed into the room and shrieked when he saw the blood on the floor. "Murder! Murder! Stop her! She's killed Fourth Master."

A crowd quickly gathered, all shouting "Murder!" Eventually they learned that Hanzhang had plunged a pair of scissors into Fourth Master. Some men from the Zhao clan wrapped him in a sheet and made for the town's clinic. In the meantime, people were rushing out of the noodle factory. When Baopu and Zhichang reached the main street, they saw Erhuai fire his rifle into the air to stop people from surging toward the site.

Baopu pushed his way through the crowd, ignoring Erhuai, who shouted and fired into the air again. Calling out for Hanzhang, Baopu dashed around, but there was still no sign of his sister. It was getting dark and the streets were painted red by the setting sun. Citizens yelled as they moved east one moment and west the next; militiamen put on their ammunition belts to guard the entrance of every street and alley. "Don't let the murderer go!" Erhuai shouted. A militiaman whispered something to him, prompting him to run west. The faster onlookers took off after them all the way to the river.

Willow saplings were swaying in the breeze, and everything was dyed blood red in the sunset. All they could see were the waving willows until a militiaman pointed and shouted, "Look!" Turning in the direction of his finger, they saw a girl whose hair was flying as she leaped and ran among the red willows. Confused shouts erupted. It was Hanzhang, all in red, bounding and jumping as if on horseback.

"Haaan-Zhaaang!" Baopu shouted as he ran, closely followed by Li Zhichang.

As they ran, a shot rang out behind them, and Hanzhang fell. She quickly got to her feet and continued running, bathed in the sunset.

Erhuai knelt on one knee, took aim, and fired again. This time the leaping red figure swayed, like the willow saplings in the breeze, and fell.

The two men ran up and cradled her in their arms.

＞＜

Fourth Master's condition was upgraded from critical a week later, although he was told to remain in the hospital. Hanzhang, who had been hit in the leg, was detained by the public security bureau.

Wali was suddenly facing its most terrifying and unsettling moment in years. After surging into the streets and screaming, the people retreated into their own alleys and lanes. When they met they opened their eyes wide, bit down on their lips, and nodded before quickly going their own way. Erhuai patrolled the streets with the militia, while mobile guard posts were added outside the Sui estate. A deadly silence loomed over the town, affecting even the animals. All this reminded people of the days after the temple burned down. Machines in the noodle factory continued to run, but the workers moved in hurried steps, hands in their pockets, cautious and apprehensive.

Fourth Master's sons rushed home, one from the city, the other from the county town, accompanied by their sobbing wives. They went to the local prosecutorial offices, demanding a swift and severe judgment against Hanzhang. Wattles Wu put aside his regular work at school and spent a day and a night drafting an eyewitness report. Someone managed to see it but could understand hardly a word of it, although one line stuck in his mind: "Anon, fresh blood flowed in torrents." Everyone agreed that the Sui girl was done for, all but Guo Yun, who refused to join in the discussion. As for Fourth Master's injury, he gave his evaluation in a few words, saying that the man "needs three years to regain his health and eight years to reestablish his constitution."

After repeated visits to see their sister, Jiansu and Baopu finally got a complete picture of what had been going on between Hanzhang and Fourth Master over the past twenty years. Beating their chests and stomping their feet, they were beside themselves with grief and bitterness. Baopu told her to wait patiently, for they would find a way to have everything resolved satisfactorily. Upon returning home, he sat down to write out a bill of accusation, which would play a deciding role in Hanzhang's future, a thought that seemed to add tremendous weight to his pen. Jiansu, Zhichang, Daxi, and Naonao often came to see him, but each time they quietly backed out of the room when they saw the glum look on his face and the pen scratching the paper in a frenzy. Yet Baopu did not ignore his duty at the factory; instead, he worked doubly hard, cautious and attentive to every detail. The serious look on his face earned him even greater respect from the workers. Even Lu Jindian and Li Yuming repeatedly showed their concern, which touched him deeply.

He continued to work on the indictment whenever he could find the time. Late one afternoon, when Zhichang, Jiansu, Daxi, and Naonao came by, he unfurled the rolled-up accusation, surprising everyone with its length and its contents. Naonao found the opening and began to read, but she hadn't gotten far before she choked up. The others cried too, all but Baopu, who paced the room and chain-smoked, his gray-streaked hair flickering under the light. After a while, they concluded that the bill of complaint traced the origins of the incident and provided iron-clad evidence, but that it would not save Hanzhang, since its length alone exceeded the legal limits. A discussion ensued, after which Baopu followed Zhichang's suggestion that they present to the court only those sections directly concerning Hanzhang.

Baopu felt that a load had been lifted from his shoulders after filing the complaint, and now all they could do was await the judgment.

Li Zhichang repeatedly asked Baopu to convey to Hanzhang his unyielding love for her. "I'll wait for her no matter how long it takes," he said, easing Baopu's concern that the incident would ruin his sister's chance for marriage. As his eyes misted up, he grasped Zhichang's hands and said, "Wait for her then. She's a good girl who has suffered a great deal, but she will make you a good home." They spent more time talking about the noodle company, fully confident that the industry would soon be thriving. Li had decided that the revived glass noodle industry could serve as a springboard to promote other Wali industries; he had further plans to set up laboratories and find a way to develop and utilize the underground river.

"Go ahead," Baopu responded. "There are people in town who will try to stop you, but that doesn't matter. The most important thing is not to stop on your own. Each of us is bound up by an invisible chain, but I'll no longer submit to it. I'll struggle to keep moving forward, even if the chain breaks my arms or makes my hands bleed. Without that sort of fighting spirit, you cannot enjoy a life worth living in Wali. Keep that in mind, Zhichang."

One morning that autumn, the town received news that one of the young men in the Sui clan had been drafted. Baopu was dubious when he first heard the news, but it was later confirmed; the mother of Sui Xiaoqing, a seventeen-year-old boy who had just graduated from high school, came to see Baopu and said, "The boy is leaving and the town's custom is to see him off with a banquet. But Grandpa Sui has just passed away and Hanzhang is being detained, so we'll just forget it this time." Baopu considered the woman's comment and shook his head. "No, let's follow the custom. It's an important event and we have to give a banquet to see Xiaoqing off. In fact, we'll have more people this time; besides the Sui clan, we'll invite people from the Li and the Zhao families, even other families." He also decided that he'd take charge, to which Xiaoqing's mother reluctantly agreed, as she could not convince him otherwise. Baopu immediately told Zhichang to ask Zhang-Wang to serve as the chef, extending an invitation to Guo Yun, who could bring Jiansu to the farewell banquet. Li returned to report that Zhang-Wang was in a drunken stupor, so they had to hire Fatty Han, the cook from the town's restaurant.

The banquet, the first after Li Qisheng's death, began after dark. Old men walked over on the dewy road, their canes sending loud raps into the starry evening. Sui Xiaoqing was summoned back and forth by the old men, to which he answered in a young, crisp voice. Baopu studied the young man's face under the light; it was red as an apple. Still not allowed to drink, Jiansu ate only fresh vegetables. Daxi and Naonao helped out as Fatty Han's assistants and did not sit down until all the dishes had been served. At some point, a white-bearded old man raised his glass and stood up; it was Guo Yun, who suggested that everyone drink to peace and good health, and to the ruddy-faced Sui youth, another soldier from Wali. They all downed their drinks, and the banquet began to get lively. Jiansu asked the idling female civil servant to bring the cassette player from the Wali Emporium.

As the music played, they clapped their hands and asked Naonao to do a dance, a request she accepted with much enthusiasm. She did a disco dance, the vivacious and wondrous steps getting the attention of everyone, who seemed to hold their breath as they watched. Baopu felt a warm current course through his body as he looked at her charming face and her pretty jeans. In the end he rubbed his eyes and quietly left the crowd.

Walking into the evening breeze, he found he didn't know where he was going. He turned around when he heard footsteps behind him; it was Jiansu. The two brothers continued to walk in silence down the moonlit road for a long time before they stopped.

Before them stood an iridescent earthen wall—the city wall of the ancient Donglaizi state. They stood there, leaning up against the wall.

"I know you were thinking about Uncle and Hanzhang and left because it made you sad," Jiansu said. Baopu nodded and then shook his head as he began to smoke.

"I was thinking about them and how happy they'd be if they were here to watch Naonao dance," Baopu said. "I was also thinking of others, like Dahu, Li Qisheng, and Father. With the moon, the music, and someone dancing, this has been Wali's most enjoyable night in years, but none of them is here. I've thought of the factory and the tremendous responsibility I must shoulder. Is it possible for a member of the Sui clan to be that strong? Will I do right by the town? I don't know. All I know is I'll never sit idly in that old mill again. Sui Dahu sacrificed his life and Sui Xiaoqing is leaving, so I've been thinking about these good young men, every one of them from the Sui clan."

Jiansu gripped his hands. "I've been thinking about Uncle these past few days. I wish I'd spent more time with him. He was waiting for the river to rise again, waiting to sail the ocean, but he died before either of those occurred. What enraged me was how people laughed at him whenever he shouted his sailing chants."

"The river won't stay this narrow forever, and there will be others from the Sui clan to sail the ocean," Baopu said as he turned and began to walk back. But then he stopped, as if listening for something.

"Can you hear the water in the river?" Jiansu asked.

Baopu shook his head. "It's running underground, so we can't hear it, not yet."

But Jiansu heard something. It was the old millstone rumbling as it turned, like distant thunder. It was the sound the old men talked about when they related how those who left Wali for a faraway place would wake up in the middle of the night and hear the rumbling mills of their hometown. Jiansu thought he could hear something else as well, the sound of water in the river, as, in his mind's eye, he saw a broad waterway with shimmering waves as the bright sun lit up a forest of masts.